# Tomorrow I'll Love You

# Also By K. Jamila

Mine Would Be You
Golden Hour Of You and Me

# Dedication

*To those who persevere—I know the journey is long, but you are stronger than you know, and the view is always worth the climb.*

*And to myself—for moving on.*

# Playlist

the 1 — Taylor Swift
Long Time — Wild Rivers
Jealous — Labrinth
For Anyone — HER
Male Fantasy — Billie Eilish
Over You — Addison Agen
Strange — Celeste
Nobody Gets Me — SZA
Another Lifetime — Nao
It was supposed to be us — EXES
Was It Just Me — Beth Crowley
To Be Loved — Adele
Now That We Don't Talk — Taylor Swift
Friends Who Failed At Love — Chloe Angelides
Can I Leave Me Too? - The Greeting Committee
Is your bedroom ceiling bored? — Sody, Cavetown
I'd Rather Be In Love — Michelle Branch
Kiss Me — Ed Sheeran
Wildfire — Cautious Clay
My Whole Life — Alina Baraz

# Authors Note

Dear reader,

Thank you for choosing this book as your next read, it means the absolute world to me. As you begin *Tomorrow, I'll Love You*, I want to give a quick warning before you dive in to make the best decision for you and your mental health.

This book contains content recommended for those 18+ and includes mentions of mental health struggles such as anxiety, depression, discussions of suicide, and tough parental relationships. If any of these are triggering for you, please pause and consider what is best for you.

*Tomorrow, I'll Love You* is a story extremely close to my heart in many ways. As you read on, I hope you find something for yourself within its pages. I hope you enjoy it.

Thank you.

*K. Jamila, with love.*

# ISAIAH AURORA

Love was so simple before I grew up.

Back then, it was rainbows and butterflies. It was freefalling without a care in the world of the consequences, of the risks. Back then, love was like a million shooting stars. They burned bright and left their mark in the sky. They were innocent—wishes fulfilled and dreams realized. Back then, love was a ball of sunshine that was never going to burn out.

Loving Isaiah when I was younger was as ingrained in me as breathing.

When we were kids, young and infatuated with the mere existence of one another, we made a million promises. Sealed with the promise of each other's hearts and souls and a kiss on a pinky promise, we swore would never be apart. That this, that we, would always be in each other's lives. No matter what.

We weren't just Isaiah and Aurora, two separate beings, we were

IsaiahAurora. Hand in hand, never separated. Not as kids, not as teenagers, and certainly not as adults. Where one went, the other went. *We* would never not be.

But I guess…

Plans change.

Now, stuck with only the remnants of love, I wondered how I ever could have been so stupid. So naïve. And I wondered if the pain was ever going to stop. Our love came and went like dandelions in the spring. There and then gone, in the blink of an eye.

Was my heart ever going to feel like my own again? Or would it always feel like a piece of it was his to keep? Were the memories ever going to fade into a foggy oblivion? Or was I destined to keep living them, to keep replaying them over and over and over again? No one told me love didn't end just because you thought that it should.

Love was a tough little bitch. And she had claws. They were stuck, embedded in every facet of who I was. I couldn't breathe without tearing the wound right back open. And I couldn't pry her off. Love didn't care about the tears I shed or the pleas that left my lips for it to disappear. I wanted it to disappear. I wanted to be free.

But I wasn't. I wasn't free. I wasn't over it. I was stuck in limbo. In the haze of a love lost. Stuck in a maze with no way out, constantly wondering if this was how I was always going to feel.

Love was so simple when I was a kid. Now, love was a painful reminder of all the promises we broke. And every year that passed was a reminder that we failed.

That our love failed.

# Feels Like Home

*I*'ve hated kissing for the past six years.

A strange thing to admit. A strange thing to discover about oneself. You'd think, logically, there would have to be a million bad kisses for them to become a thing to hate. An infinite amount of terrible experiences. Instead, it took only one—one singular kiss with someone who wasn't Isaiah. One singular moment in time that left my heart steady and my skin cold to know that I would hate kissing if I wasn't kissing him.

Worse that now—still—I felt the remnants of our last one. Worse now, because it was fading, the edges becoming a phantom of the memory it once was. It was simple, short. Like it would happen again soon. It just never did.

Stupid. It was so goddamn stupid.

I thought I could get over it, man up, grow up, *something*—I can't.

Hence why I turn my cheek when Drew leans in to kiss me. Brushing it off by turning my lips up into a casual smile.

"Too early," I say, shrugging my shoulders.

He takes it in stride, throwing me the smile that convinced me to give him a date in the first place. It's date three, and it's fine…but that's it. Fine.

"It was worth a shot." Drew pockets his hands, still at ease. "Can I walk you to the train?"

Checking the time, I notice practice starts in exactly forty minutes. "Sure, if you want."

"I do." Drew bumps my shoulder with his. Playful. Happy.

Deep down, I want my heart to beat; I want butterflies. I want to feel like I can walk on water or touch the sky and feel the brush of the elusive cloud nine on my skin.

But I can't. I can't force those things to life.

Can't force myself to feel something for someone who doesn't belong to me.

Shrugging my duffle bag over my shoulder, I force a smile, pushing my curls away from my face. Drew adjusts his suit jacket before leading us away from the cute patio and back onto the cracked Philadelphia sidewalk. He takes up the outside, balancing on the curb every now and then before turning that warm look back to me.

Do you think it's possible to punch yourself into feeling butterflies? Just to say it happened?

"How is the season going?"

"Good." I glance over at him. "We've got a winning record. Ten more games to go before playoffs."

"I've seen your stats; you're doing pretty great out there."

We check the road and cross on the red hand. "You watch women's soccer?"

"Can't say I did before our first date." He smiles softly. "I've missed the only match you've played since, but I did some research."

"That's sweet." Internally, I'm punching myself. For not being able to give him anything more than this sad attempt at conversation. "I can get you tickets for a game if you ever want to come."

My eyes flit over to him in time to see the small flicker of surprise pass over his features. I've given him the bare minimum, so my offer seems like a gift.

"I'd like that."

Thankfully, when I look up, my Septa stop is in front of me. I turn, facing him, meeting his gentle blue-gray eyes. "I'll send over the schedule for you, and you just let me know what date works for you."

"Sounds perfect, Aurora. It was good to see you again."

"You too." I hesitate, taking a deep breath. "I'm sorry if I'm…difficult." I wave my hand, making only brief contact with his eyes. "I'm bad at this."

Drew taps my foot with his, forcing my eyes up. "You're not. You said from the beginning you wanted to take things slow. It's only date three, so as long as I can convince you for a fourth, I'll be alright." He smiles, easing the tension that I feel between us.

Whether or not my heart is in it, I can't stop myself. "That sounds nice."

Above, the sunlight reflects off the glass buildings of Center City, Philadelphia, painting shadows on the sidewalk. Early Saturday mornings are some of my favorite days in the city. Coffee and pastry shops are bustling, restaurants are setting up for brunch, runners and walkers are out searching for patches of green hidden in the sea of metal. It's early enough to avoid the weekend crowd but alive as ever. Philly always gives me that feeling—a vivaciousness I've never felt anywhere else. I always thought you could feel the heartbeat of this place when you stepped outside—through the cracks in the sidewalks or cobblestone streets of old city, it's there underneath the surface. Maybe I'm biased because it's my home or at least one of the things I consider home, but it's like no place else.

"Have a good practice, and I'll talk to you soon," Drew says, and I nod, dancing on the balls of my feet.

A moment of hesitation later, I pull him in for a quick hug, despite my stupid brain telling me not to. Despite feeling uncomfortable at the foreign feel of his skin on mine.

As he pulls away, he catches my hand and squeezes it before stepping away.

I watch as he strides down the street, weaving seamlessly into the growing crowd until he disappears. As I head to my stop, I plug my earphones in, dreading that Maazina is going to question me as soon as I step on the turf since she's the one that set me up with Drew.

But every time I close my eyes, I'm hit with flashes of the person I thought I'd be walking through life with. This pathetic phenomenon only happened when I started dating again a few years ago, sporadically and never consistently, but after every date, no matter who it's with, my mind won't let me forget it's not who I want.

Like I said…pathetic.

Holding in a groan, I rest my head back. I know I need to get out of my head and pull myself out of this hole I stumble into every so often. I don't have time to feel like this, not with games coming up, playoffs, and then possibly, *hopefully,* camp for the national team. Life is so livable in every other aspect, and I just need to live it.

Who cares if my love life is an absolute dumpster fire? Who cares if someone that used to feel like home is lost to me now?

That's just how it is. One day, eventually, it'll sink in.

Outside, the city passes, like time does, slowly and yet all at once. Passing by in a blur. I'm so used to the view it doesn't make me blink twice, exactly how I'm so used to life now, with that tiny well of emptiness

I've grown so accustomed to. The upside is, I've learned to fill it anyway I can. Enjoying even the most worn-down buildings or minuscule aspects of life. Maybe it never satisfies the void, but it does at least provide a distraction and gives me something else to be thankful for.

Like every time this distinct mood sets in, I count all the things I do have, all the things and people I'm intensely grateful for. And then, I exhale.

Reminding myself even now, with everything I've lost, I still know how to breathe.

The sight of our practice stadium makes it easier. Nothing compares to playing home games at Lincoln Financial Field now that the women's team is being given the same respect as the male soccer players in this country, but the practice field is like a childhood bedroom.

It's not the prettiest place on the block. But it's home. Decorated haphazardly with everything that once made up who I was.

The practice field is built out of the work and sweat and tears and laughter and wins and losses of a group of girls determined to live their dreams. Even when the tears fall more often than the smiles come or our lungs are burning with both exhaustion and a hunger to prove ourselves, that field holds onto it all.

I stride toward the stadium with my headphones in until I'm walking down familiar hallways and into the locker room. First to arrive, as always, I take a seat on the bench and pull out my cleats. The dim room feels safe. Safe enough to let myself lean on my locker just for a moment.

And snap out of it seconds later when the door opens with a familiar creak.

Vivian strides in on her long, muscled legs, the sweeper in our defensive diamond formation and one of my best friends. Her long micro braids fall down her back as she approaches her locker right across from mine. As usual, she's bopping along to the music in her headphones to the point where she barely notices me—but she knows I'm here. I'm always here.

She collapses on the bench directly across from me, tapping my shin with her foot. "Scale of one to ten, how bad is today going to be?"

I snort, forming my pre-wrap into a headband to hold my curls back. "Conditioning day."

"It is literally almost ninety degrees." Beads of sweat already dot her dark skin, only highlighting her point.

"And the humidity sucks."

"We are fucked." Viv falls back dramatically, dropping her cleats on the ground.

One after the other, I roll my socks on, folding them near the ankles since there will be no use for shin guards today. From my bag, I pull out a Propel, Viv's favorite, and toss it at her. "Heads up."

She lifts her chin and catches the bottle just in time. "Have I ever told you I love you?"

"Not once actually."

"Dipshit."

I crack a smile as I shimmy my feet into my cleats. The door to the locker room opens, and a cacophony of voices enter with it, bleeding loudly into one another and splitting off into their own conversations. The team settles in: forwards, midfielders, the rest of my defense, goalies, and the subs. The two other defenders take up their space with us. Sylvia collapses next to me, and Maazina pushes an unwilling Vivian into a sitting position.

Sylvia rests her head on my shoulder, letting out a big yawn. "This blows."

"So do you," Maazina chimes, a twinkle in her green-brown eyes. "Bet that's why you're so tired."

Vivian hits her on the back of the head. "You have an uncanny talent for turning everything dirty."

"She makes it too easy; it's not my fault," Maazina protests. Everyone around us is in motion, lockers slamming, cleats being pulled on, and practice jerseys being thrown around so we can be ready before the coaches enter.

Sylvia simply raises a middle finger in Maazina's direction all with her head on my shoulder and her eyes closed.

I nudge her leg. "Come on, Syl. Gotta get ready."

"What if I just quit and sleep instead?"

"That would be your dream job." Maazina smiles, shoving her foot into her bright teal cleats.

"Sleeping the day away is the greatest joy in life, and you can't tell me otherwise. Second only to sour gummy worms."

A chorus of laughter breaks out at that, the entire locker room very aware of Sylvia's two great loves.

"Wake up. Sylvia. If the coaches walk in and add extra runs, I'll kill you myself," one of the other girls calls from behind a locker, and a sound of agreement follows.

"You're all so fucking aggressive," Sylvia rumbles, finally lifting her head from my shoulder, and stretching her lean arms above her head. I stand, grab my water, and head toward the door.

"I'll be on the turf. Try to beat the coaches out there, please. Ten minutes max," I call, nodding to the other captain, Thalia, who voices her agreement.

"Yes, Dad," the entire team responds.

"Idiots," I mumble under my breath lovingly, knowing they all heard me. Confirmed with a small, *she does love us*, following before the locker door shuts behind me.

My cleats echo on the cement of the hallway, bouncing off the walls. From the end, the light streams through, highlighting the cracks in the flooring and reflecting the bright green turf that awaits me.

I love it here. There aren't enough words to describe how much I love it here—this home that I've never lost. This dream that I've never lost sight of. Soccer has and always will be the one thing that will always and forever be mine. Here, I get to forget the lingering unhappiness that lies in wait in other parts of my life. Here, I get to forget the mistakes I've made off the field, the choices I wish I could re-do, and the people who I wish were still in my life but aren't. I get to forget it all.

I step out onto the turf, echoing footsteps turn into soft footfalls, and I inhale.

Here is the one place I still feel like me.

The summer heat of the east coast is hotter than the depths of hell. No one could ever convince me otherwise. Sweat drips down my spine, an uncomfortable sensation as the sun's rays rest on each of us as we fall back in line. Shoulder to shoulder, we straighten, hands on our hips and eyes on our coaches, who all watch with poorly concealed amusement.

"I want to die," Sylvia mumbles next to me.

"Second that."

"Third." Vivian's whisper is the last thing I hear before Coach Teller's voice booms across the field.

"Last one if you all cross the line together. If not, we go again." Coach Teller crosses her arms. Even from a distance, she maintains an air of casual intimidation. She's a short, strong woman. Dark brown skin. Brown eyes. Broke a few records back when she played. She's earned that intimidation, the respect. And I can't say I mind—she's the best coach I've ever had.

Though my hatred for her and the full-field suicide runs do have me contemplating multiple crimes. We dig in, adrenaline pumping through my blood as the whistle sounds loud and clear. Too slow and we run again. Too fast and there's no way each of us crosses at the same time. But if we don't push, we run again. It's the ultimate test of teamwork; when we're tired, and burnt out, this is when it matters most.

So, we run side by side.

Touching each line and returning until we've run from one end of the field to the other.

And we cross that line in perfect unison, not a footstep out of place.

A quick succession of two whistles followed by a longer third signals the end of two hours of conditioning. Thank fuck.

We all but collapse as we form a semi-circle around our three coaches. I glance around at my team, my girls, in pure admiration. The lean muscles covered in sweat under the sun, the red blooming on all of our cheeks in an array of shades over the variety of skin tones in the circle, and most of all, the look of pride, even if it was just a practice.

"Good work out there today, ladies. Rest day tomorrow. Game on Sunday." Coach Teller glances at all of us. It's the last Sunday in July, and I'm already counting down until the summer heat leaves. "We ready?"

"Yes, ma'am."

"Good." She turns to leave, her face shielded by the visor she wears, but her eyes are piercing. Her eyes linger on Maazina, a lightness finally appearing. "Not too much trouble tonight. And if there is, I don't wanna know. Understood?"

Maazina looks at us with a smile and nods. "Yes, ma'am." When her voice is the only one that rings out, she shoots us a glare. "Way to be a team."

Coach Teller turns, her voice carrying over her shoulder, "Even they knew that question was directed towards you, Aybar. Deal with it."

"Assholes."

I bump her hip. "You love us."

Coach Matthews, my father and one of the assistant coaches, steps forward. "Captains, take it away." My dad spares me a glance and a short nod before he and the other assistant, Coach Laurel, turn to follow Teller, leaving myself and my other captain to step into the center of the circle. I brush off the look and face my team.

"Hands in."

Every hand falls in, resting on one another, and like always, on the count of three, a loud cheer of, "Royals!", echoes through the air. One by one, we clean up the field and head toward that concrete tunnel. Conversations turn into laughter. Exhaustion fades into comradery. Soft footfalls turn to echoes on concrete.

Here, at least, will always be home.

## Today, I Miss Him

"Ro, you're coming out."

My head falls back as I lean against the countertop. "I'm exhausted, Soph."

"So am I. I have two monsters for children. And yes, blah blah, you're a professional athlete, but you try dealing with these heathens. One of which is a mini you, for God's sake, and the other an exact replica of my husband." My sister exhales, causing me to smile, and I hear the clink of glass in the background. "And you have tomorrow off. I'm begging you. We don't have to do much, but I need to get out."

"Sophia—"

"Stop bitching. What are you even doing?" she asks, and I glance around. "I'd bet both my kids on the fact that you're standing in your kitchen, hungry and contemplating take-out or one of those horrendous frozen meals."

With a suck of my teeth, I look around at my kitchen. Ingredients sit unused in the fridge, which are no interest to me. Besides the bare basics like cutting fruit and cooking the same three subpar meals, cooking is not my forte. I survive off of meals from the team, take-out, or as Sophia says, those disgusting (but easy) frozen foods.

"You're so exhausting."

"I am not exhausting, I'm *exhausted*. And you love me. Kian will drop me off." Another clink of the glass. "I should be there in an hour. Max."

"Are you drinking already?"

"It's white wine."

"What about the kids?" I ask, knowing it's hopeless. Any other day and I would've given in. But after Drew and after conditioning, I'm exhausted from keeping myself standing on two feet. Two feet that are achingly tired from holding myself up and putting on a face day after day. Not that that admittance will ever make it past my lips.

Dad always says, "*Even when it is unbearable, you will not bend.*" And I will not bend.

At least not when anyone can see it.

Even if all I want to do is collapse on the couch and burrow into the cushions molded to my body, I know being around my sister will make me feel better. She is undoubtedly a part of my soul. A piece of me that, if removed, the rest of me would be slowly touched by the despair of her absence. Life would be infinitely less interesting to me if I didn't have her. The girl that knows without a word when I need to bend and catches me before I break.

"Kian is watching them since he's the whole reason we have them."

I snort. "It takes two to tango."

"No. It is all his fault."

"Alright, have him drop you off here, then we'll go. You're buying me dinner."

When she speaks, I easily visualize the smile on her face. "I expected nothing less. Love you, Ro."

In the background, I hear Kian, my sister's wonderfully idiotic husband, and the brother I never had, shout, "I love you most, Ro!", subsequently followed by an, "Oof."

"Alrighty then, love you too," I say and all that follows is the back and forth between them until I hang up. Sighing, I push off the counter and prepare a single cup of coffee.

Soft light flickers from the candles burning on every surface. Music plays softly from the TV as the nightlife starts to seep in through the windows, painting scattered shadows over the floor and onto the exposed brick hallway before they fall away. Behind me, the light above the stove illuminates the kitchen. Dark, sparkling countertops and light cabinets continue the contrast that exists in the rest of the apartment. Photos and art are hung around the various walls, framing the bookshelf that sits next to the hallway, stuck to the fridge with magnets, along with a few haphazard soccer achievements thrown in along the way.

Walking past, I toss my sage green blanket over the fluffy couch, running a hand over the soft, welcoming material, knowing that's probably where I'll fall asleep tonight. Where I can leave the blinds open just so I can see the city lights of old city Philadelphia but dwell in the darkness of my apartment. Before heading to my room, oat milk is poured into my coffee as the warmth from the mug seeps into my palms as I cross the room and head down the short hallway.

For just a moment, I collapse onto the fluffy, green comforter, looking out at the city. Living on a side street next to Market keeps me separated enough, but when I want, I can get a glimpse of the city below me. I take a sip and let myself enjoy the almost silence. Chords from the music trickle into my room, a symphony of sounds that keep me from descending into complete silence. Silence that becomes louder than I can bear.

Some days, I can't fathom being left only with my thoughts.

Wondering why I'm not further along, wondering why, when I have almost everything I could ever want, I'm still not proud of myself.

It doesn't help that the voicemail from my dad after practice still echoes in my head. "*You need to be better, Aurora. You need to be the best, be faster, be stronger. You need to lead that team. You, more than anyone, need to be prepared for the next few games. Losing isn't an option.*"

It's fine—just criticism. Except I couldn't tell you the last time the man told me he was proud of me. Today, I know for a fact I was the fastest girl in the lineup, and I've been leading this team all season, running myself into the ground to do so.

Sighing, I snap out of it. Those problems are for another day.

I make my way to my closet, paging through the clothes until I find something. By the time I'm dressed and ready, the familiar buzz rings through the apartment. At the door, I hold the button so Sophia can get up to my place.

Right as I collapse on the couch, the door unlocks—using a key that she made herself—and my sister opens the door. If Sophia was a color, she'd be pink. A soft pink. Not overbearing but welcoming. Warm but firm when needed. Sophia is blooming flowers in the springtime, standing strong through the early rains and into the bright, sunny skies.

Anyone who sees us together can tell we're sisters. Same height, the same curl pattern, the same nose we got from our mom, and the same smile from our dad. Still, we are different. Sophia has softer, gentler curves; maybe it was motherhood, maybe it was the yoga and the running and the Pilates—I always thought it was just Sophia. Soft but strong under the surface. I still have curves, my hips wider than the standard, my thighs thicker than what was trendy when I was younger, but playing has kept me strong on the surface. It just happened to leave me more fragile underneath.

Sophia strides in, her curls cut shorter than mine, framing her round, warm, brown cheeks that are dotted with blush. The midi-skirt she has on dances around her legs as she walks, pulling a bottle of wine and a small plastic bag out from behind her back.

"Did you bring that from home?"

Sophia takes a seat on the big, square ottoman in front of me. "Of course not. I made Kian stop at Wawa and the liquor store." She passes me the bottle, the one that's already open, and then tosses me the bag of mini Kit-Kats.

A grin spreads. "I knew you were good for something."

"You are so your father's child."

I pop candy into my mouth. "You were his first." Soph flips me off before flicking the top of the wine and taking a swig. "It's good to know you haven't gotten any classier with age."

"It's good to know you're still a brat."

After putting the candy in the freezer, I return, taking a seat next to my sister. My head seamlessly finds its place on her shoulder, a spot I've rested on countless times. Sophia is one of two people I willingly let my guard down around, one of two I let see the vulnerable parts of me. And she's the only one of the two I've got left.

She passes me the bottle, and I take a small sip before resting it between my legs.

"I had a date this morning."

Beside me, a careful sigh escapes her. Her hand finds the bottom of my curls like they used to when we were younger and I crawled into her room when I couldn't sleep. "With the same guy? Drew?" I nod. "How did it go?"

There is no reason for me to feel this rundown today. Over a date. Over conditioning practice. But that almost kiss… I can't stop replaying it. I can't get it out of my head—how much I didn't want it, how much I wanted it to be someone else.

How today, I miss him.

Not just the version of him that I loved, that I was in love with, but the version that was my friend. My best friend. The Isaiah that knew everything there was to know about me. Now, that Isaiah doesn't exist. Just like we don't.

It's an uncomfortable ache, one that hasn't ever fully gone away, instead something that's become an unwanted friend. One that usually I ignore, but it's heavier today. Like a flower wilting under heavy rain.

I can't shake it, can't get rid of it. It just…aches.

Shrugging, I search for what I want to say. Feeling younger than I am, like an adolescent trying to figure it all out again. "It was fine, but I feel pathetic. I shouldn't be sad after a date." I deeply inhale. "I shouldn't be sad anymore at all."

Not when it's been six years.

"Ro, Isaiah was a huge part of your life. It's okay that you feel like this sometimes." Soph's fingers twirl and untwirl the end of my curls. "It's okay that you aren't ready to kiss Drew, and it'd be okay if you wanted to stop seeing him, too. Unfortunately, there is no set amount of time for things like this, for relationships ending. It's one of those things that will always leave a mark. Anytime something like that ends, it never really ends. It's like an old bruise or an old injury. Sometimes, something pokes it and makes it fresh again. A memory, a moment. And sometimes, you don't even realize it's there."

For the most part, she's right. Sophia is usually right. But I don't tell her that I am always aware of it. That everywhere I go, everything I do,

I know exactly what Isaiah would be doing or where he'd be. It's like the injury won't heal. No matter how much time has passed.

And because she's my sister, she knows exactly what I'm thinking without my saying a word. "But Ro, it'll never heal if you don't let it." I take another sip of the wine. When she speaks again, her tone is gentler, as if her next words might hurt. "You'll never forget him, but if you want to move on, you have to let him go. You have to live your life, even if he's not in it."

No one ever told me growing up that your heart aching would be something you could feel. No one ever warned me that it doesn't feel like a twisted ankle, an aching muscle, or even a broken leg. It sits there, in my chest, aching against my ribs with nowhere to go. And no way to fix it. You can't ice it, you can't apply heat, you can't do anything…but let it fucking ache.

I'm used to pushing through injuries. To keep running when pain strikes. To keep breathing even when it feels impossible. To keep going. But how am I supposed to push through something I can never predict? How am I supposed to heal something that I can't see? That I can't mend with my own two hands?

I swallow the pain, ignoring how my chest wants to cave in, and give a shaky nod. "No, yeah–you're right." Standing, I hand my sister the bottle, avoiding the careful gaze of her knowing brown eyes and how her lips are trying not to fall downward when she looks at me.

"Ro," she murmurs, but when I turn, there's a strained smile on my face.

"Let's just go, Soph." My phone dings, showing Kian's name on my screen—which he typed in as *Kian: The Gremlin Herder*. It puts a real smile on my face.

The message is simple, a picture of Kian with the girls in the back, one in a car seat and the other practically all grown up (by grown up, I mean ten), except they don't resemble my nieces at all because my idiot brother-in-law spent God knows how long drawing them to look like Gremlins instead. With one single word typed out: *help.*

I hold the phone out to my sister. "Your husband is a rare breed of idiot."

"That's what I get for marrying the first man to kiss me."

A real laugh breaks through my lips because they may poke and prod and tease and trick each other, but I've never seen two people more in love.

"You know he bought Zaza a *Gremlin* stuffed animal? You know how many times we have to watch that movie? It's almost as bad as you when you wouldn't watch anything but *The Prince and Me* or *Brother Bear*. Or *Annie*. Fucking *Annie*." She takes a long swig, and I cross my arms.

"I wasn't that—"

"No, because you were. And Zaza is literally your kid. I gave birth to her, but she is just like you." A twinkle of mischief enters my sister's eyes. "And she's proud of it."

"She should be." I grab my purse, tossing my keys inside, and blow out the candles. "I'm leaving."

"Grouchy." The sound of her voice is followed by scuffling and the clink of a bottle being set down. By the time she reaches me, she's practically pushing me out the door. Standing side by side, Sophia tugs me. Though we're at eye level, it feels like she's looking over me. Like she always has. "You'll be alright Aurora. I'll make sure of it."

Anyone else and I'd tell them I'd be just fine on my own. But it was Sophia, and even if I tried to fight her, she wouldn't let me win. And I didn't mind losing to her.

We start walking, falling into step with one another. The night air is heavy with humidity, draping over us as we step outside. Underfoot, we navigate the old, haphazardly paved and never-repaired roads as we turn off my quiet side street. Old and new neon signs blink along the streets, painting shadows over various-sized groups on the street deciding on which bar to enter. A few blocks down, we come to my favorite one, Revolution House. The bouncer, a face I'm not ashamed to say is familiar now, nods, waving us in. Delicate string lights are hung up around the brick wall interior, the rustic but gentle atmosphere continuing up the stairs, where the walls open up and the air flows through.

Up here, they're still seating for dinner, though a decent crowd ebbs and flows as music plays overhead. Groups are scattered between the bar and the high and low-top tables situated around the porch. Sophia drags us to the host stand, who happily takes us to a table in the corner near the edge, where we can see the downstairs porch from above. We bid her thank you as she hands us the menu.

"What do you want?"

"To drink?" She nods. "Whatever you get."

"It's nice to know you still want to be me."

"How did Mom and Dad put up with you before I came along?"

Sophia rolls her eyes as my lips quirk. Before she can respond, the server arrives, and she orders two glasses of wine. In a moment of silence, we both scan the menus, Sophia's nails tapping against the lamination until we both set them down.

"Do you think I can convince Kian to bring breakfast tomorrow when he comes to get me?"

"You could convince Kian to do anything." Glancing at her, she shrugs with a soft smile, knowing that I'm right. That there isn't a thing that man wouldn't do for her. Or for his daughters. Or me, for that matter. "Tell him I want French toast."

The server returns with the wine, and we place our order. When she walks away, Sophia meets my eyes. "You can text him yourself. He answers you more than me most of the time anyway."

"Brilliant idea."

I grab my phone and send a quick message to him.

> **Me:** French toast tomorrow morning <3

> **Kian, the Gremlin Herder:** I didn't know I was taking orders.

> **Me:** At the request of your wife of course

> **Kian, the Gremlin Herder:** And you had no part in it I'm sure

> **Me:** Not one

> **Kian, the Gremlin Herder:** French toast will be there. Tell Soph she looks pretty.

Rolling my eyes while my heart swells, I show the message to her. Even now, after all these years... I remember when she came home at fourteen, I had just turned ten and still thought boys had cooties (including *him*), but Sophia... she talked about Kian like he spun the world into creation just for her. She talked about that kiss like it was the only thing that had any real value.

Never would've guessed that fifteen years later, they'd still be those two kids who had never known what it was like to not be in love with each other.

Sliding my phone back into my bag, I take a long sip of wine as my sister lets her eyes travel around the bar, people-watching. One of my favorite parts of living in a city, of life in general. But when I return my eyes to her, her features aren't one of open curiosity.

"Why are you making that face?"

Her brown skin looks pale under the warm lights, and she forces her lips into a sheepish smile, though she fails at pulling it off. "It's nothing, Ro."

But I watch as her eyes return again and again to the same spot over my shoulder. Before I can tell myself not to, I turn and follow her gaze. I wish I hadn't. I wish I believed my terrible liar of a sister when she said it was nothing. Even if it wasn't.

Seeing Isaiah for the first time in six years was the opposite of nothing.

# We Have Changed

I was staring the best and worst parts of my past in the face.

And I couldn't bear it.

My throat was tightening by the second, my stomach doing flips. I couldn't—my hands were shaking and my head was in a dizzying spin. All I felt was sick. All I could think about was that Isaiah was standing at a bar less than twenty feet away. After six years.

"Aurora," Soph murmurs, and I shake my head.

In one fell swoop, I down the rest of my wine. "What the fuck is he doing here?"

Our food arrives, but I feel physically and emotionally ill. He hadn't seen me when I turned around, and I keep myself faced away, even as every cell in my body yells at me to spin around again.

To look at him. To take him in.

To see what's different about him. To track every change.

To see if he's as beautiful as he used to be.

Sophia doesn't take her eyes off me as I try to stop myself from reeling. My fork moves aimlessly, doing nothing more than pushing the food around the plate. "Can we just eat and go somewhere else, please?" I look up, meeting Sophia's persistent gaze.

"Of course."

"I'm sorry. I don't want to ruin your night out, I just—"

She waves her hand. "Don't apologize, Ro. I get it." Her eyes flick behind me. "I wouldn't want to stay if I were you either."

I attempt a few bites, but they settle in my stomach heavily, so I give up on eating.

Sophia looks at me knowingly. I was the same way when I was a kid. Especially when Dad was disappointed in me (because he was never mad, always disappointed) and I would get so anxious, the idea of food made me nauseous.

Today, it wasn't disappointment.

It was the weight of Isaiah and all the unsaid words we'd left between us. The weight of him, which I would never completely lose.

"I'll take it home and eat it later, I promise."

Sophia nods; whether she believes me or not is a problem for another day. Thankfully, our server returns, and Sophia requests a few boxes and the check. Within five minutes we're pushing away from the table and heading toward the exit.

I was a fool to think it would be easy.

At the foot of the stairs, Isaiah stands there, looking up at me.

Looking at me like he never stopped.

I miss a step, turning into a stumbling fool. I recover and brush past him without a second glance, without a second thought, and make a beeline for the exit. It's strange running away from something instead of facing it head on. The disappointment punches me in the gut. For letting the fear take over. Usually, fear has one face. One instinctive reaction. This is a fear I don't understand. One I don't know how to react to.

I push through the crowd that's grown in size, but I've been elbowing my way through life for years, so it doesn't deter me.

I should've known Isaiah wouldn't give up so easily.

But at the same time…I don't know him anymore. Maybe he's changed. Maybe everything about the person I used to know is different now. Maybe the person following me out of the restaurant is just a familiar face and nothing more.

"Aurora."

That voice isn't different at all. It floats over my skin, searching for a weak spot, a place to infiltrate my walls and wrap me up in its arms.

I stop. I take a deep breath.

*You can do this, Aurora. Turn around and get it over with.*

Pulling my shoulders back, I find Isaiah only a few steps away.

Nothing could've feasibly prepared me for this. Seeing him standing there with his eyes on me feels like a fever dream. Isaiah looks…exactly like he used to. Seeing him there, it's as if I've walked into my childhood bedroom. Unchanged and yet different. All your favorite things are still there, plastered on the walls, drowning you in wistful nostalgia, but even though nothing has changed in the room, everything else *has* changed.

Life has gone on.

*We* have changed.

Isaiah's deep brown skin is smooth, drawn over his more prominent cheekbones, over the perfect curve of his nose, and around his dark eyebrows. Coarse curly hair that he used to either crop or braid is cut short now, curled on top and sharp around the edges. Though he's not smiling now, the image of what it looks like when he does, when the edges of his lips would start to turn up, is a perfect picture in my head.

There are two stark differences.

One, his dark, beautiful skin is covered in even darker ink. Painted and imprinted on his skin like artwork. Art that will never fully fade. It travels up from his hands, up both arms, disappearing under his shirt sleeve. One leg matches the look of his arm, almost completely covered in dark ink. It's strange and slightly insane to feel jealous of an inanimate object. A tattoo needle of all things. Knowing that sometime in the last few years, it got to touch his skin.

And I didn't.

I hate how that singular notion makes me jealous of everything else that may have learned Isaiah in those years. The rain that fell and traveled over his skin, the wind that wrapped around him wherever he was, the hands that might have decided to trace his shape. All of it. I cannot bear the jealousy burning through me at the world getting to have him for six years.

When I didn't.

The other difference is he *feels* different. IT makes me sound crazy, but it's true. He feels more refined, more mature—more everything. Even from a few feet away, he calls to me like a beacon. Like light calls to a moth and the moon calls to the sea. It's been almost six years, and yet, I still feel him like I used to.

But we have changed. Whether I admit it or not. Whether I can feel it or not. It is an undeniable fact that over the course of those years lost, we have changed.

I'm just not sure how yet.

"What are you doing here?" The words escape before I can stop them, more caustic than I intended. Sophia exhales from behind where he stands, rubbing a hand across her forehead.

Isaiah gazes at me, taking in every inch like he hasn't seen me in years. Which he hasn't. "I got a job here."

*Fuck.* "Here in Philly?"

He takes a step closer, and my heart beats wildly in my chest, but my feet are molded to the concrete. "Yeah, I start in a few weeks."

The pair of deep brown eyes I grew up looking at lock with mine. Isaiah was always quieter than I was; that isn't new. And with him, I never ran out of words.

But I open my mouth, and I have nothing to say. Because it hits me that I'm still mad at him. With a vengeance, that reminder comes right back, swirling like a cyclone without a care in the world who it might take out on its path.

I step back, my blood-chilling. His eyes narrow ever so slightly, watching me close myself off in an instant.

"Aurora, don't."

"No." I shake my head, coldly meeting his eyes. "You don't—don't Aurora me."

I break eye contact and turn, knowing Sophia will follow me as I do.

God, this sucks. Every time I have imagined seeing him again, it wasn't like this. Maybe in my imagination, I couldn't quite grasp how the emotions would take over and take control. Because this is so much worse than I ever could've dreamt up or practiced for. In my head, I told myself I'd be indifferent, that I'd play the cool girl. That I would be unfazed.

But instead, I am left walking away from him both angry and sad with no understanding of how to filter through this.

Dad would tell me this is pointless, that it isn't worth my time. Being sad or unfocused never got anyone anywhere. And Mom would tell me it's okay to feel my feelings, to let myself let it all go. But all I've ever done is walk the line in the middle of acting like I don't feel a thing when instead, I'm trying to swim to the surface to avoid drowning.

"Aurora, please. Wait." Isaiah's voice used to be my favorite song, and now it's one I can't listen to.

"Leave it, Isaiah. Not now," Sophia murmurs gently behind me.

And Sophia, the only other person who grew up with these same two people who never quite figured out how to love each other how they needed, quietly catches up with me. She wraps her arm through mine and somehow leads us back to my apartment, since I'm stuck somewhere in the abyss of my thoughts. I don't pull away, even though her arm touching mine puts me more on edge. Ironic that the person I was running away from was the only person I ever wanted to touch me when I was like this.

The moment the door is shut, I rest my back on it. Sophia takes a seat on the edge of my couch, her eyes soft with empathy and something else I've only ever seen in our mom's. Between my body and the door, I hide my hands behind the small of my back in an attempt to ignore how shaky they are.

Vulnerability all but seeps out of me. "I cannot do this, Sophia." My voice is shaky, not strong like I wish it was, but I'm not sure I could fake it even if I tried. I *hate,* more than anyone, how distraught this makes me feel. "We haven't existed in the same place for years. I can't do this."

Sophia twirls the ring on her left hand. "You can."

My eyes find a particularly interesting spot on the ceiling above me—both avoiding my sister's eyes, which also tell me *you have to,* and attempting to staunch the tears trying to creep out. For once, I wish Dad was here to tell me that crying never solved anything, that it is a useless, weak display of human emotion. Because right now, being yelled at for having emotions sounds a lot better than actually having them.

"Maybe I don't want to, then."

Sophia is a mixture of our parents. She possesses the kindness of our mother in tough situations, but she won't just tell you what you want to hear. Somehow, while I am firmly on the side of being almost exactly like our dad, she (usually) finds balance in the middle.

"Ro, he is not the center of the universe. No matter how much it feels like he is, he isn't."

Drawing my eyes back to her, I stay quiet. My mind won't stop running back to the years when he kind of *was*. It's hard to explain, harder to get my thoughts to make sense, but when you're kids and your lives are so entwined with each other, it's hard to separate them. To find where each life was lived separately, when in reality, they were lived together.

Isaiah and I first met when we were young. He was four and I had just turned five at the end of May. Spring was finally giving way to summer, and he was new to the suburb we lived in. Just him, his older brother, and his mom moving into the house a few doors down.

We were such different kids. No one expected us to be friends. And we weren't really—not at first. He was a quiet, scrawny kid with glasses who liked to read, and not that I was loud, but I'd been playing sports since I could breathe. I was rougher around the edges, formed by my father's coaching hands, and a bit abrasive, even then. We didn't mesh. Until one day, some kid—I don't even remember his name, but he was the neighborhood bully—stepped on his glasses after they fell off Isaiah's face. And I, knowing Isaiah wouldn't, retaliated for him and punched the kid in the face.

From that day on, we were inseparable.

Funny how life changes in the blink of an eye, and suddenly, you're on your own without the person you thought would be there every step. Funnier that people say time heals all, but they don't really mean it. What they leave out is that if you love—*loved*—someone, most times, the memories don't completely disappear, the feelings don't just evaporate.

No. Instead, they become a red wine stain on your favorite dress.

And we're left feeling like we know better, that they aren't the entire world, but that sometimes, standing alone in a crowded room or under the safety of your covers, it still feels like they are.

"Of course, he isn't." I try to tell myself I believe it. Pushing off the door, I head into the apartment. There's nothing to clean up, but I find myself doing it anyway. I don't get far before Sophia is beside me, grabbing the cloth out of my hand.

"Manically cleaning isn't going to make whatever you're feeling go away."

"I'm not—"

A sad, emphatic smile comes over her face. "Sometimes, I think you forget we have the same parents." Manically cleaning when upset was always dad's thing. No wonder I picked it up and she didn't. She continues, "I wasn't telling you that you had to be fine tonight. I was just telling you that you will be."

She plays with the bottom of my hair, tugging on the curls before patting my cheek. "Let's go cuddle in bed."

That gets a smile out of me, whether I want it to or not. "You'd think that someone with a husband as needy as Kian and two kids, you'd want some alone time."

"Oh, I do. Just not from you."

I roll my eyes, though the sentiment does relieve some of the pain lingering in my chest. Behind me, I shut the lights off, shrouding us in darkness aside from the lights from the city streaming in as we walk down the hallway. Side by side like we used to in the Jack-and-Jill bathroom we shared in our childhood home, we wash our faces and change into PJs before climbing under my big comforter.

The large TV on the opposite wall lights up the room as I scroll for something to watch, while beside me, Sophia pulls out the rest of the candy. "Thought you might want these."

I take them without a word and hit play on *The Best Man*. A movie that isn't comforting in the slightest given the circumstances of the plot, but one that brings me solace whenever I turn it on. I'm not sure I'd ever admit how many times I'd seen it if someone asked.

"You never get any less predictable."

"You are such an asshole."

"Least I've changed crushes in the last few years. You're never going to move on from Morris Chestnut." Sophia rolls her eyes but settles in further because she loves this movie almost as much as I do.

"Why do I need to move on from him? He's beautiful."

After a brief pause, she concedes. "Yeah. He is."

Silence settles except for the movie in the background, and in between eating more Kit Kats than I should and brushing our teeth, I find myself cuddled up to my big sister like when I used to climb into her bed after a nightmare. *Thank you* is on the tip of my tongue, but instead of speaking at all, I let the silence cascade over the room as the TV flashes. One of the best parts about Sophia—and it might be a part that is reserved for a select few—is that she always seems to know what someone might not say. And through it all, through every facet and shimmer of all the emotions I've felt in the past few hours, this is the one I hold onto as I fall asleep.

Somehow, waking up is anything but peaceful in my own apartment as my bed is suddenly overtaken by my two nieces, Azalea (Zaza to me) and Joey.

"Good morning, ladies." Blinking my eyes open, I find Kian leaning in the doorway with a smug smile.

"Giving you a key was a mistake," I say, raising my arm to make room for the ten and three-year-old as they squeeze between their mom and me. "Did you at least bring my French toast?"

"We did!" Zaza answers for her dad, her curls tickling my chin. My hands find my favorite ten-year-old in the world and squeeze her, hugging her tight to me. She squeals as I kiss her cheek and nose. "I'm too old for this, Ro."

Exclaiming dramatically, I lean back. "Too old? Nuh-uh!"

Joey, my favorite three-year-old, climbs off her mom and over to me. "I'm not!" Her words are still babbly but clearer than they used to be.

I pull her in and adjust to cuddle them both. "Well, thank God for that."

Sophia crawls out of bed and into her husband's arms. They wrap around her without hesitation and fit her into place like a puzzle. He kisses the side of her head. "Breakfast is on the table, and I started coffee."

"I knew I loved you for a reason," Sophia mumbles, patting his stomach. Kian is a large man, just like his dad, from his Samoan heritage, and he's strong and maybe even intimidating to those that don't know him. With the intricate tattoos and the muscles he built from playing sports his entire life, he stands tall and proud—he always does. But around Sophia, around his girls, even me, depending on how nice I am that day, he softens, and it's a beautiful thing to see.

Not that I'll ever say anything of the sort out loud—God forbid.

"Come on, girls. Go help your mama," he states, sparing me a glance before raising a brow at them.

Zaza and Joey kiss me on the cheek before climbing recklessly out of bed. By the way Kian remains, I know that somehow, Sophia has already told him what happened—probably after I fell asleep. I stand up and take a long swig of water before meeting his eyes. He stalks towards me and doesn't even give me a chance to fight the big hug he wraps me in.

It's almost pathetic how easily I melt into my brother-in-law, but I'll kill him before he could ever admit it. "You alright?" he asks softly, like the morning sun illuminating the rug.

"I'm fine."

"Well, if you're not and wanna let me know, I won't tell anyone."

A laugh shakes my body as I squeeze him in response. "I'm okay, really. It'll pass, and life will go back to normal."

Pulling back, Kian looks like he doesn't believe me, but he leaves it at that. He spins, throwing his arm over my shoulders. "Let's go eat."

I pause before we step out. "Thank you." I don't meet his eyes, but I know they're watching me. Whether he knows me well enough to know that a response might cause me to pull away or because he's an incredible dad with a knack for reading those around him, he lets the silence persist and leads me down the hallway.

Being greeted in the kitchen by my sister and nieces is a pleasant sight, one that doesn't happen often since it's usually me bombarding them at their house. The morning feels full. Squeals of laughter from the girls who won't leave me alone (for which I'm thankful) and horrendously awful dad jokes from Kian that somehow still make us laugh. It's not until the whipped cream can is emptied, the plates are put in the dishwasher, and I'm being hugged goodbye by my favorite people in the world (and Kian) that I appreciate living so close to them. Kids aren't something I've ever seen for myself, but when my nieces wrap their arms around my legs, my heart swells. And Sophia and Kian wrap it up in a bow when they join in.

"Okay, okay, get off. You are going to suffocate me."

Kian glances at me, not loosening his hold. "Might not be such a bad plan."

"Daddy, that's mean!" Zaza frowns and rolls her eyes like I taught her. "You can't be mean to Auntie Ro."

He narrows his eyes. "You've turned her against me."

I whisper, "Like it was hard? She was always going to pick me."

"Over her father? Are you—"

Sophia cuts in, shutting Kian up first with a pinch. "Enough you two. My God." She kisses my cheek before breaking the big, warm group hug. Before I know it, I'm holding the front door open for them as they head out, and when I step back into the apartment, I'm all by myself.

It's something I'm good at. Which is something I hate. Sure, I have a lot of good things in my life, and I'm beyond aware of that: soccer, my girls, my team, my sister, my parents. Maybe it's being freshly twenty-five and young, yet it also feels old. Like you've crossed this weird spectrum into growing up and life is different from how you once thought it might be. In some ways, it's amazing, and it's perfect. And in some, it's not.

And as much as my parents did their best to prepare me for life, I don't think anyone could've prepared me for that. For straddling the lines of being grateful and also mourning the life that you dreamed about: the one that was warm and shiny and perfect.

In a perfect life, I wouldn't have gotten so good at being alone. Maybe more people would realize how much I hated it if I was better at being vulnerable.

And in a perfect life, I'd be more willing to do something about it than concede.

There are a lot of things I hate losing. An important match, an argument, a competition. But this?

Accepting this is a lot easier than fighting it.

# PUT THE WEIGHT DOWN

Having my dad as my coach has never gotten easier.

I'm sure someone more intelligent with a degree in psychology or something could take one glance at our relationship and have a roadmap of what my childhood was like compared to Sophia's. I'm not saying we have a *bad* relationship or that I have it worse than others, but it's different and hard in its own right.

Generally, I believe we all have a bad habit of falling into the burden of comparison. In our looks, our talents, in our lives. Specifically that because someone else has it worse, by no means, under no circumstance, are you allowed to complain. And it's a trap—because it leads you down a rabbit hole of telling yourself to grow up, to be thankful, even under the weight of your own heavy clouds all because they're lighter than someone else's.

"Can we take a break?" I rub my forehead with the heel of my hand.

Dad glances at me. "You think you got everything? Formations, pass routes, sneak plays?" I nod. "Top players? And the quick ones with lazy footwork?"

Sighing, I roll my eyes. "Yes. They're a professional team. Just like us. I know the players. I know *about* the players. I've seen the tape. This," I say, motioning, "isn't necessary." Especially not when we've already studied this film as a team.

It's always been like this. When I was kid, it seemed fun—extra passes or touches after practices, running together, and then going to get Italian water ice or seeing a movie together. Then I got older, and it felt nitpicky, from helping me improve to all the ways I was failing to be the best. And compared to Sophia, who never played sports in her life, who never developed a compulsion to be competitive, and who seemed to get his love just the same, I felt I had to earn it. Even though realistically, anyone would say Dad and I are closer, and we are.

I've just always felt that to keep that spot, I had to compete for it.

We make eye contact, and I school my face into innocence. One of the hardest parts about this facet of our relationship is not always knowing when it's going to switch. One second, he's my coach, the next my dad. And after that, my friend. The daughter he calls when life isn't going his way and the daughter he used to do everything with. But also, the daughter he doesn't fully realize is now grown up. And that her time—*my* time—isn't dedicated to him. So, he reverts into the coach or the father because those roles are consistent.

"Let's wrap it up for the day then."

Exhaling, I sit back, eyes roaming around my dad's place. He doesn't live far from Mom, even though they've been separated since the day Sophia told them she was pregnant at eighteen. It was a strange day, my parents telling me their relationship was ending, while my sister's younger yet healthier relationship was thriving and making me an aunt.

His space is exactly how it's always been. Framed photographs he's had since I was a kid, the same collages of baby photos, his collection of knick-knacks from all the places he lived, mixed in with the books and DVDs on tall wooden bookshelves. It's tasteful and warm. Collections of the person he was mixed with the person he is now.

My dad is hard to read sometimes—likes to keep to himself, doesn't like to be vulnerable, all the wonderful things I share—but he also puts pieces of himself into his space, the place where he feels safe. Here, it's easy to get a glimpse into who he is and what he loves. And whether I like it or not, I'm just like him. I always wanted to be growing up before I learned that people are complex and filled with nuances that aren't as pretty as the rose-colored glasses make them out to be. Always following along, placing my steps in the ones he left for me, wondering how I would ever fill them. Now I have; we are two sides of the same coin, whether I like it or not. I filled those footsteps before I could realize I didn't want to.

"What time are we heading to your mom's?"

Checking my phone, Sophia's text indicates they're on the way now. "About thirty?"

He nods, closing his notebooks and unmuting ESPN. The familiar drone of sportscasters takes up the rest of the space in the room not held by my father or myself. I love him, but it can get tiring when often, I have to hold myself up as the person he expects me to be.

"How's everything else going?"

Isaiah is, of course, the first thing that comes to mind. Which is the last thing I'd bring up with my dad. I'm twenty-five with a sister who has two kids, and the idea of talking to my dad about a boy any more than I have to disgusts me. Mainly because his opinion, even though it pisses me off more than not, does mean the world to me. And also, he, unfortunately, was there for the aftermath of Isaiah.

I shrug. "It's alright. I spend more time with you than almost anyone, so there's not much to update you on."

Dad meets my eyes. The downside of spending so much time with him and being almost a mirror image of him is that sometimes, he knows me better than I'd like him to. Even without saying a word. "You sure?"

"Yeah, all good. Sophia came over last weekend; we went to dinner and made Kian bring us breakfast."

Dad huffs lovingly. "Boy's a sucker."

"Always has been."

We share a laugh, happy the tense moment of before has faded into the background. For a dad who taught us boys were stupid and not worth our time (as most do because they think it's the best lesson they can teach their daughters), he took to Kian without hesitation. Without a word, Dad gets up and grabs me water and some pretzels—just the centers where all the salt is because he knows I like it.

"Thank God for you."

I frown. "What do you mean?"

Dad runs a hand over his coarse, short hair. "I love your sister and Kian. But it's nice not having to worry about you." When I furrow my brows, he continues, waving his hand nonchalantly. "About boys and all that shit. You don't let it get to you. Don't let it distract you. Not anymore, at least."

Delaying my answer, I pop a pretzel in my mouth. Dad has no idea how badly I want to hide away with Sophia or rest my head on mom's lap all from just seeing Isaiah. No idea how much I despise how good I've gotten at being alone.

I force a laugh. "Yeah, I guess so. You're welcome for being the easy kid." The joke lands flat.

I want to be able to let down my guard around him—because he's still one of my favorite people—but I can't. He expects better of me.

"Let's not get ahead of ourselves." He snorts, taking a sip of his beer. "You fought with me at every turn."

"Because you taught me to."

As always, the frustration rises whenever we have conversations like this. The things he taught me to be are now other ways to criticize me. Sometimes, I can't help but think that it's because I'm not his son. Are the things he's yelling at me for, criticizing me for, traits he would praise if I was a boy?

Sophia was never going to bend to his every wish—she was softer, she had his love, and didn't need his approval or feel like she needed to earn it. I'm not sure what happened to me, but as a kid, it was like I couldn't do anything without his praise. Mom's praises weren't enough. I needed Dad to be proud of me, to tell me I was doing everything right. I became the kid who did everything by his book, only to have it turned against me when I stopped following the rules. I hate it. That because I'm his daughter, the traits I share with him, the traits he gave me—the traits so often admirable in men—are now a point of contention.

And not to bring it back to Isaiah again, but growing up, even though we were kids, it's like he saw that. He saw how it affected me, and he never made me feel ashamed of the things Dad made me feel ashamed of.

He saw me—always. When my own father couldn't.

He saw me when Sophia was distracted with her own life. When Mom was dealing with her divorce. When I felt ignored by life, I never felt ignored by Isaiah.

He saw me.

Dad's huff of laughter breaks me out of yet another spiral, his eyes on the TV. "Yeah, I guess I did."

Sighing, I lean back. Wanting so badly to scream at him how much it hurts me that he can't see how much I want what Sophia has, how much I don't want this to be my life, how much it hurts that sometimes, he sees me exactly as I am, and other times, he only sees what he wants to.

And how badly I'm still unable to do anything without his approval.

Walking into my mom's house is like sitting on my childhood couch in between waking and sleeping and feeling the warmth of a blanket being placed over top of me.

The loud voices of my nieces welcome us as we enter, along with the smell of my mom and Kian's cooking. We pass through the front room that contains my mom's radio, CDs, and a few chairs, and into the kitchen where Sophia sits at the counter. Mom takes one look at me, and I know the secrets have been spilled, which, as usual, leaves Dad the only one in the dark.

Rightfully so.

Before even my nieces can touch me, Kian bombards me with a hug and an almost painful squeeze. "What in the French toast is this? Get off of me."

Around his shoulder, Sophia shoots me a sheepish look. Whether that's from her oaf of a husband latching onto me like a leech or because she told Mom, I can't decipher. I don't really care. Sometimes it's easier for Sophia to tell my secrets. Because saying things out loud that make me uncomfortable, things that scare me, is not something I'm good at.

Sophia got the ability to be vulnerable. I got her.

Kian places a big kiss on my cheek and lets me go before I can pinch him for it. "Nice to see you too, Aurora."

With a roll of my eyes, I turn away with a smile and head for Zaza.

She's standing on a stool in the kitchen next to my mom, dumping flour into a bowl. Some of it has made its way onto her cheeks, leaving white patches on her brown skin.

"Mwah!" I say, placing a quick kiss on her cheek before she can fight me. Zaza smiles as a giggle breaks free. I lean over to do the same to Joey, who's happily seated in Mom's arms.

"Hi, hon." Mom smiles, her dirty blonde hair pulled back into a haphazard bun, tendrils framing her face. Her fair skin is clear and youthful, especially in this room, filled with the people she loves most. Even my dad. They still care about each other, even if it isn't perfect.

"Hi," I say, resting my head on my mom's shoulder. Even though I'm not always good at letting her in, she never turns me away. She has never placed conditions on her love, never made us jump through hoops. She is steady underneath my cheek, and the tension in my shoulders dissipates.

"You ready for your game Saturday?"

"She is," Dad answers for me, kissing Sophia on the cheek.

"Yes, I am. You're coming?"

Mom smiles. "Course. We all will, right, Joey?"

Joey pumps her tiny fist in the air. "Go, Auntie Ro!" Her three-year-old gibberish may be hard to understand at times, but it is goddamn cute. Mom strides around the corner and hands off her granddaughter to Dad. He happily accepts.

"Can you help me with something upstairs?" Mom looks at me, and a glance at Sophia and Kian tells me there is no use in escaping.

I nod, following my mom out of the room. It isn't until I'm seated on her bed with Oscar, the cat, curled on my chest, that I meet her eyes. Her hand lands on my outstretched knee.

"So..." She glances at me, no sympathy in her eyes, just understanding. "Isaiah."

"Yeah." Exhaling, I scratch Oscar between the ears. "I hate that he's here."

"I know you do. And I know that you're wishing it didn't affect you as much as it did. That you could brush it off and move on and act like it never happened. I know how much you hate that you can't. I don't know what Sophia or Kian said, and I love them, but I only care that you know that it is okay. It's okay if you miss him. If you have missed him for all these years. It's okay if you didn't."

She brushes a blond strand out of her eyes. "And none of us would judge you if you hated him, too. We don't know all the details, and we don't need to, but if there's a small part of you that hates him or a small part of you that still loves him…" she hesitates when she says that, scared she might scare me away, but I'm too exhausted to move. Too exhausted to act like I don't want to hear it. "That's alright, too."

My mom, a former professional soccer player, a strong woman—a vulnerable woman—makes it all seem so simple. I admire her for that; I always have. There are many days that I wished I took after her and not Dad.

She brushes a curl away from my forehead before giving me a knowing look. "Dad was never very good at giving you the space to feel your feelings or to let you figure it out on your own. I'm not blaming him, but I see how hard it is for you. And he's never been very good at putting the weight down. Neither are you, sweetie."

There is a wistfully sad look in her eyes. Maybe it's something that comes with age, with the wisdom of loving and losing people over the years, of picking up the weight of life and putting it down. Maybe it's something else. Either way, I'm happy to have that wisdom directed at me and sad that my mom has ever felt even a semblance of this before.

"Remember, that it is okay to put it down. To rest. You don't have to know how you feel; sometimes, it's okay to not know anything. Sure, right now, this is about Isaiah. But it applies to everything. The team, your life. Life is too short for you to be weighed down by it the entire time."

I wish I had something to say, but I don't. But the best part about moms, or at least my mom, is that with a single look, they know exactly what we need. She knows when words are scary, she knows the ins and outs of both her daughters, becoming a chameleon for our needs and never thinking twice about it.

Without a word, she pulls me forward into a hug. Careful not to squeeze too tight, Mom holds me in all the ways that matter.

## SEVENTEEN

If the past few days showed me anything, it was that when faced with the unexpected, I was not as steadfast as I hoped. Thankfully, today was game day. And that field, under stadium lights or the sun, was the one place I never wavered.

Once my feet hit the grass, everything else fell away.

The locker room before practice was always animated, but the locker room before a game is one of my favorite places in the world. Everyone becomes the best version of themselves. Pre-game post-warm-up rituals are frantic yet composed. Still professional. There's always an undercurrent of adrenaline in the room. It's chaos, but it's chaos that could only be created by women who all absolutely love what they get to do for a living and who all absolutely love each other. Not to say we're perfect…but on game day, it feels like we are.

Aside from practice, I haven't spoken to Viv or Maazina since all the drama. We and Sylvia don't usually go a day without talking in our chaotic group chat, aptly named the Idiot Brigade. But that doesn't mean they don't show up for me anyway. And I for them.

Sylvia, as always, is eating her pregame snack of her sour snakes and sour Skittles, while Viv sits behind her, pulling her long, black hair into a braid. Viv's already done mine, pulled the front hair into two braids and back into a curly ponytail. Maazina sits next to me re-wrapping her ankle. We've already been on the field, put touches on the ball, and seen the crowd begin to enter the stadium—now it's just a waiting game until we're in formation on the field.

When Maazina finishes, she pulls out the soft pretzel from her bag and splits it in half, handing me my section. I blow her a kiss, trying not to smile and failing when she makes a huge deal of trying to catch it.

"You're an idiot."

Maazina smiles, the freckles that dust the entirety of her face spreading as she does. "Yes, but I am *your* idiot."

"You're the entire team's idiot," Vivian deadpans. The best part about Viv is the nonchalant way she says almost everything—so only the people closest to her know if she's joking or serious. Lucky for us, we are those people.

"Yes—but I am specifically Ro's idiot first."

I wrap my arm around her neck and pull her in tight. "True. She is mine before the rest of the team's."

Vivian smiles as she finishes up Sylvia's braid, stealing herself a gummy in return. The locker room doors open. Coach Teller, Coach Laurel, and my dad enter, all eyes on them. It takes a moment, but the emotion finally shows on Coach Teller's face, her eyes lighting up as she claps against the clipboard in her hand until it echoes as she steps into the room.

"Captains."

Thalia and I stand up. "Yes, Coach?"

Her eyes flicker between us both until a confident smile pulls at her lips. "Ready to lead this team to ten wins?"

It doesn't sound like much, but women's soccer only has on average a twenty-two-game season. We've only lost two. And we currently have an eight-game win streak. The best in the league.

"Yes, Coach."

The room bustles with adrenaline.

"And all this talk of Philly sports getting so close only to lose. Getting halfway only to falter. This is the most attention this team—a women's soccer team—has gotten from its own city. Well…" Coach Teller turns, eyes landing on every one of us. "Let's go out there and give them something to keep talking about, huh?"

Teller strides back to the door, her speech kept short and sweet, and takes another look. "Shirts tucked in. Heads on straight. Eyes on the prize. I want a championship. And I know you do, too. This is one step closer. Let's get it done."

She pulls open the locker room door, and wordlessly, we exit, falling into formation in the cool darkness of the tunnel. Light streams into the dark corridor as we approach the entrance. Sadly, we might never get the roar of a crowd that men's teams do—unless it's the World Cup or the Olympics—but the claps we do get are still exciting, and seeing people in the stands will never get old. Especially little girls all dressed up in their garb, holding the hands of their parents who brought them here.

Everything from exiting the tunnel to the first whistle always passes in a blur. Lining up, playing the anthem, and getting into one last huddle, it's all just the lead-up. More time for the adrenaline to build. On game days, I swear the world is brighter. It always feels like playing for the first time.

Everyone has their favorite type of game day.

Maazina is a sun goddess. It doesn't matter how hot it is or how cold it is, all that girl wants is the sun. Sylvia likes playing in the pouring rain, but only if we're playing on grass and not turf. While I do love playing in the mud as much as any soccer player, my favorite days are the cloudy days when the sun is fighting to peek through the clouds but falling just short. Even more so, a cloudy day in the fall or the winter. The breeze, the chill in the air reminding us to stay warm—there's just something about it.

Anyway, the point is, everyone has a perfect game day. Even if someone says they don't, it's a lie. Doesn't matter what sport, doesn't matter if it's inside or out, every athlete has a favorite. Maybe for some, it's a feeling, and for others, it's the weather. But the best part, even when it's not the perfect day, some part of it is still perfect because we all get to do what we love for a living. It's not easy, and it's not always great, but it's what we love.

Taking a glance around the circle, it's nice to be surrounded by people who love the same thing I do. We all got here in different ways, we all chose the sport for different reasons and fell in love with it in our own ways, but we all got here.

Our hands come into the huddle, landing on each other in harmony. "One, two, three, Royals!"

Like a well-oiled machine, we fall into step as we jog onto the field, the other team already in position. The burnt-orange away jerseys they're wearing are speckled over the green, jarring in opposition while the sun reflects off our white home uniforms, making the deep purple accents shimmer. I take my position at the head of the defensive diamond, Sylvia on my left, Viv behind me, having my back like always, and Maazina on the right. My right-hand man.

She glances over at me, a smile on her face—as always. "Hey, your butt looks good." Then, with a swift glance to the coaches, she sticks her tongue out at me.

A laugh bubbles out, a lightness washing over me. "Yeah, I know it does." Maazina wiggles her eyebrows. "Only 'cause you tell me all the time."

She rolls her shoulders. "Somebody ought to. Love you," she sings.

"Yeah, love you, too." With a shake of my head, I turn forward, eyes on the ball being placed on the midline. I rock onto my tiptoes, the adrenaline flowing strong and steady.

The whistle is shrill, but it fades quickly as we take control of the ball. The other team is quick to follow, but right now, we're in charge. Malia, our star forward, swipes it out from under the foot of the opponent, calmly passing it to center field, landing at Kendall's feet. We control the pace. Slow and steady at first. I receive the ball and dribble it up, using the outer curve of my foot with perfect control. Kendall falls back to my position as Stella, the right mid, and I make our way up the field.

"Switch!" I shout, and we weave into each other's positions, one of this team's strengths. We all have our spots. But we've trained for moments like this—when the opportunity is presented, we won't miss it for the simple fact that we couldn't step into a position that isn't "ours."

The energy shifts, and we're past the midline. Moments like these are my favorite, when it all comes together and the game becomes second nature. With a quick foot, I send the ball to Malia, who's in perfect position, and fall back to my position. Malia and Kendall weave between the defenders, and with a sure foot, Malia strikes the ball to the back corner of the net. Boom. 1-0.

Yeah, we've got probably sixty-five minutes left to play. But…we got this.

As we line up, I let my eyes fall on the crowd.

"Jesus Christ," I mumble to myself.

Not only is Drew there in the seat I was able to get him tickets for, but not far from him or my family is Isaiah. Wearing my jersey—number 17. Exactly as he used to in high school like nothing has changed. As if years haven't passed.

With a single glance, my heart aches seeing him there.

It's almost painful dragging my eyes away and focusing on the game in front of me. The ball sits on the midline again, waiting for the ref to blow the whistle, and my thoughts spin in that singular moment before I have to play again.

Does my family know he's here? Will he talk to them? Will he try to talk to *me* again?

The whistle sounds, and all those thoughts fall to the wayside, but not like usual. Usually, during a game, any other thoughts are stuffed into a tiny little compartment, and I'm unaware they even exist. But this time, though my focus is on the game, I'm painfully aware of them lurking in the background.

The game helps. It always does. But it's different. Most of my smiles are forced. I fight to glance to the stands. My only distraction is the team opposite of us—putting up a good fight, giving me little time to stand still or to think. Or to do anything but play. Which is the thing I'm best at. It is the only thing that I am "the best" at. Not meaning that I'm the best player in the world—God, no—just that this is the one thing I know without a sliver of a doubt that I'm good at. And today, I'm so fucking grateful for the other team kicking it into gear and giving us a good game.

Ironically, it is one of the best games I've had. I'm unstoppable, the defense is unstoppable, and the entire team doesn't let up for one single second. After a few slow plays right after our first goal, everything kicked up a notch. The game was constant. Every touch, every pass—it was all spot on. By halftime, we're up 2-0.

Coach Teller gives us a quick recap of what we've done good and what can be improved. More goals, more talking—because if there is one thing about Coach Teller, she wants us to talk—and points out the weaknesses of the other team we can further exploit. Their left-wing defender is weaker than the rest, their center-mids aren't communicating. All things to get us this win.

Even my dad gave me a simple nod before going around and checking on the other girls. Sometimes it hurts hearing him compliment the others on a play they made or a touch when I get nothing. I know it can't be easy; he obviously doesn't want to show favoritism, but it would be nice. Just once in a while…it would be nice.

Today, like most days, I take what I can get.

When we exit back to the field, I keep my eyes on the ground and my girls, not letting them stray to the stands. I'll deal with *that* later.

Maazina runs up beside me, kicking up her foot to hit my butt. "Is it wrong that all I am thinking about is my post-game cheesesteak?"

Vivian, who's on my left, snorts. "Bold of you to think we think you or Sylvia have any thoughts other than food."

"Hey!" Sylvia exclaims. "I didn't even eat any candy at halftime."

"A miracle." I raise a brow. "Not that I can say much. Kian is cooking tonight, saving me from hell."

"Yeah, you in the kitchen is hell," Maazina says, smartly choosing that moment to run ahead of me.

Vivian and Sylvia laugh next to me. I give them a playful glare. "One day, when you find bugs in your cleats, don't be surprised." I blow a kiss over my shoulder as we head to our spots.

I dance on my toes, the energy coming back in full swing. For an instant, the moment of silence before the whistle blows and the second half starts washes me clean of anything else. All I know is the tingling in my fingertips and the blood pumping through my veins.

It doesn't last long, but I enjoy every damn second of it.

Until the game ends and I have to face some twisted reality, at that moment, it feels normal.

"Great game, girls. You did exactly as I asked today. As you have this entire season so far." Coach Teller surveys the locker room, a proud gleam in her eyes after ending the game with a score of 4-0. "I expect this streak to continue. Understood?"

A resounding yes echoes against the metal.

"Recovery tomorrow. I'll see you for film and conditioning Tuesday."

I stand, stretching my arms overhead, thankful to be showered and in clean clothes. Albeit it's a pair of soccer shorts and a T-shirt, but still. The coaches head into the office, closing the door behind them as the team gets ready to disperse.

The four of us always walk out together, and we're waiting on Sylvia. Around us, the rest of the team exits. We exchange words as they go, along with friendly jabs or pats on the back. Everyone has the people they're closest with—that's a given—but we're still a team, and that's what's important.

Sylvia slips on her shoe and grabs her back. "Okay, ready."

"Fucking slowpoke," Maazina says, her dimple popping as Sylvia just whacks her on the head.

With no cleats on, our footsteps don't echo on the cement floor but are quiet, sometimes shuffled, steps. Vivian nudges my shoulder. "I saw Drew out there."

I grip the strap of my bag. "Yeah, he wanted to come see. I was able to score him a ticket."

"The real question is, who was the one wearing your jersey?" Maazina tucks her hair behind her ear, eyeing me. "He's pretty."

I huff. Not in annoyance at her, but in annoyance because it's true. "That's Isaiah."

All steps stop besides my own. They know who he is; they're the only ones on the team that do.

"Guys, please. Can we do this another time? It's not a big deal."

Sylvia, my sweet gentle Sylvia, stares at me. Unblinking. "Did you hear that, guys? The boy she grew up with and hasn't seen in what—six years—is back, wearing her jersey at her game, and it isn't a big deal?"

I'm not the only one shocked at the tough love because Viv and Maazina share a confused glance at Sylvia before looking between me and her before shaking their heads. "Wasn't expecting that from you, but," Vivian looks sheepish, which doesn't happen often, "she's right."

Sylvia smiles, like she didn't say anything at all, and grips my hand. The skin prickles, but I don't let go. "It came out harsher than I meant, but Ro, come on."

I throw my head back, staring at the ceiling to avoid their eyes.

"Yeah, I mean, he's here, in your jersey. That would mess me up, too," Vivian says.

"If I admit it bothers me, can we drop this conversation and get out there so I can deal with it and go home? Please."

"We'll drop it for now, but that doesn't mean we're dropping it forever." Sylvia kicks my shoe, bringing my eyes back down.

I hold my hands up in surrender. "Fine. Deal."

Sun shines through the window at the end of the tunnel for our exit, and my heartbeat pounds the closer we get. Chatter from family and friends fill my ears when we push the door open, and I beeline for my family first, very aware of Drew off to the left and Isaiah on the right.

"Two boys waiting for you—how exciting," Kian mumbles, but his eyes are soft.

I kiss Zaza and Joey on the cheek, smiling at their jerseys and face paint.

Sophia pinches her husband before I can. "Stop it, you doofus."

"Did anyone talk to him?" I murmur, bending down to pull Zaza in my arms, grounding myself before I deal with this nonsense.

"I did."

Not sure why, but Kian wasn't who I was expecting. "And?"

"It was short—about his move and preparing for his job. I didn't want to fraternize with the enemy too long," Kian says, though he avoids my eyes. It bothers me but not enough for me to care at this moment.

"He's not the enemy; you are so annoying." Sophia backhands him on the chest before turning to me. "Just go talk to him. Get it over with."

"Okay, well, is it rude if I talk to him before Drew? Or do I talk to Drew first?"

"Who is Frew?" Joey babbles, easing the situation without even noticing.

Sophia smiles and bends down to me and the kids, but it's Mom who speaks. "Do whichever is easier for you. We can't tell you; only you know how each option might make you feel."

With an exhale, I stand up and head to Drew first. He smiles, his loose brown curls golden in the sun. "Hi, thanks for coming."

He places a quick kiss on my cheek, and my stomach flips. Though I can't tell if it's because of the kiss or because I know Isaiah saw it. "You played great—at least, from my limited knowledge."

I chuckle, ignoring the warmth on my cheeks at the compliment. "Thank you. It was a good game for everyone."

"Do you have plans after this?" Drew meets my eyes, and I twist my fingers out of his sight.

"I do. My brother-in-law is cooking dinner for all of us. I know my schedule is crazy, but give me a call later. If you want? I should be free this week if you still—"

"Aurora, I do. You don't have to feel bad," Drew says gently. Under the sun, he looks golden, and so far, he's been nothing but kind and patient, and I so desperately want it to work. "I still want to keep exploring this at whatever pace you are comfortable with."

The same conversation on a different day. I feel awful. But I keep trying, keep hoping the spark will show up. "Okay, good. Then yeah, give me a call tonight."

"Will do." Drew kisses my cheek again before turning and heading away from the stadium. And as I watch him go, I'm all too aware of who's still standing behind me.

The one with whom the spark has never died, no matter how much I wish it would. Turning, my eyes find him in an instant.

I ignore the tattoos trailing over his body and the sun shining off his deep brown skin. I ignore the flips my stomach does from seeing him in my jersey number again. 17. I picked that number because of us. Little me always wanted to be number one, always wanted to be the best, so, of course, one was my favorite number. Seven was his. So we combined them, and it's stuck ever since.

I stride over, stopping with at least two feet of distance between us. "What are you doing here?"

"I told you, I got a job."

"Don't be an ass, Isaiah. What are you doing here? At the stadium. In that jersey."

My favorite shade of brown shines in the sun when his eyes lift with amusement. "It's your jersey."

My grip tightens on my bag. "Stop being dense and answer."

He steps forward, two feet of distance down to one. "I did answer. I gave you the short version. You want the long one?" Isaiah doesn't give me a chance to respond. "I got a job here because you're here. I'm at this stadium because it's where you play, and I'm in this jersey because it's yours. And I regret every year I didn't wear it."

I swallow the lump in my throat as I try to grapple with it all. All the painful yearning mixes with hot anger. Anger that he thinks I would welcome him back with open arms like he didn't break my heart when he left. Like he didn't let it shatter into pieces on the floor and leave me the broom to sweep them up.

It's not even the leaving that pisses me off. If he told me, if he came to me, I would've given him space. I would've done whatever he needed of me. But he left and then didn't speak to me. Like I didn't exist.

"Fuck you." It's venomous. More so than I intended. "You haven't been here in six years. I've learned how to live life without you." A lie. "So, wear the jersey, show up. It doesn't matter. It won't change anything."

Isaiah remains calm, like always. The one who saw through all my shit and never let it phase him. "Believe that all you want, but I don't. I never learned how to live without you. Still haven't, never will. And I don't believe that you have either." My heart pounds, and I hate it. And I wish I could hate him. "When you're ready to talk and listen, I will be here."

He steps back, eyes glancing behind me to my family that I'm sure is watching—maybe even some of the team—before landing back on me. I see everything in those eyes, like a flashback film reel playing our history, so I look away.

"I'll be here, Aurora. I mean it."

I shake my head and wait for his footsteps to recede. Even though he's gone, his words linger in the air, settling over my skin like dew. So easily, Isaiah takes up any space that's weak enough to let him in. Which is most of me. The truth is, if he pushes hard enough, I know I'll forgive him. I know that having him back will erase the six years without him.

I hate it. I hate how much I hope that he means it. That he'll show up, that he'll be here.

That he still might be my Isaiah.

# FLASHBACK

## *Isaiah, Spring 2014*

I never have trouble finding Aurora. She's an impossible girl to miss. Especially on the field, where she comes alive. More than usual. Like all the pieces of her come together in a perfect puzzle. Aurora knows exactly who she is most times, as much as anyone can, but out there, she not only knows who she is, she becomes exactly who she is supposed to be.

In front of me, she flies down the field, brown curls flying behind her, strong legs delicately handling the ball at her feet, and a big smile on her face. Just like every day she gets to play.

The homemade jersey I have with her number—seventeen—slides easily overtop the white muscle tank I'm wearing. There aren't many others at the field since there's still an hour till game time, so I find my spot on the bleachers at the front. Swinging my backpack around, I pull my AP English book out and set it on my lap.

So far, since we were kids, I hadn't missed a single game of Aurora's unless it was out of state. Even the kiddie games at camp, I watched from the sidelines, and when she started playing travel soccer when she was eight, I either begged my mom or brother to take me, or I begged hers. And now, she'd been starting varsity since her freshman year, and I hadn't missed a single game. I didn't plan on ever missing a game.

I look up and instantly catch Aurora's eyes. They brighten when they find me, as if she's surprised every time she sees me here. She waves, and I return it before she's called back, but not before crossing her eyes and sticking her tongue out at me like she always does. Dragging my eyes away from my best friend, I focus on the book in front of me so I can focus on her when the whistle blows.

Elijah, my older brother, plops down beside me, handing me a pack of Twizzlers. "How's the book?"

His hat casts a shadow over the pages, the embroidered ivy state logo faded with wear. It's his book, the same class he took a few years ago. I'm chasing the shadow my brother left and trying to fill it. "Don't play stupid."

A big smile spreads on his face, appreciation filling his eyes as he looks at the pages. "You know if you ever need my help, imma phone call away?"

Everyone who ever met Eli knew that. He took care of anyone, especially me. Dad died shortly after I was born, and Eli was there every step, even with all the pressure Mom put on him. I wasn't going to be a burden to him, not after all he had done. I wanted him to be a college student. I wanted him to be my brother. He was already coming home every Thursday night after class and staying till Sunday as it was. Not only did he work part time in Philadelphia during the week, but he worked the weekends here too to help my mom out and such. Least I could do was manage high school.

"I got it. I ain't dumb."

"Obviously. I raised you," he jokes, leaning back onto the bleacher and turning his eyes toward the field. And in some ways, it's not a joke. He raised me as much as my mom did.

"You know you didn't have to come, right?" I ask, eyes skimming over the page.

"I know, but she's the little sister I never asked for. She's your girl. It's her junior year, and Aurora… she's going places with this," Eli says matter-of-factly. Like nothing could stop her.

We look up at the same time, and my eyes latch onto number seventeen, trailing over the details that make her, her. Eli smiles when he looks at her, pride shining in his eyes. Once again, I drag my eyes away, trying to focus on the schoolwork at hand—you know, the shit important for me to get into college, to follow in Eli's footsteps, to make sure I don't disappoint Mom.

But…

The longer I look at her, the more time my eyes spend staring at her, which I admit, has been happening more and more recently. I'm starting to think that she just might be as important as anything else.

Maybe more.

Aurora bounds over, her soccer bag bouncing behind her. Beads of sweat look like water droplets on her nose, and her curls are frizzier than they were before the game. I reach out as soon as she's close enough and grab her bag.

Like always, she wraps her arms around my waist and sinks into a hug. At this point, I'm not sure if they're more for her or me, but we both exhale at the touch. Neither of us has ever navigated toward hugs with anyone else aside from a friendly or familial obligation, but somehow, they've found their way into our relationship—willingly.

"Hi." She pulls back, her hazel eyes softening at the seventeen on my chest before traveling to Eli. "Hi!" she repeats, pulling him for a quick side hug, though Eli doesn't accept that.

He rocks her dramatically back and forth. "Nice work out there, Matthews."

"What is it with you and Kian trying to smother me to death?" Aurora mumbles into my brother's chest.

"Just the way it goes." He finally releases her, and she rolls her eyes, though her lips fight a smile. "Where are Soph and Kian anyway? And your parents?"

"Picking up the kid and working late. You should come over for dinner later. Whole family will be there."

That was one thing I loved about her family—how even after the divorce, her parents made sure they put aside any negative feelings and were there for the kids. Of course, it seems like the bare minimum, but mostly, it's horror story after horror story. It's nice that not only are they there for Sophia and Aurora but also Zaza and Kian, and even Eli and me.

"For sure. I'll be there. I'll see if Mom's up for it, too."

"Sounds perfect. Thanks for coming, Eli."

My brother almost looks sheepish at the praise, bordering on uncomfortable. I don't think he hears it too often, even as simple as a *thank you.* "Anytime," he says before kissing her on the cheek. "You two have fun. I'll see you later." He turns and waves, leaving the two of us.

"You played great, Rora."

Her smile is bright. "Thanks. Now, can we go? I'm starved."

Our aftergame ritual includes milkshakes and a giant order of fries at the diner not too far from here. "'Course." I throw my arm around her shoulder, pulling her in.

She likes a bit of quiet after a game, especially after talking to the parents and the coaches. I let her have it until we get to the diner—let her pick the music in the car, usually consisting of sad pop songs, which I've come to enjoy, and let her decide if she wants to talk or not. I'm here to enjoy the ride.

By the time we get to the diner, she's back and full of life. The adrenaline is now a simmer, and she bumps me as we enter the old place. The usual customers are here, including us, seated at the countertop on pale pink stools or in the booths, where we take a seat.

My eyes find hers, bright hazel in the sunlight streaming in through the windows, the crewneck I had in my backseat covering her skin. I'm not sure what it is today, but I can't keep my eyes off her. Today, Aurora is radiant.

I'm pretty sure she always is, but today, for me, she is blinding.

The curls, her brown skin, the warm eyes, the strong personality, she is the star of the show—everything about her is brilliant.

Adjusting in the booth, my legs stretch out, trapping hers. "Do I have something on my face?"

My brows furrow. "No, why?"

"Then why are you staring at me, Isaiah?"

My mouth goes dry, and I attempt to swallow the lump in my throat, but thank God I'm saved by our order being placed on the table.

"Thank you." Aurora smiles at the server and grabs a fry, licking the stray salt from her lip. My eyes linger a second longer than they should.

"Are you gonna share with me today?"

She kicks me under the table. "I don't know what you're talking about. I share with you all the time. My friends, my sense of humor, my addictive personality that you can't stay away from."

I raise a brow. "You are literally hogging the fries as we speak."

A huff of laughter escapes her, and she pushes the plate to the center of the table. "Sorry, I get excited." After a few more fries, she meets my eyes. "Did you submit the poem?"

I exhale. "Rora, please."

"Don't Rora me. You promised." She leans forward, pushing her milkshake my way so I can try it. Even though I've tried it a million times, it's routine. "You promised that if I got an A on that stupid science exam, you would submit it."

Talking about poetry with anyone but Aurora makes me nauseous. She's the only one that I even try with. I trust her more than anyone, but this is hard—attempting to submit a poem to a contest and living in fear of being rejected for something so personal. Seems like hell. Which is why she made the deal in the first place.

"You're too talented not to, Isaiah. Please."

"You flatter me," I deadpan.

Aurora smiles—sunshine on a cloudy day. "Flattery is my strong suit."

"No, it isn't."

"Okay, you know, you could fan my ego every once in a while."

I smile at that, pushing my milkshake her way. "I do enough." She kicks my leg again before she draws her leg up and rests her elbow on her knee. Rora doesn't say anything else, just hits me with those eyes, and I know the first thing I'll do later is submit the stupid poem. "Fine."

"Thank you. Now that that's handled, we can play hangman."

I huff and watch as she pulls out the notebook from her bag—a notebook only filled with whatever games we decide to play in this diner. This month, it's been hangman. Leaning back, I let my eyes fall on her again since she's focused on the notebook. Under the table, my knee rhythmically taps hers, and every touch feels brand new. Like I've never touched her before.

There is nothing extra special about today. Nothing happened at school in the hallways or at lunch. We've done what we do every day. It's not an extraordinary day in any particular way.

But it's different. Aurora feels different.

Even though I've spent pretty much every day with her since I moved here, I feel like I'm noticing things that I didn't before—or maybe things that weren't significant to our friendship. Today, I can't help but notice she has a freckle in one of her hazel eyes and one on the tip of her nose that sort of looks like a star. There's a tiny little scar on her bottom lip, and when she focuses on something, her nose wrinkles the tiniest bit. I've never noticed these details like this before.

Not with this level of awareness or attention.

My chest is tight and blood-heavy. Under the table, I rub my palms together, ignoring how clammy they feel. It's all fucking weird. And not at all awful.

When I look at her, I swear time moves in slow motion, but she's at full speed. As if I can't be bothered to give anything other than her even a fraction of my attention.

*Fuck.*

I've always *seen* Aurora, even when we were kids. She's my best friend, for God's sake. She's a part of who I am. I know everything there is to know about her—what she hates, what she loves, what she loves to hate and hates to love. I know it all. And I thought I knew myself and exactly how I felt. But this is new. This is weird.

Because I didn't know it was possible to see her in a different light when I already knew her in every shade.

Today, Aurora is impossible to miss in a way I didn't know was possible.

## Keepsake Box

**M**emory Lane is a shit fucking place, and I'd fight anyone who disagreed.

The keepsake box won't stop staring at me. I know it's an inanimate object, but it hasn't left me alone all day. I've had it since I was a little girl; it's moved houses with me, and it has pieces of every part of my life… of course, pathetically, regarding Isaiah. Bigger things, like soccer or my nieces, are in picture frames on walls or showcases with trophies. This box is pretty much everything else.

For years, I've forgotten about it—haven't added anything to it.

Now, I can't stop fucking staring at it.

Nostalgia is absolutely my worst enemy, forcing me to remember days and moments in vivid detail when I'd rather forget them. Life would be so much easier if I could live in the present more, especially considering, most days, I love where I'm at. But I can never escape the spiral of those days I'd kill to relive. A gentle touch I'd kill to feel again. A smile or a laugh I'd kill to have directed at me and my annoyingly fragile heart.

Nostalgia creeps in gently until it decides to sting.

Still, knowing that bite is coming, I pull the keepsake box closer.

My fingers curl around the edges, grazing the cracked paint. Somewhere out in the world, Isaiah has one that looks similar. We got them together at the Goodwill in our town. Originally, it was part of a larger chest, but it was broken and splintered.

Our moms had gotten together and made these for us. Sawed and sanded the wood, placed new locks on them, and handed them over. With Eli's help, we both carved the number seventeen on them. And our names next to each other on each box. Because *God forbid* we did anything separately.

Then, we made them our own. Isaiah painted his in shades of green since that was his favorite color and delicately painted some of his favorite poetry as he got older. Mine was more chaotic. Shades of whatever color were my favorite at the time, jagged flowers or shapes that I liked, a crappy shoreline, a scrawled version of the Philadelphia skyline, and whatever else I loved.

Without thinking, my fingers find the number on the upper left corner of the box. I trace it, wondering if I could transport back in time. Back when I wasn't angry or hurt or left behind by Isaiah; I was just with him.

I open the box and find the lid painted with all the things I forgot about. Memories flood; when we got to high school, maybe at the end of sophomore or beginning of junior year, that's when it all started—it's when we both started painting the inside of the boxes with things we didn't want the other to see. I have no idea what's in Isaiah's, but my tiny paintings are very clearly all related to him.

An outline of his glasses that he didn't like to wear, the title of his favorite poetry book, *Windless Sails*, and milkshake cups from our time at the diner. Those were just the paintings.

Inside, I find more. An old Twizzlers wrapper since Isaiah could eat them for breakfast, lunch, and dinner. A copy of the poem that won in a competition I forced him to submit it to. Pictures of us taken after my games, at the diner in our booth, or in the street or yard as kids. Pictures of us with each other's families, at dinner, on our first day of school—everything and anything you could think of.

Jesus, it was fucking endless.

I flick through, ignoring things I know are guaranteed to hurt more than I can handle. Like more of his old poetry or the stupid notes we would pass in class. There are some random things in here that aren't related to him—things like old friendship bracelets from my early soccer teams or pins I won at the tournaments.

But the little pouch tucked under it all clinks together, and I know exactly what it is. Turning it over, I tug until the jewelry falls out. The first is a thin, gold chain Isaiah used to wear. The memory of him placing it around my neck after getting MVP in the championship game comes to life as soon as I touch it.

The second is a ring—a gold signet ring with a slight dome polished to perfection. It was a family ring, passed down from his grandfather (maybe even beyond that) to his dad, to Eli, and then, to him. On the signet, a tiny *B* is engraved for their last name.

I remember when he gave this to me, too. Or really, left it. It was the end of summer after we graduated, and we weren't really talking because of Eli. He left it on my desk with a poem that's tucked away because I can't bear to look at it. Part of me hates this ring. It seemed that in every story I'd heard after it was given, whether intentional or not, the person left. His dad gave it to Eli before he died when Isaiah was a baby, then Eli gave it to him before disappearing, and then, he left it to me.

Still, part of me loves this ring.

I slip it on my middle finger where I used to wear it. Spinning it three times…it just feels like it never should've left that spot.

God, look at me, fucking sentimental over a ring. That's not mine. That I haven't worn in years.

Pushing away the box, I lean back into the bed. Pressing my palms against my eyes doesn't do much to alleviate the sting building, but I don't want to cry over this. I cried over this for two years and haven't since—but here I am, all over again.

I want what he said to be true. And yet, I'm infuriated by it.

Before I fully succumb to whatever torture my thoughts want to put me through, I step out onto my balcony with my phone in hand. For a second, I consider not calling anyone—not letting anyone in. But it's not doing me any fucking good as it is.

Humidity dampens the air, and the sun scorches the skin of my shoulders. Warmth spreads over my cheeks and lightens my shoulders, clears my lungs. I wouldn't describe myself as a summer child, but part of me has always thought it was the closest to Heaven any of us might understand. The smell of fresh cut grass or clouds heavy with the scent of rain. Maybe it was the nostalgia that summer brought, the freedom we felt. Or maybe it was that under the sun, the weight of the world didn't feel as heavy.

Scrolling through my favorites, I land on Maazina's name. She answers on the second ring. "What's cooking, good looking?"

I snort, huffing out a laugh. "You are a special character."

"Don't I know it," Maazina says warmly before her voice turns gentle. "What's up?"

My arms rest on the balcony railing, the heat distracting me from the stinging in my eyes. "Are you busy tonight?"

"Not at all."

"I need to get out of the apartment."

"Me, too."

I check the date, and low and behold, it's August second. A year ago, her mother passed. A month later, her fiancé broke up with her. Left her a note on a Post-It.

"Maazina, are you okay?"

"Yes and no. Like always."

Maazina may be the jokester, but under that comedic surface, she is far more nuanced than she wants people to believe. No one else on the team—not even Sylvia and Viv—know how deeply she dealt with depression after her situation. There were nights I stayed up with her so she could sleep. If I couldn't be there, I was on the phone. Sometimes, she slept here because she couldn't bear to be in her own apartment. She is one of the most caring people I know and is someone who feels more deeply than many. I'm terrible at handling other people's vulnerability; she excels at it. Knowing exactly what to do with it, knowing exactly what different people need.

But Maazina can forget about herself sometimes. She knows how to be strong for everyone else, how to create a safe space for their emotions, but she forgets that she needs that, too. I think she gets so lost in the current of other people's wants and needs, she pushes her own aside. More willing to let herself suffer than those around her.

Whereas I excel in sitting in the sadness, floating down the river of what-ifs, and overthinking. So when she finally gets to the breaking point, I never let her do it alone. I think that's why we gravitate toward each other—two souls who need one another more than they could ever know.

"Well, come over. I need someone to hold my hand," I say, knowing she needs that, too.

"Let's do it. Should I bring anything, or did you have something in mind?"

"No. We can go out. Maybe dinner? Ice cream? Just text me when you're on the way."

"Coolio." I laugh softly. "I'll see you later, loser."

I give another snort. "Yeah, alright."

The phone beeps, and I exhale before turning back inside. I pick up all the items sprawled out on the floor and shove them back into the keepsake box before heading to my closet. Carefully, I tuck it back where I found it, only to stumble upon two new items that fell to the floor.

An old sweatshirt of his and two tiny stuffed animal octopi. The first, he gave me for Valentine's Day in middle school, and the second, he won for me at a carnival in high school. I leave the sweatshirt and the first, smaller stuffed animal on the floor. But I take the other—a pink and purple octopus—and roll it around in my hands.

Isaiah knew how much I loved them, so whenever he saw anything octopus related, he got it. It wasn't often, but I do have a small collection of items because of him. This one just meant the most. I leave the other behind but this one, I pull close to my chest before tucking it under my comforter.

I'll analyze that decision another day.

Four long, sporadic buzzes let me know Maazina's arrived.

"Well, hello there!" She grins, leaning against the door frame. You'd never know that she's having a bad day.

"Let me just finish up, and then, we can go." I jog back to my bathroom, swiping the mascara over my lashes and dabbing on lip gloss.

Maazina sits on the couch upside down, legs thrown over the back with her phone in hand. The sight stops me in my tracks.

"What the hell are you doing?"

"It's comfortable, duh." Her eyes focus on me, and she contorts herself off the couch. "You ready?"

With a nod, I grab my bag and close the door behind us. Maazina eyes me. "Come on, grumpy, cheer up." She nudges my shoulder until my lips pull into a smile. "There it is."

"You talk to me like a child."

"Sometimes, you act like one."

If my eyebrows could touch the sky, they would. She's right but damn. "And you don't?"

Her green-brown eyes twinkle. "Yeah, but in a different way. I'm all child wonder and immaturity." She motions her hand to me as the elevator descends. "You're all temper-tantrum-like and moody."

I can't help but laugh. "God, I hate you."

"I believe the word you're looking for is love. It's spelled l-o-v-e. Have you ever heard of it?" Instead of answering, I start walking. "Where are we going?"

Above, the sky has turned dark and gray, the smell of rain overwhelming.

The clicking of our heels pauses at the crosswalk. None of us wear them often, but sometimes, when I'm feeling small, the additional height makes me feel like I'm on top of the world. Maazina just likes the sound. "One of my favorite bars is doing an open mic type thing. Usually, it's small bands, and honestly, it's always good. They don't do them often. Is that okay?"

Excitement blooms on her face. "Of course, that sounds good. They have food, right?"

We cross hand in hand when the street traffic stops. "Of course. I'm starving."

We approach the restaurant and pay the small cover fee that gets split between anyone who goes up on the stage tonight. Most times, they all decide to donate it to the charity of choice that the restaurant chooses for each event, and even if they do keep it (as starving artists should), the restaurant donates whatever the amount would've been. More often than not, they double it—if not more. I love this place. They care about their staff, their customers, and those that come here and are brave enough to get on the small stage.

The host, Nelli, smiles as I enter. We've got a good relationship. I've given her a few tickets to some games. She takes my constant take-out orders without judgment and gets me a good seat for these events.

"Hi, Ro! Good game!" Nelli pops out in front of the stand with a big smile.

My cheeks warm at the compliment. They always make me feel strange, no matter who they come from. "Thank you, Nelli. How's school going?"

She waves her hand. "You know, it's school." I raise a brow. Nelli is currently double majoring with plans to pursue med school right after, all while being on the division one soccer team. She shrugs at the look, gathering menus in her hands. "Come on. If you don't ask, I'll make them comp something."

"You're in charge here; I'm merely a humble customer."

Nelli stops in front of a two-top table off to the side of the stage but with a great view. The dim chandeliers placed around in a pattern create warm lighting over the floor. "You're my favorite though."

"I know." It's at that moment Maazina steps fully into view, and I fight my grin. Nelli is a huge fan.

Nelli's eyes widen, and her mouth gapes ever so slightly. Frantically, her eyes jump between me and Maazina, who's grinning ear to ear. "Hi."

"Oh, my God, Maazina Aybar? Aurora, that's Maazina!" Nelli's voice takes on a tone I've never heard. "I mean, of course, you know that. She's your teammate. Oh, my God." She swallows, forcing herself to breathe. "Hi. Imma huge fan."

"Oh, that's sweet. Thank you. It's wonderful to meet you." Maazina shines at the compliments, at the attention. Confident, not cocky. A fine line that she walks well. "We'll have to get you to the next home game or two—maybe onto the field? What do you say, Ro?"

"Sounds good to me. Nelli?"

She squeals. "Please? I would die!"

"No dying," Maazina says. "But absolutely."

Nelli hugs me, and before she can stop herself, she hugs Maazina, who laughs. "Thank you so, so much. I'll let you be now. It starts soon. But really, thank you." She practically dances back to the host stand before we can even say the words, "You're welcome".

It's not often that we get crazy fans like the other sports in this city. I doubt we ever will, but it's not about that. It's about the fact that we get to do what we love for a living, and it's about girls like Nelli. Neither of us says it, but we sit in silence for a moment, and I know Maazina is soaking it in, too.

Outside, the sky darkens, and the warm, yellow lights cast shadows over the bar. We order drinks and an appetizer to start, existing in a peaceful quiet with the low hum of other voices. But when Maazina hits me with a gentle look, I know she's going to ask.

"So...do you want to talk about it?"

"I mean, not really. But I should. Do you?"

"Absolutely not. Please talk to me about this. It's fresh and new, and

I didn't come so you could feel guilty for being upset." The warm lights illuminate her freckles and the natural highlights in her long, brown hair. "You know I would never say anything. Anything you tell me stays with me. And if it's about Drew, don't think that because I introduced you that it has to mean anything."

I sit back, crossing my leg over the other. "I know that. Soph knows—"

"Of course, she does," we both say at the same time. My lips raise briefly before falling again.

"It's Isaiah. It's about Drew too, but not really," I say, exhaling. "I found an old keepsake box today just filled with everything from when I was a kid, in high school, and almost all of it related to Isaiah. He has one similar because we made them together. We did everything together."

I swallow, taking a sip of the mocktail in front of me. Around us, the restaurant has filled up, couples sitting at tables with warm smiles, friends sharing laughs over the table.

"We did everything together, and then, he left. No explanation, no real goodbye. One day, he was there, and he was my best friend, and…" *More.* My eyes burn. "The next, he was just gone. And now, he wants to show up and say that he's here for me? He hasn't been here for six years. And this, all this, makes me feel fucking crazy. I go from missing him to furious to this emotional mess."

My voice is quiet, but the words are sharp, the hurt spilling out of them like a bleeding heart. Maazina listens intently, never taking her eyes off me.

"I just—he wouldn't let me be there for him back then, and now what? What am I supposed to do? Fight it? Let it happen? Keep dating when everyone I talk to falls short because they aren't him?"

The next few words are ones I've thought of, kept to myself because out loud, they sound pathetic, but they're fighting to escape. "How am

I ever supposed to try to fall in love again when I'm not sure I've ever stopped loving him?"

Maazina takes a long sip of her drink, blinking rapidly, and I pretend not to see the water building in her eyes.

When she looks at me again, her eyes are clear. "I don't think you have to make that decision right now. Or any decision. You don't have to know how to feel about him being here or try and work through that all at once." She hesitates, then clears her throat. "You don't have to stop loving him if you don't want to. I know some people would tell you to get over it or move on, but sometimes, when you know, you know. And if that doesn't work out, who's to tell you how long it'll take to move on? Who's to tell you if you should? You don't have to know what you want, Aurora, or what any of it means. My God, I wouldn't. Just cut yourself some slack. I know you're shit at that, but just do it."

We share a smile at that, but her words are on a loop in my head.

*When you know, you know.*

I knew.

At eighteen, I knew everything, and now, I don't know anything.

## Still You

The conversation strays after that. We don't ever talk about Drew. Not that there's much to say besides he doesn't deserve to pine after someone who's not sure she wants to be pined after. It's a waste of his time and careless of his feelings in a way I don't want to be.

But I can deal with that on my own.

Fresh drinks are in front of us with plates of food waiting for the lights to dim.

Maazina mumbles around the bite of nachos, "These are delicious."

"Remember when you had the nerve to call me a child earlier?"

"Yup, and I would do it again."

I laugh for the first time since we pretended Maazina didn't cry at the table and I didn't voice my fears of never falling in love again. I pluck out a chip that's mostly just cheese, glancing up. "Thank you, for earlier," I say, clearing my throat.

"You don't have to thank me for being your friend," she says, side-eying me before focusing on the food again. "That's the whole point."

"Shut up and accept the thank you, Maazina."

She smiles as the lights finally dim. Claps echo around the packed room as the manager, Cleo, takes the stage. "We've got a few great acts tonight, everyone, if I do say so myself. Some readings, some singing, some bands. You know, a mix of everything. First up is our very own Nelli, reading a short story piece that was published in her college's creative arts magazine because she is determined to leave no stone unturned at that school."

Nelli approaches the stage, cool and confident as she takes the center. The story she reads is about her mother and her grandfather, and somewhere along the line, it turns into a story about her and her father. How the relationships mirror each other and how we sometimes become the people we try the least to be like. It resonates with me, how she touches both the negative and the positives of it. She gets a standing ovation when she finishes, and there are fewer dry eyes than wet ones.

Cleo returns, hugging Nelli before she returns to work. "Next up, a new addition to the city of Philadelphia. He's a poet and a professor starting this fall, and tonight, he'll be reading from his debut poetry book coming out in two weeks titled, *Someone Else's House*."

*What the* fuck.

"Welcome, Isaiah Bryant."

Maazina chokes on her drink.

I would laugh if I wasn't frozen in my seat.

"Aurora, what the fuck?" she whisper-yells as everyone else claps.

"What do you mean, what the fuck?" I glance at her, blinking. "What the fuck."

Isaiah steps on stage, and he looks beautiful. I want to die. Whether that is in correlation to him being here or him looking that good, I'm not sure. Low lights cast shadows over his brown skin, gorgeously highlighting the ink that I wish I could trace, wish I could memorize the art that he decided to memorialize.

He holds the poetry book in his hand, the title flashing like neon signs in my head as he strides up, owning the small stage. A perfect smile—one gained after years of braces—tilts his lips, and the only way I know it's not *my* smile is because his little dimple isn't there.

*Someone Else's House.* What the fuck.

It means nothing substantial to everyone else sitting here, but it means something to me. He used to say this when we were kids. When he felt alone, when he felt like he could never fill the shoes of his brother or the expectations of his mom, he used to say, *"Sometimes, I just want to go to someone else's house. Live someone else's life. Just for a day. To step away and remember why I love mine."* And while it wasn't a fix, we just always went to my house.

"Is he stalking you? Does he have your phone bugged? What the hell is going on?" Maazina says, stuffing food in her mouth because she's anxious.

"Maazina." My eyes don't stray from Isaiah as he takes a seat on the stool.

"He's a poet? He writes poetry?"

"Maazina." I hate how good he looks.

"How are you so fucking calm?"

I am, obviously, anything but.

Isaiah adjusts on the stool, resting one long leg on the step and stretching out. It's a small venue, but it's huge for him—or younger him, who hated crowds and public speaking. And reading his poetry to anyone but me. But then again, he's going to be a professor now, too. Either way, a bud of pride blooms in my chest despite wishing it wouldn't.

"I'm gonna be honest, I'd be lying if I said I wasn't nervous as hell up here," he says, his mouth barely curling. "I've only read from this collection a few times, mostly to my mom preparing for my first year of teaching college students and for publication. To be completely honest, I'm scared shitless." A small echo of laughter follows.

He casts his eyes down, focusing on the book before glancing out at the crowd. I swallow, my grip tightening on my glass, wondering if he's seen me yet. Isaiah clears his throat. "But I've written and rewritten these poems more times than I can count. And to understand any of them, you need to understand that they're about the same girl. Pretty much everything I write is about the same girl. She used to be the first person that saw anything I wrote. Now, I'm just hoping that somehow, she hears these. So, thanks for letting me get up here to be a completely hopeless romantic in front of a bunch of strangers."

"Has he seen you?" Maazina whispers to me, tapping her fingernails on the table.

At that moment, his eyes fan out over the crowd, and they find me in a heartbeat. His smile doesn't falter to the outside eye, but I see the moment he contemplates dropping it. "He has now."

"Fuck."

I look around the room, seeing everyone watching him with locked eyes, but when I turn back, his eyes remain on me. Even in a crowded room, I feel each second of his heated look. Isaiah runs a hand toward his forehead over his short-cropped hair. I notice every tiny detail, even from afar. The thin silver bracelet around his wrist contrasting against the ink, the very slight tightening of his fingers on the book, and the way his foot taps nervously on the stool.

"The first I'll be reading is called "West View High"."

It's a prose poem, he explains. He always loved those. Getting to let his thoughts run without the constrictions of a certain form or line requirements. He loved stricter poem forms, too, but I used to watch him write prose like his hand was on fire. He couldn't get his thoughts out quickly enough. I used to love his prose poems.

But right now, I have no idea how I'm going to feel.

How I'm going to feel about any of these—because I realize, these poems, from these six years of distance, are the only ones in his life that I haven't read first.

A piece of my heart aches, curling in on itself.

The poem starts. Isaiah's voice slows and deepens, and chills dance up my spine. It's a long prose poem, but it's enticing—the way he tells the story, the way he repeats phrases, the way he paints his life.

He turns the page, the end approaching. "I never wanted to go to West View High. A static public school stuck in the suburbs of Pennsylvania with lockers of gray and poorly painted walls. Heaving myself out from under warm covers to push through crowds of people who never saw me, all while wishing for a life that I was too naïve for. Even now, there is one thing I miss—the early dawn mornings, the sky painted pink, the house with green shutters, and the girl who lived within. I never wanted to go to West View High, but I always wanted to walk there with her by my side."

It goes on, and my eyes never leave him as he reads it. The whole thing is simple yet beautiful. Maybe that's why the line that I can't forget is the simplest of all. *I never wanted to go to West View High, but I always wanted to walk there with her by my side.*

Maazina's eyes are burning holes in my cheek with her stare, but I refuse to look. I'm scared if I even blink, tears will fall. Isaiah glances up, locating me in seconds as the crowd claps at the end of the first poem. Even from a distance, in his eyes, I see all the other memories we made as teenagers. All the jokes we told on the early morning walks to school, all the times he carried my soccer bag, all the times we worked on a poem together. And I remember all the times I wanted him to hold my hand.

Below the table, I intertwine my hands together tightly to stop them from shaking.

"The next one is a poem form known as a cinquain: a five-line, twenty-two-syllable poem. Short and sweet. I realize that sounds nerdy, but bear with me, it's one of my favorites." He smiles; the crowd smiles back. "It's called "Still You.""

*Life was…*

*Jade green, sweet smiles.*

*Sunshine on brown skin,*

*Hands that brushed, eyes that shone. Life is*

*still you.*

A poem of simple phrases, all of which hit like a shot to the heart. The cadence of his voice, how he emphasizes, pauses—it feels like he's speaking directly to me in a room full of people.

Tears streak out of my eyes without my permission.

"I'll be outside…I've gotta…" My words are jumbled, lost in the sound of clapping hands, and I'm not even sure if Maazina hears them. I quickly push away from the table and make a beeline to the street, where the rain has finally started in a slow drizzle.

My blood is pumping. Two simple little poems did this to me—God knows what else is in that book. Hot air causes the misty rain to stick to me, and the tears roll over my cheeks. The brick wall at my back is the only stability I can find.

Of all the places to end up in, it had to be the same night he was there.

"Aurora?"

Exhaling, I open my eyes to Isaiah. "What?"

"I didn't know you were going to be here."

All I can think is how neither of us knows anything anymore.

"Obviously."

We stare at each other.

"You're crying," he says, hesitating.

I huff, more tears falling. "Clearly, Isaiah. Why did you come out here? To point that out?"

"No, I…" He sighs, running a hand over his face, disrupting the droplets of water that have landed there. "It just took me by surprise."

"Yeah, well, you being here took me by surprise."

Our eyes meet. Emotions flash in his deep brown eyes as he studies me and studies the tears that won't stop. I wonder if he can see all the hurt I've tried to hide.

I swallow anything but anger down. "I don't get it, Isaiah. You show up in this city, at my game and tell me that you're here for me." My throat tightens, but I don't break eye contact. "But where were you? You went six years without me, and you think you can just waltz in here and show up and think that fixes it? Not days, not weeks, not months…years."

"Rora…"

Hurt burns my skin. "Don't call me that. You don't get to call me that ever fucking again."

This entire thing is whiplash. One minute, I'm wanting what he said to be true, that he's here for me, that he'll show it, and the next, I'm so livid I can barely breathe. It's exhausting.

And I hate that when I look at him, I see it mirrored in his eyes. More hurt than anything. I hate the way he focuses on the raindrops on my skin, like he's jealous they're touching me, and he's not.

"I didn't come here to hurt you, I—" He pauses and inhales. The frustration is visible on his features. I know how much he wants to retreat because I used to be where he retreated to. "I came here to say I'm sorry. To find out if you were happy—"

"Happy?" I step forward, straining my neck to look at him. "Do I look happy to you?"

The pause is heavy, weighed down by the truth that he doesn't want to acknowledge. I'm not sure I really want him to either.

Wiping away the tears is pointless, but I do it anyway, rain drops taking their place until more fall. I attempt to stride past him but don't get very far. Isaiah's hand curls around my bicep, gentle yet firm enough to keep me in place.

"Aurora, wait."

"Wait? Wait for what?"

His hand is a brand on my arm, each finger burning its own imprint. Every inch of his skin that touches mine is heated. And familiar. And yet, it is also foreign.

Swallowing, I pull my arm out of his grip.

His eyes are full of emotions I don't want to dive into. "I miss you."

A shot to the heart would hurt less.

My chest caves in; my heart grows claws that dig for safety.

"I will explain everything if you just let me. I will apologize until you tell me to stop. Just please believe me when I say I miss you, that I've missed you every single day," Isaiah pleads while I stare at him.

I believe him because there wasn't a day I didn't think of him. But that doesn't mean it's all okay. In fact, it feels even worse.

My head shakes on its own accord as I step back. I swallow as I try to talk around the lump in my throat to no avail. He doesn't push. Instead, he waits. Eyes filled with hurt become patient as I try and search for my words. For any words at all.

I turn my eyes up to the sky, letting them close as the rain patters against my skin. When I open them again, Isaiah is still looking at me. Finally, I choke out the words, "I need some time. You want to explain—

fine. But I need time. I will find you when I'm ready."

With that, I step away and place one foot in front of the other like it isn't shooting pain in my chest with every step. Maazina waits in front of the door. I was so distracted by him that for a second, as terrible as it is, I forgot I wasn't here alone.

I hate that I'm crying and she's here to see it. She doesn't like seeing people cry, and she never really knows what to do when someone does—much like myself—but she walks by my side, holding the umbrella over both of us as she takes the lead towards my apartment.

Before we turn the corner, I can't help but look behind me.

How could I not with Isaiah's stare burning holes in my back? Sure enough, he's still standing in the rain with his eyes on me.

He stands, waiting there, knowing he has to keep waiting until I decide to end the torture.

I leave knowing that he missed me. After wondering constantly, staring up at the ceiling in the middle of sleepless nights—

He *missed* me.

# 8

## No Escape

The internet has become my best friend.

It was something that I had avoided in terms of Isaiah during our time apart. I had no desire to know what he was up to. If he could disappear without a word, with a ring and a poem as a goodbye, if he could live without me—then so could I.

In the two weeks since he read the poems, I had discovered everything I would've known had we stayed…friends. He graduated in three years with his BA in English Literature with a minor in history and then went on to get his MFA. The poetry book came out Tuesday, and he starts teaching at a local University next week—the end of August—as a poetry professor. There are no girlfriends that I can find, at least no pictures of any on social media. It's mostly Isaiah, a few friends, and his mom. One thing I notice is the lack of his brother. Eli was always so involved, and now…it's like he never existed.

I rub my eyes, tired from staring at the screen as I move the ice around on my thighs. Next to me sits *Someone Else's House*. There are bits and pieces of us both on the cover. It's a deep jade green, but the tiny house sitting in the center is molded after his childhood home. A simple, two-story, brick home with shutters and a big tree in the yard. It's simple. It's beautiful. It's the only part of the book I've looked at besides the 'about the author' section on the back.

My phone rings. "Hello?"

"Your sister told me that if you're still staring at that book, I am required to drive up and take it from you."

"Kian," I sigh, "why are you scared of my sister?"

"It's less about the fear and more about the state of your sanity." He pauses. "Not that you had much before. Not that either of you ever had, but that's beside the point."

"I hate you."

"Are you still staring at the book?"

"If I am, are you actually going to drive all the way up here just to take it?"

"Well, probably not, but come on, Ro." He sighs. "He wants to explain, to let you in."

I furrow my brows. "To let me in? He's the one who shut me out. And how do you know that the explanation is perfectly reasonable and will make up for everything? What—has he talked to you all these years?"

He hesitates. "That's not—"

"I don't want to talk about this, Kian. I'm gonna be mean, and I don't want to be. Can you just tell Soph that I'm fine, please? Love you. Kiss the kiddos for me." I don't wait for his response before I hang up.

I exhale heavily as I run a hand down my face. A takeout box with a half-eaten turkey burger and sweet potato fries sits to one side of me and the book to the other. An old record spins on my vinyl player as I sit there in Isaiah's old hoodie.

Thank God I live alone. If anyone walked in on this sight, I wouldn't even blame them for speed dialing a therapist.

I reach over, grabbing the book.

In my hands, the cover is a smooth matte, and the pages have that classic book feel I know Isaiah used to love. And even though I can't bring myself to open it, I toss it in my bag for the away game that has come at the perfect time. I love this city, but I need to get out. Ever since he's shown up, it's felt too small.

Right now, I need a moment to breathe.

Sweat drips down my nose as I backpedal. We're up by two but with probably ten minutes left. Houston, the home team, is pushing hard. The heat is scorching, and this game has been non-stop on both sides. But even though my chest heaves and my legs burn, I feel amazing. I've played a great game, the team has played a great game—we're on fire. As hard as Houston tries, they don't recover, and the game ends in our two-nothing win.

My dad falls into step beside me as we walk to the locker rooms. "Nice work out there." I glance over as he adjusts his hat. "You were a little slow when you had to cut back in on the left. That knee okay?"

The tiny piece of hope that never fully bloomed recedes. "It's fine. I tweaked it in practice, but I've got it covered."

Dad pulls the locker room door open for me. "Make sure you do. Don't want it slowing you down any further."

*God, just once, would he leave it at nice work?* Is that asking too much? Asking for him to be a dad and not a coach? For one split second?

I head in with a parting nod, packing my bag and already thinking about the shower I can't wait to take at the hotel. This escape hasn't been much of an escape, aside from the ninety minutes on the field. On the plane here, it was dad pointing out every mistake I made twice over from the previous game. In warm-ups, a hard pointed stare that caught every touch, every pass, every call. And now this. Maybe to someone else, it would be nothing out of the ordinary. But this was my life. All the time. Wary praise followed by an observation that was less than ideal, followed by a comment that might have meant well but never landed that way.

Everything good I did was overshadowed by a mistake.

I sit, dropping my head in my hands and massaging my temples. Viv takes a seat next to me. "You alright?"

Whether I am or not, I say, "Yeah, just exhausted." I fake a smile. I know she sees right through it. The girls know our relationship is rocky. But now isn't the time or place, and she knows that, but I'm thankful for the check-in.

She rubs a hand down my back before giving me my space. I'm thankful I did my post-game speech on the field and spoke to all my girls because I don't have it in me now. The coaches give their final thoughts before herding us onto the bus back to the hotel. I've never been more thankful to be back in the room. Even though I hate hotels and the fact that I can never trust how clean it is or how comfortable I feel, it's a relief to be away from other eyes—aside from Maazina, my roommate.

I wanted to escape home, and now, I want to escape here.

After unplugging my ear pods, I turn off do not disturb to see a text from an unknown number. I already know exactly who it is.

> **Unknown:** Aurora, it's Isaiah. I assume you deleted my old number, but either way, I got a new one. I hope your game went well—I'm sure you played beautifully; you always do. I want to give you your space, but I really want us to talk. Please think about it. Safe travels home.

Immediately I call Sophia. "Did you give Isaiah my phone number?"

"Uh, no. Why?"

"Because he texted me, and I certainly didn't give it to him, nor did any of my teammates," I say, setting my curls free from their bun. Maazina watches me from her spot on the bed.

"Oh."

"Put Kian on the phone."

Sophia sighs, mumbling to herself, "fucking idiot", before calling loudly for her husband.

"Hello?"

"Kian."

"No, Sophia! I don't want to talk to her."

I rearrange the pillows behind me, getting comfortable since my idiot brother-in-law thinks he can put this off. There's a bit more shouting in the background, Sophia yelling that he can suffer his own consequences and Kian threatening to cry, but eventually, I hear a reluctant sigh.

"Are you done being a baby?"

"How pissed off are you? Scale of one to ten."

It's a fair question, but I don't know. Honestly, right now, I just feel worn down. "Because I'm tired, it's a three. Do not ask me tomorrow."

"I'm sorry."

"You're not. Don't apologize when you don't mean it. Just…why?" I ask, and Maazina silently comes to sit next to me, scrolling on the TV and looking at the room service menu.

Kian paces in the background. "I…well, he was distraught, Aurora. He practically begged me."

"Having kids made you weak."

"I don't deny that."

"Good." Any fight I do have left dies. My head falls back, and my eyes close. "I'll talk to you guys later, okay?"

"That's it? You're not gonna—okay. Sounds good." He pauses. "I love you, Aurora."

"Yeah, uh-huh. I love you, too."

After hanging up, I stare at the text message. I knew I couldn't avoid it forever. I just would've preferred it to be on my terms. Then maybe I could've pushed it off further.

I read it until I have it memorized, until I can recite it.

Finally, I type out a weak response. Telling him I'll be in contact shortly after I get home and then place my phone down.

Dramatically, I groan. "I hate him."

"Isaiah? Or your brother-in-law? Who, you know, is a beautiful man."

"Gross, Maazina. You know he's married. To my sister."

She nods, popping a candy in her mouth. "Yeah, who is arguably far prettier than him. But together? It's simply not fair."

"I'm surrounded by—"

"Don't finish that sentence, or I won't give you any candy."

I hold out my hand, and candy is dropped into my palm. "To answer your question: both." I wish it were true.

"Would be easier that way, wouldn't it?"

My head falls back. "So much."

A knock on the door connecting us and another room sounds before it opens. Vivian and Sylvia stand in the doorway. "Can we come in?"

"Of course."

They make themselves comfortable in the room, specifically on the bed we're on.

"He texted her," Maazina says, shoving candy in her mouth. I pinch her arm. "What? You were gonna tell them eventually, and if you're gonna talk to him, may as well talk to us first." Her words are jumbled and barely decipherable, but we all understand.

Sylvia gives me a gentle smile. When other people do that, it's so obvious that most times, they're trying to hide their pity. But Sylvia makes you feel understood. "She told us about the poetry."

"Don't remind me." I haven't stopped thinking about it since. The book, though I can barely fathom opening it, is tucked away at the bottom of my bag.

"I mean, my God, you guys should've been there. He only read two… but that was some of the sappiest shit I've ever heard. I loved it."

"Why don't you buy the book then?" I mumble as Viv laughs.

Maazina raises a brow. "I did."

"Traitor."

"To defeat your enemy, you must know your enemy."

Vivian stares. "You are…terrifying." Her eyes flick to me. "When did we decide he was the enemy?"

"We didn't. I'm just assuming that's how Aurora feels."

I roll over and grab the candy. "I never said he was my *enemy*. And is reading the poems really going to help you? Actually, you know what? I don't want to know."

"Are you sure you don't want to know?"

"I do," Sylvia and Viv chime in unison.

"They're like straight out of a romance novel or some grand rom-com, Ro. I can't make this up," Maazina says.

I groan. "Can we talk about something else?"

"Sure, like Drew?" She couldn't hold the laugh in even if she tried.

"You are the fucking worst," I bite but can't help but laugh.

"Ah-ah, *best*."

I roll over on my back, laughter still reverberating through the air. My thoughts are sure to return to Isaiah the moment it's quiet again. And

I probably won't stop thinking about him until I'm speaking to him. So, I'd rather enjoy my friends and not panic and fret about something I can't control.

I curl up with two pillows. I know when I get back, there's no more avoiding it.

It's time to face the music.

# ANSWERS

The arts building on campus is gorgeous. All brick, large cathedral windows and vaulted ceilings. I can picture Isaiah here so easily.

Though, if I just grew a pair and entered, I wouldn't have to picture it. I could just see it.

*Fuck it.* I take a deep breath and push through the doors. It's quiet on campus, later in the afternoon with less students milling about, but I happen to know he's coming to the end of his last class.

Perks of having a fan who works for the school.

I walk slowly through the halls, doing my best to blend in as a stray student and most likely failing, until I find the large lecture room. Through the small window, I see Isaiah leaning on the desk, tattooed arms crossed against his chest, and a gentle smile on his face. When we were kids, teaching was never something that crossed his mind, but it makes sense. He's a good listener, he's encouraging, and he's incredibly smart. He's also brilliant at anything he puts his mind to.

The book feels like a heavy weight in my bag. I know it contains pieces of Isaiah I don't have, that I don't know about—him deciding to teach feels like that, too. All it does is make me wonder what other parts of him are new to me? What other parts of him bloomed after he left?

What parts of him are left from when he was everything to me?

Soon enough, the students file out, and before entering, I ensure they've all left, shutting the door behind me. The click draws his attention.

His eyes widen. "Ro—Aurora. What are you doing here?"

I watch his tattooed hands move nervously over the desk, cleaning it up and closing books. "I'm here to talk."

Isaiah runs a hand towards his forehead, over his curls. "You could've given me a heads up."

"Yeah, well, you left on your terms; you showed up here on your terms. I'm doing this on mine." I cross my arms, acting like my heart isn't beating out of my chest.

He dips his head. "Alright." Isaiah leans on his desk, and I stride in, sitting atop a desk directly across from him. I glance around. There's a poem up on the screen, a book sitting open on the desk.

"What do you want to know?"

I snort, hanging my head back before meeting his eyes. "What are you willing to tell me?"

Isaiah's expression is serious, though his eyes remain warm as they look at me. "I'll tell you anything you want to know."

"Everything?"

"Everything." He uncrosses an arm, motioning to the room. "I'd rather not do it here, but I will tell you everything."

I swallow, reaching into my bag and pulling out the book. "Let's start with this."

He fidgets, his fingers spinning the thin chain around his wrist. "You bought it?" Isaiah studies me, his eyes taking in every inch, heat singing my skin where his gaze lands.

Flipping it open, I thumb over the pages, careful to avoid the words. I still haven't read it. "Felt like I had to."

"Can I—one second." He kicks off the desk and moves around to his bag. The sound of rustling follows, and he pulls out another copy. One with the spine cracked and the pages folded, one that's well read. He steps towards me, closing the space, and holds it out. "Take this one."

"Why?"

"Aurora, just take it."

The moment he gets closer, I grab it from his outstretched hands to stop him from getting any closer. It's no use. He's a beacon. His cologne infiltrates my space, and even after all these years, he just smells like home. There's no use trying to decipher the scents; it's just…home.

"I think we should talk about the book after you read it." He grabs his bag. "But for right now, can we talk in my office?"

I'm frazzled, but I follow him out of the room and down the halls. Our shoulders brush once or twice, and each time, Isaiah glances down at me and me up at him.

*I miss you.*

The words bang on the inside of my head like a hammer. He's standing right next to me, and I miss him… I've never missed anyone in my life like this.

We reach his office quickly. It's decorated with bookshelves that are filled with poetry, fiction, and art books. There are papers scattered on the desk, meeting times written on his calendar on the wall, and a few pictures in frames I don't linger on. The door shuts behind him, and we're left alone again.

"Why did you leave?" I ask before the courage leaves as quick as it came.

Isaiah exhales, stepping into my line of sight. Sunlight streams in through the window, highlighting the man in front of me.

"Are you going to look at me?"

I hadn't even realized I'd looked away, deciding to focus on the linoleum floors instead. Wordlessly, I meet his eyes.

"I left because of Elijah."

"What?" My mind spins, spiraling as it tries to find the reasoning. Elijah left and never looked back at the end of our senior year. Isaiah himself left and stopped talking to me shortly after. But I never thought to connect the two—maybe I was dumb, but I couldn't see the correlation.

Isaiah sighs, crossing his arms. "There's no point in trying to figure out why. There isn't an excuse. I just did."

I narrow my eyes. "I'm going to need more than that, Isaiah. You're just creating more questions."

Silence stretches in the space between us. He fidgets, and as strange as it sounds, it makes me feel better. That something as simple as that hasn't changed.

"I've never talked about it with anyone, Aurora. Not the reason, not the why… just give me a second," he says gently. The sound of his voice is a soft caress. Even if he is frustrated, he's never let it show verbally. He's never pushed it on to someone else by yelling or shouting, at least in my experience.

"Okay." I swallow, tugging on a loose thread on my tank top. His shoulders rise and fall as he takes a few deep breaths. From here, I see his eyes pause on a photo frame on the desk before they close. After a moment, he turns back to me.

"When Elijah left, everything fell apart. Like the world had been ripped out from under me. When he left, we were still in school. You know there were distractions. Your final season, graduation, and whatnot. But after…I don't think I ever let you see how hard it was."

He didn't. I remember it—him acting like everything was fine.

"Mom wouldn't talk about it. She went to work early and came home late. She cracked down on grades and preparing for college, but we never talked about that he was gone. I was trying to fill his footsteps, which, until then, had been perfect. But it was too much. It all…" Isaiah swallows, exhaling as his eyes close.

My chest aches. I knew he was hurting; that was easy to see, but it was the first time in our lives he wouldn't let me in. When I pushed, he pulled away. When I tried to let him be, he was frustrated. There wasn't a win. There couldn't have been with his brother walking out of his life.

"It was too much. Trying to exceed her expectations and my own… it was unbearable. And I'd never had to do anything without him. I couldn't wrap my head around it, what life had turned into with him gone. He raised me; he was my best friend, aside from you." Isaiah lets out a humorless laugh. "And he just left. Left most of his stuff like it meant nothing."

My eyes water at the unsaid. Eli left him too and seemingly left him behind like it was easy.

I turn away, shutting my eyes. When I open them, I'm grateful that no tears fall.

I can't imagine the hurt he felt. But I do know how hurt I was when he did a similar thing to me.

"Why didn't you let me in?" My voice cracks, and his jaw clenches, foot tapping as he stays put. "I will never be able to know what that was like for you. I will never understand the pain then and the pain now. But you had me. You… I was in—" I stop, scared I'm going to cry right here, right now if I don't take a deep breath. "You were my best friend in the world. I would've done anything for you. But you just shut me out. Day by day."

Pain flashes over his features. "I didn't know how to talk to you."

"I didn't need you to talk to me. I wanted you to let me be there for you in any way that would've helped you. You could've yelled at me, you could've said you didn't want to talk, and I would've let it happen. I would've dealt with anything you threw at me, Isaiah. But leaving at the end of it? You'd already shut me out, but I guess I thought you would've let me back in."

Tension thickens the air, and a small kernel of regret lands in my stomach. The reality is, it wasn't about me.

"I'm sorry, I didn't mean to try and make his leaving feel less significant."

"You didn't." Isaiah begins to step forward but thinks better of it, leaning back against the desk. He pockets his hands in the fitted slacks and looks back to me. "He hurt me, yes, for reasons I'm not sure I'll ever uncover. But just because he left doesn't mean I should've left you. And for that, I'm sorry, Aurora."

The number one most present man in my life is my dad. And he has never, in my memory, apologized to me for anything. I can't help it if someone saying they're sorry makes my emotions churn. It hits different coming from Isaiah since he knows—used to know--the ins and outs of that relationship. The knowing look in his eye tells me he still remembers.

"I know you are," I say, the tension dissolving. But exhaustion takes its place. And the sadness I've felt since that day sits heavy on my shoulders. "But you did hurt me. I can't understand what you felt. I can't understand the darkness you were walking through. But you left me. You made me feel as though our friendship, our…" I swallow, waving my hand. "You made me feel like none of that mattered. That all those years, our lives together, our entire relationship meant nothing. The reality is, you did leave me. You *left* me. And you didn't look back."

He heaves a sigh. My throat tightens, and I'm not sure if I want to throw up or cry.

I continue, "I'm not saying this to take away from what you felt. I don't want to be an extra burden you carry. I just want you to know how I felt. How I feel."

Isaiah's eyes are piercing and full of pain. "You still feel that way?"

"What? Lonely and sad? Everyday." My voice cracks. "You being here doesn't immediately make that all go away. It's not magically going to fix it, Isaiah. Those feelings have been my friends since the day you walked away."

Silence falls. His honesty and the apology were enough to control the fire, but it's not done burning.

With cautious steps, Isaiah moves toward me. Slumped against the chair behind me, I watch him. When he's an arm's length away, he stops. If I reached out, my fingertips would be able to brush against the simple, black linen shirt. Might even feel the heat emitting from him.

I keep still.

"I'm not going to walk away ever again. I'm not going to leave you ever again."

"And how do I know that?" I want to shout; it would be easier, but my words are weighed down with pain.

For a moment, he stares at me. I'm not sure what he's looking for.

"I have to show you. And I will." Isaiah's voice is soft. "I meant what I said. About being here for you." *I never learned how to live without you.* "Leaving was a mistake. A mistake I'll pay for as long as you want me to. But there is no future I imagine without you in it. There is no life I envision without you. I'm here for you."

"Okay."

"Okay?"

I tip my head back. "That's all I have to give, Isaiah. I can't…" Again, my stupid voice cracks. "There's nothing left to say right now."

Right now, I want to hide. I want to lock myself in a room, wrapped in a blanket and shrouded in darkness. I don't want to feel this way—vulnerable and wide-open.

"Can I ask you a question?"

"Sure. I'm not obligated to answer."

Isaiah takes a breath. "Is there any chance you'll ever forgive me?"

My heart stings. His voice is gentle, quiet. Quiet enough that if anyone else was here, only I would've been able to hear it. Back then, he did that all the time. Lowered his voice so only I could hear him. Made us feel like the only two people in the world.

My eyes travel over his face. The sharp shape of his hairline, the curls on top. The way his nose perfectly fits his face with a tiny bump on the bridge and the tiny silver stud on one side. I can't help but take my time on his jawline and the full lips that turn into a beautiful smile. Eventually, I look up, finding my favorite shade of brown looking at me.

I want to tell him—I want to scream at him, "of course, there is!" I want to take away his hurt as quickly as possible. But the prickly, self-protective instincts I have left don't let me. Because if he hurts me again… I won't recover. I won't bounce back.

"A chance."

And I swear, even that makes him stand straighter. He's close enough that I could easily memorize all the visible tattoos if I took the time. Could find out the parts of him that are different—older. But right now, it's too much. The proximity, the heat emitting off his body, the light smell of cologne. The way he's looking at me.

"It's going to take some time," I say, pushing off the chair and taking a step back. "And you should know, I'm seeing someone."

Guilt swells that it took me this long to remember Drew. And at the fact that I only mentioned it to put some space between me and Isaiah.

"The one at your game," he states, and I nod. "Okay."

I stand. He's too close. He's too…everything. And I'm scared if I spend another minute here, I'll forgive him right now. "I'm gonna go. Sorry to bombard you here and demand answers." As I move, I stumble, frazzled by the short but illuminating conversation. Undone by the feelings running rampant.

Isaiah catches me, fingers gently curling around my arms. His thumb draws a slow circle on my skin. "I'd rather you demand answers than not speak to me at all."

Nerves fire rapidly, trying to process the feel of him touching me and the sincerity behind his words. I remain captive to the soft grip on my skin for a moment longer before stepping back.

"Can I walk you out?" he asks.

I mull it over, and the silence that fills the space is heavy and awkward. I love silence. But I hate it with him. It's not normal. We never walked on eggshells around each other. We were never fearful or hesitant. We just were.

And now we…

I don't fucking know, but I hate it.

"I think I just need to be alone, Isaiah."

Isaiah dips his head. "I understand." We stare at each other. His eyes rake over me, taking me in. I wonder if I'm the same girl he left behind. Are the parts of me he likes still here? Or have they been eaten alive by this ridiculous, dramatic misery? I sigh and break my eyes away.

But he's not done. "I'll be at your next game."

I stop a few feet away from the door. Everything feels like it's crashing down right now. My anger and the hurt and the pain—they're all dragging me to the floor step by step. And now this. He says he's going to show up for me. I can only wait and see.

"Okay."

Isaiah says nothing else but moves toward the door, holding it open for me. I step into the hallway alone, my eyes forward, but with every step, his gaze remains locked on me. I can feel the heat of it, the pressure. The resolve to fix what's broken.

His words ring in my head over and over again. I hope he means them. I want nothing more than for them to be true. For him to show up for me now.  But it's going to take more than what he gave me today. I can't just let him back in, no matter how much I want to. I can't act like I haven't felt alone every single day since he left. I want to forgive him.

I hope he gives me a reason to.

# Never Really Over

## Isaiah

*I*'ve known Aurora's dad for a long time.

Coach Matthews is how most people know him, especially his daughter. I grew up with him, so I know what he is like off the field. I know him as Aurora—and Sophia's—dad, as the overprotective father when Kian came around, as the ex-husband of their mom, and all the other facets of who he is.

There's a difference in the way he interacts with Aurora and Sophia. I think a lot of it is that Sophia never played competitively. It was never her entire life. It has always been Aurora's.

Aurora loves her dad deeply, but I think a part of her also resents him.

My forearms rest on the cold, silver bar of the stands, my eyes latched onto her during warmups. Her dad watches her from the sidelines, arms crossed and an unreadable expression hidden behind sunglasses. I watch her face go from a bright, wide smile, to a straight line when her father calls her over.

I get that he's doing his job as a coach. He's done the same throughout the warm-ups with the other players, as all the coaches have. But no matter what anyone says, I don't think you can be both a father and an unbiased coach. It's not possible. By the frustration on her face, it seems not much has changed.

I respect her father, but I don't necessarily like him.

Whether I have that right anymore or not, it doesn't matter.

"Hey, man." A familiar voice distracts me, and I find Kian behind me. "What's up?"

He leans over the railing. "You look deep in thought over here." I shake my head, finding Aurora as she resumes warm-ups. "Does she know?"

"Know that you've kept in contact with me almost the whole time?" I stare at him, and he turns sheepish. The guilt settles further into my stomach. "No. I'm certain she would've killed you if she knew."

"Why just me?" Kian asks and then shakes his head. "Never mind. Are you going to tell her?"

"Are you going to go into witness protection?"

"I'll be fine. Sophia will protect me. And if she doesn't, that's a problem for me. That's what witness protection is for," he says, and I snort. "The problem here is you."

I sigh. "I assume you know she came to the school to talk?"

"'Course. Sophia told me."

"We just talked. We've barely opened the door to… I don't even know if she's going to forgive me, Kian. Isn't telling her going to slam it shut before she even lets me in?"

Kian looks out to the field, finding his little sister. Technically in-laws but realistically not. He's her family. Her big brother. "If you don't tell her and she finds out, isn't that going to be worse?"

"Yes."

The sun is hidden behind the clouds above us, a few rays peeking through. Obviously, I have to tell her. But I can so easily picture the disappointment in her eyes, and the thought of disappointing her again, of hurting her anymore, wrecks me.

He looks at me. "Then, you know you have to do it."

A shrill, young voice breaks the silence. Kian's youngest daughter, Joey, barrels down the stadium stairs and into his legs. He picks her up, and she smiles at me. I've only met her over FaceTime whenever I was able, but it's nice to finally see her in person. Her curls bounce around her brown cheeks, pieces of Sophia (and therefore Aurora) in her features and of course, from Kian.

"Sup, munchkin?" I hold out my hand, and she gives me a high five, her small hand fitting in my larger palm.

"Are you here for Auntie Ro?" she mumbles, the words tumbling out at lightning speed.

"I am." I smile, glancing down at her toddler-sized jersey that has Aurora's number on it. Just like mine.

Joey's hands shoot up in excitement, her cheeks widening. "Good. She's the best."

"You're right about that, Jo." She beams at my nickname and stretches her arms out. Kian wastes no time handing her over, and she settles into my arms easily. Her eyes are glued to her aunt on the field, but after a minute, she turns and looks at me.

"Are you Auntie Ro's boyfriend?"

Kian chokes on the water he just sipped. "Where did you learn that word?"

She shrugs. "Mommy said it."

My heart beats inside my chest, faster than it should since the question was asked by a three-year-old. Even Kian is looking expectantly, albeit amusedly, as he waits for my answer.

"No, I'm just…N o."

Joey hums like she doesn't believe me, but she ends her investigation there. Kian chuckles to himself. Slowly, the stadium fills up. Time ticks by until warm-ups have finished. The girls prepare to head into the locker room, and my eyes, like earlier, are glued on Aurora.

I've missed enough. I don't plan on missing another second.

Before she disappears with her team, she spares the briefest of looks in our direction. Even in the distance, I know she's looking at me.

They linger for longer than I expect, and what I don't anticipate is how much that stings.

How many times did she look only to find that I wasn't there?

I swallow it down—the guilt, the frustration; it won't do me any good. I can't turn back the clock and undo my leaving. Can't undo the pain I caused.

But I can move forward and show up for her now. After I learned how to show up for myself when the chips were down. It's time to step up for the person who got caught up in the aftermath.

And prove that I have no plans to leave.

Watching Aurora today is even better than it was when we were young.

The clock ticks down, the Royals up by two, and she never stops. She commands her defense and supports the midfield and the offense flawlessly. Aurora is a force to be reckoned with. A summer thunderstorm that comes in with a vengeance and gets it done quickly yet beautifully.

Out there on that field, she looks as free as ever.

Beside me, her nieces cheer her on, jumping up and down on the stadium benches. Sophia sits next to me with a proud smile on her face. The only person missing is Aurora's mom, who couldn't make it. But it's nice to be sitting here with the rest of her family—I had missed them, too.

"You know, there's rumors she's going to get pulled for the national team training camp," Sophia says, glancing in my direction.

"You're serious?"

"Very." There's a pause. "I don't mean to go all big sister mode, Isaiah. You know I love you. I missed you too, wherever you were. But if this is some weird pitstop or something else, please leave my sister out of it."

I take a sip of my water. "I understand, Sophia."

She rambles on, "It wouldn't just distract her, you know? It would… all that hurt that she buries and tries to hide, it would come right back to the surface. I can't see my sister like that again, okay?"

The words sit there between us, floating in the air. Despite it, Sophia reaches over with her free hand and grabs mine, giving it a squeeze.

"Aurora isn't a pit stop. Not in the slightest." That's all I can say.

Words are pointless if I don't follow through. Promises are empty if there isn't any ground for them to stand on. I squeeze her hand back just as the whistle blows, signaling the end of the game.

We stand, but Sophia turns to me, pausing us for one more moment. "I'm glad you're back, Isaiah."

I nod, and she squeezes my hand again before letting go and picking Joey up. Azalea holds her dad's hand as we make our way down the stands and toward the lot where the players exit. In front of us is the guy Aurora is supposedly seeing, walking in the same direction. I take a deep breath despite the annoyance with a man I've never spoken to flowing through my veins.

The team exits, making their way toward their families, and Aurora appears next to the same three girls she walked out with last time. Their eyes land in our direction, specifically on me, and from here, I can see them turn cautious. Though I can't blame them, it still hurts.

Exhaling, I focus on the cement until the invisible pressure on my shoulders lifts.

"Isaiah?" Azalea's voice breaks my concentration.

"What's up, kiddo?"

Her brows furrow. "I'm not a kid; I'm ten." Behind her, Kian snorts.

"Duly noted. Kiddo's just a nickname. I promise."

She nods, her hazel eyes big and wide, just like Aurora's used to be. I remember when she was born. Aurora and I were thirteen, Sophia and Kian were freshly eighteen, but even though they were scared and everything was changing, Azalea was a breath of fresh air. She and Aurora were two peas in a pod, best friends from the first moment Aurora held her.

Because of my choice, I've had to watch her grow up over sporadic FaceTimes and pictures sent in the mail. She was the closest thing I had to a niece or younger family member—another part of their lives the Matthews let me into.

"Are you gonna come with us for ice cream?"

I smile. "Not tonight. But maybe next time?"

The ten-year-old practically stomps her foot. "Why not? I'm sure if you asked Auntie Ro, you could come." Azalea grips my hand in both of hers, pouting. "Please, pretty please?"

There's a burning pressure on my back. When I glance in that direction, I find Aurora talking to *him* with her eyes locked on me. Her cheeks flush, and she averts her eyes.

"Don't you wanna spend time with your family? And your aunt?"

"I see them all the time. I wanna spend time with you, too."

Kian speaks up behind me. "Did you hear that, hon? Our daughter is already getting sick of us."

Sophia huffs. "More like sick of you."

I can't help but laugh, turning my focus back to Azalea. "I promise, if it's okay with everyone else, I'll come next time. Deal?"

She contemplates it for a moment before smiling. "Deal. But you have to pinky promise."

And pinky promise, I do. When I'm finished making a deal, I turn around to find Aurora looking at us both with amusement. There's a warmth in her eyes I wasn't expecting. Behind her stands someone I'd rather not see since he's apparently hovering. My eyes are drawn back to Aurora when she stalks toward me.

"You can join, if you want," Aurora says, bending down and opening her arms as her nieces rush into them.

My eyes glance up behind her. "No, it's okay. Really. I got to see you play. I can come next time."

I know that we aren't there yet. We're barely anywhere. Me showing up today is just the beginning.

But still, Aurora tries to clear the tension. "Are you sure? Really, if you want to come, you can."

I shake my head. "Enjoy your time with them. There'll be other chances for you to invite me," I say teasingly. Hoping to draw anything out of her. Even a twitch of her lips.

And they do. Barely. No one else would notice a thing. But I do. I pocket my hands and try to fight my own smile.

Aurora's curls float in the breeze that passes between us. "Okay, um… I guess I'll talk to you soon?" Her eyes rake over my crouched form, pausing on the ink wherever she can see it, like they have every time she's seen me.

It's awkward, learning how to navigate whatever our relationship is. Friends? Friends that haven't spoken in years, friends with a history of not just friends. It's all pretty fucking weird. I see it reflected in Aurora, too. In the very slight tension in her shoulders, the way she carefully thinks about everything before she says it.

"Sounds good." We both stand, the girls hanging onto her legs. "You played a great game, Aurora."

Her cheeks flush again. "Thank you."

I rub the curls that flow off the heads of the little girls hanging onto their aunt. Sophia pulls me in for a hug that feels like it did when we were teenagers. Kian mouths, "tell her," quickly so no one else sees, and I toss my hand up as I head to my car.

As I settle in the seat, I rest my head back. The past six years have been hard. Challenging in ways I wasn't ready for. Sometimes, it feels like I'm far older than I am, that it was ten years instead of a mere six. Dealing with the aftermath of Elijah disappearing from my life and the wreckage that was left behind took its toll on me.

Somehow, this—Aurora—feels harder. Maybe because before, we were always something to each other. When I left, I turned that to dust. At first, I thought there was no chance I could convince her to be a part of my life again.

But the heat of her gaze still lingers. The warmth in her eyes shines when I doubt she's even aware of it. The tension that zaps to life the moment we're near each other… There's a lot to be done, a lot of dust to be cleared, but it's not over.

Aurora and I could never really, truly be over.

# In Another Life

**D**rew is everything I could've wanted.

He is kind and patient. He listens and understands. Consistent, trustworthy, honest. It doesn't hurt that he's pretty to look at too—a gentle smile, warm eyes. He's perfect.

Or…he would be, if he was someone else.

I'm trying so hard. But it's simply not enough.

The air is warm, but the humidity has dwindled with the setting sun. We're hand in hand, and my skin prickles but not in the way it should. It's like a flashing warning sign telling me to let go and run away. Every time we touch, all I can think about is Isaiah. Like a virus invading my brain.

Luckily, we reach the gelato shop quickly, and he lets go to open the door. I flex my hand, welcoming the freedom it's gained back.

"Thank you." I walk inside, trying to piece together the right words to say to him.

"I am going to need you to finish the story about your sister telling your parents she was pregnant the first time."

I snort as we get in line. Part of the reason I even started telling it was so that I didn't blurt out that this has to end.

"It might've been the funniest day of my life. She snuck Kian in and pushed him to my bedroom for him to hide. She had this whole plan to call them down to the living room or whatever, but my parents beat her to it. Suddenly, they wanna talk to us both. So, Kian's in my room, we're in the living room, and our parents…" I laugh, able to picture it so clearly. "And our parents tell us they're getting divorced. Sophia's face was priceless. Not because she was surprised; we had talked about it for a while. But because I'd never seen her so shocked. She didn't often need to be the center of attention, didn't ever like it. But this…she was young, but she was excited."

"How old was she?"

We move up in line, both eyeing the flavors. "She was eighteen; I had just turned thirteen." Drew nods but motions for me to continue. "Anyway, the rest is short, and it's probably way funnier since it's my family. But she gets up and *yells* at them. She yells at them for deciding to tell us that day and that they were selfish, and Sophia goes, '*You guys suck, and you should've gotten divorced years ago. And by the way, I'm pregnant, but thanks for making today about you.*' They had no idea what was going on, what she was even saying, and then Kian pops his head out from the hallway. It was all very dramatic. But I have never laughed so hard in my life."

Drew chuckles beside me, touching the small of my back. "I can't imagine being thirteen and sitting through that. I assume you already knew Sophia was pregnant?"

"Of course. Even at those ages, I was glued to her hip. She couldn't have gotten rid of me if she tried, so she had to tell me."

"It's nice that you have such a good relationship."

I smile, giving a small nod. "Yeah, it is." We move up to order, and I slip my card to the cashier before he can stop me.

My heart pounds as we carry our very full gelato cups to a seat outside. Small talk isn't going to make it any easier. We sit in silence for a moment, enjoying the first few bites and the breeze. I let my eyes glide over him again. The blue-gray of his eyes that have only ever been warm and understanding. How he never pushed, never tugged, just gently walked beside me as we began dating. He was so understanding, and I feel so fucking stupid.

I swallow the lump in my throat.

In another life…he might've been the one that got away.

In another life, he'd be perfect.

But in this life, it isn't going to work. Not with who I am, not with what I'm feeling.

Drew glances up at me, and I swear there's a knowing look in his eyes. I clear my throat but let out a dry, humorless laugh. "I have to tell you something."

"I know."

Under the table, my foot taps sporadically. "I need to end this." I take a deep breath. "God, I hate that I am about to say this, but it really, truly is not you. Nothing you have done has been anything shy of perfect." Swallowing, I look up, only to find kindness in his soft smile. "I'm not ready. I thought I was. I wanted to be at the time, but I'm…I'm not. And I can't force it; I don't want to. You deserve so much better than what I've given you, Drew."

Behind him, the sun reflects on the glass doors of the gelato shop. Drew gives a small shrug. "All anyone deserves is the truth, Aurora. You gave that to me." He reaches over, a quick brush of his fingers over my hand. "I enjoyed getting to know you as much as you let me."

My eyes prick. Couldn't he, I don't know, tell me he hates me?

"Thank you."

"I didn't do anything." He leans back, taking a bite of gelato.

Maybe if it had gone farther or if I could stomach being vulnerable, I'd tell him his kindness and his patience meant more to me than is probably healthy.

"Now, how 'bout we finish these, I'll walk you home, and then we'll call it?"

I laugh. "Sure. Is it too awful and too soon for me to say, friends?"

Drew shakes his head. "Not at all. Friends sounds good."

The basement gym at my dad's house is a dream and a nightmare. It has anything and everything you could ever want for a home gym. But more often than not, I hate it. There isn't the same distance between my dad and I that I can cling onto on the field.

"Come on. Thirty more seconds."

Sweat drips down my brow. Frustration wins out over the burning in my legs. The time ticks down slowly, but after what feels like minutes, the timer goes off. As soon as I stop, my legs shake until I collapse onto the mat with my arms slung over my face.

"You're distracted."

I exhale. "I'm tired. And my knee is fucked. I'm not distracted."

Dad rolls a cool water bottle into my side. "Your mom told me Isaiah's back."

"So?"

"I'd call that a distraction."

"Because everything unrelated to soccer is a distraction? Why can't it just be life?" I sit up, downing half the bottle, and stare at him.

"If it's not important, if it's not getting you any further, it's a distraction."

My chest burns. Referring to Isaiah as unimportant infuriates me. "Just because it isn't important to you, doesn't mean that's true."

Dad sighs. "There's a lot coming up. Playoffs. Selection for the national team. I don't want you to lose focus. I don't want you to let up."

I take a deep breath. Focus. I hate that word. Ever since I started playing, it's been about focus. Trivial things that bothered me were brushed aside. Sometimes, I needed it—to be reminded that those things wouldn't matter after a minute. Other times, I needed him to be my dad. Not my coach, not my friend. My dad. Like he was unfailingly with Sophia. When she came to him, he listened to her, gave her advice, and he was gentle with her. More so than he ever was or ever has been with me.

"I haven't lost focus for fifteen years, dad. Can you cut me a break?"

"Why? Why are you so tired? Why are you so burnt out? You're twenty-five, and you have everything going for you. This is everything you ever dreamed of, why should I cut you a break?" Dad says, his unflinching gaze highlighted by the harsh features of his face.

"Because you never let up! You never let me breathe. You never consider anything might be wrong because all it is to you is a distraction that I shouldn't care about." I'm pacing now, my cheeks hot with anger. "I love what I do more than anything. If I seem burnt out to you, it's because I can never, ever, let you know something might be wrong. I'm burnt out of trying to act like the daughter you want me to be. The player you want me to be. Can't you just…" I swallow, angry tears pricking my eyes. "Can't you just be proud of who I am?"

Heavy silence blankets the room, filling every crevice. The urge to run is overwhelming, but I stare back at him. There's more I could say, more I want to say, but I wait. Wait to see if he has anything to say at all.

Dad rubs his hands against his sweats and stands. His expression is unreadable, like always whenever we fight. "Well. It's a shame you feel that way," is all I get before he turns and heads up the stairs.

My hand tightens on the water bottle as my chest heaves. Above me, I can hear him moving around, probably cleaning to avoid it all. I grab my bag and storm upstairs before I think better of it. We stare off.

"That's all you have to say?"

He leans on the wall. He's looking at me, but it's more like he's looking through me. "What do you want me to say?"

I bite my tongue. I'll argue, and I'll yell, but I will not beg him to care, to apologize. Not if he doesn't even mean it. The metallic taste of blood fills my mouth. "I…nothing. It doesn't matter."

Turning on my heel, I head out the door before I do something stupid and beg him to give a shit. My car door slams shut behind me. I admit I don't use it much, but it comes in handy for visiting my parents and Sophia. And it comes in handy when I need to cry and have a breakdown in the safety of its doors.

I scroll through my contacts, pausing very briefly over Isaiah's name, my heart beating faster when I do, urging me to call him. To crawl into his metaphorical arms like when we were teens. Common sense kicks in, and I find Sophia's name instead, hitting dial as I start to reverse, the phone ringing through the car speakers.

"Hey, what's up? I thought you were at Dad's?"

"I can't take it anymore, Soph." My throat tightens. "He makes me feel like a robot."

In the background, I can hear Joey's babbling and Zaza asking her dad for help. It's so stupid, but I can't help but be incredibly thankful for

Kian and the father he is and will be to them.

"What happened?"

"Just the same old shit. I guess Mom told him about Isaiah, but of course, to him that means I'm distracted and I have no focus. He thinks I'm lazy and burnt out." I exhale. "And I'm not—not with soccer. But it's like I can't even be around him anymore. I'm not sure how we got here, but I feel like…like he doesn't even like me."

"Aurora, I'm sorry."

A few tears streak down my cheeks without my permission. "You're using your mom voice," I say, my voice cracking.

"You're crying. What else am I supposed to do?"

"I don't know—make me stop?"

"We all know that's Kian's specialty."

I huff, my lips turning up. "That's only cause he's so annoying, he makes you forget."

"Exactly," Sophia says. "But I am sorry, Ro. It's not fair. You are an incredible girl, one I'm very proud to have as my sister and someone who is an incredible role model for my kids. I can't speak for your dad—"

"Your dad, too," I interject before she can continue, laughing through the tears.

"Anyway…I can't speak for him, and nothing I say will erase that. But you're amazing, Ro. You're a human being, and I'm sorry he won't let you be one."

My chest constricts. "Okay, enough."

"Stubborn idiot."

"Hey!" I wipe the tears away, blinking to clear my eyes.

"Why don't you come meet us at the diner for dinner? I'll make Kian buy your food and an extra milkshake for you."

"You promise?"

"What are sisters for?"

I'm not sure why, but I wonder if Sophia knows just how much she means to me. As a sister, as my friend, as one of my favorite people in the world. "Thanks, Soph. I'll meet you guys there after I shower."

After she tells me she loves me, I hang up and turn the volume up. It's strange how empty and alone I feel after that conversation, or lack thereof, with my dad. Even with everyone that loves me, it doesn't make the cut made by my father heal any faster. Not that I expect it to; it's been an open wound since I was a teenager—Isaiah would know. He tried to bandage it up as often as Sophia. And it doesn't help that I want to call him, too. Now that he's back, I should be able to call him up and act like years haven't passed. But I can't. That wound's been bleeding since he left.

Sometimes, I feel like all my time is spent trying to bandage myself up, to staunch the bleeding someone else caused. How many times am I going to have to patch myself up and carry on? And is it even working? My heart still aches; the memories still sting. Are these the cuts that will always bleed? Will it ever stop?

Everyone struggles. I know that, but…why does it feel so goddamn lonely all the time?

# FLASHBACK

## *Aurora, Summer 2014*

Isaiah has a way of making everything feel okay.

Like the world could be falling apart in my hands, and for him, it's as simple as reconnecting the puzzle pieces.

I could be having the worst day, and Isaiah shows up and washes it away. Maybe because with him, I don't care whether I'm at my best or my worst—I simply exist. Which isn't easy to do at seventeen. But he doesn't care what version of me he gets. He doesn't shy away from all the messy parts or the jagged edges that I'm still learning myself.

Almost everyone else, I think, I keep at a distance. Most times, it's not even a conscious choice I'm making; it's my natural defense mechanism kicking in. That if I don't get close, I can't get hurt.

They can't decide they don't like that I'm a raging hopeless romantic, that I'm wistful and nostalgic, that at the same time, I'm deeply competitive and stubborn and sarcastic. They can't decide that I'm being clingy when I show how much I might care about something. It can't be used against me. If they don't know me; they can't hurt *me*. They can only hurt the version I've presented.

But Isaiah's such an integral part of me at this point that he sees through it. So, there's no use in trying to hide it.

His car pulls into the parking lot, and I bound over with my soccer bag slung over my shoulder.

"Hi," I say breathlessly. "Thank you for picking me up."

"Always. You okay?"

I lean back into the seats, my legs already sore from today and my nose sunburnt. "For the most part."

Isaiah reverses the car, swinging his arm behind my seat. "Any reason you stayed an hour and a half longer after practice?"

The words my dad strung at me a few days ago ring clear in my head. How I'd gotten too slow over the summer, that my footwork on my left wasn't good enough, that I seemed unfocused and unmotivated. Given the fact that I played travel year-round, my school team in the spring, summer, and winter leagues, along with school and an occasional part time job… I'm not unfocused.

I'm exhausted.

The hurt still seethes under my skin. The words still reverberate in my thoughts at every turn. It's annoying how long it lingers. Feelings are so strange. Sometimes, the effects last seconds, minutes maybe, and are gone the next. And sometimes, they stick around no matter how hard you try to get rid of them. It's not like I can fight with Dad; he'll just shut it down. There's no use in arguing; there's no use in crying. There's just no use. So, I live with it.

"Dad thinks I've gotten slow."

Isaiah rolls his eyes as we pull up to the stoplight. "Is that it?"

I tug at my lip, pulling at the skin sharply. "No," I say, sighing. "But can we drop it?

"For now." His face turns gentle. "What do you wanna do?"

"I don't care. I just don't want to go home." I check the clock. It's only ten A.M. on a Saturday. The whole day is ahead of us.

"What if we drove down to the beach? Just for the day?" he asks, and I smile.

"That's what I was going to ask. You wouldn't mind?

"Nope. Not if it's what you need." Isaiah reaches over and squeezes my thigh. Heat spreads out from his touch, making my already warm skin even hotter.

The line between us has certainly blurred from just friends. More touches, more longing glances, more butterflies in my stomach. But we haven't kissed. Haven't talked. Haven't done anything to solidly make it something more. It's just there, hanging on a tightrope.

Whatever.

I sink into the seat of his car and into the lingering touch. I roll my head against the leather so I can spend the drive looking at him.

He wrinkles his nose. "You stink."

On instinct, I hit his chest. "Asshole." I roll down my window, letting the breeze in.

"Kidding, kidding." Another squeeze of my thigh. "We can stop at my place and grab a change of clothes. You have some there, right?" I nod. "Alright then."

The volume of the music increases, and I enjoy the air on my skin. It's probably a placebo effect, but simply being around him releases some of the tension from my shoulders. Releases the exhaustion sinking into my skin. Isaiah just makes things feel not so overwhelming. The comments, the criticism—they fall to the wayside with him. It's always been like that. Knowing when the other needs something and being there.

We either drag each other out of the hole, or we sit there in it together.

When we were younger, it was as easy as pushing each other on the swing set.

As we've gotten older, it's turned into watching crappy reality TV all day or raiding our parents' pantry for snacks. We've learned to recognize the signs and the tells.

For Isaiah, it's a smile with no dimple. Brown eyes with no warmth. It's when paper balls litter his bedroom floor because he can't write. That and when it was completely silent. He works best with a constant noise in the background—TV, music, anything—because it keeps him focused. For him, it is most often after visiting his father's grave with Eli and his mom. So, my job became quietly picking the trash and throwing it away until he could see the floor again. We usually end up at the park in our neighborhood, with me pushing him on the swings like we're kids again.

Mine is simply smiling so hard my cheeks hurt. Or finding any means to distract myself—like working myself to exertion or playing the music too loud. Isaiah has taken to noticing when my smile looks forced or the exhaustion is literally painted on my face. Usually, I get snippy or snarky with him. Ironic since he's the one person I shouldn't take it out on. But that's the way the cookie crumbles. He knows I don't mean it, knows it's not a reflection on who he is. I usually end up begging him for a hug shortly after anyway and mumbling an apology he says isn't necessary into his chest.

I steal a glance at him and exhale.

For me, Isaiah makes it easy to be human.

Above, the sun is high in the sky, the late summer heat maintaining a hold on us even though it's September. "Come on, please," I say, turning my eyes on Isaiah. He blinks open an eye, brown eyes molten under the sun as they look at me. My heart flutters, all the stress and the exhaustion dissipating every second we spend together. "One last swim for the year?"

Isaiah groans, rolling over and throwing his arm over my stomach, his face tucked into my side. "I'm comfortable where I am."

I smile, inhaling him along with the salt air. Sandalwood and sea salt invades my senses as it always does. Nudging him, I say, "Pretty please, for me?"

He sighs, and a small puff of air lands on my bare skin, sending goosebumps down my spine. "Fine," he mumbles, his lips so close they almost brush my skin.

Isaiah jumps up, his arms next to my head, like he's going to do a pushup, blocking out the sun from above me. "You owe me."

"Owe you what?" I ask, my eyes flickering to his lips and back up.

"Not sure yet, but I definitely get something for getting you to smile after earlier."

Said smile fights to re-appear. I roll my eyes, ignoring the flush over my skin. "Help me up," I say. Isaiah stands fully now, reaching out a hand. His fingers wrap around my own, and it feels solid, steady.

The sand is soft underfoot as we approach the waves. I pick up speed as I approach, crashing through the calm water on the shore and diving in as soon as I'm able. Salt water sticks to my skin and soaks my curls as I swim up. When I turn, water droplets splash onto Isaiah, who stands behind me, the waves swelling at his waist.

I swim over and pull him in. He rolls his eyes, fighting a smile. When he's far enough in that he has to swim, I latch onto his back.

"This doesn't seem fair. I'm doing all the work." Isaiah's hands are firm on the back of my knees.

"You are." My arms are wrapped around his chest, getting fuller by the day. It seems every time we're together, I notice something else about him that's changed as we keep growing older. "Thank you," I say, resting my head on his shoulder, the sun reflecting off the water on our skin.

He hums, and a wave approaches us. "Ready?"

I grin. "Ready."

As the waves crest, Isaiah dunks me under the water with a smile on my face. We surface together just in time to float over the next wave.

Here with him in the water and under the sun, all the worries and the insecurities fall away.

I'm just me. And that's enough.

## I Missed You

The diner is packed.

Families take up almost every booth, and loud chatter echoes throughout. Luckily, I'm quite attuned to the tone of Joey's babbling and more so, the inflictions in Zaza's voice when she has an attitude.

I slide into the cracked, blue, leather seat, right next to Joey's booster seat, where Sophia was just seated. Before anything else, Kian pushes a metal cup toward me.

"Milkshake number one," Kian says, stretching out across from me. Zaza sits between him and Sophia with quite the pout on her face.

"Thank you," I say, turning to Joey. "Hi, honeybun." Her golden-brown cheeks widen at that, a rosy pink taking place. "What's with the pout over there, Zaza?"

She huffs. The grip on her crayon tightens, and she continues angrily coloring in the picture. I glance at her parents and mouth, *"What's wrong?"*

"She's related to you," Kian snarks, and I kick him under the table.

"Hey," Zaza and I say at the same time. Her lips quirk, but she pulls them down before she shows any signs of happiness.

"Alrighty then." I glance at Sophia, but she just spoons ice cream into her mouth.

"Auntie Ro, will you help me?" Joey mumbles, haphazardly pushing crayons toward me. When she does, Zaza huffs but continues, angrily grabbing a magenta crayon from her dad's hand.

Sophia sighs. "We ordered for you. I hope that's alright. I just couldn't deal with the hungry gremlin over here."

"I am *not* a gremlin."

Sophia twists the curl in her daughter's hair. "I know, sweetie. I was referring to your daddy."

I snort, helping Joey color in a dinosaur, and take a spoon of ice cream. Kian smiles anyway, even though his daughter is admittedly taking after me and his wife is picking on him. Instead of saying anything, he reaches over Zaza and gently tugs Sophia's ear, making a kissy face at her.

"Ew, Daddy, stop." Joey frowns, pointing her crayon at him.

"Yeah, ew," I encourage. I already feel better now that I'm here. Even if I'm avoiding it all, I'd rather do it with them.

"And we wonder where this one," he points to Zaza, "gets it from. Or actually, where either of them gets it from."

"I don't know what you're talking about. I am a wonderful influence and a perfect aunt." Even Sophia can't keep it in at that one, laughing after her next bite of ice cream. "Joey, why are your parents so mean to me?"

Her brows furrow in the cutest way, and she purses her lips. "I don't know, Auntie Ro. But I love you." Joey leans into my side, and my heart swells. Over her head, I stick my tongue out at the so-called parents.

"I love you, too, Joey."

"What about me?" Zaza cries out, her pout trembling. They aren't exaggerating when they say me and Zaza are one in the same. Similar moods, similar attitudes, similar in most ways.

"Zaza, baby, you know I love you. So much."

"I wanted to sit next to you." She tosses her crayon on the table. I see her eyes glistening, but she doesn't let any tears fall.

I reach my hand over the table and grab hers. "How 'bout we switch after we eat? You can come sit with me, and we can draw something together."

"Fine, but I don't wanna sit with Joey."

Her sister is unfazed, which makes me laugh internally—not externally, unless I want to be the next recipient of Zaza's scorn. "Okay, we'll work it out." She nods and squeezes my hand back before she holds out her palm, and Kian oh-so-carefully places a crayon in it.

He doesn't let go. "Azalea, what do you say?"

She looks up at him, and his eyes soften when she does. "Please."

Kian sighs and sits back, fingertips dancing over Sophia's shoulder. "So, I see we've all had fantastic days today."

"I have!" Joey's toddler speak tumbles out.

The three of us chuckle softly. Joey's always been a happy baby, and she often makes us smile even when it feels like we can't. Even Zaza and her attitude makes me feel better. Something about the deep, intense problems of a ten-year-old.

The bickering settles, and I relax into the seat. Chocolate melts on my tongue with the next spoonful.

"Can I ask a question that may potentially upset you?" Kian asks.

I raise a brow. "I suppose."

"How are things with Drew?"

"I ended it yesterday, actually."

Both Sophia and Kian frown. "I'm sorry, Ro—"

I wave them off. "Stop. It's okay. He was super nice about it. There was no use in putting it off. Maybe I could've given it a bit longer if you-know-who hadn't shown up, but he deserved better than someone who had to force herself to feel butterflies," I say, dryly laughing.

Rather than say anything, Kian kicks my foot under the table.

"Do you want to talk about it—"

"Nope." I stare at him until he raises his hands in defeat.

The smell of food wafts toward us, and seconds later, our waitress appears with a tray on her shoulder. She smiles as she hands out the food, Sophia taking and distributing further. I'm handed a plate of chicken tenders and French fries, of which I certainly won't complain about.

Kian goes about collecting the crayons and the coloring pages, of which is his first obvious offense when Zaza narrows her eyes. Then, he splits a large platter of chicken tenders onto two plates—one for Joey and one for Zaza. Joey doesn't mind, immediately pawing a French fry, but Azalea has other plans. I can see the fire brewing in her eyes, and I grab some fries to prepare.

"I don't want to share with her."

"Oh, brother," Sophia murmurs.

Kian frowns. "Why not? When I asked earlier, you said that was okay."

She crosses her arms, her brown cheeks turning red. "Well, I changed my mind." Tears pool in the corners of her eyes. My heart aches. I'm not sure if she's tired or having a bad day, but it's a lot of emotions, and it makes me sad to see her sad.

"Hey," I say softly, meeting her eyes. "What's wrong? Can you talk to me? Want to come sit with me now?"

Most times, if she doesn't want to talk to her parents, she will talk to me. Zaza hesitates, but eventually, she gives a tearful nod. Sophia lets her out of the booth so she can crawl in next to me, where I've placed her portion of food.

"Thank you."

I wrap my arm around her waist and kiss her cheek. "Of course. Do you want to tell me what's wrong, or do you want to eat first?"

She exhales and grabs a fry, and the rest of us all take a deep breath. For the next five minutes, everything is calm. Joey talks and talks, some words less babbly than the others, and we listen intently as if we understand all of it. Zaza is quiet, but there aren't any more tears in her eyes.

But then, she taps me. "Can I ask you a question?

"Of course."

"Do you hate Isaiah?"

I blink in surprise. Kian blows a raspberry. "No, of course not. Why would you think that?"

"Why didn't you invite him?"

"Tonight?"

She shakes her head. "After your game, for ice cream."

"I didn't think about it, but he can come next time."

"You just don't want him around."

I have whiplash from how quickly kids can go from one mood to the next, but I school my features. I'm not sure when or how she's picked up on the tension between the two of us, but obviously, she has.

"That's not true, baby."

Azalea huffs. "Yes, it is. He talks to Daddy all the time. And he talks about you all the time. But he's barely around, and when he is, you act all funny."

My body turns cold.

Sophia drops her fork and turns to stare at her husband.

Kian sighs. "Oh, shit."

Joey frowns. "Daddy, bad word."

I watch in frozen disbelief as Kian rubs his hands over his face. I stare until he looks at me. "Would you care to explain, Kian?"

"Is there an option B?"

Anger runs red hot. Tears prick my eyes. "I can't…believe you." I turn to my niece, my voice shaky. "Can you let me out, baby?"

Confusion floods her face. It's not her fault, but I need to get out of here and away from Kian. Zaza doesn't say anything but scoots out to give me room. I stand, almost spilling my water as my limbs tremble. Without looking back, I stumble outside. The air is no relief. It's hot and sticky, and it's suffocating.

Today has gone from bad to worse. I wish I could bottle it up and shatter it, act like it never happened.

"Aurora."

My head whips around to find Kian exiting the diner. I turn and walk toward my car, digging through my purse for my keys, but he catches up and steps in front of my car.

"Aurora, please."

"What? What do you want me to say?"

He looks distraught. But that's how I feel. "I want you to listen to me."

"I don't know if I can do that, Kian." For the second time today, tears fall without my permission. "How long?"

Kian sighs. "Since he left. Or a few months after he left, I guess. A while."

"A while?" I choke out, a painful laugh escaping me. I want to fucking scream. My mind is spinning, and it won't focus on anything. "You've been talking to Isaiah for six years? The same six years that I've been a fucking mess about it?"

Guilt appears for a split second when I look at Kian's face, but my anger overtakes it in the next breath.

"And how in the hell did you hide that from Sophia?"

He leans his head up to the sky. "He asked me not to tell anyone."

"So you told the ten-year-old?"

"No one said I was a star pupil." Kian shakes his head, the joke falling flat. "She didn't see him much at the beginning, barely remembered who he was. But in the last year or so, there's been more calls. Joey met him, too. It's a mess; I know that."

I swear I can hear my heart beat faster as realization blooms. "Did you know he was coming here?"

Silence.

"Kian." My voice cracks.

"Yes. But—"

"Please let me leave," I say, my hand tightening around my keys.

He steps toward me, and I squeeze my eyes closed, unmoving. If I cry another fucking tear today, I am going to go sit on the highway.

"I didn't do this to hurt you, Aurora. I did it because he needed someone." My heart burns, the pain getting worse with every pulse. "He wanted to tell you. Please believe me when I say I would've come to you the moment I knew that he told you. The last thing I expected was for my daughter to spill the news over chicken tenders." Kian squeezes my arm. "I'm sorry."

I nod, stepping back. My fight or flight is in full effect, and I've never wanted to run so badly.

"Do you know his address?"

Kian studies me with a sad look. "Yes."

"Will you text it to me please?"

He nods, and I get into my car, sinking into the seats. I keep my eyes closed until I'm positive they're dry. Outside, Kian stalks toward the diner, pausing outside for a moment. Sophia won't be that mad considering she's not good at staying mad at people, but she'll put up a good fight—mostly on my behalf. I stay put until my phone vibrates with a text.

Outside, the sun still shines in the blue sky, but the colors of the sunset are starting to reflect on the clouds. I wait until my heart doesn't feel like it's going to grow talons and rip itself out of my chest before plugging in the directions.

I stare at the brick wall of Isaiah's apartment building. It's not far from my own, but it's charming—all brick with a small garden in the front and a pathway that leads to the apartment entrances. I bet there's exposed brick on the inside and built in bookshelves filled to the brim. The idea of his living space comes together so easily in my head, and it's easier to stand out here and make it up than to take a few steps toward finding out what it's really like.

I thought being angry would've made this easier. Instead, I'm overwhelmed. My fingers pull on a loose thread on the bottom of my shorts until it tears.

I find his door, knock three times, and wait.

Isaiah opens the door, black-framed glasses over his eyes. Almost instantly, his face clouds with confusion. "Aurora? What are you doing here?"

"We need to talk."

"Okay, come on in," he says, holding the door open. The smell of Isaiah wraps around me like my old, favorite blanket.

It's as if the city of Philadelphia made this place specifically for him. I kick my shoes off and stride in. On the right, there is a fully exposed brick wall that accents his living room and leads to a hallway. His desk is up against the wall, his laptop open and a notebook with a pen close by. The kitchen overlooks the living room with a breakfast counter adorned with candles and photo frames. A rusty orange chair sits next to his couch with a blanket folded over the back and a book open on the arm.

"Is everything okay?" He wipes his hands on his cotton shorts, the edges of which touch a large tattoo that accentuates the shape of his thighs. Good God, I was not prepared.

Not for Isaiah at home. In his glasses and in his element.

I wrap my arms around myself. His eyes survey the movement before meeting mine. "Kind of. Not really."

Isaiah sighs. "Let me get you some water. Sit down, and we can talk."

He leaves me standing there, and I can't take my eyes off him. The simple, gray t-shirt accentuates every muscular curve. Stark, black lines of tattoos decorate his visible skin, and those glasses frame his face perfectly.

Fuck me. The glasses.

He hated them when we were younger, especially in middle school. Hated the way they fogged up when it was humid and how he always had to push them up when he was reading or writing. Hated being picked on for them. In high school, I was the only one that saw them. When we were together in the safety of our homes was the only time he felt comfortable enough to put them on.

I've never not loved him in glasses. The way they frame his angular face and highlight his eyes. Now, as an adult, who is comfortable in his body, the confidence visible in every step, the glasses just…hit different.

I tear my eyes away and force myself to sit on the couch, ignoring the warmth building in the pit of my stomach. The rug underfoot is soft. There's a candle burning on his coffee table and a mug on the table next to his chair.

"For you," he says, startling me. He sinks into his chair.

"Thank you," I murmur, trying to find the anger I had when I drove over here.

Isaiah leans forward, resting his elbows on his knees. I swallow when we lock eyes. I swear my heart rate slows, and my brain clears. Even when I'm supposed to be mad at him, being around him makes me feel safe. Even after all this time.

"So, you talked to Kian all these years?"

His face falls. "I was supposed to tell you."

"Yeah, well, personally, I wish there wasn't anything to tell."

"Rora—" he says, and I flinch. The nickname still stings. "Aurora, I'm sorry. I didn't want you to find out from anyone but me. Kian wanted me to tell you, so I understand if you're mad at him, but everything he did, everything he didn't tell you, is because I asked him to."

I take a sip of water. All that boiling anger from earlier is now a simmer, which has made way for all the hurt that was hiding underneath. Hurt that I have pushed down and tried to ignore when, in fact, it's been eating me alive. Waiting to strike. Isaiah needed someone to talk to, and he chose Kian.

Sadness envelopes me. I hate that he was going through something like that. And yet, it stings that I wasn't the one he needed.

Especially considering, I always needed him.

"Why—" I interrupt myself when a sob escapes from my throat. "Fuck me." I turn my eyes to the ceiling, willing myself not to cry. My eyes blur anyway.

"Hey," Isaiah says, and I blink my eyes to see him start to stand.

I croak out, "Please don't. Or I will never get through this." God, I want to punch myself. "Why did you choose him? I know that you said you couldn't talk to me," I hiccup, "but I just…I don't understand *why* you didn't want me to talk to. I don't understand why you didn't need me."

Well, there it is. I left my bleeding heart on a blank page and handed the book straight to him.

"I want nothing more than to give you an answer that makes it okay. But I don't have one. I was so lost after he left." Isaiah leans back, his eyes flickering across the room. I follow, to find a picture of him and Elijah on his desk. "I had never felt that way before. That…down. That broken. And it wasn't that I didn't want to talk to you. I couldn't. I didn't know who I was anymore. I didn't recognize myself in the mirror. And I felt ashamed of that, and the idea of *you* seeing that, seeing that weak version of myself…I couldn't do it. I didn't want to be broken in front of you."

My hand tightens on the glass. I wish I had a magic wand and could go back and fix it. Make it so Elijah never left and make it so that Isaiah never felt this way.

"When Elijah left, there was this space missing. This *thing* that followed me around. And life—you know, life went on. But I didn't know how or why. I would go to tell him things, something that made me laugh or passages that interested me, and he wasn't there. He *always* used to be there, and he just wasn't." Isaiah's voice is soft, but the hurt…the pain, it's on every word. "It wasn't that Kian was a fix all or filled that space. No one could ever fill the space Elijah left. I just needed a way to stay connected. And half the time I called, we sat there in silence because I never knew what to say. I wasn't ready to come back, and I wasn't ready to really deal with what I may have left in my wake." He looks at me. "But I still needed to know that everyone was okay."

I shook my head. "I wasn't."

"I know that now." Isaiah moves, albeit slowly, toward me and takes a seat on the ottoman in front of the couch.

His long, dark legs trap me in, and I'm mesmerized momentarily by the ink on them, by how close they are to mine. Before I can stop him, Isaiah reaches up, tilting my chin up with his finger until I'm looking into his brown eyes. His eyes are open and honest and one of my seven wonders of the world. And I have missed them so fucking much.

"I'm sorry that I hurt you. I'm sorry that I left you. I would do anything to erase the pain I caused you."

His touch is a gentle comfort. A crutch. A grounding force.

"I'm sorry if I ever made you feel unwanted or unneeded. That is the furthest thing from the truth. Because I need you to know that I always want you. I always want to talk to you. I always have and always will need you. I needed you every day for the past six years. It's my own fault that I did that, I know, but it doesn't make it any less true."

Isaiah wipes away a tear I didn't know had fallen. How could I pay attention to anything else when he's gently taking my bleeding heart and starting to piece it back together.

I may still need some space, some time to let go of the hurt, but if we're going to have anything—be anything—whether that's friends or more, I have to stop acting like his being here means less than it does. I have to acknowledge how much I want him back in my life, in any capacity.

Before I can overthink, I lean forward, my knee brushing his, and wrap my arms around his neck. The sheer act of touching him lifts the weight off my shoulders, eases the pit in my stomach. I find warmth in the crook of his neck, and I can breathe again. It takes him a moment to catch up, but eventually, his arms circle me. Isaiah moves with care, with hesitancy, but soon enough, the weight of his arms settle on my back, his fingertips brushing the side of my ribs, and I exhale, tears falling from my eyes and onto his shirt.

"I'm sorry that he left." My words are whispered, and he tenses for a moment, letting me know that he heard them. But he relaxes and tightens his hold. "And I missed you so much."

"I missed you."

I squeeze him harder, breathing him in before I sit back. With the back of my hand, I wipe my cheeks. "Sorry I cried all over you. And I'm sorry I stormed over here."

Isaiah reaches up, his thumb tracing a tear track. "I told you I'd rather you yell at me if the alternative was not talking at all."

"I didn't yell," I say, and the corner of his lips turn up.

"That is true."

"Still, I should've just listened."

"You did."

"I'm sorry if I'm being insensitive about it. It's a lot to process, and I'm sorry if it's all bringing it back up for you."

Isaiah raises a brow. "You've said sorry four times in less than two minutes." He puts a finger over my lips when I go to speak. "I appreciate them, Aurora. I accept them. But I don't need them. You're not being insensitive. It's all been thrown at you in quick succession. I've had years to process Eli and you and all of it. But…if we could table the Eli talk for tonight, I'd appreciate that."

He takes his finger away. "I'm sorry," I say, and he chuckles. The sound tickles my skin, like a million little tiny kisses. "Can you point me to the bathroom?"

Isaiah stands, grabbing my hand and pulling me with him. He stands taller by a few inches, and we're close enough I can see the rise and fall of his chest, feel the heat emitting from his body. And all I am aware of is his hand holding mine.

"Down the hall to the left."

The hallway is short with just three doors, a bathroom, a closet, and his bedroom. As soon as the bathroom door is shut, I turn on the faucet and slide to the floor. My chest aches, and I don't know if it's good or bad or both, but I can't stop the sob that escapes. Today has been hit after hit, emotion after emotion, and I was going down one way or another. I try to muffle the sound in my elbow as my body shakes, as all the emotions forge their way out.

Being broken down by my dad is one thing—an unfortunately expected thing. I'm used to it. I'm used to the criticism, the heedless pressure for me to be the best, the silence when I say something he doesn't want to hear. But the Isaiah information has felt like standing in front of a dart board and being hit dead center each time. Opening old wounds that never healed because I refused to acknowledge them. After a while, they became a part of who I am. Anytime they reopened while he was gone, they bled and bled, and I picked and picked until it scarred. And the process repeated. The grief of losing him for no apparent reason was going to be by my side for the rest of my life, like a phantom. A ghost with unfinished business. But I had forgotten what it was like to have him in my life. Now, these wounds are reopening because he's back. But he's *back*. He's here with the same warm eyes of my childhood, the same steady hands, and I don't feel so alone.

When breathing doesn't feel impossible, I focus on the things I can see, the things I can feel, and count until my heart rate calms. The sound of movement breaks me out of my spell, and I exit to see Isaiah at the edge of the kitchen.

I come to a halt. "What is that?"

Ears perk up from the cradle of his arms, sharp and pointy. "A cat."

I blink and step closer. A bundle of black fur is curled tightly in his arms. There are spots of white—on the tip of the ear, on the paw hanging over the edge of his arms. Isaiah studies me, lingering on my swollen eyes and my red cheeks, but doesn't say anything as I reach out a cautious finger.

A slightly pink nose reaches out to sniff it, showcasing its green eyes. "Hi, there."

"Her name is Raven."

"Teen Titans or Poe?"

Isaiah laughs. "Both."

My eyes are sore, my head is pounding, and my throat is scratchy, but the little lady nudges her head into my palm, and I can't help but smile. Her tiny body rumbles with a purr before he sets her down and steps back into the kitchen.

Raven curls her body around my leg before collapsing on her back with a meow. I look back to Isaiah, who's standing over a recipe book on the counter. There is an undercurrent of awkwardness in the air—maybe because I just sobbed in the bathroom, or maybe it's all that's transpired—but it'll never go away if I don't try. If we don't.

I lean against the doorway. Raven wiggles on the floor until her paws touch my ankle, making me smile.

"So…you're a cat daddy?"

Isaiah places his palms on the counter, and another laugh rolls through his body. His shoulders shake, and a smile forms. "I suppose that's one way to put it."

My fingers spin the signet ring I've been wearing since I pulled it out of that keepsake box. His eyes lock onto the movement, but he doesn't acknowledge it. "Here—that's for you." He points to my glass of water, the two tiny pills next to it, and the washcloth on a small plate.

It has been my post-crying routine forever. Especially if I reach the breaking point, I always end up with a pounding head and swollen eyes. "You remembered?"

"I remember everything," Isaiah says nonchalantly. Inside my chest, my heart twists and swells. I swallow the ibuprofen and press the cool washcloth underneath my eyes. Moments pass in silence; the only sound is the knife on the cutting board and the music playing softly from his computer.

"Do you want to stay for dinner?"

Despite the fact that the idea of going back to my empty apartment and eating some crappy frozen meal from my freezer and sitting on my couch alone makes me feel sick, I'm also still on edge. One wrong move and I'm bound to burst into tears for the umpteenth time today.

"I think I'm gonna head home in a few. Believe it or not, this is not the only confrontation I've had today."

"Wanna talk about it?"

"Not tonight. Just Dad stuff." I wave my hand because it's always Dad stuff, but his eyes narrow anyway. "It's fine, Isaiah, I just need to…um."

"To sit?"

I press the washcloth into my face, hoping the pressure will alleviate. "Yeah."

With quick steps, he stalks toward me until I have to bend my neck to see him. "I'm glad you came."

"Yeah… me, too."

Without even thinking about it, I drop the washcloth and wrap my arms around his waist, immediately sinking into him. Isaiah exhales as his arms curl around me, and for the first time today, it genuinely feels like things will be okay.

Back then, with Isaiah around, everything always felt okay.

Maybe it'll feel like that again.

# All Over Again

Whatever I thought about Isaiah's poetry before fell to the wayside. Because what it has become is beyond my wildest fucking dreams. I practically throw myself back on the couch. It's not the one he gave me—the annotated one. *That* one is something I need to prepare for.

"Told you it was insane," Maazina says.

I glare at her, but her focus is fully on the cake pop in her hand. Practice this morning was brutal, especially considering I didn't look at my dad once, and we came here after to fully rot in my apartment. Sylvia is currently asleep next to me on the couch, and Vivian is stretched out on the floor watching *Modern Family*.

"You didn't say it was this bad."

Maazina raises a brow. "Well, considering the entire thing is about you, I would hope that I was not as emotionally wrecked as you currently are."

"That's such a good point," Viv muses, stretching her arms up in the air.

"I don't know why I thought reading these with you losers here was a good idea."

"We're here in case you feel the need to jump off any tall buildings." Maazina snorts.

Next to me, Sylvia rises from the dead. "So true," she says, hand in the air but eyes closed.

I roll my eyes but return to the book, which I'm only about halfway through. I've had to read every poem twice to digest them, and I'm sure there is more that I'm missing, but I haven't even opened the copy he gave me yet. Two nights ago, after I got back from his place, I flipped through it to see handwriting and tiny sticky notes on the inside and immediately shut it. So, it's currently sitting on the kitchen counter, waiting for me to grow a pair.

When I turn the page, I find the next poem titled "Seventeen" and immediately close it. The last two have been more about his life, about his brother, and the pressure of life, and I've taken in a lot, but I'm not ready for that.

I pick up my phone again, like I have almost every hour, searching for a notification I won't have. Like an hour ago, there's still no text or call from Dad. Hasn't been since we fought, and there won't be. I place it face down on the coffee table.

Viv clocks the actions. "All good?" I shrug. "You can talk to us, you know. In the four practices we've had since the game, you haven't looked at your dad once."

"It's not a big deal. You don't need to worry. It won't affect his coaching on you guys." I kick my legs out and head to the kitchen, rifling through my snacks.

"I'm not asking because I'm worried about his coaching."

"That's not what everyone thinks." Pretzels clank into a bowl. "It's not a big deal, okay? I don't want to make it a big deal. He's my dad, yes, but he's your coach. He's the team's coach."

It's not that I don't get along with all my teammates, because I do. Sure, they aren't my best friends in the whole world; they aren't Maazina or Sylvia or Viv, but I do love every single one of them. And what I overheard during practice wasn't mean, per say; it was just them discussing the idea of this being a distraction. The last thing I want to do is be a distraction.

"Dude, not to be like completely biased, but there is no way anyone on that team can call it favoritism." Sylvia sits up, running a hand through her long, black hair. "If anything, he makes it that much harder on you when he does get involved. For the most part, you know, he leaves it to Teller and Laurel, but when he doesn't…" She shakes her head. "I don't know how you do it."

I furrow my brows. "It's not that bad."

Maazina scoffs. "Maybe if he genuinely was just your coach, sure. Everyone gets critical now and then. But this has been your whole life, Aurora."

With a sigh, I join Viv on the floor, leaning my back against the couch.

It's not that Dad is evil. Or that he's overtly mean. Just continuous digs that have repeatedly dented my self-confidence. If I didn't feel confident about my skills, skills *I* built with my own hard work, if I didn't feel the way I did about the game, I would've quit. It was worse in high-school and college. After my regular practices or when I was home on breaks, we were back on the field. Making me do exercises he thought I could improve on. Throwing in back-handed compliments after reminding me how poor my left foot touch was, how poor my form was on a certain kick, and so on.

Now, it's all about what more I can do because it's never enough.

"It's been my whole life. I'm used to it," I say, my tone sharp enough that I hope it leaves no room for further conversation. I hate talking about my dad with them. If he wasn't their coach, it would be different, but he is. And despite my feelings, he's a good coach to all of them. My issues with him shouldn't matter.

We all have our things. The things we should open up about but skate around at times. This is mine.

"Well, we're here for you as your friends, not just your teammates, if you ever want to talk,"

I nod, my eyes glued on the TV. "I know. Thank you."

Maazina walks behind me and places a big kiss on the top of my head. "Love you, grumpy."

Maazina stalks to the kitchen, disappearing from view. I hear the quick patter of her feet from behind me and turn to look, only to find her standing directly in front of me, holding the book I've been avoiding. "What is this?"

I stare straight ahead. "I don't know what you're talking about."

"Aurora, are you joking?"

"What? What is it?" Sylvia and Vivian are highly intrigued as Maazina fans through the book.

"Oh, my God, he wrote in it? This entire book is marked up, Aurora. The cover is different? This is an entirely different version. Oh, my fucking God." Maazina sits next to me in a dramatic fashion, holding up the poetry book like it's made out of gold.

And it is, but it's *my* gold.

I snatch it and hold it to my chest. "Stop. I haven't read it yet."

"Why not?"

"A girl can only handle so much at once, okay?"

Sylvia twists her lips. "Yeah, that's a good point."

I scratch my forehead. "And he's coming over later anyway, so it's just not a good time to read it. I'll be all gross and sensitive and—"

"Aurora, shut the fuck up. He's coming over? To your house?"

Maazina looks shocked.

"Like you invited him?" Sylvia blinks, and Viv stares at me.

I throw my hands up, almost throwing the book in the process. "Yes. Invited. I invited him. We talked two nights ago."

"You bitch," Maazina exclaims. "And you didn't tell me?" Viv slaps her arm. "I mean us—you didn't tell us?"

"You have more energy than both my nieces combined."

"I take that as a compliment—thank you."

"I promise I will tell you all the details after tonight," I say in an attempt to appease them. Maazina stares me down with her eyes, the green shining through today, and makes a huffing sound.

"Fine, I accept those terms." She rests her head on my shoulder. Viv and Sylvia nod in agreement, and I exhale, finally free from the inquisition.

"Wait—"

"I will quite literally burst into tears if you ask me another question."

Maazina pokes my side. "It wasn't about you… It was about Isaiah." Helpless to do anything else, I laugh. "When is he coming over?"

"I think I said five."

The sun is still streaming through the windows, the AC blasting to combat the summer heat from seeping into my apartment. We've been rotting here most of the day, so I genuinely have no idea what time it is.

"Oh, boy," Viv muses.

"What?"

A buzz coming from my door answers my own question.

"No. It cannot be five."

Sylvia collapses face down onto the couch behind us, holding up her phone screen for us all to see. Five o'clock in big bright letters shine in all our faces. "Unfortunately, it is time."

A chaotic energy enters the room, one that makes it seem like we're all in college and our roommate's crush is coming over for the first time as pure panic ensues.

"Oh, my God, we get to meet him?" Sylvia's eyes brighten, and she claps her hands.

"Do we actually like him? Or are we still mad at him? Do we hate him on principle or…I need more information."

I press my palms to my temples. "Can we all just act as close to normal as we can get?"

Viv snorts, tossing her arm over Maazina, and that says it all. I take a quick glance in the large mirror leaning on the wall and decide the cropped t-shirt and biker shorts are good enough. As soon as I'm close enough, I press the button to let him up.

I turn around to find all three of them staring at me. "Sit down? Pretty please."

They chuckle but thankfully do sit on the couch right before he knocks at my door. I take three deep breaths before I open it. Isaiah appears with a tote bag over his shoulder, sunglasses hanging off the short sleeve button down he's wearing. Tattoos peek out between the panels of the shirt on his chest, and the pale green looks gorgeous against his brown skin. The tan shorts complement both colors and show off a majority of the tattoos on his legs. One leg is fully covered, and the other has ink placed sporadically.

All of it is hot. Unfairly hot. I-need-to-be-standing-in-front-of-an-industrial-fan hot.

Behind me, someone clears their throat and brings me back to the present.

"Hi, come in." I stand aside so he can enter. "These are a few of my teammates. I lost track of time."

Isaiah smiles. It's warm and gentle but still draws every eye to it. "Hi, everyone."

I stand by his side and point as I talk. "That's Sylvia, Maazina, and Vivian. They're with me on defense."

He shakes each of their hands, and when he's not looking, Sylvia fans herself and makes googly eyes. "It's nice to officially meet you guys. You all play wonderfully together from what I've seen."

"Thank you!" Maazina chimes, smiling brightly. "We're getting ready to head out, and we'll be out of the way."

Isaiah waves his hand. "Not at all. I can come back if you'd rather, Aurora."

Vivian steps forward, shaking her head. "That's not necessary, really. We've been here all day." He smiles and sets down the tote bag on the stool under the counter.

The girls pack up fairly quickly, sliding their shoes on. Vivian and Sylvia wait at the door, but Maazina pauses. "I was with Aurora at the restaurant when you read some of your work. I wanted to say I thought it was beautiful, really."

Isaiah dips his head. "Thank you, Maazina."

She smiles and then plops a kiss on my cheek. "Be nice to my girl," she says with a wave of her fingers that somehow looks slightly menacing directed at him.

"Get out." I point, and she laughs as she shuts the door behind them. I turn. "Sorry about that."

"Nothing to be sorry for. She's funny."

I stalk to the kitchen and stand across the counter from him. "She is. She's one of the happiest people I know."

Which is deeply ironic considering the shit she's been through. Despite it, she walks around with her head held high. Like the sun is out shining just for her. Most days, I don't know how she does it, but she gets up and keeps moving forward.

"Happy people love you."

I snort, pouring him some water. "Yeah, must be the raging pessimistic attitude they can't channel on their own."

Isaiah shakes his head. "You're not pessimistic, and you know it. I'm sure she does, too. You always wanted everyone to think that of you and apparently still do."

"When I invited you over here, it wasn't to be psychoanalyzed."

He pouts. "Where's the fun in that?"

There's a lightness to the air today. I'm all cried out and having everything—or almost everything—out in the open makes it seem a bit easier to navigate.

"I was thinking we could just start this whole friendship thing again," I say, staring at the marble pattern in the countertop. "Have dinner, watch a movie, or something?" Even saying it out loud makes me feel slightly ill.

"Friendship sounds nice." The corner of his mouth turns up, and my cheeks heat for no reason. "Whatever you want that sounds good. What did you have in mind for dinner?"

"Well, I have nothing of substance in my fridge, and I can't cook, so we can order out?"

Isaiah laughs. "Why don't we go grocery shopping? I can cook."

"Why?"

"Because it concerns me that you have nothing in your fridge. And I'm scared I'm going to open it and see a bunch of frozen microwavable dinners. And it could be fun." He scratches his chin and runs his hand over his face. "And…I want to cook for you."

"I resent the frozen meal comment," I say, "but that's fine." No one besides my family has cooked me a meal in a long time. And maybe it doesn't mean anything, or maybe it means he's just as nervous as I am. "Let me just grab my shoes."

I run into my bedroom to grab my sneakers. The octopus I pulled out from the closet is front and center on my bed since I couldn't bear to put it back. I leave it and step back into the front room.

Isaiah's eyes trail over my form as I step into view. They roam around my face, my cheeks that are currently turning hotter by the second, before panning down over my shoulders and my arms, goosebumps rising on my forearms as he goes. He takes all of me in, every inch down to the shoes on my feet before meeting my eyes. Like he hasn't been able to all the other times.

I wonder if it's sunk in for him that we're here. That only two days ago, I was in his apartment, and today, he's in mine. My heart beat goes from slow to fast in a matter of seconds thinking about it. Especially with him looking at me like that.

"Ready," I breathe out.

We head toward the door together, but he beats me to it, pulling it open. The keys jingle in my hand as I step out, and his hand finds the small of my back. The contact lasts for less than two seconds, but my body sings. Sinking into his touch, having the contact after years of living without, feels a bit like coming home. It's a new home, one we have to learn how to navigate, how to re-enter each other's lives, but it doesn't diminish that comfort. How instant it is, how—that even after tears and fights—Isaiah still feels like home.

And that I was right to think he probably always will.

"Do you even own a spatula?"

I cross my arms, hip hitting the shopping cart that is so full, it's fucking heavy. "This is getting ridiculous."

"What's ridiculous is the state of your kitchen. I'm highly concerned."

"You know, when you said you wanted to cook, I didn't hear you say that you wanted to berate me over the lack of utensils I have."

Isaiah throws a spatula and some other things into the cart. He takes over pushing it down the aisle and smiles at me. He looks so carefree. Of course, I want to think part of that is me. He was always more open and comfortable when it was us versus a large group. I got to see sides of him that others didn't and vice versa, and it feels like that's coming back out. Without even thinking of it.

"Isaiah, what else could we possibly need?" I whine when he stops to examine the shelves. I rest my head on his shoulder for a moment before I snap my head back up.

"Almost done, promise." He brushes against me as we start moving together in step. We turn up the freezer aisle. "The chocolate drumsticks still your favorite?"

"Yeah, but they don't make the all-chocolate ones anymore, or I can't ever find them. Do you still like that weird, frozen chocolate cake?"

Isaiah grabs two pints of ice cream. "It's not weird; you liked it. But only on special occasions. I bought it for myself when I got the book deal and when it was published."

"That must've been exciting."

We move up the aisle together. "It was, and it wasn't."

"In what way?"

"I celebrated alone both times, so it was anticlimactic in a sense. There was no one around to really be excited with me."

My fingers itch to reach out to him, but I keep my arms crossed. "Where was your mom?"

There is a long line at the checkout counters, so we merge together at the end of one. "We weren't talking that much when I got the deal. I even went a bit MIA on her, too in the beginning, so it was still a bit of a sore spot for her. For the publication date, we just couldn't be in the same place."

"I'm sorry you celebrated alone. Those are huge accomplishments, Isaiah," I say, his eyes flickering when I say his name. "I'm proud of you. I wish I could've been with you."

"Just promise you'll eat the next frozen chocolate cake with me?"

Gentle, comforting heat drapes over me. "Promise."

If someone had asked me a month ago if I thought I'd be standing in a grocery store with Isaiah, I would've said they were on an acid trip. Even if they asked me if I thought I'd be talking to Isaiah, I would've laughed in their face. But here we are.

"What do you want me to make tonight?"

I raise a brow. "You're the one who insisted on adding the entire store to the cart. Why are you asking me?"

His head falls forward, the nose ring glimmering in the light. "I don't want to make something you won't like."

My insides turn to mush at the almost imperceptible shake in his voice, his own nerves shining through. "You won't."

We hold eye contact for a moment. Every time I look into his eyes, I find something I forgot about. The little eye freckle he has, the black of his eyelashes. How warm those eyes become when they're looking at me. A soft smile forms on his lips—a shy smile, possibly my favorite smile of his.

It never sunk in how well you have to know someone to recognize these things: the different types of smiles they have, what the scrunching of a nose means. Maybe they've changed since we were last together, but I could still pass the Isaiah test. Standing here together, instead of feeling hopelessness at having missed all these years, I find myself excited.

Roused at the prospect of getting to discover new things, to memorize him all over again.

# A Chance

## Isaiah

My radar for Aurora's attention is as strong as ever.

I'm hyper aware of her eyes on me as I move around the kitchen. I can sense her tracking each movement. I'm aware now as we sit on the couch with plates on our laps. The TV is on, but I'm not paying much attention, not when she's sitting next to me.

Her glass clinks as she taps her nail against it, and my eyes flicker over again. Probably the fifth fucking time in two minutes. Aurora brings her glass to her lips, and I'm clocked on to her movement. The slow raise of the glass, the way her lips form to the rim—she's mesmerizing, and she doesn't even try. For me, all she has to do is exist.

My eyes find the gold ring on her finger—the ring I left for her. My pulse races. It might mean nothing. But I don't think it does.

"I know you always liked cooking, but when did you learn to cook like this?" Aurora is wide-eyed as she takes another bite.

"After I left," I say, swirling the drunken noodles. I take a sip of my own drink, which happens to be apple juice since Aurora didn't want to drink. "It became an escape, a way to take my mind off of everything. I had a lot of days when writing was insufferable, so I spent time cooking. I learned how to make everyone's favorite meals that I could remember. Tried new things. Whenever I needed to clear my mind, whenever I needed to be creative in a way that didn't require depending on my own inspiration, the kitchen was it. Found I really liked it, you know?"

"I'm happy you found something." She re-adjusts to sit cross-legged. Immediately, my eyes latch onto the warm, brown skin of her legs. They're strong and thick, and I can only imagine running my hand up and down the curve of her thighs, smooth skin under my fingertips. Tracing every dark freckle like constellations.

"Thank you for making me dinner," she says. Her curls cascade over her shoulders; her hazel eyes gleam under the gentle lights, and there's a softness to her face. A freedom on her features. The past few times we've seen each other, she's obviously been guarded. Those walls aren't gone, but she's at ease tonight.

I know she said friends; I know she's seeing someone. But I didn't come back *just* to be friends. If that's all she can offer me, I'll take it with open arms. It's more than I deserve.

But I've never stopped loving her. I never stopped being in love with her.

"You're welcome," I say.

"I was thinking we could watch the new Teenage Mutant Ninja Turtles movie? It just came out, and I haven't watched it yet."

"Yeah, that sounds good. Do you remember—"

"That time we got drunk and decided to watch the cartoon for like six hours?" Her hazel eyes lighten playfully, long lashes brushing her cheeks.

My shoulders shake with a laugh. "It was fucking trippy. Remember you wouldn't stop talking like Raph for like an entire week?"

Aurora laughs. One of my favorite sounds then, one of my favorite sounds now. It's melodic and earnest, cheeky and full of life. "Oh, my God, everyone hated me," she says, still laughing with a small snort. I love it. I want more of it. "I kept it up at family dinner once, and Zaza and Kian thought it was the funniest thing in the world, and Sophia wanted to strangle me."

"And didn't you accidentally do it in front of a teacher, too? Or your coach?"

She almost chokes on her apple juice, cheeks turning pink. "Yes, holy shit. I think it was my high school coach, and I didn't do it to be an ass. It literally just happened, and he stared at me for a good five minutes in complete and total silence."

I run a hand toward my forehead, laughing. I remember picking her up from practice to go get milkshakes and her getting in the car and instantly bursting into tears.

"And every time anyone gave Leo a hard time, you just got so defensive."

I raise my hands. "All he wanted was to be his best, alright?

"Whatever you say." She grins. "Do you want more of the finest wine in the world before I hit play?"

I snort and finish my apple juice. "Sure, thank you." Aurora stands and practically glides into the kitchen, sliding over the hardwood with her socks, and returns moments later with two very full glasses. Our fingers graze when I take my glass, and I watch her rub her fingers together afterward as she sinks onto the couch.

It's impossible not to stare at her. No girl I've ever met has ever captured my attention the way Aurora has. No one has those hazel eyes or deep brown curls. No one has her heart or her humor. No one has ever come close to Aurora. No one ever will.

Her cheeks turn slightly pink, as if she's all too aware of the fact that I'm staring. I turn back to the movie and try to keep my attention there. And I do for a while—as we finish eating and emptying our glasses. Silently, I take each of our plates to the kitchen, and sitting there on the counter is the book I gave her.

My mind whirls with a million things. I wonder if she's read this version—any version—of the book. Has she seen the pencil scribbling in the margins? My thoughts, my edits, my changes, my notes. And not ones I made for me—that copy is entirely for her. I annotated it for her, wrote everything I was feeling out for her. I couldn't have stopped if I tried. If anyone opened it, they'd see clearly how much I love her. How much not being near her broke me a million times over.

A hand touches my shoulder. I spin, locking eyes with Aurora. "I haven't read it yet. Not that one, anyway."

I swallow. "You don't have to. I gave it to you because it's yours."

She fiddles with the ring and takes a minute to meet my gaze. Longing dances in her eyes. A feeling I'm sure reflects in mine. Outside, the sun has fallen and taken the heat with it. But it feels like it's inside this kitchen, sparking between me and Aurora. A curl pops free from behind her ear, and all I want is to tuck it back. We're not touching, but we could be. If I extended my arm, if she stepped closer—the spark would turn to a flame.

Aurora exhales a soft puff of air. "It's not that I don't want to; I do. I have to take it slow. I'm reading them, but I'm entirely positive that when I open the one you gave me, I'm going to cry. I need a minute." Her lips curl up, but her cheeks pinken.

"I'll bring you tissues."

That gets a laugh out of her. "Thank you. I'll be sure to text you 911 the moment I turn the cover."

I pocket my hands, my eyes roaming over her again. Can I tell her that's exactly what I want? I want her to feel comfortable enough to call or text any moment for anything. If she laughs at something on TV, I want to know. If she cries, I want to know. If she's angry, even at me, I want to know. Because I used to. I used to know everything, and I want to know everything again.

"Now, come on. Let's do the dishes and finish the movie. Unless you think I have some chance of burning the kitchen down while doing that, too."

"If you managed to do that, I think you would deserve an award," I say, tapping her forehead and moving toward the stove. "I made you enough for leftovers."

"Isaiah."

"Don't argue. Just get over here and help me with the dishes." I hand her a dish towel and finish spooning the leftovers into a Tupperware container. Aurora grabs her drying rack and mat and places it next to the sink.

"I guess I'll just stand here and look pretty while you do all the hard work. Aren't I the best company you've ever had?" Aurora smiles cheekily, leaning against the counter.

I chuckle before turning on the water and grabbing the soap. The fact is, she *is* the best company I've ever had. She doesn't even have to try. As for looking pretty…my eyes trail over the column of her neck, over her shoulders, and down her arms. Her waist tapers and flares to her hips and accentuates her strong legs that my fingers itch to wrap around.

Well, I'd be happy for her to stand here and do that as long as she wanted.

After soaping and scrubbing, I hand her the first dish.

"How many tattoos do you have?"

I glance over. "Too many to count. A lot. Not enough."

She dries the second dish and holds her hand out for more. "Do you have a favorite?"

"A few, probably." The ones that come to mind are the ones that remind me of her. And the few I got for Elijah. "Most of them don't mean much. They were just nice to look at." I shake my hands off and point to the one I think of when anyone ever asks my favorite.

It's a playing card but with a single number inside—seventeen.

"This one comes to mind."

I watch Aurora's hazel eyes widen as she wraps her fingers around my forearm. Her fingernails are painted in a light pink, and they trace over the outline of the tattoo, her nail scratching lightly over the number in the center. A chill trickles down my spine.

"Isaiah, what…" Her voice turns scratchy. "What is this?"

I shrug, trying to act like the heat from her touch doesn't have all the blood in my body rushing south. Like my heart isn't accelerating rapidly at her tender touch. "It's my favorite tattoo."

"Don't be dense," she murmurs, but her eyes are watering.

"It is."

A tear falls down her cheek, and I reach up, wiping it away with my thumb. Her hold still hasn't loosened on my arm. "I don't have any tissues with me, unfortunately."

"You are so stupid." She wipes her face with the back of her hand before hitting my chest.

Aurora continues to examine my arm, and I wonder if she'll pick up on anything else. The small ones hidden within the larger pieces are usually the ones that mean something to me. My mom's initials and Elijah's. My favorite novel. Lines from some of my favorite poetry.

I watch her study me. Her fingers trace the fine lines tattooed into my skin with a gentle touch, so light I might've thought I was dreaming if I wasn't watching her. Her eyelashes are long and black, fluttering on her cheeks. She moves up my arm, pushing my sleeve up to see it all and then back down towards my wrist, and when her eyes widen, I know she's seen one of the others.

It's our birthdays over one another. May 30th for Aurora over September 30th for me.

"I think I hate you." Her voice is quiet and shaky.

"I suppose we should've saved the tattoo tour for another day," I say, trying to lighten the mood. Even though nothing is going to lighten how I feel about her.

Aurora turns those hazel eyes up at me, glistening with tears. "I'm never going to stop crying at this point."

I chuckle. "I'm really sorry. You should've seen me when I got them."

She hasn't let go of my arm, her thumb resting on the two dates. "When did you?"

"I got the dates on my birthday after I left," I say, chest tightening with the memories.

I was a wreck when I got the dates. Freshly eighteen and depressed because I was alone. Part of it was my fault, and part of it wasn't. Elijah was gone, my mom and I weren't speaking, and I walked away from the one person who understood me when I didn't understand myself. After that tattoo, I went home and slept for almost three days because I couldn't get out of bed and didn't care to. I passed my classes by the skin of my teeth. That whole first year was focused on dragging myself out of a hole I'd partially dug.

Her eyes soften when she hears all that I don't say. Clearing my throat, I continue, "I got the card after you graduated and started playing for the

Royals. I remember looking at the current roster and hoping there wasn't already a player with the number seventeen so you could take it. And when your team photos were posted and you were wearing seventeen, I went and got it the next day."

"You looked me up?"

I raise a brow. "Aurora." Sure, I talked to Kian, but I never stopped following her career. Or what I knew would become her career.

"What?" she says, exasperated. "You might not have. I didn't."

"At all?"

Her thumb rubs against my skin where the tattoo is. "I did the first year, but you didn't post anything. After that, I assumed maybe you blocked me from seeing things or had new accounts. I don't know. And I was scared that if I kept looking, I'd see something I didn't want to see."

My heart pounds. "What wouldn't you have wanted to see?"

"Anything, if I'm being honest. If you posted and were happy, I would've wondered what I had done wrong. If you posted and were upset, I would've kicked myself." Aurora swallows, grip tightening on my wrist. "If you had a new best friend or a…girlfriend, I'm not sure I would've handled it well."

"Kind of like how I'm handling you seeing someone right now." I meant for it to sound light, but it falls flat, jealousy getting the best of me. Aurora sighs and lets go of my wrist. "I'm sorry, I shouldn't have…" I run a hand over my face. "Can we forget that I said that?"

"Said what?" She smiles. But there's a tension in the air now, not as sharp as it has been, but it's there, slinking in the shadows. Aurora takes a deep breath and interlocks her fingers. "I love the tattoos."

My eyes rake over her. "I'm pretty fond of them, too." We stare at each other for a second longer. "I'll finish up the dishes if you want to get the ice cream out, and then, we can finish the movie?"

Aurora nods, and we descend into silence. I work through the rest of the dishes and clean the sink, wondering why the fuck I had to open my mouth. Around me, she skates through the kitchen, grabbing bowls and spoons, pulling toppings from her cabinets. I wipe my hands on a towel and turn to see her waiting patiently.

"Go ahead. I'm gonna run to the restroom."

Her slight smile falters, and I exhale, walking down the hall to the bathroom. I pass the door to her bedroom that's pushed open to see one of the stuffed octopi I got her years ago sitting squarely between her pillows. I pause, unable to tear my eyes off it.

I won that for her at a carnival. Even now, I remember how her eyes lit up, how her teeth pulled at her lip. I remember everything.

Eventually, I make my way to the bathroom and lean against the closed door. I need to pull it together. Tonight wasn't about anything else except her having me here. Fuck. I hate myself for even mentioning her seeing someone. I hate that deep down, I know having to settle for being her friend will wreck me. I hate that if that's the case, it will be my own fault.

But she's Aurora; she is *my* Aurora and always will be. The curve of her lips when she smiles at me, the twinkle in her eyes when I make her laugh, the freckles and the scars I used to have memorized—not to be a complete prick, but the thought of someone else discovering those things burns the anger red hot.

Even so, I know that I have to walk out there and act like being her friend will be enough for me. Because if that's what all this leads to, if she can only be friends with me, I'll suck it up and be her best friend again.

And I'll be happy with it, even if I'm not.

Halfway through the movie, Aurora's eyes start to droop.

From the moment I stepped out of the bathroom door, I pulled it together. Enough to eat our ice cream on the couch and fall into a sense of normalcy like we once had. The dishes have all been cleaned, including our dessert, and a candle is lit on the countertop. For the most part, her apartment is dark, aside from the soft white lights she's strung up and the glow of the TV.

And now, she's stretched out sideways on the couch, her sock covered foot brushing my leg. She rests her head in her hands, but every few seconds, her eyes stay closed for longer than before. Every time they do, my eyes fall back to her.

I carefully stand up when her eyes close and grab a blanket from the basket near the TV. Gently, I drape it over her legs and crouch down beside her.

"Aurora." I rub her arm until her eyes blink open.

She rubs her eyes. "I'm sorry. Practice was brutal today."

"Don't be. I'm glad I could come." I pull the blanket up further until it's at her waist, fingers quickly brushing her skin before I pull my hands back. "We can finish the movie another time."

A tired smile forms on her lips. "I would like that. I liked hanging out. It was nice."

"All you gotta do is ask, and I'll be here."

Aurora turns, facing me a bit more, her head resting on the arm of the couch now. "My next game is away, but the one after that, are you going to come?"

My blood heats at the hazy gaze of her eyes, and hope unfurls, even though it shouldn't. "Wouldn't miss it."

"You should know, Zaza insists on you coming with us to get ice cream the next time," she says, letting out a big yawn.

"She is your twin."

That gets a quick laugh. "Everyone seems to think so."

I pat her hip on instinct, not thinking anything of it. "I'll get out of your hair. I'm gonna blow out the candle before I go." I go to stand, but she reaches out, her delicate fingers wrapping around my wrist.

"Isaiah," Aurora says, her fingers moving in tiny circles on my skin. The way she says my name, half-asleep but with just as much importance, sends a chill down my back. "You should know, I'm not seeing anyone anymore."

My heart stops, and I think I stop breathing for a second. "Okay."

"I should've said it earlier, but I wanted you to know."

I shake my head. "You didn't have to tell me anything. But I'm glad you did."

"Me, too."

I don't know what it means—but at the same time, it means everything.

"Want me to do anything else before I leave?"

"No, but text me when you get home?" She curls further into a ball.

"Of course." My hands itch to reach for her, to tuck a curl, to run my finger over her cheek. Instead I stand, blow out the candle, and grab my things, pausing briefly at the door. "Goodnight, Aurora."

"Goodnight."

Her tired smile is the last thing I see, and her words pound in my head. I try not to get too far ahead of myself, that the timing is just a coincidence, that it just wouldn't have worked. But it's useless.

All I want is Aurora.

All I need is a chance.

And I think she just gave it to me.

## One Half of a Whole

Kian answers the door with a surprised look.

"Hi," I say. In my hands, I have a Funfetti cake I made from a box and a bag of all his favorite treats.

"Hi."

"Can I come in?"

"Am I liable to die?"

I roll my eyes, hiding a smile. "Not today."

"Then, by all means, come in." Kian moves to the side. I follow him upstairs of the split-level home. "Your sister and the kids aren't here." He moves over to sit on the couch, ESPN currently muted on the television. His work laptop sits open in front of him.

"I know," I say, following him in and setting my stuff down on the coffee table. My knee cracks when I take a seat, causing me to flinch. "I'm sorry for last weekend. It wasn't fair of me to take it all out on you."

"What's in the bag?"

"Um…a box made Funfetti cake and like three bags of sour candy."

"You're forgiven," Kian says, reaching for the bag. "But you had every right to be upset. It's not like that was easy to hear. I'm honestly surprised you didn't hit me."

"Believe me, I thought about it." I pull my knees up onto the recliner and lean into the cushions. "It was just a lot. But we talked, and you know, he told me he wanted to be the one to tell me, and it shouldn't have happened that way."

"It shouldn't have. I could've tried harder to get him to be okay with me telling you sooner. It wasn't fair."

"Him needing you wasn't about me. I get that. Thank you for being there for him, Kian."

Now that the anger is gone, all I can be is thankful Isaiah had someone. No one should have to go through anything like that completely alone.

We share a knowing look, and Kian stands. "Bring it in."

I don't hesitate to walk into my brother-in-law's outstretched arms. If Isaiah wasn't a factor, I'd say that Kian objectively gives the best hugs. He's a big bear of a man and has a way of making you feel like everything is okay.

"Okay, get off so we can eat the cake."

I plop down next to him on the couch, pulling out the cake and handing him a fork. "No plates?" he asks.

"Plates are overrated."

Kian chuckles but takes the first bite. "So, you talked? How is it going?"

I take a bite, getting as little frosting as possible. "Good. I stormed over there after the diner. He handled that better than I deserved. But I think it helped. I really missed him, you know?"

Kian bumps my shoulder. "I know."

"But then, he came over the other night—"

"To your apartment?" Kian practically chokes next to me.

"Please relax. Yes, to my apartment. It needed to happen, and it was nice."

Even though he's not here, my cheeks turn warm thinking about it. He looked beyond perfect in my kitchen. He was at ease, he was comfortable, and I couldn't take my eyes off him. Not that I really ever can. There were moments when the intensity was more than I expected. The book. The reminiscing. The tattoos.

Those fucking tattoos. Both of them are burned into my brain for the rest of my life. Every time I think about them, my legs turn to jelly, and I understand why my heart is fighting to break out of my chest and walk right into Isaiah's arms.

"It was nice?" Kian exclaims. "*Nice?*"

I eat more cake. "He made me dinner. It was nice."

"You're so full of shit."

"You're a child."

Kian cackles next to me. "Nice. You and Isaiah, in a room, and it's nice. You two could barely function without reaching for each other when he showed up at your games. There's so much pining in your eyes, it makes me want to vomit, and it was *nice*?" His laughter echoes ridiculously through the room.

I throw my hands up in exasperation. "Shut up, Kian."

He points his fork at me. "Fine, but just know, I see through you."

"Well, I told him I wasn't seeing Drew anymore."

"You did?"

Leaning back into the couch, I rest my head in my palm. "I did. It doesn't mean anything, but he deserved to know."

Kian makes a beeping noise. "That's my bullshit radar going off by the way."

"Okay, fuck off. We're just friends. We're just learning how to be friends again."

At that, he falls back into the couch manically laughing, and I sit there with my arms crossed, trying to convince myself my words are true. Obviously, they aren't, but I'm choosing to be delusional.

That light that bloomed in his eyes when I told him I wasn't seeing anyone made me feel like I'd given him the world. It was how I felt when he showed me the tattoos. Like everything I ever wanted—Isaiah—was in reach.

Instead of accepting that, I sit there on the couch and tell myself we're just friends.

It's probably far too stalker-like to show up at Isaiah's place of work again. Probably worse that I snuck into his class at the very back and have been here the entirety of his final class of the day.

The payback is discovering that he also reads from his own book here. Not too much and it sounds as if he only does so if it's relevant to the lesson. Unfortunately, the lesson today was about evoking emotion. He read from a poem I hadn't gotten to on my own, "Can I Leave Me Too?" It was as if he twisted a knife in my chest, and all I could do was sit there and watch.

He mused on about a person he loved and couldn't hold on to.

It was a prose poem that felt like a story, a look into his past life, and it held every single student entranced. That was when he noticed me sitting here, too. He had glanced up from where he leaned against his desk, shock filtering quickly over his features before they settled.

I sat there as the students analyzed the word choice, the sentence structure, and so on and so on. He wore his glasses, which had sent my heart careening when I first noticed, and he stood proud in front of the room. Relaxed but maintaining the air one needs to keep students interested.

Eventually, the students were dismissed, and we were the only two who remained in the class. Isaiah sat on top of his desk as I walked down the stairs.

"How did you find the class, Miss Matthews?" Isaiah hits me with a focused gaze. The low timber of his voice sends a shiver crawling down my spine.

My eyes take him in. He crosses his arms, the tattoos that are on display moving beautifully as he does. Lean muscles ripple under the material as he sits cool, calm, and collected. This is his element.

"Hm. I thought it was well done. You might want to consider providing snacks for emotional damage, but that's just an idea."

Isaiah smiles, not quite enough for the dimple but enough for me. "I'll make sure to make a note."

I step forward, running a finger over the desk, eyes landing on the poetry book on top. "So, you read them here, too?"

He tracks me and my slow pacing. I make sure to never put less than two or three feet between us. "I read them everywhere, Aurora."

"What happens if some girl decides they're about her and becomes obsessed with you?"

Isaiah stands, tucking his hands into slacks. "There's only one girl I want obsessed with me." My heart goes pitter-patter in my chest like a cartoon character who's trying to keep it contained. "Her name's Azalea. Have you met her?"

Laughter breaks out. "You're stupid," I say. "And you don't need to worry about that. Zaza is plenty obsessed with you. Uncle Ziah." That's what she used to call him, even though she only knew him (in person) very briefly.

"What about Joey?"

"I thought you said one. You're getting greedy."

He shrugs. "I gotta weakness for the Matthews girls. Even though I suppose some of them are also Esera."

"They're Matthews at heart. No need to worry about Joey either."

Isaiah hums, moving a step closer. "And their aunt?"

My throat is dry, and I'm all too aware of the dwindling distance. The warmth emitting off his body, the heat slowly burning in his eyes, and the way my stomach is putting on an Olympic-level flipping act. "You'll have to ask them." His lips curl, and he nods. "So…are you busy tonight?"

"Not if you're asking me not to be."

I cross my arms. He crosses his. "Isaiah."

"Aurora."

"I'm serious."

"What makes you think I'm not?" he asks, cocking his head.

The way he looks at me… Isaiah makes me feel like I'm the only one in his orbit.

"Well, I was going to head to the Y, where I volunteer with some young players as often as I can, you know, to help out the coaches or whatever I can do for the kids. But I thought you could come with me, and then, we could go to dinner? You know to—I don't know—spend some time together," I muse, focusing on a scrape in the wooden desk.

"That sounds great. Let me just pack up, and we can go?" He moves swiftly, grabbing his books and phone, placing them gently in his shoulder bag.

"Take your time. It's actually not far from here. Do you mind walking?"

Isaiah shakes his head and swings his bag up. "Ready when you are."

We walk through the halls together, his hand finding purchase on my lower back when he opens the main door. Heat spreads from each of his fingertips and through my shirt onto my skin. Outside, we're hit with a blanket of heat, but it doesn't compare to his touch. The fifteen-minute walk passes quickly.

He tells me about some of his favorite students and some of the works they've turned in. Poems about their parents, fictional poems based on a short story or myth of their choosing, and how he likes seeing the improvement the most. That it makes him feel like he's successfully providing to the kids in the best way he knows how. It makes my heart swell, seeing him flourish.

"How'd you find this program?"

Our arms brush on the sidewalk, my fingers itching to touch him, but they remain at my side. "Coach Teller. Her wife is a teacher, and one of the women she works with set this program up. We come as a team a few times a year, to have more time to interact with the kids and what not, but I enjoy coming as often as I can. It's always really fun. They're so young and excited, and it's nice to see that." I glance up at him. "It's nice to be able to contribute, you know? Even if it only makes a tiny difference."

"That sounds great, Ro. I'm sure they love it," Isaiah replies as we reach the door, pulling it open and letting me step inside first.

We reach the door, and the familiar scent of the YMCA is immediate. Cleaning supplies with the faint smell of rubber and something that can only be described as *gym*. I sign us in at the desk before heading through the back to the gymnasium. Echoes of kids' voices bounce around the halls as we get closer. One of my favorite people is standing outside the door with a clipboard.

"Hi, Miss Loren," I smile, leaning in for a quick hug. Miss Loren has lived in the neighborhood her whole life. She grew up at this Y. Her brown skin wrinkles when she smiles at me.

"Aurora, so good to see you!" It takes her a split second to notice the man standing behind me. "Who is this?"

I grab his hand, pulling him forward. "This is Isaiah. We grew up together, and he just moved here. Thought I'd bring him along."

Miss Loren reaches for his hands. "Lovely to meet you, son. Any friend of Aurora's is welcome here."

"Thank you for having me." Isaiah smiles warmly. His hand falls out of hers and instantly grabs mine again. It takes me by surprise, but his palm against mine feels perfect.

Feels like they should've been together instead of apart for six years.

Her eyes flicker between us. "You should know, she's quite the fan favorite. Few of the kiddos have some mighty large crushes on that one."

My cheeks flame instantly. "Miss Loren!"

"What?" Her big, bouncy curls flounce as she looks between us. "He should know. Keep him on his toes."

"They're kids!"

"I've seen the way they look at you. Those boys have their first big crush. Some of the girls, too."

"Oh, my God," I mumble. Isaiah laughs beside me.

"Thanks for letting me know. I'll be sure to keep an eye out."

Miss Loren pats his shoulder. "Smart boy." Of course, that isn't enough for her. Leaning into me, she whispers, "That's a handsome boy, Aurora. Feel free to bring him as often as you'd like. Sure the coaches and the kids wouldn't mind."

We may as well call a fire engine because my cheeks are liable to be a fire hazard.

By Isaiah's faint smile, one he is poorly attempting to hide, he heard her. Not that Miss Loren can really whisper anyway, and why would she try if it means poor old me gets to be the resident tomato? She strides away, a cocky lilt to her walk, and leaves us alone.

"I wouldn't take what she says to heart." I step away, the loss of his hand jolting.

Oh, how I love the way his eyes shine when he's amused. "You mean about my being handsome? Or you being a hot commodity?"

"Both."

Isaiah closes the distance I fought for, fingertips brushing my arm. "I already knew those things. And both just happen to be true."

I love coaching. One day, whenever my playing days come to an end, this is what I want to do. The kids are all so fresh and excited. It's the game that keeps them going, the fun of being on a team and working together. There's something insanely special about that.

Growing up I had a lot of different kinds of coaches—not including my father. Some great and some not so great. Some that ignored us, that thought because we were young, we couldn't know what we wanted and pushed us into positions we didn't care for. But the ones that I remember, the ones like Coach Teller, were the ones that knew how to walk the line. How to be a coach and still treat us like we had autonomy.

That's what I want to do.

Isaiah has been watching from the sidelines of the gym with a few parents. No matter where I was or what I was doing, he was watching.

A few kids currently have me pulled aside, begging me to show them a move from last time. Who am I to say no to smiling young faces? Most of the kids play on another team outside of here—either recreational or travel—but this serves as both after school care and a little extra attention from the community. Usually the coaches shy away from specific skills, but today is, in fact, a skill day.

I pull the tiny size-four soccer ball toward me. It's a classic turn meant to fool a defender by using the inner part of your foot to pull it back. And let me tell you, nothing makes your confidence boost like a bunch of ten-year-old's being insanely impressed by you. Their tiny cheers are like straight adrenaline.

One of the girls, Paige, steps up first. "Please teach me that, Coach Matthews?"

"Of course!" I pull her to my side and show her the move in slow motion. The other kids look on with pure thrill in their eyes.

Getting to do this is always fun for me. Zaza plays, but I don't like to interfere too much since we're family. I don't want to risk the relationship that way. Not like me and my dad. But here, I get to let go of that fear, work with other kids, and do what I can. By the time the coaches whistle the session to a close, Paige and her friends are almost perfect on the skill. As perfect as ten-year-old's can be, at least, and that's pretty phenomenal.

"Coach Matthews, are you guys gonna make the play-offs?"

I crouch down. "It looks like it. If we win our next few games, we'll be there."

The kids explode in excitement, bringing a smile to my face. "And you'll still come here, right?"

"Of course. I'll see if I can get the whole team out again soon, alright?" I respond, and I'm greeted with bright eyes and excited faces. They start to disperse into their closing tasks—groups the coaches created to clean up the gymnasium. After a quick goodbye to the coaches and the girls, I prepare to leave.

Isaiah and I walk out side by side. I pause, stretching my arms over my head. A tight muscle in my shoulder twinges with pain as I do.

"Coach has a nice ring to it," Isaiah chimes as I lead the way toward the restaurant.

"Let's not think too far ahead. I've got some good years in front of me." I bump him playfully.

"No doubt about that." The sun has taken its place lower in the sky, painting it technicolor. Today, a cool breeze weaves between us and wraps around us. "I see what Miss Loren meant about my competition."

"Jesus, they're literally ten."

He raises a brow. "So, you admit there *is* a competition?"

My mouth gapes as he sends me flustering. Once again, my face is hot, and my heart starts sprinting. A slow smile spreads on Isaiah's face, the remaining sunlight framing him in gold. I whip my head back around, saving myself from the intensity of his gaze.

"No, that is not what I said."

"But it was implied."

"Do you want to compete with ten-year-old's?"

Isaiah huffs in humor. "Absolutely not. I'm just saying, I'm not sure I've ever seen so many googly-eyed kids in one room."

"You flatter me," I deadpan.

There's a neon sign that blinks *open* and a chalkboard outside. We enter, and the space opens up in front of us. In the back, there's a pool table and a ski-ball machine on one side, and on the other, my personal favorite, an air hockey table.

I lead Isaiah to the bar, white twinkle lights hanging above and music playing in the background. He takes a seat on the barstool next to me. Quickly, the bartender slides us waters and menus.

"Is that what I think it is?"

"A menu?"

Isaiah shakes his head. "You're such a smartass."

Laughter trickles out. "Yes, that is an air hockey table." He hums, his face turning inquisitive. I turn in my chair, resting my feet on his barstool. "Why are you making that face? What bright idea are you cooking up there?"

"I say we place a game of air hockey–"

"Or five. Or six. Or ten."

He smiles. "And for every win, that person gets a question that has to be answered. I've, uh—I've been thinking about it since dinner at your place, but I think we need to learn how to be us again." Isaiah averts his eyes, his fingers tapping nervously.

I tap his leg gently until he looks at me again. "I think that sounds like a good idea."

We've been separate for so long, and I genuinely thought that was going to be the rest of my life. One half of a whole, searching for ways to fill in the empty spaces as best they could.

It's starting to feel like that isn't true anymore.

"Good to know you're still the sorest loser I've ever met."

I huff. "Shut the fuck up, Isaiah."

He laughs, and even over the music, I hear every note. "Don't be bitter because you're losing."

The air hockey table is mocking me. That's the only explanation. Because I simply cannot only have won two of six. One of our favorite movie theaters growing up had an arcade section, so we'd always go early to play some games, and we always ended up playing air hockey. And I almost always won.

So, I'm feeling very betrayed.

I take a deep breath and grab the puck to start a new game. Across the table, Isaiah scratches his forehead, but slowly drags an L shape across before letting his hand drop back down.

"You're such a shithead."

A confident smirk takes over his face. His eyes are alight but focused. "At least I'm not a loser."

I take the puck and set it so we can get started. We volley it back and forth until I get a good hit and slam it, making the first score. The puck slinks over the table with every following hit, but since I'm quite literally enraged over air hockey, I finally win another game, making the tally three to six. Isaiah marks it down on the back of a coaster.

Isaiah picks up his beer bottle, fingers wrapping around it and interrupting the condensation. He takes a short pull. "How do you feel about saving the questions for another night?"

"Works for me," I say. "How many games did we say?"

"Best out of thirteen."

"Hm."

"Worried Aurora?"

I flip him off and point to the table.

Luckily, I win the next one, making it six to four—Isaiah.

But Isaiah comes back and wins the eleventh and twelfth.

The moment he gets the puck first in the final game, I have a bad feeling. And that bad feeling is right. Every time he hits the puck, he scores, and I'm left standing there—a loser.

"This is bullshit." I cross my arms.

Isaiah walks—excuse me—*saunters* toward me until he's right in front of me. "I missed this." I blink up at him. He pulls me in for a playful hug, one where I keep my arms crossed because I am, in fact, a sore loser and where he just rocks me back and forth—gloating—because he is a sore winner.

"Come on, Ro, you can't be mad at me. We made a deal." His lips are mere centimeters away from my ear. So close I can practically feel them. As usual, my heart goes wild.

"I'm not mad at you. I'm mad at myself for losing," I mumble into his chest. Eventually, I soften into the embrace. I missed hugging him. I missed touching *him*. It's like a drug—one that I'll never get enough of.

He squeezes me tight before letting me go. The bar has slowly populated over the past two hours.

"Do you wanna head out?"

The song changes, and I'm instantly transported to the past. It reminds me of late-night drives and trips to Wawa, loading up on snacks and soft pretzels and Twizzlers for Isaiah. It reminds me of lying on the floor of his room while he was trying to write. It reminds me of myself post-game, him driving me home and giving me control of the radio.

"After this song?"

His eyes soften, flickering to my lips before landing on my eyes. I'm thrilled when he wraps his arm around me again, pulling me back into his chest. Like this, I track every inhale, every tiny movement he makes, and I swear I feel his heart racing against my back. We both feign looking at the TVs above us, some baseball game playing, but I know that we're both fighting not to look at each other.

For a second, I stop fighting. I take a long look at him. I wish I could blame it on the bar lighting, which I'm convinced makes people more attractive, but I can't. Isaiah is simply that beautiful. So much so that my heart literally aches at the sight of him. The long black eyelashes, the curve of his nose, the full shape of his lips.

He's not an imposing person, not the biggest guy in the room, nor the most insanely attractive. Isaiah is the double take. You see him and you recognize that he's attractive, but something ticks in your brain, saying *ah, you missed it*, and you have to look back, and you're struck by how fucking beautiful someone could be.

I see it—girls strolling past us to their seats have given him long looks all night. Now, I wouldn't say I was a jealous person, but I'd be lying if I said a little green Aurora didn't rear her head when their gazes lingered too long.

But there's an extra layer for me. I grew up with him. I can recognize every single change, no matter how minute. An extra wrinkle, a new freckle, a new mannerism. Every new piece of information is locked away in the recess of my brain that is solely dedicated to Isaiah. I've kept it locked away for so long, begging myself not to dwell on it in fear that I would never crawl my way out. Now, that door is wide open. Accepting new information and storing it away where it belongs.

Isaiah's arm wraps around my shoulders, his fingers playing with a curl. I'm not even sure he knows he's doing it. I only know that he feels comfortable enough to do so. At that, I sink a tiny bit further into him. Into the warmth, the familiarity.

And I notice, we're swaying. Barely. Probably imperceptible to an outsider.

But I think right here, right now, if the room was burning down around us, I'd be content to let it.

As long as I got to do it with him.

## Hair Pin Drop

*C*oach Teller stands with her hands behind her back, gazing at all of us. We're seated, uniforms tucked in and cleats laced up, but there's an excited gaze in Coach's eyes today. One that means good news.

"Alright, ladies. Game day. Are we ready?"

In unison, we say, "Yes, Coach."

She nods, rocking on the balls of her feet. "Good. Are we planning on winning?"

"Yes, Coach."

"Well then. I've got some exciting news to share." Her eyes land on me for a split second, and my heart careens. "Two of you have been selected for the National Team showcase."

Loud cheers and claps ensue, but I'm too nervous. The showcase is like a try-out. But on a much larger scale. With much larger stakes. Like the Olympics or the World Cup. I lock eyes with Kendall, one of our best forwards and the other favorite. She rolls her lips and does a little dance with her shoulders.

She's twenty-two and an absolute superstar. The National Team needs a forward like Kendall. Quick and smart but sure-footed and confident. Someone who knows the field and knows when it's her chance and when it's not.

My dad and Coach Laurel stand beside Teller, their faces giving nothing away. I continue to avoid my dad's eyes and turn my focus to Coach Teller.

"Kendall Sabla and Aurora Matthews, get your asses up here."

Maazina shoves me off the bench, breaking into loud 'whoops.' Coach Teller rolls her eyes, but a small smile grows anyway. "Congratulations, girls. We all know you're going to get there and absolutely smash it. I'd like to talk to you both before we head to the field, but for now," Coach Teller says, checking her watch and looking around. Everyone is poised to explode off the benches, awaiting the go ahead. "You've got ten minutes. Have at 'em."

My eyes widen in surprise as Kendall and I are bombarded. From her delayed reaction, it's clear neither of us have processed it. "Holy shit," I whisper, not thinking she'll hear me, but somehow, under the commotion, she does.

"Holy shit!" she shouts, grabbing my hands and pulling me into a hug. This might be the best pre-game of my life. The team is acting like seven-year-olds given too much sugar, practically jumping off the walls. You would've thought we won the championship. Vivian steals me from Kendall, pulling me into a tight hug and rocking us back and forth.

Maazina decides that's a good moment to catapult herself at me, launching herself onto my back so I'm forced to catch her. "Let's fucking go!" she shouts, hands pumping the air like she was the one selected.

Coach Teller pokes her head out of the office. "Language."

Above me, Maazina clears her throat. "Let's freakin' go!"

I laugh, and she leans down, planting her face next to mine. "I'm so proud of you, Aurora. I've never been so honored to be someone's own personal idiot." She plops a kiss on my cheek.

"Maazina, you've got ten seconds to get off her back before I make you," Coach Teller shouts. Maazina quickly climbs down but doesn't let go of me.

I've got nothing to say. I'm overflowing with emotions—elation, shock, love—from all of these girls who have been nothing short of family to me. They mean the entire world to me. Even though I know some of them are sad, as I would be, they don't let that get in the way of what this means to me and Kendall. I can't wait to step on the field and play with them today.

Through the haze, Isaiah comes to mind. God, I want to call him. There's a yearning blooming in my stomach, begging me to walk out and go find him in the stands.

Eventually, the celebrations calm down, and game mode switches on. Coach is speaking to Kendall at the moment as the girls around me slip right back into their normal pre-game routines. Outside the office, my dad stands there, talking quietly with Coach Laurel. As if he can sense my gaze, he looks up.

As expected, his face is stoic.

He's never broken first after a fight in my life. I'm the one to apologize, even if I've done nothing wrong. I feel every beat of my heart as we stare at each other. I swallow. He says something to Coach Laurel, who nods, and takes a few steps, and for a split second, the ache alleviates. My back straightens. He can't ignore me today, right?

Wrong.

He stalks right out the door without a lingering glance, without a word. My chest caves in. I thought, at the very least, I would get a nod. A pat on the back.

Instead, I get nothing.

It doesn't matter what I do. Whether I'm on top of the world or hitting rock bottom. If his pride is threatened, he won't give in. For a moment, I thought this would do it. Get him to bend. But I guess it doesn't matter. He'd rather break than give me his praise. I guess it's too much for him.

The numbness smooths over my skin like a cold gel.

I'm used to it, but it never hurts any less.

There are eyes on me, three pairs who know exactly what happened, and I pretend they aren't.

When I turn to face them, there's a smile on my face, and I take my seat on the benches. Sylvia rests her head on my shoulder, eating her pre-game candy. No one says anything, and I'm grateful. Regardless of how I feel, we've got a game today.

I reach in my bag until I pull the tape from the bottom of the bag and cut it into strips for my knee. Coach Teller calls me into the office moments later, and my cleats click on the floor as I make my way over, moving on autopilot.

She wraps me up in a hug. "I'm so proud of you, kid. You've worked so hard for this." When she pulls back, her hands remain on my arms. "You've come so far. You've earned every single bit of this. This is what you've worked for. I hope you believe to the fullest extent that you were made for this."

Her words mean the world to me, and I try to focus on them over everything else. "Thank you for everything you have done for me," I say. Coach Teller has been there for me from the moment I graduated college. I tore my hamstring my first year playing for her, dealt with an almost tear in my knee and knee strains, but I never gave up. And she never gave up on me.

"Proud of you. You're gonna rock that team." Coach Teller sniffs, reaching for her clipboard.

"Are you crying?"

"Get out, Matthews. We have a game to play."

It pulls a genuine laugh, and I do as she says. "I always knew you loved me."

"Out."

Even though my heart is breaking in my chest, Coach Teller is far from the reason.

She follows me out of the office and holds the locker room door open. I shake out my arms and my legs, the blood still flowing from warms up, and put on my game face. I don't have time to fall apart, even if a part of me wants to.

This should be one of the best days I've ever had, and I'm going to make it so.

We're dominating this game.

Every play is ours. Every touch, every pass, every call. Currently, it's 3-0—us. And it doesn't look like we'll be stopping anytime soon. The moment I walked out of the tunnel and took my spot on the field, I found my family and Isaiah. I swear we locked eyes for a moment, and in that moment, everything was okay. That no matter what, he'd be excited for me. He'd know what it meant.

Even now, over halfway through the game, I know exactly where they are, no matter where I stand on the field. I move the defense up a bit, as the ball is in the other half, and spare the quickest glance to my right. Even from a distance, I know his eyes are on me.

Maazina cuts inside, a few feet away. The sun hits her cleats just right, shining on the sharpie where she writes her mom's name. "How goes it with lover boy?"

"Shut up, Maazina."

She shrugs, eyes on the play in front of us. "What? You're the one all goo-goo ga-ga over him."

I can't help but laugh, adjusting the pre-wrap holding my curls. "Have I told you I hate you recently?"

She hums. "Not that I can remember."

"Good. Use that as your reminder." I yell to fall back seconds later as play starts to descend.

Besides me, Maazina gets into position, since it's coming to the right. I step up, the first line of defense if it's needed, but the ball goes astray, coming straight toward me, the opposing players too far behind. I take it, rolling it across my foot and passing it wide left to Sylvia as we take control again. We switch the ball across the field before sending it up to our midfield.

It says up for a minute, but it appears the opposing team has found their stride. A ball is passed across the field, but I step up, intercepting the pass. It's light on my foot, an extension of my body as my team gets into position. There's an opponent coming my way, but I have time. I move with the ball swiftly, sure on my feet.

I don't even see the tackle coming.

One second, everything is perfect.

The next, I'm on the ground, and my knee is in excruciating pain.

My knee is on fire, screaming with pain as agony blooms and expands in throbbing waves.

"Aurora? Hey, Aurora." Maazina's voice sounds from nearby, but I can't open my eyes. If keep my eyes closed, I can pretend it isn't happening.

That this isn't *fucking* happening.

Around me, everything's stopped, and I can feel the presence of others standing over me. I feel a touch on my arm. "Aurora, talk to me."

Coach Teller's calm voice in the middle of the panic is the reason the first tear falls. "This can't be happening," I say, my voice wet and my throat threatening to close up.

"We've got you."

I blink my eyes open, and though her face is composed, her eyes give her away. She is devastated. At my knee, the trainers block my view, their fingers gently prodding, but even that is agonizing.

"We're going to get you off this field, okay? We've gotta stand you up. If you can't walk, we'll help you."

Seconds later, I'm being lifted. The jostling is awful, but I school my face. No one else out here will see me cry. My girls are watching me— calm yet wide-eyed. My gut hollows out, my heart ripping itself to shreds.

Tentatively, I touch my left foot to the ground, trying out the knee, and have to bite my tongue from crying out. Coach Teller is under one arm, a trainer under another. "Keep it off the ground."

Carefully, I'm helped off the field, and it's so quiet, you could hear a hair pin drop. But all I can hear are the cracks in my chest. Because on the day that I'm selected for the National Team is the day my knee gives out.

I couldn't make today better if I tried.

# You Always Will Be

"Please get me Isaiah."

The padded table is cool beneath my back, and a cool towel rests on my forehead. All I can do is stare at the plain, white ceiling above me.

"Ro," Sophia muses gently, hand on my shoulder, "are you sure?"

Kian and the kids are standing by the door, my mom with them. I don't know if dad ever came in the room, but I know he's on the sidelines finishing the game. I tell myself I don't care. *Ha.*

"Please," I plead, my voice cracking. "Please bring him back here."

Sophia kisses my cheek without a word before retreating. Silence returns, aside from the rummaging of the trainers. I'll need an MRI to confirm anything, but in the meantime, they'll wrap it and ice it as best they can. The silence is pounding in my ears, and all I can hear are my own thoughts. Which are, admittedly, not very positive. I press my palms to my eyes, hoping they'll absorb the wetness.

"Aurora?"

My chest heaves when I hear his voice, and he's by my side before I can inhale. His fingers brush my temple, a gentle swipe under my eye. I blink them open to find his brown ones filled with concern.

"Hey there," he murmurs tenderly.

"Hi."

"How you feeling?"

My knee throbs, but I shrug. "Could be better, I guess." I wrap my fingers around his wrist, keeping his hand on my face.

"You look pretty good from up here."

"Even teary eyed with a fucked-up knee?" My voice trembles.

"Even then, Rora, even then."

The nickname breaks me. For the first time since he's returned, I don't fight it. Tears start pouring out, and Isaiah soothingly pulls me up into a sitting position, cupping his hand in my curls and holding me to his chest. It's not long before my tears are soaking his shirt. My fingers are curled tightly into the fabric, wishing I could melt into him and disappear.

Isaiah whispers calming words, gentle shushes, and just holds me.

"Will you take me home?" I ask when I can breathe again.

Isaiah swipes his thumb under my eyes and pushes my curls away from my face. "Of course."

He walks over to the desk, where the athletic trainers are so kindly acting like they didn't see my break down. They stand, making their way over to me all together.

"Hey there. You ready to go home?" Thomas asks, papers in his hand.

"Yeah. Thanks, Thomas."

"Anytime. So, we've scheduled you to get an MRI tomorrow, alright? We'll get this figured out so we can get you back on the field as soon as we can."

I nod, taking the papers. "Do I need to wait for Coach Teller?"

"No, you've got the clear to head out."

Thank God. If anyone got a look at me right now, I might crawl in front of a car.

Thomas looks to Isaiah. "You're taking her home?" He nods. "Okay, crutches are over here. If you can put pressure, go ahead but lightly. We've got some tape, ice packs, and a knee brace in here for you. It's still swollen, so don't force the brace on it too soon. When the ice melts you can re-ice it or wrap it so you can sleep, and keep it elevated."

Isaiah listens intently, and I'm only half paying attention. I've been injured before, so I file the information away.

"You know how to take care of yourself. Just make sure you give yourself some grace in the meantime. Address for tomorrow is there," Thomas says, finishing up.

"Got it. Thank you." Isaiah looks between us two, looking ready to take on the world of injury.

"Thanks, Thomas."

Isaiah steps in front of me. "You ready?"

Exhaling, I nod, and he hands me the crutches. I adjust to them in a few seconds, and Isaiah is never more than a step behind. In the hallway, everyone else waits with my stuff. They don't even know I was selected today—unless Coach told them, which I doubt. Sure, this is devastating, but they don't know why it's eating me from the inside out.

"Auntie Ro, are you okay?" Joey babbles, her big eyes wide.

My lips tremble. "I'll be okay, baby. Isaiah's gonna take me home and patch me up." She moves toward me and gently hugs the leg that isn't wrapped up, Zaza joining her.

"Careful there." Kian steps up, prying them off.

I shake my head. "It's okay. Love you both, okay?"

They give me sad eyes but step back. Mom steps up and hugs me. "You'll be alright. You'll be back sooner than you know it." Her touch makes me want to collapse, and I choke down sobs. Isaiah's hand lands on my back, rubbing up and down softly, grounding me.

Sophia and Kian say something similar, Sophia holding my hand while we stand, squeezing it, letting me know she's right there. Like she always is. In the tunnel, I hear the whistles and the faintest sounds of my teammates' voices.

I look back at Isaiah, and he exhales, reading me like only he can. "Alright, let's get you out of here." Sophia squeezes once more and lets go of my hand so I can use the crutches properly. They help me into the passenger side of Isaiah's car, placing my bags and the crutches in the back seat.

Sophia palms my cheeks like she used to when we were kids. "I love you so much. Call me if you need anything," she says, directing the second sentence to both Isaiah and myself, and then kisses my forehead.

"Love you."

The door closes, and I watch through the window as they head to their own cars before sinking into the seat. The idea of going back to my apartment alone, left to stew in my own thoughts, makes me sick.

When I turn, Isaiah is already looking at me. "Is now a bad time to tell you that I got selected for the National Team Showcase before the game? And now—" I shake my head, a few tears falling out. "Now, my knee is fucked. And this…. this was everything I ever wanted."

Even if he wanted to, he couldn't hide the way his face falls. "Aurora." He reaches over, his hand cupping my face, fingers finding purchase in my curls. "I'm sorry, sweetie. I'm so sorry."

I close my eyes, tears leaking like acid down my cheeks. "How am I supposed to—how am I—"

"Hey, hey. Look at me," Isaiah demands. His eyes are sad but firm. "Breathe. In and out." I do as he says, even though I'd rather scream. "Good. Again. In and out." The tears slow. The aching in my chest continues but fades to the background. I focus on Isaiah. "You're okay. You're going to be okay."

There's not a single waver to his voice. He says it like he means it. We sit like that for who knows how long. It's probably minutes, but it feels like hours until I can speak.

"Can I come to your place?" I swallow thickly. "I don't want to be alone."

His brown eyes soften. "Of course. Do you want to stop at yours for anything?"

I shake my head, wishing I could curl up and hide. Isaiah reaches over, intertwining his fingers with mine. Instantaneously, the steady pressure diminishes the loneliness. Without his hand holding mine, it felt like I was lost in the limitlessness of space, destined to float endlessly with no destination. Isaiah is my anchor—holding onto me and holding me here. Even in the darkness, he'll be there to keep me from disappearing. His thumb smooths over the back of my hand in repetitive motions.

"Let's get you home."

Home. It has so many different meanings, can be so many different things. That field is my home—even though it just royally kicked me off. My apartment, Sophia and Kian's house, my mom's, my dad's. They are all homes in their own right.

But Isaiah holding onto me, Isaiah being the one I wanted… Right now, he feels more like home than any of the others. I've been homesick for so long without him, and right now, the only place I want to be is Isaiah's home.

Isaiah is attentive, and dare I say it, close to hovering. To my surprise, I don't mind it. I'm not sure in recent years that anyone has hovered over me when injured or sick. Paid attention to every little movement, every noise, every step. It's nice to be cared for, to have someone there instead of having to pull myself together and take care of myself.

He sets down my stuff, Raven currently weaving her lithe body between his legs.

I lean against the back of the couch. "Can I shower? Do you mind?"

"You're okay to shower?"

"Yeah, but I might need help undoing the ice."

Isaiah approaches me. "Can you stand, or do you want me to run a bath?

With apprehension, I try to bend my knee, only to fail. "Would you hate me if I said bath?"

"I could never hate you."

My head falls forward, finding the firmness of his chest. His arms wrap around me, rubbing my back without hesitation. "Thank you."

"Always. I'll grab some clothes for you. Give me a second, and I'll come get you when it's ready." Isaiah pulls back, placing a kiss on the crown of my curls.

I watch as he moves through his apartment and the sound of running water starts. Raven sits on her haunches a few feet away, green eyes focused on me. Since I can't move, I give her a smile, assuming the cat can recognize facial expressions, and it seems to work. She lets out a soft mewl and rubs her body on the crutch and somehow, around my good leg.

After a moment, she trots down the hallway in search of her dad, and I track carefully behind her. Isaiah is exiting his bedroom with a pile of clothes in his hands when he sees me. "Come on in. It's almost ready."

A few more movements and I settle myself on top of the closed toilet with my leg straight out in front. Isaiah places the folded clothes on the sink next to lotion and athletic tape. He bends down in front of me, fingers reaching for the ice wrapping.

"I'll take this off and then go if you think you'll be okay?"

"I'll be fine."

"If you aren't, that's okay, too."

I tuck a curl behind my ear and nod, my eyes focused on where his hands touch my skin. With deft fingers, he starts unraveling the plastic that's keeping the ice on my knee. Round and round the tape goes, cool drops of water traveling down my leg. One hand wraps around the back of my calf, keeping it steady. It has the opposite effect on my heart, which is anything but. Each finger is like a spark on my skin.

I'm saddened by the loss of his touch when he removes the bag of ice and places it in the sink. I barely have time to miss it because his fingers are back, gently roaming the swollen and already bruising knee.

"I can't fucking believe she tackled you like that."

With a shake of my head, I feel my own knee. It throbs under my touch. "I doubt it was that bad."

Isaiah turns his eyes up at me, and I'm surprised by the anger there. "She instantly got red carded. It was a dirty tackle, and everyone knows it."

It's nice. To have someone else be mad for you. To be upset with you. It's nice to not have to be feeling all of these things alone. Which is why I almost smile. "I'll be okay, Isaiah."

He turns his attention to my knee again, his big hands still covering most of my skin. "I know you will be." At that, he reaches over, touching the bath water to check the temperature.

"Thanks for the bubbles."

Isaiah exhales, some tension finally leaving his shoulders. "You're welcome."

Our eyes meet, and there's an abundance of things that pass between us. In the warm light of his bathroom, his eyes twinkle like a million little shining stars. Isaiah looks at me in a way that no one else ever has. With him here, I can breathe deep. I can inhale and exhale, and it doesn't feel like my world is falling apart.

Still, when he shuts the door behind him and I carefully make my way into the tub, that doesn't stop the sobs from racking my chest. I muffle them as best I can, and my tears melt into the water, but that doesn't stop Isaiah from sitting outside the bathroom door.

I needed the door shut so I could let it out without being more of a burden.

Isaiah knew and still decided to be close enough if I needed him, too.

His clothes smell like him.

Obvious, I know, but it's overwhelming. Clean and warm. An undertone of musk. It's all him, and it's everywhere. The shorts are huge but allow my leg room to breathe, and the long sleeve goes well past my fingertips, but it's cozy.

When I hobbled my way out of the bathroom, he had pushed the leather ottoman closer to the couch, placing pillows for elevation. A candle was lit and the TV on. But what I really paid attention to was the way he studied me from head to toe. His eyes took a leisurely path over my body, lingering on the way his clothes hung on me, the shape of my legs, leaving behind a wake of heat over my skin. As if he was touching every single part of me with his eyes.

Now, almost an hour later with my leg elevated, I still feel it—the heat left over from his gaze. Add that to the fact that he made me dinner again and has been generally doting, I'm unsure I'll ever cool down again.

Isaiah is finishing up the dishes in the kitchen, and the sink stops. "You want dessert?"

"Of course."

He chuckles, and the sound finds every weak spot I have and burrows. Raven is nestled on my right between the arm of the couch and my body, her tiny paw that has a streak of white resting on my leg. Isaiah returns with two plates and forks, large servings of chocolate cake on each, and takes up his spot on my left.

"Is this the frozen chocolate cake?" I ask, digging in my fork.

"Well, it's thawed now." He takes a bite, and I blink at him. "Yes, that's the one."

I poke at it. "Not sure there's anything to celebrate, Isaiah." My knee is tightly wrapped, disguising the bruises that have already bloomed. It's swollen, but the pain is kept at bay by the ibuprofen Isaiah gave me.

"We can still celebrate your selection for the National Team," he murmurs, giving me a searing look. "But it also serves as an anti-celebration cake." His tongue swipes at a crumb. "When something bad happens—cake."

I can't help but smile. "Anti-celebration cake. I like that."

"Is this a bad night to start with one of my air-hockey win questions?"

This time, I can't help but laugh. Maybe my first since the injury. It feels light and airy. Nice. Isaiah's face lights up at it. "No, I think this is a perfect night."

"Why'd you ask for me tonight?"

"I see we're starting off easy," I say, taking another bite, buying some time. "Come on, Isaiah, you know why." My throat feels tight at the idea of being vulnerable when I'm already physically weakened. I can't run away; I can't avoid it.

"I need you to say it, Rora." His eyes are pleading. He needs to hear it.

I lick my lips. "I needed you. I didn't want anyone else near me, not even Sophia. I laid there, staring at the ceiling, and all I could think about was how much I needed you to be next to me. To tell me it would be okay. To hold my hand." The room is so quiet, I'm scared he'll hear my heart racing. "More than that, I wanted you there. You always knew how to make something awful feel better. You always understood exactly what I needed, and you still do. You probably always will."

Isaiah is staring at me. He's so still that I'm half-sure he's not breathing.

"Isaiah?" I whisper, and he exhales. In the space between us, his free hand reaches for mine.

"Yeah, just need a second."

I intertwine our fingers this time, threading them together. Today has been a whirlwind of emotions. Up and down and fucking flipped around. But holding his hand might be the best part of it all.

He gives my hand a gentle squeeze, opening his eyes.

"I should've kept my mouth shut, huh?"

Isaiah chuckles but gives a firm shake of his head. "No. It's nice to know you still need me."

*Still.* Even when I was telling myself I didn't, I did.

"I always have, Isaiah."

The sheer weight of his gaze is enough to make my heart thump. Whoever came up with the opinion that brown eyes were inferior had obviously never looked at someone with brown eyes. Never cared for them. Because there is no way that the warmth, the softness, the endlessness of them could be anything close to inferior.

"For a minute, I thought you'd never forgive me. Never look at me like that again. I thought I might've really lost you."

It's funny because, at one point, I thought the same. All that anger, all the pain—I wasn't sure I'd be able to let it go. How stupid I was acting like I could've ever held onto that. How stupid I was for thinking I could ever look at him and not forgive him.

"I never could hold a grudge against you," I murmur.

The grip on my hand tightens. "You tried." He gives me a cheeky grin.

"I failed."

"Not to celebrate a failure, but I am grateful for that one." His voice is filled with humor and also the utmost sincerity. "I'm not sure I would've known what to do if you succeeded."

I turn to look at him, unable to adjust how I'd like because of my fucking knee, but I try my best. My eyes notice that the space between us is incrementally smaller. Like he's not aware of it but has to be closer to me. "I'm not sure either."

His lips turn up in a closed mouth smile that is just as enticing as all his other ones. I rub my thumb against his hand. "My turn."

"Choose wisely. You've only got four."

"You're such a sore winner."

"But I *am* a winner."

"Jesus Christ." I run my free hand over my face, a gentle laugh escaping past my lips. "You're insufferable."

"Just like you when you lose—" he starts, and I cut him off by placing the hand that was holding his over his lips. They curve into a smile on my palm, setting the sensitive skin of my hand and the rest of my body on fire. The brief touch has turned his eyes molten. Warm enough to send tingles over my skin.

"Are you done?" I ask, and he nods. I remove my hand. "So…why now? Why'd you come back now?"

Isaiah doesn't look surprised by the question. Instead, he looks contemplative. He stretches his arms up and behind him on the couch, the ink stretching over the lean muscle, his t-shirt riding up, exposing the smooth plane of his stomach.

He fixes me with a heady stare. "Six years was as long as I could go without you. And it was six years too long. I know that now. The first two years, I was lost, and I couldn't stand to show up. I was struggling to stand on my own two feet. The third and fourth were better in a way. I graduated early and was writing. Then, I got the publishing deal. All I wanted was to call you; I was just so ashamed. And so anxious that there was no fixing what I broke." Isaiah turns his head up to the ceiling, taking a deep breath. "And since I couldn't get out of my own way to call you, I wrote about you. Almost every day. I would try not to, and every day, you'd end up on the pages anyway. The last year, I just couldn't do it anymore."

I'm not sure I've ever seen his eyes look so firm. Unwavering.

"I couldn't fucking handle not being able to call you and tell you things. Bad, good, whatever. All of it. At that point, I didn't care about my own fears, whether you'd let me back in your life or not. Whether we could ever repair it all. Because if I didn't try, I was never going to know. And that was unfathomable to me. So, I started looking for jobs immediately. Took a while but I got here, and that's all that matters."

"Can you help me up?"

Isaiah looks momentarily confused, but he does as I ask. I make sure to keep my foot only lightly on the ground, using his arms for balance. Once I feel stable enough, I throw my arms around his neck. There were no words forming in my brain, no coherent thoughts, just…Isaiah.

I feel like a fucking teenager with a brain-eating bacteria called a crush.

His arms wrap around my back, holding me up and holding me steady. His hands spread over his t-shirt, as if he needs to touch as much of me as possible.

"You asked for my help getting up to give me a hug?" Isaiah asks, his breath hitting my neck, sending goosebumps down my spine.

"Yes." I swallow. Vulnerable words are begging to escape, and there's fear in my chest, wanting me to hold them back, but I have to stop that. "You never stopped being my best friend. Even when I tried to hate you, you still were. You always will be."

One hand crawls up my back and wraps around the back of my neck, tangling in my curls. I'm fairly certain he can feel the rapid beating of my heart, but I don't care. We stand like that until my knee starts aching again, but when we sit down, the space between us on the couch is almost non-existent. My leg is a hair's breadth away from his.

It's so much easier letting him back in. And doing so makes my life better. Even on a day like today, where everything else has unraveled before me, Isaiah is doing the opposite.

When he left, while he was gone, I said it was like missing one half of a whole. There were all these empty spaces in the shape of him, where only he could fit. Like a puzzle with missing pieces. Those spaces were like ghosts, phantoms in my life that would pop up when something reminded me of him.

Isaiah is slowly taking back those empty spaces that once belonged to him. So effortlessly.

It feels like coming back to myself after being lost. Like taking a deep breath after being underwater.

It feels like coming home.

# FLASHBACK

## *Aurora, Fall 2014*

The carnival was in full swing when we arrived.

I barely noticed the drive because I spent the entire time staring at Isaiah in the driver's seat.

Sighing, I drag my eyes away. Not that it helps. He is seared into my brain, branded into my memory.

Bright, colorful lights break up the night sky, and high-pitched voices fill the silence. The smell of popcorn and funnel cake is as prevalent as ever as we pay the small fee for admission. It's definitely geared for younger kids, but it's a tradition. We've come here every year since we were kids. First with our parents, then with Sophia and Kian, and now just us.

Other students from our school come too, babysitting younger siblings like Sophia used to do or needing a reason to get out of the house, but it's pretty fun for everyone.

"What are we starting with?" I ask, tugging the sleeves of my crewneck over my fingers.

"Water guns?"

"You're going down, loser."

He gives me a crooked smile. "So aggressive when losing is at stake."

We walk side by side toward the first game of the night. Our fingers brush, and I try to act like that touch doesn't make my skin tingle. But it does. Clearing my throat, I say, "It's not at stake because I'm not going to lose."

As we arrive, we take our places at the back of the short line. Isaiah leans closer to me again, bending down and bringing us eye-level so I can see the warm gleam in his brown eyes. "That's what you say every year." Isaiah taps my nose with his finger, and my heart stops. "And yet every year, you lose at least twice."

I reach up with a quick hand and pinch the back of his arm.

He curses under his breath. "God, you are evil. Who made you?"

"Not sure, but they knew you needed me," I chime.

With a cheeky grin, we step forward and take our spots. We absolutely take this too seriously as we take aim, and all the chatter quiets. The buzzer sounds, and the water starts. Of course, Isaiah takes perfect aim, so of course, I kick my foot out and try to get the back of his knee.

"Old tricks, Rora, really?" he asks, never faltering.

"Can you blame me for trying?" I watch, annoyed as he wins.

Isaiah smiles brightly, a dimple on his cheek. My smile. My favorite smile. "You are such a sore loser."

My mouth gapes. "Okay, well, don't be an asshole."

He imitates me, crossing his arms and pouting. "Well, don't be an asshole." It lasts all of five seconds before the laughter starts. "You should've seen your face."

There are no good prizes at the water guns, so I turn and start walking away from him. He catches up to me instantly, wrapping his arms around me from behind and lifting me off the ground. My stomach flips upside down and all around as he does. Though I try to fight it, the laugh escapes my lips anyway.

"Put me down."

"Only if you promise I'm still your best friend."

I roll my eyes, my heart fluttering a million miles a minute in my chest, and I'm just hoping he doesn't notice. Ever since this year started, my heart can't stop fluttering when he's around. It doesn't matter what we're doing—laying in our rooms watching a movie, at the diner with milkshakes, singing in the car, swinging at the park—if Isaiah is there, my heart may as well be a butterfly that just got its wings.

I've been going crazy. I can't function around him anymore. The solid weight of his arms around my body makes me lightheaded, every single nerve in my body feels like it's firing at the same time. Every time he looks at me for longer than a second, my cheeks turn warm, and it feels like the full power of the sun is shining directly on me.

And in turn, I've become a suncatcher, spinning around and around, searching for the light so he doesn't take his eyes off me.

Stealing a glance to his face, pressed close to mine, I exhale. Sometimes, I still have trouble understanding this is the same boy with broken glasses at the playground and the same lanky fourteen-year-old. His arms around me now are strong and steady, his voice is deeper, and he's developed this intoxicatingly quiet confidence, and honestly, I'm not sure what to do with any of it.

I may as well be a pink-cheeked, googly, heart-eyed cartoon when I look at him.

It's a miracle he hasn't noticed.

Or maybe he has and is doing me the kindness of not breaking my heart. A heart that usually, I pride myself on not being fragile. But not with him. Now, it's putty in his hands.

I feel like some days, my day is based on Isaiah. If he smiles at me a certain way, if he says something that my brain can spin into something that was possibly, *maybe*, flirty. Do these things suddenly mean something different now? Does he feel the same way? And it's ridiculous since we've spent almost every day together since we were kids.

Is this what being a teenager in love is? I hate it.

Wondering if he feels an inkling of the same thing—if he ever will.

Isaiah squeezes me. "Earth to Rora? You in there?"

I blink the heart-eyes away. "Yes, sorry."

"Are you gonna answer the question?" His arms are still wrapped around me as he basically walks us through the carnival.

"Of course, you're still my best friend."

Stopping us, his head falls dramatically so my shoulder. "Thank God. I was getting worried for a minute."

"Get off of me," I say playfully, trying—but not really trying—to get out of his grip.

"Come on, I'll get you whatever you want. Funnel cake? Popcorn? Soft pretzel?" He smiles, pressing a finger to my cheek, trying to get me to smile. "Ice cream? Or is that for later?"

"Pretzel, please."

"What a surprise."

I let him lead us to the food stand, unable to do anything but stare at him. He's always been my Isaiah, but this is different. Around us, couples from our school hold hands. Some kiss after playing a game together or stand quietly together in their groups. Our hands hang between our bodies, so close to touching and yet so far away. My pinky brushes against his, and I inhale sharply. Then, I blush, hoping he didn't hear it. Hoping he can't hear how fast my heart is beating in my chest.

Pathetic.

I don't even notice him handing over cash to the attendant. I'm pretty sure I don't blink until he's handing me a soft pretzel and a water.

"Thank you."

He hums in response. "Alright, you think they have any stuffed octopi?"

Trying and failing to hide my grin, I shrug my shoulders. The pretzel and the salt melt on my tongue as we walk through, looking for the games with any stuffed animals. We were eight or nine, I think, when he learned how much I loved the animal. No reason really. Isaiah thinks it's because of *Finding Nemo*, and I think it's because I saw one at an aquarium, but I suppose to each their own.

Around us, I notice eyes on him, lingering longer than usual. From girls who have never ever paid attention to him before. Or maybe I was too focused on him to even notice. I try not to frown, but the urge to hold his hand grows stronger with every step. Though, Isaiah doesn't look at a single one of them.

"Found it! Come on," he says, grabbing my hand without a thought, and it's like a bolt of lightning straight to my heart. My palm turns sweaty, and I can't think or do anything but feel his hand in mine. "Which one do you want?"

"You're so confident you're going to win, aren't you?"

Isaiah raises a brow, a cocky smile on his face. Not often does this fun, playful side appear in such a public setting. But that smile makes my heart race each time I do see it.

"Yes, I am."

Crossing my arms, I scrunch my nose. "Pink and purple one."

It's the basketball hoop game, which doesn't usually have prizes, but I'm not one to question it, and I enjoy watching him anyway. For the prize, he has to get a certain number of points. Leaning back, I take another bite of pretzel and enjoy the show. Isaiah palms the ball and takes the first shot as soon as the buzzer goes off. One by one, they go in.

Isaiah doesn't play for any team at school or pursue any sport seriously, but he and Elijah grew up shooting hoops or tossing a football or racing each other. He's athletic, even if that's not his focus. And if it's happening in my presence? I'm watching.

He's flawless. Shot after shot, I watch the basketball fall into the net. After he's halfway through, he looks to me with a quirky smile and confident eyes. I swallow, trying to figure out where my air went. Where my common sense went.

But they are lost, swept under the spell of Isaiah Bryant.

The buzzer sounds, ticking up his final number of points. And of course, it's enough for any prize of his choosing. I step forward as he selects the pink and purple octopus and hands it to me. There's a smile on his face, and in my obsessed, crush filled mind, I swear his eyes soften and his hands linger a second too long. I hug the stuffed animal to my chest, a smile unraveling on its own accord.

"Thank you," I say, turning my eyes up at him.

With his arm around my shoulder again, he leads us through the carnival. He squeezes my arm a few times in a searing grip. "Anything for you, Rora Jade."

Sighing, I feel my heart melt into a puddle for the millionth time today. For a second, I let myself lean into his touch. Whether it's friendly or something more, I don't care. It feels nice to be held like this. More so, being held by him.

Under his arm, I let him lead us to the photobooth. There's no line, so we squeeze right on in. We are touching *everywhere*. Our thighs are pressed together; his arm is still wound around my shoulders playing with the ends of my curls. Isaiah is everywhere. In my thoughts and my dreams. I can't escape him. I don't want to.

"Ready?" he asks, his lips upturned in a smile, his small dimple shining through. I nod, unable to do much else.

The countdown begins, and Isaiah pulls me closer. Each flash captures a different version of us. Playful and friendly with smiles. Teasing and silly when he holds up a stupid peace sign behind my head. And something…more.

Right before the last photo, I steal another glance at Isaiah. I know that we'll be friends forever.

But I can't help but hope we become more.

# Zoo-Wee Mama

The black brace on my knee is such a glaring contrast to my skin.

If I look too long, I start feeling nauseous. I've replayed the injury a million times in less than twenty-four hours, and I wish I could scrub my brain clean. The crutches are quiet on the floor of the locker room as I make my way through. Coach Teller is waiting in her office for me, the door wide open.

"Hey, Coach."

Her head whips around. "Hey, come on in. Please sit. How are you doing today?"

I shrug. "Could be better but could be worse." I slide over the papers the doctors gave me. Of course, they'll send her the results and images of the MRI and all the details later. "It's a grade two MCL tear. They want me to have surgery in two days on Monday."

Coach Teller looks over the papers. They mostly just detail the surgery, the recovery, and what can be expected. No high impact work, pain (obviously), a brace at all times until the surgery and shortly after, and physical therapy. Twelve weeks is the expected recovery time. By that schedule, I'll be back on my feet by the end of January. That leaves me almost a month and half to prepare for the first training camp.

*If* all goes well.

"I'm sorry, Coach." I cast my eyes down. Logically, I know this isn't my fault, but that doesn't automatically erase the guilt of letting my team down. Certainly not the guilt of letting myself down.

"None of that, Matthews. You didn't do a damn thing to apologize for." The papers rustle as she sets them down. "You have gotten through setbacks before. And you'll get through this."

Heavy. That's how it feels. Another injury, another setback. I know I'll get out of this funk once I'm working toward getting better, but the days before recovery starts are bleak. Hours of mulling over it until you drive yourself crazy.

"Yeah, okay." I look up to see her firm smile. Like she believes it, even if I don't yet. "Once the surgery is over, can I still attend practices? I wanna be there for the girls."

"Of course. But you'll take this weekend off. And get settled first. Make sure you don't push too fast. You listen to everything the physical therapist says, you understand?"

My lip twitches. "Yes, Coach."

"The team is important. But so are you. And you're going to be at that showcase."

Coach Teller may be a typical coach—you know, all stoic, focused, and never one to let us in too close. But she loves us. She believes in us. And her confidence in me makes me sit up straighter. "You think so?"

"I know so, Matthews. Now get out and go home."

"Yes, ma'am." Gradually, I stand, still getting used to the feeling of the crutches under my arm. The hallways are empty as I head back toward Isaiah's car.

He's been…so attentive since yesterday. This morning, I woke up in his bed despite falling asleep on the couch. Raven was cuddled next to my leg that had been elevated, and I decided that Isaiah's shoulder was better than any pillow. He was warm and steady. Solid underneath me, even in sleep. I'd much rather have stayed there all day instead of going to doctors appointments and scheduling surgeries.

The sweatshirt of his that I stole this morning falls past my hips, his shorts hitting right above the top of the thick brace on my knee. When the outside air blows across my face and twists my curls, I immediately find him. Although, he isn't alone.

Maazina, Sylvia, and Vivian stand with him. They seem to be laughing or, at the very least, having a pleasant interaction. It takes me a bit by surprise. Not that they have really been anything but supportive or kind, but when I first told them more details, they were definitely skeptical. Though, after I tell them about the past few days, I'm sure any skepticism will fall away.

I crutch my way over.

"Hey," Isaiah says, taking my bag out of my hands and throwing it over his shoulder. Maazina wiggles her eyebrows behind him.

"Hi. Thanks."

He hums in response, eyes tracking over me quickly. They linger for only a second, yet leave a solid warmth behind.

Before I can say anything, the girls hug me.

"You look sexy with a knee brace."

"You wear those crutches so well."

"Want me to find that girl and hit her knee *I, Tonya* style?"

All of us that aren't Maazina look at Maazina with wide eyes.

"Maazina, you can't just say that!"

She shrugs. "What? It's not like you're going to say yes, and I wouldn't *actually* do it."

"Have you been psychologically evaluated?" I ask, even though my lips are curling into a smile.

"Maybe. Maybe not." Maazina whips around and looks at Isaiah. "Just so you know, I'm the one you should be scared of."

Isaiah blinks and deadpans, "Yeah, that's been noted."

Sylvia and Vivian chuckle. "We thought we could accompany you back home, watch movies, and hang out. Is that okay with you?" Sylvia bounces on the balls of her feet.

"Yeah, I'd like that."

Isaiah opens the passenger side door and the back door. "Everyone, hop on in." Maazina is the first to slide in like a baseball player in the backseat, causing him to huff out a laugh. After the three of them squeeze in, he helps me in the passenger seat.

"Did you do this?" I ask quietly when his hand lands on my waist. Our faces are so close, they might touch. The space between us is charged. Out of the corner of my eye, I see all three girls leaning forward with wide eyes.

"What makes you think that?" There's a twinkle in his eye, and he uses his fingers to squeeze my waist. I can see every freckle, every eyelash, every scar. Every inch of his beautiful, dark skin that is shining under the sunlight.

My heart swells. "Thank you."

Isaiah doesn't say anything else, just wordlessly helps me into the car and closes the door after me. He opens the back door once more. "You girls mind holding these?" he asks, referring to my crutches.

"Not at all."

The door shuts again, and in the mere moments where he is outside the bubble, I hear, "Jesus Christ, Aurora, that man is—"

"Zoo-wee mama," Maazina mumbles. I think she might be googly-eyed.

"Shut up." I shake my head, trying to hide my laughter.

Isaiah climbs in seconds later and smiles as if he doesn't have a care in the world. "Ready?"

"Ready."

In my lap, my phone vibrates. It's the Idiot Brigade group message.

**Vivian:** Good god, Aurora, he is so…

**Maazina:** So 'sir, yes, sir'?

**Vivian:** Exactly.

**Maazina:** I'm ready…. (SpongeBob voice).

**Sylvia:** Alexa, play…*Ready For It (Taylor's version).*

**Me:** I hate every single one of you.

**Maazina:** Except him.

Except him. Yeah. That's the truth of it.

Maazina is upside down on the couch again. Sylvia is spread out next to her, and Vivian and I are on the floor, my leg elevated, as usual.

Since Isaiah dropped us off almost an hour and a half ago, it's been a full lazy day. We've watched almost two episodes of some trashy reality TV show that Sylvia found and haven't moved since except to fill up waters.

Which is why the apartment buzzer makes no sense.

Vivian jumps up, her long braids swaying as she does. Soon enough, there's a knock. I lean over, peeking through the crack in the door. "Thank you?" she says, muddled. When she turns, there is a large bag of take-out food in her hands. "Did anyone order this?"

We all shake our heads, and she finds the receipt. "Well, lookie here. Somebody is in love."

"No, he didn't."

"Oh, yes, he did."

My cheeks warm in an instant. "And he is not in love. Stop."

"I'm swooning," Maazina says, catapulting off the couch. "And I'm not even the one he's in love with."

I push myself up. "Unbearable."

Sylvia comes to my side and helps me the rest of the way to gather around the counter. Viv lays out the food, copious amounts of take out from my favorite Vietnamese place.

"Can I be serious for a minute?" Sylvia asks, plucking a spring roll from the dishes.

"Please do." I shoot a look toward the other two, who grin sheepishly.

"How are you feeling about the whole thing?"

I mull it over, taking the time to serve various dishes on everyone's plates that Viv pulled out. All that comes to mind is how much fuller my life already feels with him in it. How my heart aches at the sight of him, begging to escape and go to him instead of staying in my chest where it belongs. How the desire to touch him is so overwhelming, sometimes I can't think straight. How easy it feels to know I could call and tell him anything, and it would feel like it once did.

"Better than I thought I ever would." I glance around, finding no judgment in their waiting eyes. "We talked, and he was honest. About everything. He didn't make me feel like I was crazy for feeling the way I felt."

"In love?" Maazina wiggles her eyebrows, taking a bite of her noodles.

I flick her nose. "Isaiah listened to me. More so, he heard me. I think that was something I really needed. It's obviously been very brief, but it's crazy how much it feels like nothing has changed. Like yeah, there are things I guess I might not know about this version of him, but I'm kind of excited about it. Getting to know him again." I shrug my shoulders, casting my eyes down and trying to act like there isn't warmth rushing to my cheeks.

When I glance up, Sylvia looks love struck—elbows resting on the counter with her face in hands with her soft, brown eyes wide. "Okay there, lovebird. Take a deep breath." I point my chopsticks at her.

She smiles, crossing her legs on the stool. "Sorry. I'm just really happy for you. That the friendship is still there. I know, even though you never ever wanted to talk about it, how much it weighed on you. More than you probably ever let us in on. So, it's nice to see the proverbial weight starting to lift off your shoulders."

Maazina looks between us. "Ditto what she said."

Vivian raises a brow. "Sorry we can't take the weight of Maazina's insanity off your shoulders, too."

"Hey, I am a lovely, lovely girl, and she should be honored that her shoulder is my other home."

I blink. "Really, so grateful." In response, she draws a heart with her hands. "Can we talk about someone else's life now? I'm sorry it's been very much all about me."

"Shut up, Aurora," Vivian chimes. "But we can appease you. I'll go first. I have a date on Wednesday. I expect it to go horribly. But she's pretty. We met on the way to the movies, both alone on the bus, and ended up at the same film."

"And you think it's going to go horribly, why?"

Viv twirls her hand in a *duh* motion. "I mean, when do dates ever go well? For me, especially?" Ironically, we do have a running joke that on every date Viv has gone on, guy or girl, something utterly embarrassing happens.

Maazina bursts out laughing. "Remember that time your drink came out of your nose?"

Vivian sighs. "Unfortunately because you never let me forget it."

"Oh." I chuckle. "And the time the waiter spilled your dinner on you?"

"Okay, and moving on. Sylvia, your turn."

"I've got nothing but my stuffed pig and sour candy. And the occasional hook up with that guy from the men's team. I am in need of a really good crush." Sylvia turns to me. "Isaiah have any friends here besides you? He's gorgeous, obviously, and surely, he could help a girl out."

I deadpan. "Yes, I'll be sure to bring that up." She purses her lips dramatically in thanks. All eyes turn to Maazina.

"Aurora is my sugar mama; we all know this. Why would I let anyone else distract me from that?" Sometimes, she says things so seriously, so convincingly, I worry that one day, she will run the world. Probably by accident.

Deep down, I know it's more so she hasn't really tried dating much since everything happened, and she'd rather laugh about it than acknowledge it. She's talked to us all individually, but I think the pressure of the three of us can be scary.

"I'm not very rich."

Maazina winks at me. "But you are very cute."

I can't stop the big, genuine laugh that snakes its way out. Aside from Isaiah, it's the first real laugh I've let out since the injury, and it's no surprise it happens with them. They are my rocks. In a sense, they are my three found sisters, girls I hope will be a part of my life at every turn and I a part of theirs. Without even trying, they have turned today around. A day that could've stayed dark, they made the sun peek through the clouds.

It's a reminder that even when he wasn't here, I had them. And it proves that through it all, I will always have them.

# Jade(p)

"Scale of one to ten, how do we feel today?"

I'm lying on the PT table, waiting for the therapist to return. Even though it's only day three, he's already become very familiar with Sophia. My phone rests on my chest on speaker, which is where Sophia's voice is coming from. "A seven. Mostly well, I suppose. Starting PT has been a Godsend to feeling like my life isn't wasting away."

Kian shouts from somewhere, "Can't keep a girl down for long!"

"I hate your husband sometimes."

Sophia chuckles. "Yeah, me, too."

"Liar."

"Says who?"

"Says me? You've got two gremlins with the guy."

She hums. "Yeah, yeah. You've got a point." I smile. "I just wanted to check in on you. Mom said she'll probably call later."

"Sounds good. Isaiah's picking me up, and then we're going somewhere?

A movie or something. I'm not sure. He's been taking me to all my appointments since they don't affect his class schedule."

"Aurora and Isaiah…sitting in a tree," Kian sings, voice fading in and out of the phone. Mere seconds later, I hear a *huff.* "Ouch. Jesus."

"Shut up, Kian," Sophia says, but I can hear the smile in her voice. "So…have you spoken to Dad?"

"No. Not planning on it either since he couldn't be bothered to say anything about the National Team Selection, nor has he checked on me once. When he's man enough to talk to me, I'll listen."

"Alright. I'm here if you want to talk about it, okay?"

"I know. I love you," I say, and she responds—Kian, too—before hanging up.

I mean it about my dad. If he wants to talk, I'll talk. But I won't beg him to look at me, to care about me, to be proud of me. And especially not to love me like he should. Not when I have so many people who love me without conditions.

Exhaling, I prod my knee with my hands, pulling it back and releasing it, like I'm allowed. If there is anything about a knee injury to be thankful for, it's how quickly they instruct you to get back to PT. It still absolutely sucks, but at least I can do something other than elevate and ice. Shortly after, I'm set free with my crutches, brace, and new exercises to run through. It's sore from the bike work and all the stretches, but I'm able to walk at times, and I'll take what I can get.

I find Isaiah leaning against his car for me. My heartbeat jumps in milliseconds.

All I know is that since the injury, since the surgery, I hate not being around him more than I thought was possible. My body feels like it's constantly searching for its other half. Post-surgery, I spent two days at his house because I didn't want to risk an extended period of time without him.

When I did eventually go back home, he showed up that night with the key that I gave him with two large bags filled with food. He walked in and said he made enough for me to not have to eat my crappy frozen meals, to not have to order out if I didn't want to, and he made me dessert.

I read his book for longer than was probably good for my mental health, and I cried every time I turned the page.

He came over once a day at least, usually for dinner, and every time, his hands would end up on my knee with a gentle touch. Massaging the sensitive area with the utmost care and stealing bits and pieces of my heart at the same time.

Every time he looks at me, my brain short-circuits and has to re-route before I can function. He touches me, and I turn into a puddle. And he takes care of me without complaint or obligation, but because he wants to.

Isaiah shows up for me.

"Long time, no see." He smiles, and I swoon. Like a cartoon character with a crush.

"How do you function without me for an hour and a half?"

Isaiah blows out air, taking my bag from me. "It's not easy, really. I usually drive around missing you. Then, I drown my sorrows in some ice cream. The usual."

"Hm. Sounds about right." I look up at him, only inches away. We stand closer together every time we're near each other.

"I'm sure that makes you happy."

"Absolutely."

My grin grows when he leans down and places a kiss on my cheek. When he pulls back, he runs his hand up the back of his cropped hair. "Ready?"

"Sure." He pulls the door open for me, and I climb in. "So, what's the plan for this boring Tuesday evening?"

"I actually have a reading tonight. I thought you could come? We can get dinner after or something else. And you don't have to—"

"I want to. Can we stop for a snack first?"

"'Course."

Isaiah moves into action, a shy smile gracing his lips as he heads out of the parking lot. We reach the convenience store quickly, and I crutch my way in, grabbing a Gatorade, a soft pretzel, and a pack of Twizzlers for Isaiah.

"Got you these." I hand the candy over, and he breaks into them in the next second.

"Thank you. I haven't had them in a while."

"How is that possible?"

He leans back, the ink on the back of his neck peeking out when his skin stretches. "I've been trying to cut back."

"To what? A pack a day instead of two?"

Isaiah scoffs, leaning over and pinching my thigh. "Such a brat."

I pull my normal leg up on the seat and rest my cheek against it, smiling. The squeeze of his hand lingers, and I take the time to stare at him. Something has shifted. All the years of pushing down everything. Acting like I wasn't in love with him when he left, acting like it didn't break my heart—it was all for nothing. Because all the facades have faded away, leaving me without a shell.

Reminding me that I never needed one with him.

"Why are you staring at me, Rora?"

"Want to make sure I don't miss anything else."

At the red light, he looks over at me. Yeah, there's no way anyone who loved someone with brown eyes would've ever said a single negative word. "I don't plan on you missing anything ever again."

The silence that follows is comfortable and easy. Like it used to be.

Time is passing so quickly. It feels like yesterday Isaiah just showed up. Now, it's mid-September, and I have a bum knee, but I also have Isaiah back. The drive is quick, the breeze slinking in through the open windows and the sun starting to set. The restaurant is in Fishtown, which always has an array of events going on if you know the right places. Inside, it's brick walls and neon signs. Seats are arranged to face the tiny stage with a stool. We take our pick of the seats, choosing a spot to the left of the stage but close up, and waiter drops off waters and menus.

Isaiah pulls out his book. "I'm third in the line-up. It should start in five minutes."

"Sounds good."

"Do you have a favorite yet?" He slides the book toward me. It's not my copy. The one that's underlined and marked in red pen in the margins.

"Right now, it's "Seven"."

That one's about him. And Elijah. It's about their relationship, and I know all the little details that make it even more heartbreaking. About how Elijah was born on the seventh, and his lucky number was seven, and because Isaiah idolized him, seven became his own favorite number.

He gives a small shake of his head. Under the table, his leg is curled around mine. "Can I ask you a question?"

"Is this counting as an air-hockey question?"

"I suppose it can. I have some to spare." Isaiah leans back in the chair, an assured air about him. "How would you feel about a date?"

Taken aback, I blink. A date? A date. With Isaiah.

"A date?" I'm having trouble forming words, thinking, anything.

A gentle smile captures his lips, and he leans forward. His fingertips brush the top of my hand. "A date."

"Why?" I sigh immediately after the words escape my mouth. Only he could make me flustered. The humor in his eyes tells me he is fully aware of that.

"Because I want to. I think you do, too." Isaiah swallows, nerves flickering briefly over his face before they disappear. "You're my best friend, but that's not all there is here. At least, I don't think so. Is that what you think?"

Do I think we're *just* friends? No. We never said it back then; we just…were.

I was in love with him when he left. Deeply and unshakably in love with him. The boy with brown eyes who turned into the man sitting in front of me.

"No, that's not what I think."

"And I'm not planning on going anywhere." Isaiah's eyes turn serious. The pressure of his touch deepens.

I swallow, nodding shallowly. Funny how poised with something you know you want, the fear of everything before comes rushing back.

"I know you aren't."

Isaiah leans in further, like there isn't a table between us. Like we aren't in public. No, with him looking at me like that, it's just the two of us.

"Then let me take you on a date. Please, Aurora. I can't—I don't—just want to be your friend. Let me show you."

"Okay," is all I can say. The influx of emotions has stolen the rest of my words.

I watch the tension dissipate from his shoulders. He takes my hand and intertwines our fingers again, his thumb rubbing gently back and forth.

"That absolutely counts as one of your questions."

Isaiah chuckles. "I expected nothing less."

Shortly after, the first performer is announced. We adjust our chairs to better face the stage, now sitting side by side. Isaiah's hand finds my leg and rests gently on my thigh. In turn, I rest my head on his shoulder, the warmth transferring from his body to mine. That's how we sit until it's his turn to get up there. Isaiah walks with confidence, and his slacks fit him perfectly, accentuating the strength in his legs, curving over his backside (he's got a great butt), and tapering at the waist. Tattoos are on display from the sleeve down, silver jewelry glinting in the light, and he slides onto the stool.

There's less formalities at this reading. Brief introductions but for the most part, all of them have jumped right into it. Isaiah does the same. This poem, "Cracks In the Sidewalk", is another heart-wrenching favorite of mine. It's a poem inlaid with childhood wistfulness, how soul crushing it is to love someone as a teenager. There's a line about how he used to count the cracks in the sidewalks that led to my house, alluding to the idea that he memorized them. There's another line alluding to the idea that he lost that path, that he lost all his paths. I know that he means Elijah and perhaps the depression that followed.

*"Cracks rose from the cement, taking on physical bodies*
*beside me. Step by step, I started to wonder*
*would the times of the past release me?"* he reads.

Despite the sorrowful tone of some of the lines, I love the poem, how it tracks him from childhood to part of his adulthood.

I'm locked onto him, the way the words flow off his tongue, the quiet yet commanding voice that has everyone hooked. During his reading, aside from the occasional glance to the crowd, he looks at me the entire time. It's like having a spotlight directly shown on me but one that I bask in. It's heated; it's a gaze full of life and wonder and a gaze that scorches every place it lands.

His fourth and final poem of the night is titled "Jade[d]". Jade is my middle name. He used to call me that sometimes— *"Aurora Jade,"* he'd say. It was a surefire way to get a smile out of me. Isaiah treated it like our secret, and it was—no one else has ever called me that.

"*Is the world still beautiful with a Jaded gaze?*" is the first line of the poem.

I've only read it twice myself, and each time, it makes my chest cave in. We were two people who were everything to each other, and then, we weren't. Despite the reasons, the why or the how, being without the person who made your world colorful was like being thrust into a black and white movie. Suddenly, it was noiseless and gray.

I think we did our best on our own. Still accomplished some of our dreams. But I think we both know that this, being together again, is living life on the full spectrum of vivid colors.

It's terrifying to think this is only the beginning.

It's also beautiful—feeling like life is available in every shade again.

I hope it never goes dark again.

# Make a Wish

## Isaiah

Aurora and I have never been on a real date.

I've never been on a date in general. No one had a chance at capturing my attention like she had. So, there was no point in even trying. Tonight is a first of many in more ways than one. For me, at least. I know she's dated other people, so I'm determined to blow this one out of the water.

Make her forget that other people are even an option.

I show up at her apartment and knock instead of using my key this time. Though that key is never far; I know exactly where it is in my wallet—tucked right next to a picture of the two of us from a carnival when we were young.

Aurora opens the door, and I can breathe freely again.

Her curls are loose and wild around her face, her cheeks are slightly flushed, and her freckles are poignant after so much time in the summer sun. "Hi, come in. I'm almost ready."

I step in, unable to pull my eyes away. A black patterned skirt hugs her hips and her butt, accentuating the curvature of her body before falling loosely over her legs. A long slit is cut up the left side, showing off the skin of her leg and the black brace that takes absolutely nothing away from her beauty. She wears a simple, high-neck top, but when she turns around, the strappy back reveals itself, baring much of her skin.

It's as if the world stops turning when I look at her.

My heart rate slows, yet my blood rushes. A paradoxical feeling that somehow completely makes sense when she's the reason.

Every inch of her calls out to me. Skin begging to be touched, lips that I want badly to kiss. Hips that my hands want to call home. And so much more. I want her trust, her thoughts, her new dreams, and her fears.

She stops at the counter, turning to face me again. I lean down and kiss her on the cheek, enjoying the blush that rushes to them. "For you." I hand her the tiny bouquet of blue flowers, one of her favorite colors, and the bag of mini Kit-Kats.

"You didn't have to do that."

"I wanted to."

Aurora smiles. "So did I." She turns and hands me a bag of Twix.

"Thank you."

"Mhm. Let me grab my shoes, and we can go." Before she does, her eyes slowly track over me from head to toe. She swallows, heat creeping up her neck. I say nothing. Instead, I take it all in. That she's looking at me like that with desire blooming in her eyes. Aurora clears her throat and quickly scurries away, making me chuckle.

"No need to run away."

"Shut up, Isaiah," she calls from down the hall. When she returns, she has black and white sneakers in her hand and a sweater. She sits down to put her shoes on, but I reach for them.

"Here, let me help."

"Why?"

"Because I want to."

"Isaiah—" she argues, but I stop her.

"I know it's annoying to bend with the brace. I know you're in PT, but just let me help." I meet her eyes, and after a brief hesitation, she nods, letting go of her grip on the shoes. I chuckle when I see her socks, printed with some Disney character, and she kicks my chest gently with her foot.

I slip on the right shoe easily, my fingertips grazing over her skin, goosebumps following in their wake. When I move to the left, I'm careful not to jostle her knee too much, far aware that I'm probably being gentler than she or her physical therapist is. If I know anything, I know she's pushing herself as hard as she can.

My hand wraps around her leg, and my fingers find the space where the brace disappears and brush the back of her knee. With my other hand, I carefully slip on her shoe. The skin under my fingers is soft and warm, smooth and supple. I want to find out if the rest of her skin feels like that, though I'd bet my life it does.

I pull myself away and stand, holding out my hands. The hazel eyes that look up at me are wide as she places her hands in mine. With a gentle hold, I pull her to her feet.

"Ready to go?"

Aurora nods, her lips parted. I smile as we head out, never taking my hand off the small of her back on the way to the car. There's a welcome chill in the air and the nostalgic feeling of fall present.

"Where are we headed?"

I look over at her at the stoplight. "You'll see."

Aurora rolls her eyes, making my blood rush, and leans back in the passenger seat. "Tell me."

"No. Ask again and it'll be a waste of a question."

"Evil." She rolls her lips.

"Smart."

Aurora lets out a soft laugh, barely a twinkle, but it warms the space anyway. The city lights are shining through the early night sky, cars passing and people walking on the sidewalks. I drive until we reach the signs of the festival. It's small, but there are a few rides, the largest being a Ferris wheel and plenty of games. Reminiscent of our teenage years.

Pure bliss spreads over her face. The smell of popcorn and funnel cakes creep in through the open windows and the sounds of laughter from the crowds with them. I only found this place through a flyer at work, but I'm grateful I did.

In moments, we're climbing out of the car. Aurora wastes no time in threading her arm through mine, setting the pace. Since she has me to lean on, she only has to use one crutch.

"What's first, superstar?" I ask. On my arm, her fingers dance over my skin, tracing the ink that created the artwork. Her smile makes the world go round—at the very least, mine.

"Water guns?"

"You're on."

"Or do you want to hit the basketball game first? You know," she says, her eyes narrowing playfully, "to warm up."

Without hesitation, I pinch her waist, a squeal escaping her lips. With a steady grip, I pull her into my side. It's easy; it's playful. It's how I always imagined. "Watch that attitude. Wouldn't wanna talk a big game and then lose again, would you?" I say, my lips almost brushing her skin.

She loosely attempts to pull away from me, but when she sinks into my side, I know it was all a facade. We find the water guns, and I eye the array of stuffed animals as a prize option. I'm thrilled to see a tri-colored octopus as one of them.

We take our places, a serious look on Aurora's face, and wait for the buzzer. Her aim is good, but she slips just so, and I take the lead, the water never for a second leaving the target. The bell rings, my light blinking as the winner, and I sit back, enjoying the youthful frustration on Aurora's face. The unenthusiastic booth attendant tells me to select a prize, and I point to the octopus.

Aurora cuddles it instantly, pulling it into her chest. "Losing isn't so bad when I get something in return." I throw my head back, laughing, my heart pumping at the sight of her smile. "Thank you."

She threads her arm through mine again, finding her balance as we approach the hoop.

"Go on."

I raise a brow. "What's in this one for you?"

"Just want to stare at you."

Blood rushes, and I pocket my hands. "What do I win?"

"Depends on the score."

"You drive a hard bargain."

Aurora's eyes track over me in a slow heat, and she shrugs. I take the ball and wait for the game to start. When it does, with her watching me, I hit basket after basket, missing only a few when the basket adjusts. But when the score is in the mid-seventies, I feel pretty good.

"How's that?"

"Good enough."

I step forward, forcing her to tilt her head back to look up at me. "What's my prize?"

"I'll let you know when I figure it out," she says, her lips curling.

"You little—" I wrap my arms around her waist, lifting her from the ground, crutch included.

"Isaiah, put me down!" Ignoring her, I start walking towards the food and picnic tables. Not a care in the world. "Isaiah, people are staring."

I smile as we pass the amused faces of younger kids and young adults alike. Some older couples chuckle themselves as if pining over a memory.

"No can do."

"Ice cream or popcorn?"

Aurora huffs, her arms no longer flailing, instead going limp. "Ice cream."

I pat the back of her thigh. She's not quite over my shoulder, but her butt rests on my arms, and I think she's given up at holding herself straight.

"Was this just an excuse to put your hands on me?"

"You'll never really know."

I slide her down, keeping her skirt in place, until her feet are touching the ground, but my arms stay where they are. Reaching up, I brush an eyelash from her cheek, enjoying the way her eyes flutter closed.

"Make a wish." I hold my thumb up for her.

Aurora blushes. Her hands brush over the fabric of my shirt, though they may as well be on my skin. "I don't need to."

"Make one anyway."

The warmth of her breath on my thumb sends a chill down my back. We step into line for the ice cream, and she keeps her arm wrapped around me, her hand under the soft fabric of my shirt resting directly on my skin. Every time Aurora gently brushes the skin of my back, my heartbeat skips a step.

"Can I use one of my questions?" Aurora looks up at me.

"By all means."

She worries her lip with her teeth. "You haven't said much about your mom since you've been back, since we've been doing…whatever. How is she?"

My hand is still where it rests on her waist. "Mom is okay. It was rough for a while. We didn't talk a lot after I left. And I get it now; she was mad because I went away without much of a word. And I was mad because she didn't understand why I needed space. She didn't even want me to pursue writing anymore. Told me it was a waste. So, I was mad at Elijah, and then, I was mad at her. All these expectations and dreams she had for Elijah became my burden. I had to be perfect. And I was the furthest thing from that." I squeeze her twice, reminding myself Aurora is still next to me.

"Isaiah, I'm sorry."

We step up in line. I squeeze her side. "It's okay. Now, at least. Most of college was spent fighting or just not speaking. When the depression hit, I couldn't talk to her at all. I didn't want to. I doubt she wanted to talk to me. But everything…it just changed our relationship. She's my mom; I love her. She's done everything for me—but there was a time I didn't feel very loved in return."

Aurora doesn't say anything, instead placing a soft kiss on my bicep and resting her head there. Her hand leaves my back but finds my own, intertwining our fingers between our bodies.

"I know it doesn't fix any of the hurt, but I hope you know that the person you are, the person you were, was—is—always worthy of love. You were always just supposed to be you. And I think you're pretty great."

The ache in my chest alleviates some. Aurora never expected me to be anyone but who I was.

I continue, "We're better now. We talk more often, and we don't fight. But we also don't talk about Elijah." There's a sadness in that. The only person that understands what it was like is the one person I can't talk to about it.

"You can talk to me about it. I know it's not the same, but I imagine there are times when you need to, and I hope you know you can come to me." Aurora's voice is firm.

"Thank you, Ro." Leaning over, I press my lips to her temple, leaving them there longer than is expected. Every time, it gets harder and harder to pull myself away. "What flavor are you getting? Chocolate or the peanut butter swirl?"

Aurora hums, the sound vibrating against my body from where her head rests. "Peanut butter swirl. And you? Coffee chip?"

"Yup." I smile at the ease in which the memories come back, the details that haven't changed. I order for us when we step up and hand over my card. We're handed two cones—a waffle for her and a cake for me, overflowing with ice cream. I lead us and the octopus to a table as she murmurs a thank you.

"Did you give it a name yet?"

Aurora glances at the octopus sitting on the table next to us. Its colors are a deep red, pale yellow, and purple. "I'll have to think about it."

When she looks up at me, she crosses her eyes playfully, tongue reaching out to taste the ice cream. I watch her without constraint. Aurora is here on a date with me. I take the time to memorize the new details of her face. New freckles that weren't there before, how her laugh lines have deepened. I take the time to appreciate the things that haven't changed. The shape of her lips and the slope of her nose.

"My turn for a question."

She waves her hand. "Have at it."

I could've gone for an easier question, one that wasn't so heavy on our first date, but when I open my mouth, the words that come out are, "Did you ever stop loving me?"

Hazel eyes that I love widen. Ice cream drips down the cone. I see her pulse speed up in the hollow of her neck, and her cheeks flush.

"Isaiah…" Her voice is breathy.

I exhale. "I know. But I have to know, Aurora. Because I never did. Not for a second."

Aurora never takes her eyes off mine. It's a heady stare down, a tightrope drawn between us, and we're both dancing on it. A room deciding whether to burn or not, the flames flickering at the window but not yet breaking through.

"No, I never did. I loved you when you left. I was…in love with you when you left. And as hard as I may have tried to drown it, suffocate it, make it stop hurting so much, I never stopped loving you. Not for a day, not for an hour, not for a minute."

Her vulnerability is a gift, and it's not one I'll ever take for granted again.

"Do you think you could fall in love with me again?" My heart pumps. Scared and exhilarated for the answer. I think I know it. I see it when she looks at me with adoration and desire, and I feel it when she touches me.

"This is some first date," she jokes, taking another lick of her dwindling ice cream.

"I guess I thought I'd stop beating around the bush."

Around us, the buzzer and bells of the games go on. The stars are out somewhere above us, hidden by the lights of the city. Even still, she's the only thing that has my full attention.

"Yeah, Isaiah, I think I could." Aurora speaks softly, barely audible, but I hear every word. It's the last drop of hope I need, the final coin in the bank.

I'm unable to help the smile that forms on my face and unable to stop myself from leaning forward, placing my lips beside her mouth. I taste the drop of peanut butter ice cream that landed right above her lips and her skin, and it all breathes me back to life. My lips linger for a moment, wanting badly to truly kiss her, but I leave that to her, and I pull back.

Her cheeks are beet red when I do, but her hazel eyes are shining.

Looking at her is like seeing the sun for the first time after years spent in the dark. Aurora is the light at the end of the tunnel, the midday sun after endless rain. Life was so bland without her. A white, blank page with no color. She was my muse, even when life was bleak. In the dark, in the depths of a depression I barely got out of. Aurora was on every page. In every thought, in every beat of my heart, she has been there. And she has never left.

I have loved her every day for as long as I can remember.

I will love her everyday as long as she lets me.

# 21

## No Going Back

"**I**'ve never seen the city like this." I look out from the Ferris wheel, and the lights of Philadelphia shine back.

"Yeah, it's pretty up here," he says, but he isn't looking at the city. Isaiah's looking at me.

"You didn't even look." I nudge his leg, my body warm.

"Didn't need to."

I roll my eyes but scoot closer. Our bodies are pressed together in every way. Since getting ice cream, we've played more games—the ring toss, horseshoes, skee-ball—and since, Isaiah's made sure to touch me at every turn. His hands are never far from my body. Whether that's keeping our arms threaded as we walked between the game stalls, his hand on my hip or waist, or intertwining our fingers tightly while he helps me walk. Isaiah hasn't gone far at all. Right now, his hand is resting on my leg between the slit of my skirt, his fingers playing with the skin above my brace.

I'm trying to focus on things that aren't the gentle roughness of his fingertips sending goosebumps over my skin. Spoiler: it's not working very well.

Because all I can think about is falling in love with him. All I can think about is kissing him.

I told him I could fall in love with him again. I didn't say that I *knew* I could.

That I *was*.

But I am.

All the parts I loved then are still here. But better. His kindness, his thoughtfulness, his determination to be the best version of himself he can be. There are new things, too. Things that I'd bet were there then, but I didn't get a chance to see fully develop. How much he loves to care for people, how intently he listens *and* understands.

I knew it would be different with him. The dates I went on previously, the anxiety never stopped, and my stomach never stopped settled. But with Isaiah, there is only peace. Of course, he makes me feel emotionally comfortable, but so does my body. The butterflies are light and fun, not panicky and erratic. My skin sings when he touches me, and I miss him when he isn't.

"Thank you for tonight," I murmur. Isaiah looks over, his eyes soft and earnest.

"Of course. You look beautiful, Aurora. You always do."

I rest my head in my right hand, unabashedly taking every inch of him in. "You're pretty handsome yourself." My eyes track over the ink, and I so badly desire to trace every inch. Memorize every single piece of artwork he has.

"Are you flirting with me?" Isaiah smiles.

"Yes, I am."

"Took you long enough."

I tap him with my foot. "That is so not true." I laugh lightly.

"Yes, it is. I've been begging you to flirt with me."

I raise a brow. "I haven't seen you beg once."

"I can start." Isaiah leans in with playful eyes.

"Don't you dare."

"Why not? You can't run away from me up here, can't act like it's not happening…" Isaiah muses, his lips getting awfully close to my cheek. The tip of his nose grazes my skin, and heat blooms like tiny flowers around my body. My stomach flips, and shivers dance over my skin.

"Aurora," he teases, fingers splaying over my leg.

I turn my head, our noses brushing. "So, I say I might fall in love with you again, and this is how you behave?"

Before tonight, there was still a boundary. A line—a dim, waning one, but it was there. But now…the floodgates have officially opened.

Isaiah smiles, and it's blinding. My own personal light, a mini-sun shining directly on me. "Pretty much. I have to turn that could into a did. How else am I supposed to do that?"

"I'm not sure, but leaving you to your own devices seems dangerous."

The Ferris wheel continues, and we're back on the ascent. "Hm… what should I beg you for?"

"Jesus Christ." I lay my head back, eyes turned up toward the sky.

"There are so many options—"

I place my hand over his mouth because I don't want to burst into flames in public. Isaiah's eyes are devilish, and I feel his body shaking with laughter. But then, his tongue sneaks out and licks the center of my palm.

"Gross! Isaiah," I whine, drawing my hand back but laughing all the same. He lets out a big laugh beside me. This is the side of him that others don't get to see.

An unexpected wave of jealousy hits me—has he shared this with other people? Did he date? I mean, I'm sure he did, but…did they mean something more to him than he might admit? I turn away, my brows furrowing of their own accord.

"Woah, what happened over there?" Isaiah asks, but I'm staring out over the city.

The ride has stopped spinning, and we're only two from the top, so I focus on the view. Trying to ignore the jealousy burning my gut. I try to speak, but I swallow it down.

Isaiah reaches up, gently turning my chin to face him. "Rora, what's wrong?"

I huff, annoyed at myself more than anything. Annoyed that he can read me so easily. "It's nothing. I'm just being crazy."

"I doubt it, but tell me. What's making you feel crazy?"

The hold on my chin loosens, but his hand palms my cheek. "Did you date anyone seriously when you were gone? I know I don't have much room to ask anything since I was seeing someone, but…I just need to know. Because I didn't. I never made it past five dates. Kissed one person and I hated it. I can deal with physical; I tried in college, but—" I say, shaking my head. "Sex…I can—I understand, if you tried to move on or whatever." And that's true.

Isaiah and I were each other's first. It was nerve racking and exciting. It was gentle and playful, and it was perfect because it was us. Even now, I still remember the soft smile he gave me, the touches that were more tender than anything I'd ever felt before, and the way our noses brushed, and how we couldn't stop smiling like idiots.

But the truth of the matter is, shortly after, he was gone.

So, in college, I tried. But I hated every second of it. The kissing, the way they touched me. They weren't him. We never even got there, and even then, I knew they would never be him. Never touch me the way he could. And I've dated since, obviously, but nothing else. But all of that, the physical shit, isn't what I'm scared of.

"But I couldn't stand the idea of someone knowing me like you did," I say, the word vomit quite literally not giving me a chance to breathe. "I won't be mad at you. I just want to know if there was anyone like that."

A loud, cranking noise blares out. We break eye contact and notice the Ferris wheel has completely stopped. The attendants seem to be talking down below, but we're too high to hear them.

Perfect time to ask a question I'm not sure I want the answer to.

"Aurora." Isaiah's voice is firm, but now, I'm a scaredy cat shaking in my metaphorical boots. "Aurora, I'll answer when you look at me."

Exhaling, I revel in the feel of his hand that's still on my leg. I turn to meet his eyes. There's a serious gleam there, but he also looks partially amused. As if the stupid question is even stupider than I thought.

His hand finds my face again, my face fitting perfectly into the palm of his hand. The city lights reflect in his eyes, making the brown glisten. His fingers are soft, his thumb brushing over my cheek.

"Maybe once or twice, Ro, I tried. But it was only physical. It's shitty, but I was only trying to use them to move on. I'm not proud of it, but I imagined it was you touching me. That it was you I was with, even though I knew that wasn't true."

I nod, even though every part of me aches—not that it happened but that we were so lost without each other, and we never even knew it.

"In every other way, Aurora, no one ever stood a chance. I never dated. I never tried. I have never known anyone the way I know you. Never let anyone get close enough to me to try." Isaiah swallows. I see his heart rate speeding up in the crook of his neck. "I couldn't love someone the way I love you if I tried."

Oh, man.

Isaiah's words are like an arrow with a direct path to my heart. And oh, does she melt. My limbs feel languid, and all I can do is stare at him. Whether he means the love of a friend who knows you better than you know yourself or the love of being another half of someone else in a way that no one else could ever be, or somewhere in between, I don't care. Right now, I know he never stopped loving me and never loved someone else.

That's enough.

"Can you say something so I know you don't hate me?" he whispers, his lips so close. So tempting. My melted heart still beats, and it only beats for him.

Of course, my eyes are watering, but I ignore them. I've never been so happy to be stuck on top of a Ferris wheel. Staring at him, I wonder, what the fuck have I been waiting for?

I lean forward, my lips about to brush his. So close not even air could slip through.

"There's no going back after that, Aurora."

My smile is soft. My hand comes up to cup his own cheek. "There was no going back from the moment you got here, Isaiah. I'm not going to change my mind about you. You are the one thing I'm sure of."

I press forward again, and he lets me.

The first touch is merely a spark. Two lips that haven't touched in so long, wondering if they still know how. If they—if we—are still as desperate as we once were. It's a caress, our lips moving together cautiously, patiently. My shoulders fall, tension dissipates, and all I am is the person being touched by Isaiah.

Isaiah exhales, and his fingers find a firm purchase on my skin. They bury themselves in my curls, pulling me as close as he can have me. I press closer. He already has me. Without thought, my fingers grip his shirt.

"Isaiah… closer."

He laughs against my lips, pressing three quick kisses against my lips. I can't breathe. I can't think. I can't do anything that doesn't revolve around him. Good God, he's the sun, and I would fly too close every day if it meant I could feel like this. His free hand lands on my legs, gripping the outside of my thigh tightly and pulling me as close as he can on this tiny seat. And his lips—they are soft and sure. Moving over mine with ease, nipping and pulling. Heat pulses between us, pulses over my skin like tiny fireworks as his lips claim mine.

No wonder I hated kissing. I'm pretty sure I would hate the whole world if Isaiah wasn't a part of it.

My skin is on fire every time his fingers move, pressing and releasing into my skin, sending sporadic shockwaves down my spine. He's everywhere, yet it's nowhere near enough. Heat unfurls in the pit of my stomach, blooming outward, my nerve endings tingling without any sign of stopping.

His tongue brushes my lips, and I go boneless. In my chest, my heart skips and restarts itself as he presses forward, giving me as much of himself as he can. How do I tell him that my heart belongs to him and it always has? A soft sound escapes my lips when his hand slides down my leg and cups the back of my knee in the way only he ever has. It's a gentle caress of skin that is rarely ever touched, and when he touches me, I come to life. The calluses on his hands create friction over the most sensitive of skin, destroying every thought I've had that isn't him. My hand reaches up, cupping his face, feeling the smooth skin, and my teeth pull at his bottom lip.

The two of us—it's like setting off fireworks over a small town. It takes over the sky and fills it with bursts of colorful light. He lets me lead for a moment, lets me set the pace and take control, pulling him toward me and leaning into him until he doesn't. A sure press of his lips, a swipe of his tongue, a soft sound that leaves my lips for him to catch.

"You're the best part of my life, Aurora, even when you weren't in it." Isaiah's lips don't leave mine; he practically whispers the words into my mouth, and I can do nothing but drown in them. His hand tightens, pulling my head back just so, putting me fully at his mercy.

And merciless, he becomes. Kisses are placed on my cheeks, my nose, my temple. His teeth tug at my earlobe and plants kisses over the skin of my neck and the edge of my jaw. Those gentle kisses feel like sunshine. Around and around he goes, touching all the places that have missed him for so long. In doing so, he solidifies himself as the only one I've ever dreamed for.

The only man I'll ever want because I do not come alive for anyone else.

In the dark, he's my guiding light.

In the burning sunlight, he is my shade.

Isaiah makes life worth living.

We are exactly what the other person needs. Even time and distance and anger couldn't change that. This—this love —has been many things. It has been youthful love —pure and innocent, friends forever. It has been teenage crushes—shaking hands and nervous words of two kids who had no idea what to do with that. It has been strong and unyielding. It has been cradled and nourished. It has been set on fire, burned down until only loss and resentment was left, leaving us both wondering if we'd ever find it again.

It was good, it was bad, it was missing. But this love never really left, even when we tried to let go. This love was always going to come back to us. It was only a matter of time.

Isaiah kisses me like he's thinking something of the same. How could the two of us ever believe any different? He finds my lips again, and it's needy. All that there is between us is need. Needing to feel the other person—their touch, their lips. Needing to know that this is it.

It doesn't get better than this.

He tastes like coffee ice cream, and he feels like mine. My hand flattens over his heart, and I find it beating as fast as my own is. Isaiah adjusts my head, pulling me closer, our noses brushing at every movement, his tongue finding mine at the right time, and he never lets go. Not even for a second. Under my palm, his skin is hot, burning up like mine is.

The air seems to close in on us, a bubble around us, reminding us to breathe. We pull back, our lips still brushing together but enough for us to take in air. Though I'm sure we both would've been content to go on without it.

My lips are swollen, my cheeks are flushed, and I've never been happier in my life.

I wrap my fingers around his wrist, finding our tattoo—or one of them—and trace where I know the numbers are. Isaiah touches his forehead to mine, his breath fanning out over my face, and I lean forward again, pressing my lips against his. Just a touch this time. Because now that I can, I never want to stop. I have years to make up for. *We* have years to make up for.

"I've been waiting for you to do that." He presses his lips to mine again. "Much better than having to beg for it."

I smile against his lips, feeling them turn up with my own. Both of his hands come up to cup my cheeks, pulling me back in for a smooth, simple kiss. Isaiah holds me preciously, like I'm something vastly important to him. I sigh into the touch, annoyed that I can't get any closer. Annoyed that I can't kiss him forever.

"Is it ever going to feel like enough?" I ask, blinking my eyes open to find him already watching me.

"Not likely, is it?" he murmurs, placing a kiss on my nose. Heat fans out over my cheeks as his eyes track over my face. He looks at me like I could turn his world upside down and he'd be content to let it.

The creaking sound returns, and we lurch forward. I lean back, exhaling. "I guess that's the end of that."

"For now." Isaiah sits back but places our hands together.

Reaching over, I run my thumb over his lip, swiping away some of the gloss that survived. "Do you remember our first kiss?" I ask as we slowly descend.

A smile comes over his face. "Of course, I do. You basically attacked me outside the diner—"

"You're such a little shit," I exclaim. "That's not true! You kissed me."

The smile transforms to a smirk. "I know." He raises our hands, kissing the back of mine.

I rest my head on his shoulder, transported instantly back to standing outside our diner, him placing his hands on me for the first time that didn't feel…friendly. It was cold, mid-November, and he'd tugged his sweatshirt over my head without a second thought. I remember it all too well. We were so nervous and unsure, and it was still the best first kiss I could've asked for. Isaiah had held me gently, like if his hands were too pressing, I'd run away. It was as if I would've known how to kiss him if my life depended on it.

"Daydreaming over there?"

We're two stops from getting off, but I could stay here forever. "Yeah. The kiss, our first. I loved it."

"Me too." Isaiah kisses my forehead. I wonder how long this will last. This obsessive need to be touching at all times. "But it doesn't have to be a daydream anymore."

The attendant appears before us, raising the bar. Isaiah steps off first, holding out his hand for me as I step down with caution. We find my crutch. My left arm is threaded with his and hugging my octopus to my chest. He looks so carefree, so at ease. This is real life.

"I know. It isn't one."

"And besides, I can give you far more to daydream about than a measly first kiss."

Heat blooms in my cheeks. "Oh, my God."

"I didn't say anything. Your mind did that all on its own."

I raise a brow. "So, if I say give me something to dream about, you don't have a few ideas in mind?"

Isaiah's eyes darken in the lights. "I have plenty of things in mind."

He stops us at his car and pulls me into his chest. I look up as his hand snakes up and around my neck, fingers curling into the base of my curls. Blood rushes through my veins like it's on fire. The rest of the world falls away when he's there.

The grip of his fingers softens just so. "But I plan on taking my time. Because we have time, and there is so much I have to learn, to relearn."

My breath hitches. "Like what?"

His thumb presses my bottom lip. "How you liked to be kissed now, for one. What touches make you tick. What makes your heart speed up. How to make you blush like that whenever I want."

I almost tell him it's just him. That's it. However he kisses me is how I like it because he knows me, and however he touches me is perfect. And him standing in front of me is enough to make my heart rate skyrocket.

But I also like a little fun. The idea of acting like he has to work for anything is enticing. So, I stay quiet.

"How does that sound?" Isaiah teases me, keeping our lips centimeters apart.

"Sounds like you have your work cut out for you."

"You're not work, Aurora. You're the path my life was always supposed to take. Now, I just have to show you I deserve to be there."

What the fuck am I supposed to say to that? I've never felt wanted like this. Never felt desired. Never thought anyone would ever care like this if it wasn't him. I had accepted that my life was going to continue without him. I wasn't happy, and I wasn't coping—but I had accepted it. That acceptance became a brick wall to protect myself. If I knew it was there, it couldn't hurt me.

Isaiah's back and made it clear that I don't have to accept that anymore. He's here to show me that I no longer have to walk that path. I no longer have to live my life without him. Brick by brick, he's removing the wall, tearing it down with his actions, with his words, and leaving me vulnerable again.

I think underneath the surface, I'm a pretty fragile person. I once thought I had thick skin, but I don't. I heal fast—but I bruise easily. Being vulnerable wasn't something I allowed myself to be very often because all it did was make it easier for people to find pliable spots to turn black and blue. Despite his leaving, standing in front of him, as vulnerable as can be, I don't feel anything but safe.

And because his words have left me speechless, all I can do is rock up on my toes (as best I can) and press my lips to his. "Let's go home, Isaiah."

## Kiss Me

*I*saiah's eyes darken behind his glasses when I appear in the doorway.

A faded t-shirt of his falls to my thigh, and my curls tumble down past my shoulders. I stalk toward the bed, where Raven is curled up at the foot, and the covers on my side are already pulled down.

"I like you in my clothes," he says as I climb in, my bad knee first. "I like you in my bed more."

"This version of you is a lot more vocal."

"Probably has something to do with the fact that I'm not a teenager," he says, taking a sip of water, a book open in his hand. "And the fact that I'm not scared I'm going to push you away."

"You're not?"

"Not anymore. I'd just chase after you."

I snort, but I secretly love it. Turning on my side, my leg brushes his. "Thanks for letting me stay over." I let my eyes roam over his bare chest, which is also mostly covered in ink, some even dipping into the waistband of his boxers, before it continues down his leg. There's so much to be discovered.

"Come here."

For a second, I hesitate but then scoot closer. He lifts his arm, and I move into the space like it was made for me. I exhale when my head finds a home on his chest and my hand on the smooth planes of his stomach. Isaiah closes the book and places it on the nightstand, his now free hand taking mine and tugging me.

"Isaiah, I can't get any closer."

He raises a brow. "Yes, you can."

"What? You want me to crawl on top of you?"

"Yes, exactly." He doesn't give me a chance, instead just arranges me until I have to finish the job. Isaiah cradles me as I rest my chin on my hands that are now on his chest. My legs are intertwined with his, and there isn't a part of us that isn't touching. My knee aches, but I don't care.

"Greedy."

"You're damn right I am." Seconds later, I'm attacked with an onslaught of kisses. Over my hair, on my forehead, over the bridge of my nose and the apples of my cheeks. There's a hand resting on my butt that is making my brain short-circuit and eyes that are looking at me like I'm the only star in the sky.

"Would you care if I kissed you until we fell asleep?"

"Not at all."

"You tell me if anything I do makes your knee hurt."

In response, I crawl up his body until I'm straddling him. It pulls the muscle but nothing more than I'm allowed. "I'm fine. Kiss me. You've got a lot of time to make up for."

His head leans back into the pillow, eyes light with amusement. "I know I do."

Hands pull me down until our lips touch. I sigh in relief instantly, my body sinking into his. A soft groan escapes his lips, and it crawls down my spine, leaving goosebumps in its wake. My hands cup his cheeks, my thumb tracing over the sharp cut of his jaw and holding me to him.

Isaiah pulls back but only enough to kiss me everywhere else again. Down the curve of my neck, my collar bone, my shoulder and back. Leaving a trail of heat behind with each tiny butterfly kiss. His teeth nip gently, and my breath hitches. My brain is a hazy place where its only care is Isaiah.

We kiss, and we kiss. And Isaiah proves to be a very fast learner. Learning exactly what to do with his lips and his tongue that make my body sing. At some point, I'm pressed into the pillows, Isaiah hovering over me and blocking out the rest of the world.

"Everything about you is perfect, Ro." He places butterfly kisses on my cheeks and down my shoulder.

I sigh, my brain not working properly. "This is so much better than when we were young."

Isaiah laughs, his teeth tugging at my lip before pulling back. A gentle hand pushes my hair back. "You okay in there?"

"Don't look at me like that. You're the one kissing me stupid."

A beaming smile tilts his lips. His eyes soften a second later. "I could kiss you forever."

"Sounds nice."

And that's that.

Isaiah kisses me until we fall asleep together in the dark.

Sunlight streams in through the blinds.

Reality strikes in waves.

I'm practically burrowed into Isaiah's side. My leg is thrown over one of his, and my arms are tucked against his ribcage. There's an arm wrapped around me and a steady rise and fall of a chest under my cheek.

I have crawled over him like a koala.

Slowly, I unfurl a bit, my hand crawling over the lean, smooth planes of his stomach. A sigh escapes from him—a big exhale—and I bring my head up to look at him. He's still asleep from the soft flutters of his eyelids. I could sleep longer if I wanted, but I'd rather stare at him while I have the chance. At the foot of the bed, Raven is curled between his legs, her eyes tired but watching us.

The light coming in lands in streaks over Isaiah's brown skin and black ink, and I take it all in. Unable to help myself, I trace over some of the artwork with a featherlight touch. They're so intricate. Fine lines and details make up every piece of artwork he has. There are nods to all his favorite things intertwined in larger pieces—ones I assume he let the artist have creative vision or things he liked the look of—but I recognize all the tidbits.

A nod to *Dead Poets Society*, nods to Toni Morrison and Langston Hughes, to Maya Angelou, Sade, Tracy Chapman, and Stevie Wonder. Even with only black ink, there are fun ones, too—candy hearts, ghostly figures hiding in the background, and some other odd ones that I'll have to ask about.

"See something you like?"

"Jesus Christ," I say, my heart practically jumping out of my body. His hand squeezes my side underneath his t-shirt. Heat spreads from palm to fingertip into my skin. I tip my head up, seeing tired, heated, brown eyes looking back. "Give a girl a warning next time?"

I'm given a lazy smile. "Noted. Good morning."

"Morning." I press a kiss to his shoulder before resting my chin on his chest.

"I want a kiss."

I scrunch my nose. "No, I need to brush my teeth first."

He rolls his eyes. "I'll get it one way or another, Ro. May as well give in now." Before I can answer, he tugs me up himself and presses a sweet kiss to my lips. My body relaxes instantly. With a quick hand, he reaches to the nightstand, putting his glasses on.

Heat rushes over my skin. Dumb how hot glasses can be. Could just be him, though. Isaiah turns on his side, trapping me in further. Our bodies are like magnets, unable to pull away. He plays with the curls falling over my face, twisting and untwisting with gentle fingers.

"You want coffee?"

"Please."

"What about breakfast? French toast? Pancakes? Waffles?"

I laugh, filled with such youthful joy, I can't contain it. "Be careful. I could get used to this."

His eyes are locked with mine. "Yeah, me, too."

In the corner of my eye, I see the semicolon tattoo on his wrist. So tiny, it's no wonder I hadn't seen it until now. My eyes are stuck on it, and after a few moments, I think he notices.

"Ro?"

"Yeah?" My voice cracks. Isaiah nuzzles me, pressing a soft kiss to my temple. "Can you—will you tell me about this?"

His face softens, and his brown eyes go molten in the early sunlight. "It was about three years after Elijah left. I had just graduated and…" he sighs, taking a moment. "Nothing had gotten better. The mountain felt taller than ever; the climb was endless. And I couldn't figure out how to take another step." Isaiah pulls me closer, tighter. As if I'm going anywhere. "It was pills. My roommate found me."

I swallow, unable to take my eyes off of him.

After a moment, he continues, "After that, I got help. I told Mom. I went to therapy. I started writing. Every day. Every minute. Writing… saved me. Then, I got the book deal." Isaiah smiles—barely but enough. "That doesn't mean everything is perfect. There are days, moments, months where it's hard. Where it feels like I'm walking through quicksand, but these days, I want to be here."

My heart aches, wishing it could wrap him up itself. I lean up, brushing my lips over his. "Thank you for telling me."

"Anything, Aurora. I'll tell you anything." His fingers find purchase in my hair, holding me to him for a moment until I settle back.

I exhale, trying not to think too long or too hard. Trying to just be here with him. But it's reminded me that there are still going to be things we don't know.

"Are we crazy?" I ask, my fingers tapping his side.

"Aside from the obvious, how do you mean?"

I turn onto my back, and he follows me. There's a residual ache in my knee but nothing of concern. Isaiah's arms rest over my chest, fingers toying with the sleeve of his shirt, brushing over the skin of my arm.

"For rushing into this, I guess? I mean—I don't know. Should we take more time? Slow it down?"

"Realistically, all we've done is kiss."

I let out a soft laugh, appreciative of how he makes a seemingly tough conversation feel easy. "Isaiah…"

He exhales, contemplating. I lay there as his eyes roam over my face. "All we can do is do what feels right, Aurora. And this, being with you, laughing with you, even fighting with you, it all feels far more right than before. If we slow down, what do we gain? The way I see it, there are things we missed out on that we can't get back. What's the point in missing out on anything else when this—being with you, in any capacity—feels more right than anything else."

"You make it sound so easy." I know what I'm feeling is just fear, but I can't push it down.

Isaiah brushes back my hair with his other hand, his thumb rubbing over my forehead. "It is. It's you; it's me. It was hard when I wasn't here because we obviously weren't together. But now, we are. And when has anything ever been hard when we were in it together?"

I admit, for someone who hasn't been in a real relationship, never successfully dated for obvious reasons, I have a lot of anxiety about what I think they should be. How to act, what to do. Isaiah sees that and responds in the best way he knows how.

"It hasn't."

I love his gentle smiles, how they make me feel cared for. "Alright then. You tell me if it ever feels like too much. We can slow down if you need. We can take our time. It's up to you. We can talk it out. You can ask me anything, whatever you need—I'm not going anywhere, Aurora."

My hand finds his cheek. "I don't want you to." I give a small sigh, "I don't want to change things. To slow them down or anything, I was just in my own head."

"I know that. You're allowed to be in there, allowed to feel those things. It doesn't make you weak, Ro. It makes you human. With feelings."

We both know I have issues with that. Feeling weak. Feeling like I'm not good enough or not excelling. And just like before, Isaiah removes the weight of all that pressure and reminds me I don't have to walk through life feeling weighed down.

"Thank you," I say, tapping his nose. "Can you kiss me again?"

Needy. A needy, clingy person is what I turn into the moment I'm allowed to.

"Thought you'd never ask," Isaiah murmurs.

Before I can blink, he's kissing me again, pulling me into him and making it all feel like a big dream. He kissed me to sleep, and he's going to kiss me into delusion if I'm not careful.

But reality is overrated. I'd rather be kissed into oblivion with him anyway.

# FLASHBACK

## *Isaiah, Winter 2014/15*

Aurora was a beacon amongst the intimate crowd.

The cafe was forty minutes outside of our hometown, diminishing the possibility of running into anyone from school. Therefore, she was the only familiar face. Though, really, she was the only one I ever looked for anyway.

Above, the stage light is tiny, but I hear the buzzing of the lightbulb as I settle in front of the small crowd. Clearing my throat, I begin.

I'm only up here because I lost a bet to Aurora because she wants to see me embrace it. It's terrifying reading words I wrote in front of other people that aren't her. My voice turns shaky a few lines in, and I find her to steady myself. She gives me a thumbs up and a silly smile, easing my nerves. With a deep breath, I push on. Aurora has confidence in me at all times. And in my work. No matter how many times I throw it away or edit it or say a negative word, Aurora's there at every turn. My voice calms, turning slow and methodical, the way I've practiced, and I watch her beaming smile turn into something gentle. Something proud.

When I finish, I step off the stage to an echo of gentle claps and snaps and head straight for her. And Aurora is a beaming ray of sunshine in a dimly lit room. Her hands are waving in the air like my own personal cheering squad. As I approach, she wiggles her eyebrows and makes a heart with her fingers. My lips fight a smile only to fail instantly.

"You're such a goof." I sit, placing my work down on the table, and take a sip of the coffee she got me.

"You did great. I really loved those." Aurora sets her chin in her hands, turning those doe-eyed, hazel eyes up at me.

Sheepish, I shrug my shoulders. "They were alright."

She hits my chest with the back of her hand. "Stop it. They were great." The brief touch sends heat spreading through my veins. Her eyes are warm under the soft light, golden brown and specks of green—a color that I've never seen anywhere else. "You need to stop being so hard on yourself."

"It's a lot more fun this way. What kind of writer would I be if I didn't doubt myself at every turn?"

Aurora crosses her arms. "A smart one."

"Are you saying I'm unintelligent?" I lean toward her, cocking my head as our eyes lock. Her pulse jumps in the crook of her neck, and her cheeks flush. Something that's been happening consistently for the past year. A touch, a lingering glance and her cheeks turn pink instantly. My lips quirk, and she rolls her eyes.

"I'm saying you're a pain in my ass."

"Someone's gotta be." I stand, holding my hand out for her. "Come on. Let's go. I'm starving."

She grabs my hand, her tongue flicking over her lip. In my palm, heat flows from her hand into mine as we head outside. I can't stop thinking about her. Haven't been able to stop for so long now. Thinking about Aurora is the one constant I can count on. In the morning, in class, at night. All the fucking time.

All I think about is her curly hair brushing her shoulders or being held back by pre-wrap on the field. Her eyes and the various colors they take on under different lights. Melted bronze or deep gorgeous brown like old, classic literature books. And specks of green that shine like leaves in the summer time. About her smile when she sees me or when she steps off the field after a win. The way she always sits with her knee up on her chair to lean on. How she sleeps on her left side more than her right and that she loves still doing the monkey bars but hates callouses.

And it *feels* like she feels the same. The constantly pink cheeks, the way her pulse skitters, the way I catch her looking at me a little longer than she used to. I mean, things have changed for me. Have they changed for her?

Is that a risk I can take?

What if I do and it goes wrong? What if she doesn't feel the same?

I'll have lost the only true friend I've ever had. My best friend in the world.

"Isaiah," she says, her voice dancing over my skin. I look at her, and I easily see the rest of my life. "You okay?"

Coming out of the haze, I realize we're by my car. I have no idea how long we've been standing here in the cold, but I know her hand is still in mine. She looks content to keep it that way.

"Sorry," I say, eyes flickering to her lips. "Got distracted."

The sun has mostly set, leaving us under the dusk sky. Stars start to twinkle in the sky above, but the brightest one is holding my hand.

What if I do take the risk and it goes right?

My pulse skyrockets.

"Distracted by what?" She furrows her brow, adorably at that, and gives me a half smile.

Swallowing, I say, "By you."

"Me? What—"

Instead of answering, I hold up our intertwined hands. Not just palm to palm. Our fingers are threaded together. I watch her cheeks turn bright red.

She tries to pull her hand away. "Sorry, I shouldn't have…I didn't mean to hold on," Aurora mumbles, but I don't let go. Instead, I place my notebook on top of the car and tug her closer. Our bodies don't touch, but I feel it all the same.

"I don't want to let go."

Aurora stops. Just like that. I'm pretty sure it's shock, so I try not to laugh, but her eyes latch onto the way my mouth twitches. A million memories pass between us and flash in my head. Mostly of this past year, of all the times we've brushed fingers, all the times our skin has touched.

"Isaiah…"

I meet her eyes. "I mean it, Rora. I don't want to let go." I brush my thumb over her knuckles. Our breath puffs in the air, little white clouds dissipating in the cold. Reaching up, I tuck a curl behind her ear, watching as her eyelashes flutter.

"You're my best friend."

Aurora nods, the tips of her boots touching mine. "Yes."

I hesitate for a brief moment. The what-ifs pound. Over and over, knocking at the door to get in. But only one remains.

What if it works?

"What about more?"

"More?" she basically squeaks. I smile.

"What if I wanted more?" I ask and watch her fluster. It's funny given that she is often not. Aurora is steadfast and sure. Confident. Not flustered. I like it.

I take a deep breath. "Can I kiss you?"

Her hazel eyes are wide, looking up at me. I take her in. A beanie keeps her curls contained and her ears covered, a hoodie of mine is draped over her shoulders under a jacket, and leggings hug her hips and her legs. She's beautiful. Always has been. Always will be.

But it's more than that. Aurora is as beautiful inside as she is out. She's tough but kind. A hard shell with a soft, mushy inside that likes baby animals and watching rom-coms on repeat, but who also likes watching horror, even though she gets scared. That cares about people more than she lets on. She's funny but only when you really know her. And I know her. I really know her.

"Aurora?"

She blinks and swallows thickly. Then nods frantically. "Yes."

I smile and don't miss my opportunity. My free hand finds her neck, cool from the cold air, and my fingers find purchase in her hair, brushing the spot under her ear. Our noses brush first, and the moment they do, my pulse calms, and my skin settles. Between us, our breaths mingle, and I watch her watch me until I close the space. Our lips touch—soft, gentle. A simple exploratory brush at first.

Aurora leans closer, pressing them more firmly. It's simple. Until it isn't. She exhales, "Oh."

*Oh* is right. I tug her closer—as close as I can get her. Oh.

Our lips find a rhythm with zero effort, like they've been waiting for this. Her fingers grip tightly onto my sweatshirt, holding me there. As if I was going anywhere else.

Kissing Aurora is like coming home.

It all makes sense. Everything. It makes everything make sense. Together, our lips move. My tongue teases her lip but goes no further. She tastes like coffee and chocolate from her mocha, and I drink it down. It feels like the whole world was blurry, and now, it's not. Now, it's a perfect picture. My heart beats steadily in my chest. Her pulse beats wildly under my fingers, and I don't think either of us are breathing.

All we're doing is kissing, but it feels like so much more. Both my hands cup her cheeks, brushing over her cheek bones, her skin hot to the touch. I need to breathe, but I don't want to stop, even for a second. Eventually, we do. Aurora pulls back—barely but enough to breathe.

Her eyes stay closed. "Oh."

I laugh, and she blinks up at me. A slow, gorgeous smile spreads across her lips. I can't help it—I lean back in to press another kiss to her lips. She sighs, leaning into me as I do. It feels good, knowing she's comfortable, that she trusts me. I pull back, pressing a kiss to the tip of her nose.

Aurora's eyes are bright and her smile more so. Her eyes track over my face, dancing from my lips to my eyes, while her hands stay gripped tightly on my shirt. "So, what now?"

I raise a brow. "We go get ice cream."

"And?"

"And we do that some more."

She laughs, a twinkling, warm sound. Her hands move from my shirt and reach up to cup my face, her fingers brushing over my skin, leaving sparks behind. "I've been wondering if we were ever going to do that."

"Me, too," I say, tugging a curl. "Should've done it sooner."

Aurora blushes but nods. For a second, she rocks on her tiptoes, and then, she presses her lips to mine again. I sigh. Kissing Aurora will never get old. I think I'd be content like this for the rest of my life.

To kiss her forever.

# LOVEBIRDS

"**A**urora!"

I'm met with an onslaught of excited voices as I walk into the locker room. It's the first game I've been at since the injury. They had two away games and a bi-week between then and now, and though I'd been at every practice since starting physical therapy, game day is always different.

The brace is more of an annoyance at this point, but I walk steadily through. I still use the crutches more than not, but I wanted a break.

"Hi, girls." My smile is a bit forced. I'm still sad about not being out there with them, but I'm hoping they can't tell. "Ready for today?"

Thalia approaches me, grabbing my hands. "Better if you were out there with us." The captain's band is wrapped around her arm, the only one since I'm not there. They could've chosen another, but they didn't.

"You'll be great. You've been great without me, and you'll continue to be."

Thalia nods, a flush on her cheeks. Our team isn't very complimentary, more often reaching for jokes and sarcasm. But I mean every word.

The coaches exit the office, my father included, but I focus on Teller.

"Can I be on the sidelines today?"

Coach Teller's lips twitch. "Only place I'd have you if you're not on the field." Her eyes flicker between me and Dad. My stomach drops. "First, can I speak to you two? Laurel, get the girls out on the field for me?"

*Fuck me.* I do not want to get scolded by my coach. In front of my father, who happens to be my other coach. We follow her into the office, the door closing behind us. We stand almost six feet apart, so there's no chance of us having to interact.

Teller waits until the team exits. She leans on her desk, crossing her arms. "What exactly is happening here?"

"What do you mean?" I ask.

"Don't play dumb with me, Aurora. I'm not blind. I've spoken to Coach Matthews here, and he insists everything is fine." Teller raises a brow, daring me to disagree.

This may not be the way other teams—other coaches—handle things, but Coach Teller has never liked playing completely by the book. And it's not often a player and a coach are related in the professional leagues. There isn't an instruction book for her to go off of.

"Everything is fine, Coach Teller."

My anxiety lands like a pit in my gut. I'm hyper aware of my father standing as still as a statue next to me. Anytime this happens between us, he acts like everything is fine. Like nothing could penetrate him. And I turn into an anxiety ridden pit. My body is begging me to fold and break down, to apologize, to talk to him. But not this time. I won't.

"Coach Matthews, can you go join Laurel please?"

From the corner of my eye, my dad gives a short nod and heads out the door.

"Sit down, Aurora," Coach Teller instructs, and I listen. "What exactly is going on?"

His silence when I begged him to tell me he was proud of me rings in my ears. The cold stare, the lack of emotion. It all comes rushing back.

"Coach, it's nothing. Just a fight between a dad and his daughter. It won't affect the team."

"I'm not worried about the team. I'm worried about you."

I sigh. "I promise I'm okay."

Coach Teller takes a deep breath. The look she gives me lets me know she doesn't believe me for a second. "Whatever it is, I'm sorry. But if you think I don't see the pressure you put on yourself, the pressure you carry, you're wrong. You're not just a player to me, Aurora; you're a person. And I can see what you're doing to yourself. Distractions, hyper focusing on things you can fix," she says, pointing to my knee. "I see through the act. I can see that you're struggling. I'm just worried about you, is all—with the injury, the team selection, and whatever the hell is happening between you and your father. I'm here for you if you need me. Not just as a coach but as someone who cares about you."

I hate that she's right. I hate that it feels suffocating to have someone outside my immediate circle care about me, that she's so easily able to see something is wrong.

"Thank you, Coach. I'm working on it." I twist my hands in my lap.

"Alright then. I'm taking your word for it for now." She holds out a hand and helps me up. "Let's get out there. Those girls have missed you."

Light from the field streams down the tunnel, and when I step onto the turf, it greets me soft and steady. Like getting on the couch under your favorite blanket. Even so, there's a sense of distance—a sense of loss not being able to play. An undercurrent of fear that when—if—I do come back, it won't be the same. That I won't be the same.

I know my team will welcome me back. But what if the game doesn't? Where will that leave me and my dad?

Where will that leave me?

Isaiah and I wait in the parking lot together before heading to Soph's for dinner.

His arm is hung over my shoulder, his fingers intertwined with mine as we lean against the car.

"You alright?" Isaiah murmurs against my temple, placing a kiss there.

"Can we talk about it later?"

He gives me a look but nods. "Of course."

I exhale, relaxing into his hold. My hand is snaked under his t-shirt, fingers splayed over his skin. Isaiah makes the rest of my life better, more manageable. But he can't help with how I feel about the field or the game or my place in it.

That's up to me, and I have a history of burying things until there's no more room left in the grave.

"I know you don't plan on coaching for years to come, but you looked pretty hot out there."

I snort, hitting his chest. "You're so dumb."

"I'm just saying, if you ever wanna practice on anyone—you know, being bossy or shouting orders—I'm happy to be of assistance." Isaiah places kisses on my neck, nipping the skin with his teeth as he goes.

I swallow, attempting to control my breathing, but he swipes his finger under my chin, tugging it upward. His lips hover above mine, our noses touching just so, until he kisses me soft and slow. I sigh into him, letting all the anxiety and the restlessness fall away so I don't miss a moment.

"Well, howdy do-da day. Look at this show we got over here, girlies." Maazina's voice is like a siren calling in the middle of the night. There is no ignoring it.

Isaiah laughs against my lips, his forehead falling to mine. "I'm worried she's batshit crazy."

"She's way past batshit. Really, she should be institutionalized at this point." I pull back as Maazina, Sylvia, and Vivian approach, all three wearing big smirks. Along with many of the girls lingering behind them, who heard Maazina's screech.

"Hiya, lovebirds."

I turn to Isaiah. "That's the last time I kiss you in public."

Isaiah huffs in disbelief, pinching my side, but stays quiet.

"I never thought I'd see the day." Sylvia pushes my cheeks together.

"Get off me," I try to say, but my words come out jumbled. When she does free me, I say, "Good game today. You guys are holding it down back there. Just like I expected."

"It's not the same without my sugar mama, but it'll do." Maazina beams, and Vivian chuckles.

"Sugar mama?" Isaiah asks, eyes shining with confusion.

"Don't ask," Vivian and I say at once.

I love that they feel comfortable enough to be themselves with Isaiah around. It's not that I expected them to ever hide or shrink themselves for him or for anyone really, but it can always be a bit strange when suddenly, there's a significant other around.

Maazina changes the subject. "So, what did Coach want to talk to you and your dad about?"

I lean on the single crutch. "She noticed something was off."

Vivian frowns. "Are you and your dad still not speaking?"

In my peripheral vision, Isaiah's eyes lock onto me. I haven't told him. It's not a huge deal but…his eyes are burning into the side of my head, regardless. "Nope."

"I'm sorry, Aurora," Viv says, reaching out to tug a curl by my cheek.

Shrugging, I say, "It's alright. Not much I can do about it, so please don't waste your time worrying about it. I don't want it to affect you at all. It'll work itself out." All three of the girls frown at my words but don't press.

Isaiah's hand grows firmer, fighting off some of the tension piling up in my gut. "Not to change the subject, but my birthday is coming up, and I was planning on having dinner with Aurora and her family. From what I know, you guys are part of her family, so would you like to come?"

Sylvia dramatically places her hand over her heart. "I would love that."

Vivian smiles. "I'd like that, as long as we wouldn't be intruding."

"Will her hot brother-in-law be there?" Maazina asks, catching Isaiah, who usually rolls with the punches, quite, well… off-guard.

"The married one?"

"That's the one."

"Um…. yes?" Isaiah turns to me. "Was that the appropriate answer?"

"There is never an appropriate answer for that one." I run a hand down my face and find Maazina smiling as usual.

Isaiah chuckles. "I'll have her pass on all the information."

"Sounds perfect."

"We have to get going but, seriously, good game." I call them in for a group hug, like we do on the field, and my heart swells.

"We miss you out there," Viv says, patting my back.

"I'll be back."

We pull away, and they make their way to any lingering family or friends before heading to their own cars. A breeze wraps around me and Isaiah, brushing against our skin. He turns my cheek, bringing our eyes together.

"Your dad?"

"I'm sorry. It's not that I'm keeping it from you. I just haven't wanted to talk about it."

Isaiah nods. "I understand that. But can you tell me about it later? If you're able."

It makes my heart ache that he cares about how it might make me feel. It's the bare minimum, I know, but it's just not something I give myself. It's nice.

"Yeah, I can do that." I lean up, pressing a kiss to his cheek. On the other side of the parking lot, I see the man himself making his way over to his car. "It's stupid, but part of me wants to go over there."

Isaiah's eyes darken. He's always on edge about my dad. More concerned with me than what my dad would ever think of him. I assume it'd be similar if Elijah ever came back.

"It's not stupid, but do you think it'll make you feel better?"

My smile is sad. "No. Not at all."

"Why don't you save it for another day?" he asks, running a finger down the side of my face.

Across the mostly empty parking lot, my dad throws his bags in the car. He turns, as if he can sense me staring at him, and looks in this direction. Isaiah's other hand tightens on my waist, his fingers splaying over the skin under my shirt. Even though I can't see my father's eyes, I feel the glare from here. Can imagine the coldness in them. The palpable disappointment. Neither of us wave or make a single movement. We just…stare at each other. It stings that he is seemingly okay without me.

He did this to my mom when they were together, to me and Sophia growing up. Shutting down instead of talking. Shutting us out and giving us the silent treatment and turning us into the villains, even though we were the ones that broke and apologized. But as a kid, I never understood why Mom would get so angry, why she was so hurt—usually, as a kid, I understood him more, and now, I understand her perfectly. Because her fate has become mine.

Being Daddy's little girl didn't save me. It just prolonged the inevitable.

Maybe the love my dad has for me has conditions. And maybe I'll never be able to meet them.

I swallow and look away—look back to Isaiah, who is the solid ground beneath my rocky feet.

"Yeah, I can do that. Let's just get to Soph's."

Isaiah takes a long look at me as if he can see all the fragile, sharp edges I've been hiding. I've always kept them sharp to keep people out. To keep people that are more likely to leave from seeing the vulnerable parts. Isaiah looks at me like he'd walk across broken glass just to get to me. Like if I was on the edge of a cliff, he'd go with me just so I wasn't alone.

I'd do the same for him, so I recognize it.

Love is so strange.

The idea that we'd bleed ourselves dry to keep the other person safe. The way in which their needs, their wants, their emotions become yours. For a while, I thought the love we had for each other died. I hoped it did, so I could move on. But it didn't.

It'd been buried under the dirt, un-watered and neglected. But it never died. Now, the sun is back, its rays landing on something that was once beautiful, that seems as if it will be beautiful again. And it's slowly starting to bloom again.

Maybe, some of the petals of what was once a strong relationship I had with my dad are dying. Those petals dry and brittle.

But Isaiah and me—that will never die. From here on out, it's clear to me we won't let it.

So, let the rest of the world fall apart. Let the foundation crack. This love remains.

# Head in Hand

"**U**ncle Ziah!"

Isaiah beams and catches Joey upon entering. Even Zaza hugs him first. I look over their tiny heads to Kian. "What am I? Chopped liver?"

Kian snorts. "Welcome to my world." Sophia appears behind him, hitting him upside the back of the head. "Ouch. Why am I being punished for telling the truth?"

I laugh and lean over to where Joey is holding onto Isaiah like she's never going to let him go. *Me, too, girl. I get it*, I think to myself. "Hiya, gorgeous," I say and place a big kiss on her cheek. She giggles, and I lean down and wrap up my mini me.

Zaza fights a smile because, you know, she's a ten-year-old and can't be bothered, but she fails. "There it is. How are we today?"

"Good! We made cookies earlier."

I raise my brows. "Cookies? Take me!"

Zaza happily does so, leading me down the hallway. When I pass Kian, I pat his chest. "Guess you're the only one left on the chopping block."

"This is outrageous." Kian sighs and enters the kitchen behind us. Mom is there, sitting at the counter. I lift Zaza up onto the stool and go over to hug my mom.

"Hi, sweetie. How are you doing?"

"Getting there."

Mom nods, blonde strands falling out of her haphazard bun. Her face warms when Isaiah walks in. Joey is still hanging on, but that doesn't stop him from walking over to my mom. "Hi, Miss Lindsey."

Mom stands up to wrap him in a big hug. "It's good to have you back."

Isaiah meets my eyes, and I give him a soft smile. "It's good to be back," he says, never taking his eyes off me. To my right, Kian places his hands on his hips and mouths, "Just *friends*?", and then fake gags.

I flip him off and turn on my heel, heading next to Sophia. Instantly, I rest my head on her shoulder. "Whatcha doing?"

"I was trying to knead this bread, but now, you're on top of me," she says, and I stick my tongue out and quickly hit her cheek with it. Sophia doesn't even flinch. "You're disgusting."

"You act like that bothers you. Look at who you're married to."

Sophia snorts, patting my cheek. "You make a good point."

"Do you need any help?"

My sister shakes her head. "No. Kian's got the grill going, and everything should be done soon. Would you mind getting juice out for the girls though?"

"Got it." I skate around the kitchen, while Kian and Isaiah play with the girls. My heart does a little tug and pull inside my chest at the sight. He wasn't just missing from my life; he was missing from everyone's, and it's nice how easily he fits back in.

A knock on the door grabs my attention. "Who is that?"

Mom and Sophia share a look, and my stomach drops. "I'll get it," Mom says, practically running out of the kitchen.

"Soph."

She swallows, kneading the bread like her life depends on it and avoiding my eyes. "Please don't hate me."

"Why?"

"It was mostly Mom's idea. I just…went along with it. We figured the only way to get you two to speak was if we put you in the same room."

My lips flatten. I know they mean well, but I wanted to come here and not think about him, or the game, or anything of substance, and now, I don't have a choice. I sense Isaiah's gaze on my skin.

"Do you hate me?" Sophia asks.

I rub a hand over my forehead. "No. But I'm not happy."

Sophia frowns but doesn't push. I go and stand by Isaiah, my hand tightly wrapped around my own glass of orange juice. Kian gives a wide-eyed look over the room, where tension is buzzing like a live wire.

He tosses a thumb over his shoulder. "I'm gonna go check on the grill. Yeah… I'll be outside if you need me." I snort as he practically runs out of the room.

Isaiah leans down, placing his chin on my shoulder and placing a kiss on my neck under the curtain of my hair. "You okay?"

"I am right now. Can't say that'll be the case in a few minutes."

He squeezes my waist twice. "Say the word and we'll leave."

The sound of the front door closing grabs Joey and Zaza's attention, and they light up when they see their grandfather down the hall. Their little footfalls echo over the floor as they quickly exit the kitchen.

"Oof! Look how big you've gotten. I barely recognize you," my dad says, still not in my view. He does this every time he sees them, and it never fails to bring a laugh out of Joey. Zaza's getting harder to impress by the day. Dad comes in carrying both the girls with a big grin on his face.

He's so good with kids and so bad…with the rest of us.

As expected, his smile drops when he sees me. "Lindsey." His eyes land on my mom, who is unfazed. They may be friendly, but she has long stopped giving a shit about offending him.

"Work it out, Matthews." Mom finds her spot in the kitchen with Sophia, checking on what I hope is Sophia's lasagna.

Dad sets the kids down, encouraging them to go back to what they were doing, and approaches us. "Isaiah." He holds out his hand, and Isaiah shakes his hand in return firmly, but I see the reluctance. "Good to see you, young man. You doing alright?"

Isaiah pockets his hand, standing staggered behind me, our shoulders touching. "Doing good, sir. Best as I can."

Dad looks at me, his eyes completely unreadable. "Talk outside?"

"Sure." I clear my throat and follow him out to the porch. The porch where Kian is lying flat on his back in the sun. "Kian."

He jumps up, sheepishly smiling. "Nice to see you, sir."

Dad chuckles. "You, too. We're gonna talk out here, if you don't mind."

Kian holds up his hands. "Not at all. Have the whole yard if you need it." My brother-in-law gives me a kiss on the cheek as he passes. He's all too aware of what these conversations look like, how these fights go.

"You wanted to talk?"

I frown, crossing my arms. "I didn't ask for them to invite you here. I certainly didn't want to do this today."

"So, then why are we?" Dad looks bored. Like he'd rather be doing anything else than acknowledge he has done something wrong.

"You literally just asked if we could talk outside, but somehow, this is my choice?" I huff. The laugh that seeps out of my mouth is dry. "What is your problem?"

"I don't have a problem, Aurora."

Exhaling, I will the fury tightening my chest to leave. There is nothing and no one else that can hit my anger like a light switch. I don't know if it's the indifference or the blasé attitude, but I can't take it. He knows exactly what buttons to push and pushes them even more when he acts like he has no idea what he's doing. Like if he can manipulate people into being angrier, he's proven to himself that he's right.

And I lose it. "You have got to be fucking kidding me."

Dad's eyes snap to mine.

"How do you do this?" I wave my hand between us. "How do you walk around like nothing's bothering you? Like nothing is wrong?"

He fucking shrugs. "Never said nothing was wrong. You haven't called, haven't come to the house."

"Why would I have called you? I asked you to tell me that you're proud of me. Not my accomplishments, not what I do, who I *am*. And you said nothing. Better yet, then I get selected for the National Team. And you said nothing. Then, I got hurt. And you said nothing. Not as my dad and not as my coach. What am I supposed to do with that? Beg you to give a shit?" My eyes prick with hot anger.

"I'm not asking you to do that." He rocks back and forth on his feet, exhaling. "You know, I only ever wanted what's best for you. Didn't know that was a problem."

It's like talking to a brick wall, though I'd prefer that.

I scoff. "You know, that may be partially true, but you don't just want what's best for me. You want and have always wanted for me to be the best. And I have tried my hardest. But anytime I've ever fallen short, you don't give me any grace. The pressure never stops. You don't let me reset; you don't let me breathe. It's always, go-go-go. Trying to keep up with your expectations is running me into the ground."

"So, me wanting you to be the best there is—that's a problem?"

I press my fingers against my forehead. "You are infuriating."

Anger flares in his eyes. "You have so much potential; do you get that? You always have, and you still do. Pressure is what drives people to keep fighting. To keep learning and to keep improving. Why is it so wrong of me to expect more of you? To push you to be better? Pressure is a necessary factor of life and especially as a professional athlete. It's not my fault you can't handle that."

My jaw clenches. "I can handle the pressure, Dad. I cannot handle the fact that you might never look at me the same if I don't succeed."

He just…stares at me.

"Why didn't you come check on me after I got hurt?"

"Didn't think you needed me there. You had Sophia, Isaiah, your mom." He shrugs.

"I needed my dad. And nothing I've ever done has made it seem like I don't need you. So, why can't you show up for me?" I swallow, feeling my heart break off into tiny fragments. If he was holding a glass statue of me, he's dropped it and watched it shatter on the floor. "Or is it that you don't know how to talk to me if it isn't about soccer or a goal I can reach? If that isn't there, what would you even say to me?"

We stare at each other. A dad and a daughter who used to do everything together. The movies, coffee and hot chocolate at the bookstores, shopping for new cleats, running—we even used to laugh together. Now, where has that all gone? Is it because I grew up and life got bigger? Is it because I grew up and needed him less? For so long, I was his little girl, and then one day, something changed. And I don't know how to fix it. I can't stop getting older, and I can't force him to care.

I meet his eyes. "Do you even like me?"

"I love you, Aurora."

"Do you like me?" I plead, wondering if I even want to know the answer. Wondering if I even like him anymore. Dad stands there unflinching and silent.

I'm pretty sure anyone listening can hear the shattered pieces of my heart breaking.

He can't admit or can't accept that he's done anything wrong. That he's hurt me. And I'm no longer willing to stand by and apologize for his own missteps. No longer going to sweep up the pieces of me and give them back to him only for them to be broken further. If I do, soon enough, I'll only be specks of glass on the floor too small for anyone to see.

"When you want to fix this, you come talk to me. When you care enough to remember at the end of the day, I'm your daughter, you can come find me. Decide whether you like me enough to care."

I turn away before he sees the tears pooling in my eyes—not that he would care—and head around the yard. Going inside isn't an option for me right now, to face all their wondering, pity-filled eyes. Even the thought feels suffocating.

So, I walk down the street and through the neighborhood, wiping away tears that won't quit until I come upon the playground. It's empty today, so I plant myself on the swings.

I blow out a series of short breaths, trying to quell the anxiety pooling in my gut. When did I get here? A person who begs for her father to treat her like a person? Why do I have to beg for that? What do I have to do to get his attention? This idea of being the best…of having to be at the top is like a friend that I can't separate from. It's bad for me, it haunts me, and I can't shake it. I can't get it off of me.

And it's so frustrating when everyone else thinks I'm doing enough and am enough. But it's Dad's opinion that is stuck to me like glue—no matter how much I peel and scrape, it won't fucking leave my skin. It's Dad that makes me second guess myself.

I want it all to stop.

I want my self-worth to stop depending on my dad.

I want my dad to be my dad. Not my friend. Not my coach. My dad.

I want to not second guess people. To not worry they're all eventually going to leave.

Sighing, I let my head fall forward into my hands. No one's left in a long time; logically, I know that. But what if they, like Dad, decided that one day, I'm not meeting their expectations, their conditions? And it all stops.

What happens if it all stops?

I force myself to inhale. To take deep breaths and actually take in the oxygen. To stop the spiraling thoughts, but I don't know how to get out of my own head.

I want out. I want out. I want—

"Aurora?" Hands land right above my knees, strong fingers wrapping around my thighs. "Baby, can you look at me?"

Isaiah's tone has me listening. I blink my eyes open, tears rolling down when I do, and find him crouched in front of me. There's anger in his eyes, but when it dims, I know it's not directed at me.

"I'm a fucking idiot."

Isaiah shakes his head, a hand moving up to cup my cheek. "Hey, stop. That's not true."

"He's never going to see me. I'm not sure he's ever tried," I say, though the words come out with a sob. Isaiah doesn't say a word, just brings me to my feet and wraps his arms tight around me.

I'm losing track of how many times I've sobbed into his chest, but I can't stop.

His hand buries itself in my curls. I'm pretty sure in my teary haze, he's carrying me, my toes not even touching the ground, and I see I'm right when he lowers us. Isaiah adjusts us. Another time and I might be embarrassed that he's cradling me in a neighborhood playground, but I've lost all my common sense when it comes to him anyway.

Gently, he tugs my head out of the crook of his neck, his thumb swiping under my eyes. "I know he's your dad, but it's his loss. Choosing not to give you what you need, choosing not to see how wonderful and intelligent and funny and all other things not related to soccer you are, is his loss. I'm sorry that you're suffering because of his actions. I'm sorry that he's causing you pain." Isaiah sighs. "I wish I could take it away, make it hurt less."

"You are," I say, my thumb circling his inner wrist. "You being here, holding me, is taking the pain away." Isaiah is leeching the pain out of my veins, making the air breathable. I reach for him and press our lips together. It's soft, tender—a caress that encompasses more than I could ever express. "Thank you," I murmur against his lips. "You've got to stop letting me sob all the time."

"Oh, so now your tears are my responsibility?" Isaiah smiles against my lips, leaning in for another kiss.

"I think so, if you don't mind adding it to the list."

Isaiah kisses my cheeks, my nose, my forehead, and my lips again. "You are the entire list, Aurora." He sets me on my feet in front of him, his hands running up the outside of my thighs and resting on my hips. My hands find his shoulders, thumbs running over the strong column of his neck. His heartbeat moves with my own. Solid, steady, in sync. Like we are. In a burning room, we'd still be standing if we were holding onto each other.

"You are too good to me, Isaiah Bryant."

"That's not possible. You deserve to be cared about, Aurora—unconditionally. Me doing so isn't doing anything extraordinary."

Oh, but it is. His hand finds my bad knee, wrapping around the back of it. It's those moments—those small, maybe insignificant moments—that make it extraordinary.

"It is." I press my finger over his lips before he can argue. "I guess we should head back?"

Isaiah looks around. "Or we could hang out here for a bit. Be kids again."

"Will you push me on the swing?"

He gives me a small laugh. "Anything you want."

We make our way to the swing set hand in hand, like little kids. I sit down, and he moves behind me. Isaiah bends down, placing a kiss on my shoulder, then playfully nibbles his way up to my cheek, pulling a giggle out of me when the ticklish sensation fans out like a feather over my skin.

"Isaiah," I say, with a lilt to my words, "stop."

"Can't." He continues his feather-like kisses and playful bites until my cheeks hurt from smiling.

"Okay, okay!" I can't get away from him—not that I really want to—and he places his hands firmly on my hips to lean around and give me a sweet kiss on the lips.

With three squeezes of his hand, he pulls back. "You sure you're alright?"

I'm not, and yet…I am. I'm happy here with him. I'm sad about what the relationship with my father is becoming. My eyes feel puffy and swollen from the tears, and my heart is fragile. Grief is clawing at the surface, and anxiety is waiting in the shadows.

But I take Isaiah in. The warmth in his eyes, the love in his touches.

How with him, the fragile pieces don't feel so breakable. The ground doesn't tremble. My mind doesn't whirl. With him, the world is still, and reality isn't so bad. Simplicity seems beautiful, and all the other stuff will work itself out. That's what standing here with him is like. Anything that comes our way, we'll face it hand in hand, together.

I look at him and say, "I will be."

## THE LETTER

**I**'m not sure there's a better sight than Aurora curled up in my bed. Raven is coiled tightly into the curve of her legs, and Aurora is burrowed underneath the covers and holding tight to the pillow I was previously using. Her curls are a haphazard halo around her head, and her lips are slightly parted.

The heat from my mug seeps into my palms. It's only eight A.M.. Usually, she's up with me by now, but it's a Sunday. The team is off, and she doesn't have physical therapy, so I don't wake her. Ever since the injury, we haven't spent more than two nights away from each other. It's not even something we've discussed; it just happened. It's been a real fucking sight to see her open up to me again.

I set down a second mug on the nightstand and bend down. "Rora?" She stirs, arms stretching out, but burrows her face further into the pillow. Leaning down, I brush a kiss over her cheek. "Coffee's on the table, and I'll make you breakfast whenever you wake up." She mumbles something incoherent while I bring the covers up and make sure her brace is still on.

Taking my coffee, I leave Raven and Aurora curled up in my bed where I'd rather be. But I can't stop thinking about the letter I got in the mail yesterday, and I can't bring myself to sleep.

It's funny how when everything seems to be going right, things suddenly decide to go wrong.

Aurora's dad was first.

The letter is second.

Elijah's scrawl is the same. I don't recognize the address, though I suppose that's insignificant, but the messy, quick hand, half-print-half-cursive is the same. An insignificant detail but one I can't stop focusing on. I haven't told Ro, simply for the fact that I haven't opened it. It hits me that he must have spoken to Mom because she's the only one with my address.

Something I learned in my six years was that you can prepare and do the work as much as you want. But when something takes you by surprise, it's hard not to fall into those old ways. I let my head fall forward, running my hands forward toward my face. The bitter taste of the coffee lingers and so does the fear of opening that envelope.

All the fights with Mom come rushing back.

All the conversations I had with Elijah before he left are instantly replayed. Wondering if now that I'm older, I'll remember something I missed back then.

All the unanswered calls, emails, messages won't let me breathe.

All the thoughts I had, wondering what I did to him to make him leave me, sink right back onto my shoulders.

I knew Elijah felt a lot of pressure from Mom from the moment our dad died. I was a baby, barely pushing two, so I don't have much memory of him. The only pressure I had was to grow up. But Elijah... everything was expected of him—the grades, a career, help with me, a job when he was old enough, all of it. Pressures that shouldn't be put on a teenager, let alone a kid.

But I've never been able to come up with a 'why' for why he left and why he left me behind.

I send a text to my mom, asking her to call me in a bit, and run the edge of the letter under my fingertips. It's thick; I can feel the edges of paper underneath. Part of me wants to rip it up and throw it away, not even waste my time. But at the end of the day, he's still my brother. He may have left me, maybe he stopped thinking of me as his brother, but I never stopped thinking of him as mine.

"Isaiah?"

I whirl around to see Aurora holding a mug in one hand and Raven in another. I wish I had a camera so I could capture it. She looks beautiful. Tired eyes, messy curls, and my t-shirt draped over her brown skin.

"Morning."

She smiles, but it's interrupted by a yawn. I watch as she kisses Raven on the forehead, who meows, and then sets her on the ground. Aurora pads around and sits next to me on the couch, tucking herself into my side.

"What are you looking at?"

I lift my arm and pull her in, placing a kiss on her heap of her curls. "Got a letter from Elijah. Haven't opened it yet."

"A letter?" She yawns again, and I wait for the news to break through the sleepy haze. "Wait." She sits up. "What?"

I laugh dryly. "Yeah." I hold it out to her.

Her hazel eyes widen before searching for me. They soften, and she exhales. "You haven't opened it."

"No, I'm not sure I can."

Aurora nods, leaning into me again. My hand rests on her thigh, wrapping around the smooth thickness of it to ground myself.

"Do you want me to? Or do you want me to go?"

"I do not want you to go." My words are firm.

"Okay, okay. I just wanted to check. I don't want to suffocate you," Aurora says, tucking a curl behind her ear. "Are you sure?"

"Please open it."

She huffs a sad laugh next to me. "His handwriting is the same."

The aching in my ribs only grows when she notices the same stupid detail I did. I guess there aren't many other details to notice, but still. The only other detail is his address being somewhere in Massachusetts. The tearing of paper and the rustling that ensues draws my eyes back to her hands, where she's pulling a thick wad of paper from the envelope.

She unfolds it, and his messy scrawl is everywhere. After a second, Aurora looks at me. "I think you should read this, Isaiah." Though she tries to hide it, her eyes water. I rest my head on her shoulder now, feeling her hand come up around me, a soft palm on my cheek. "I'll be right here."

I take the letter, feeling the marks of the pen on the paper.

*Isaiah,*

*There is no way for me to start this letter off. A simple apology doesn't encompass the full range of emotions I feel writing this, but regardless, I am incredibly sorry for what I did to you. I want to start off by saying the reasons I have for leaving do not excuse the pain I caused you in doing so. It won't change what I did or how that made you feel. There are a million things in my life I wish I could re-do, a million things I wish I could say or unsay, a million things I would do differently. But leaving you the way I did is number one.*

*I also want to make it clear that you should not feel the need nor any obligation to respond. I admit that this letter is selfish. For me, I suppose, since the result of my choice is not knowing how you are.*

*I left because I had to. For me. There was no air left for me to breathe—around Mom, at school. Every time I came home, I lost pieces of myself in the process. Lost sight of the things I wanted and the person I wanted to become. And I couldn't remember how to fight for them. My grades were awful, my social life was non-existent, and I was just…so tired. I couldn't take the pressure from Mom. When Dad died, we were too young to understand what death is, what it does to the people left. And Mom didn't know how to live without him. I had to be responsible every day for the years to come. My childhood left when he did. I'm not mad at Mom anymore, but I was. For what she did—forcing me to grow up before I even knew who I was. Forcing me to meet expectations that were skyscrapers. Forcing me to be an adult and a caretaker instead of her son. And I was angry at myself when I got older. For losing myself, for pressuring myself to be everything. A role model for you, a student, valedictorian, the degree, friendships, work—you get the point.*

*I left because I knew if I didn't, I was saying goodbye to a life I'd barely had time to dream about. I left because I wanted to become more than what I was. I wanted to be someone to be proud of, and I couldn't do that there. Driving back and forth, prioritizing everything except myself. I wanted to be something— be someone. To make something of myself. To stop putting myself last. I was indifferent to my life and that…I couldn't let that be it. I left for myself.*

*In spite of the consequences, in spite of the pain it might cause, I left because if I didn't, my life would've never begun. I wish I had done it differently. I wish I had told you. And I'm sorry.*

*I'm sorry for abandoning you, for leaving you behind.*

*One thing has never changed, Isaiah, and that is that I love you. Even if you hate me, even if you never want to see me again, I will love you for the rest of my life. If there is one thing I hope you take from this letter, if you stop reading right now, I hope it's that—that I love you. And always will. Even if I haven't always done a good job of showing it. You're my brother. You will always be my brother.*

I don't even know my eyes are watering until a drop lands on the page. Quickly, I place them down because I don't want to ruin them. Tears leak out of my eyes. A war rages between wanting to rip those papers to tiny shreds and wanting to keep reading despite the deepening hole in my chest.

"Oh, Zay." Aurora pulls me into her, her body becoming a safe haven. "I'm sorry. I'm so sorry."

I wish I didn't understand what he felt then, but I do. Because I felt it when he left. Fuck. I want to hate him. But I can't because he's my brother, and he couldn't ever let us know he wasn't okay because we were the ones looking to him.

"I wish I hated him."

She adjusts to look at me, her bad leg resting over my lap and caging me in. No place else I'd rather be but surrounded by her. Especially when everything else feels like shit. Her fingers curl around the side of my face, tears rolling over her thumb.

"I know. But that's not who you are." Aurora has this way of seeing people, even when they don't want to be. Like she did when we were little kids. Like she has every day since. She tries to hide it. Make herself seem tougher than she is. I've always seen right through it. Because I have a way of seeing her.

"I've been telling myself I'm indifferent for years. That I was over the anger and the hurt because I didn't have a choice. What the fuck am I supposed to do with this?"

Aurora rubs her thumb back and forth on my cheek. "I don't have an answer. I wish that I did." She sighs. "I know it wasn't easy, but you got through it then. You'll find your way through this."

"Barely," I whisper, attempting a deep breath.

"What?"

I open my eyes and find hers waiting with questions. And a deep sadness. "Barely. I barely made it through, Ro." It feels like there's a giant rock on my chest, darkness seeping in at the edges of my mind. "It sounds like he was drowning, that he stopped wanting to breathe. That's what I felt when he left. I felt that way every day for almost two years. I didn't care about anything. I didn't want to *be* anyone. The meds help, but I don't want that to happen again. I don't want to feel like that again."

Pain glimmers in her eyes and over her features.

Aurora grips my face firmly. "If it happens, you will get through it. You aren't alone." I'm not sure what she sees in my eyes, maybe the fear that it's happening again, maybe something I'm not sure of myself, but she continues. "You get to decide what happens next, Isaiah. Whether you keep reading or shove it in a drawer for later. Whether it means something or it doesn't. Whatever you decide is okay. He's your brother. I get that; I understand that it probably feels like you owe him something. It's your life. You've lived it on your own for the past six years; you know yourself best. You do what's best for you."

Isn't it strange how hard doing what's right for you can feel? How hard it can feel to put yourself first?

Her words are like an anchor, and I latch on, pulling myself back to Earth and to reality. Shame rushes through my veins at letting her see this—this fragile state that I'm in.

"Hey. Don't you dare pull away from me. If you need space, I'll give it to you, but I'm right here. For you. All versions of you. In all the shitty parts of life. Not just the pretty parts. I'm right here. You're not alone." There's desperation in her voice, and I huff.

Stupid of me to think that this girl, my Aurora, would ever turn away when I need her.

Our foreheads touch, and I place a kiss on her forehead, letting my lips linger. "Thank you. I can't thank you enough."

Aurora makes it so our eyes meet. "You don't need to thank me. You're my person, Isaiah. I want to be there for you. I will always be there for you."

Abandonment fears run deep in this relationship, a thread of connection between the two of us. One that could hurt us at any moment. But she isn't going to abandon me. And I'll never leave her again. If there's anyone we can count on, it's each other.

I choke down everything that isn't useful to me at this moment—the guilt, the fear, the pressure. It's not helping. It doesn't matter.

Right now, I have a letter from my brother.

Right now, I've gotta take it one step at a time.

I stare at the front door of Aurora's dad's house.

She's currently at the field with Maazina doing her exercises, getting in some exercise on that knee. I'm almost positive she arranged that so she could give me some space, even though I didn't explicitly ask for it. The letter sits in the backseat, where I still haven't read another word.

But all that anger I attempted to extinguish has come rushing back. I'd always planned on coming here, to her dad's, whether she knew it or not—whether that's smart or not. And maybe today isn't the best day considering, but I'm way past giving a fuck. I stalk up the sidewalk and only hesitate a moment before knocking.

Mr. Matthews appears in the doorway, surprise flickering over his dark brown skin. "Isaiah, what can I do for you?" He gives me his usual firm smile. Guilt pokes its head out since he's always been kind to me.

"How are you doing, sir?" I ask, and he nods, motioning for me to continue. "Do you have time to talk?"

Mr. Matthews steps aside, and I step in. There are photos everywhere—of him and Aurora, and Sophia, and the grandkids. But it's him and Aurora that sticks out. Her as a baby on his shoulders while he coaches, him helping her put on shin guards and cleats, them together on Halloween and Christmas. Aurora napping on his chest, him doing her hair, walking her to school. They are everywhere. That's the dad Aurora deserves.

"Can I get you anything?" Mr. Matthews leads us to the living room. The pictures and knick-knacks continue, details of his own life sporadically spread through the house. He takes a seat at the office chair.

"No, thank you." I sit on the big ottoman. Images of Aurora flash in my head. Mostly of her trying to put on a brave face whenever her dad is brought up. I can see the fissures cracking in the surface. And I hate how much I can't do anything about it.

"What can I do for you, young man?"

I exhale. "You can't do this to her."

In an instant, his face turns cold. "That's not your business."

"Actually it is. She's my business." I rest my elbows on my knees and meet the cold expression on his face. "You will regret it, Mr. Matthews. If you do this to her, if you let her believe that you don't care about her beyond her accomplishments, you will never forgive yourself. And you will hurt her. More than you already have."

"And what do you know about that?"

It stings. That's what he's good at. He may not be my father, but I know him well enough. "I know what it's like to be left. You may not be leaving her physically, but you are leaving her. Leaving her to interpret how you feel about her, if she's done enough to earn your love, if she will ever do enough. All she's ever wanted was your attention, your approval.

You realize that right?"

He leans back, surveying me. "That's not true. She manages just fine."

I cough out a dry laugh. "Manages? Manages what? Feeling like everything she does isn't enough for you? Besides that, you want her to what…just *manage* to get by? Just manage for the rest of her life?"

"I'm not really sure what you're trying to get at here, Isaiah." He maintains the cool air about him, as if he's unfazed by it all. But I see it brewing under the surface. It'll ruin him if he lets it—the pride. The need to maintain ground that is crumbling.

He'll lose his daughter if he lets it.

"What I'm getting at is that you need to grow up," I say, uncaring at the angry shock in his eyes. "Your daughter asking you to express that you're proud of her isn't a weakness. Her wanting you to care about her beyond the field isn't stupid. It's human. She loves you. She wants to be able to talk to you, laugh with you. Don't you see that? You're her hero, whether you believe it or not. But if you continue this, she won't have one anymore. And you will regret every single day that you miss out on her being a part of your life. I'm asking you to grow up for her sake. Figure out your shit. Fix the relationship before there isn't one to fix."

Mr. Matthews rubs his hands together, avoiding my eyes. I know I've hit a mark. "And what makes you think you can come here and tell me that?"

"Going to be honest, sir, there wasn't much thinking involved. I love your daughter. And quite frankly, seeing her hurt pisses me off. I've hurt her myself by doing what I did. By leaving, which I don't plan on ever doing again. But what you're doing? Hurting her the way you are is bullshit. Aurora tries so hard to be what other people need. To be strong when they need her to be, to be a rock-hard shell so no one hurts the people she cares about. Unfortunately, she doesn't include herself in that shell. And you are poking at every vulnerable spot she has. And it's bullshit. So, no. I don't think I had any 'right' to come here, as you put it. But when you love someone the way I love her, there isn't much thinking involved anyway. She deserves to have someone stick up for her, and I'm more than happy to do it. Even to you."

I stand, no longer wanting to be in this room with a man so unwilling to see his faults.

Mr. Matthews doesn't say anything, just watches me.

"Have a good rest of your day." I turn and head back the way I came. It's quite possible that it ruined whatever relationship I hoped to have with her father now or in the future. But I can't bring myself to care. If there's even a chance it makes a difference, it's a loss I'm willing to take a million times over.

On the way back to the field, I make a few stops to appear like I was actually running errands. A few groceries, stuff for the apartment, for Raven, and I pick up coffee for the two of us. When I'm parked in the lot, I search the fields, finding Aurora instantly. Her curls are in a high poof, blowing in the wind behind her as she does her exercises across the field, where Maazina waits on the other end.

Her cheeks are rosy, and her smile is wide. Even just touching the field lights her up inside. I know without a doubt she'll be back out there before she even knows it.

With a deep breath, I pull my eyes away and reach for the envelope, pulling out the letters from my brother. And I comb over every word.

Every detail of his life for the past six years. The ups and the downs and the in-betweens. He got his degree and went to med school like he always planned and is currently doing his residency in Boston, hence the Massachusetts address. It's funny in an ironic way that we both had similar experiences in the haze of it all—mental health, medication. For different reasons but the similarity remains.

At the end of the letter, he wrote all of his contact information should I choose. His email, his phone number, and his address again. My grip tightens on the letters when I see it. The option is there. An open line of communication. But the fear remains.

If I call and he doesn't answer, what then? If I send a letter and it goes unread, where will that leave me? Back where I started?

And if I call and he does answer…what the fuck does that mean?

Am I ready for either of those possibilities?

With a sigh, the letters float into the passenger seat, and I turn my eyes back toward the field. Aurora must have noticed me because she waves excitedly with a big, bright smile.

My nerves settle at the sight of her. There was never a moment I doubted how much I loved her. Not a split second of time where that was ever a question. That hasn't changed; it never will.

I chuckle to myself when she sticks her tongue out before turning away. Whatever happens, I know it'll happen with her by my side.

That's all I've ever wanted.

Funny how some things fall apart and other things come together.

Life has a way of testing you, and you never know when, you never know how, and you never know what's included. But as long as my life includes her, I'll make it through.

Aurora is the dawn after an endless night.

And I plan on seeing every sunrise.

## You and Me

"Get off of me!" I wiggle, attempting to get out from under Isaiah, who is perfectly content on remaining on top of me. "You're such a goon, Isaiah. Come on."

The laugh that vibrates through his body echoes onto me. His palms land on the grass on either side of my head as he leans down. "What if I don't want to?

"Well, then we're going to be late for your birthday dinner."

"But if it's my birthday, shouldn't I get to do what I want?" he asks, and his chest brushes mine when he inhales.

"I suppose." I tip my chin up, our lips brushing. "I'd still like you to get off me."

Isaiah's eyes narrow playfully. "Why? You don't like this position?"

To no surprise, my cheeks burn. "Stop."

"Stop what? I happen to like where I am."

I turn my head to avoid eye contact, eyes looking over the field from my vantage point. "We need to finish—"

"I can help with that."

"Isaiah!" I bring my hands up between us to cover my face. Heat fans out over the entire surface of my face. "When did you get like this?"

With one hand, he remains steady overtop of me and removes my hands with the other. "I've obviously had to save every dirty joke I've ever thought of for you." He kisses me on the cheeks. "Good to know they're working."

"Get off." I hear the innuendo as soon as I say it, and when his eyes light up, I know he does to.

"I plan to." Isaiah laughs and pushes up, pulling me—red-faced and embarrassed and also quite hot—up with him.

"Get away from me." I step back, attempting to put some distance between us. Ignoring the ache building when I look at him, ignoring the flickers of heat licking at my skin, begging me to go to him.

It's obviously been years since we've explored each other like that. Every day, that gets harder and harder to ignore. And it's not that I'm purposely ignoring it, but it also feels like that last guard. The last ribbon yet to be cut. Once the line is crossed—that's it. I'd be lying if I said I wasn't a tiny bit scared. That those little fears are rearing their annoying heads and whispering in my ear.

"I don't want to be away from you." Isaiah closes the space with his long legs and traps me. His chosen method of attack is to kiss me anywhere he can. All over my face, my shoulders, my neck, and all the while, his fingers tickle my sides.

"Alright! You win, you win," I cry out with laughter following, and he stops. When I look up, he's got a big grin, complete with the dimple I love so much. Butterflies take flight in my stomach, a gentle feeling when it's regarding Isaiah.

"Now, let's finish your exercises so we can go."

"You mean, exactly what I wanted to do, but you were content to lay on top of me?"

Isaiah pinches my butt, and I squeal. "Precisely."

There's a pep to my step as we go through everything together. Isaiah helps with the stretches I can't do myself and walks beside me for anything else. I do a variety of things that haven't been approved but also things that have not been *explicitly* ruled out. I know my body. If it hurts, I stop. If it's uncomfortable, I continue. Side to side across the field, walking high knees. And Isaiah does it all with me. Maybe at a faster speed, but still, he's where I am whenever he's not teaching or writing.

Currently, he walks backward beside me. "Did you get me anything?"

"You can't just ask that."

"Well, I wouldn't to anyone normal. But it's you."

I snort. "You're such an idiot."

He reaches out and slaps my butt this time as we turn around. "Can't be mean to me on my birthday."

"I'm not!" I pull my knees up one at a time as we begin the trek back down the field.

"You're being a bit of a smartass," Isaiah says, trying and failing to sound the least bit serious.

"You like it." I raise a brow, eyes lingering on his lips. Jesus, I feel love struck and love sick all at once. If it's not Isaiah, I don't care to look at anything else.

His lips twitch, and he jogs in a circle around me. "When did I say that?"

"I can just tell." I approach him, slipping my hands under his shirt, reveling when I feel the slightest shiver roll over his skin. "Wanna know how?"

"Tell me."

"Because I know you." I rock up on my toes as best I can, and he dips his chin. "Better than anything else on the earth."

My lips brush his jawline before landing on his lips. Like clockwork, they move together like they were always meant to. Fireworks go off from my fingertips to the top of my head and crackle down my spine, leaving sparks behind. Isaiah groans, his fingers wrapping around the back of my neck, which makes my brain short circuit. Red hot heat floats over each of my nerve endings, leaving me at his mercy. His tongue gently sweeps over my lips, and I don't hesitate. He's a quick learner, and I'm pretty sure he knows me better than I know myself now and has kissed me in a way that might have changed my entire life.

I didn't know it was possible to be kissed the way he kisses me. Like it might be the last chance he'll ever get. As if in that kiss, he has to show me how much he wants me, how much he *needs* me. How much he loves me. In one fell swoop. In every kiss.

Being kissed by Isaiah is like standing under a midnight sky lit up with a million falling stars. A phenomenon all its own. A piece of magic in a tiny gesture.

His lips move against mine. His hands trace my skin, and the entire world falls away. The rest of it all ceases to matter when I'm under his spell.

"Matthews, get a goddamn room and get off my field." Coach Teller's voice is unmistakable. Especially with the use of a microphone.

My entire body burns, and I pull back from Isaiah, who's actively trying not to laugh. "Sorry, Coach," I yell back as loud as I can, and she waves her stupid microphone in the air.

When she's gone, I let my head land on his chest. "Oh, my fucking God. I can't believe this." He wraps his arms around me, but I can feel his intense laughter. "Stop it! I'm serious this time. I'm never kissing you in public again."

At that, he stops, pushing my hair back and tugging my head up. "Nonsense. You'll kiss me wherever and whenever you feel like it."

I roll my eyes.

"And anyway, that was the best gift you could've given me."

"You dickhead." I hit his chest and step back from him.

Isaiah plops a kiss on my cheek. "Come on. Let's get home and get ready."

He bends down and holds out his arms, and I climb up on his back like it's second nature. As always, he cradles my left knee with care, but his fingers are firm.

I rest my head on his shoulder. The spot that he gave me when I was a little girl crying after her first meaningful loss. The shoulder that got me through school and through my parents' divorce and has absorbed so many of my tears. I missed it. I'm happy it's back.

I'm happy it's mine again.

"Just get in the shower with me, Ro."

I put my hands on my hips. "We're already short on time. How is that going to help?"

"One shower instead of two."

"You really think your tattooed, naked body is going to make it a quick shower?"

He chuckles, eyes roaming leisurely over my body. "It's my party. We can be five minutes late."

"Five minutes, my ass. What fantasy world do you live in?" I ask, turning and petting Raven on the bed. "Oof!" Once again, I'm lifted off the ground. Raven watches me with bored eyes and a tail flicking back and forth. "Isaiah, don't you dare."

He carries me into his bathroom, where the steam is already lingering on the mirrors. "Aurora," I blink, "can I take your shirt off?"

My mouth gapes slightly before recovering. "I suppose."

"Is that a yes?"

Speechless, I nod. Suddenly, I'm as switched on as a livewire. Isaiah grips the bottom of my t-shirt and slowly lifts it up, drawing it over my skin, the fabric brushing against my now sensitive skin. It's tossed against the door.

"My turn." His eyes warm when they land on my cheeks.

"You want me to do it?" I squeak out.

"Yes."

I step forward and lift his own shirt off, purposely running my fingers over the smooth planes of his stomach and his ribs and over the ink on his chest. When I rock onto my tip-toes, Isaiah helps me out, pulling it the rest of the way off.

"How is this any quicker?" I breathe out.

Isaiah reaches for the band of my shorts. "Aurora?"

"Hm?"

"Shut up and enjoy it."

I swallow as he pulls the shorts down, palming over my thighs and the back of my knees. Whether he means to or not, he kneads my calf muscles on his way back up, stopping at the brace. "Off?"

"Mhm."

He pulls the brace off and sets it on the sink. And at the slow, leisurely pace of his, his shorts come down. Eventually, it all ends up in one pile, and my brain is on overdrive.

Isaiah pulls back the shower curtain. "Let's go." Behind me, his lips brush over my ear. "It's just me, Aurora. It's just you and me." He places a kiss on my neck. "Besides, there's no expectations here. Except to get all sudsy."

"Don't say the word sudsy."

I don't know why I'm nervous. What if I've changed too much? What if my body is different and unappealing to him? What if I fucking overthink my way into fucking this up?

"Aurora, stop overthinking it."

I sigh and step in under the spray of hot water. As the water hits Isaiah, I'm transfixed by the droplets clinging to his skin, sliding over his tattoos.

Reaching out, I trace a nail over some of the art on his arm. Isaiah watches me with those brown eyes that I love so much. "I was jealous of these when I first saw them."

"The tattoos?"

"Yeah." I'm grateful that he keeps his eyes connected with mine. "Or, more specifically, I guess the tattoo gun. Whatever. I was so messed up over the fact that it felt your skin when I couldn't. That it got to touch you and I didn't. It was incredibly dumb to be jealous over an inanimate object, but I was."

Isaiah's eyes crinkle, and I wrap my hand around his wrist.

"I guess it doesn't matter now."

"It doesn't. You can touch me as often as you'd like. Make up for lost time." He reaches over and grabs the soap. "But it wasn't dumb. I would see your posts, watch your games whenever I could, and I was jealous of everything and everyone. But all of that, it…it just doesn't matter anymore."

I nod, taking in my fill of Isaiah. He gets more beautiful every time I look at him.

"I can see the wheels spinning, Aurora. What're you thinking?" His voice is gentle, like his hands as they roam over my skin with soap.

Glancing down, I look at my own skin, my own body. We've been through a lot—ups and downs. Periods where I hated it, where I didn't understand why it was built the way it was. As I've gotten older, I usually view it through a neutral lens. It's usually under the scrutiny of someone else that I become aware of it again. It took a lot to understand that it was just a body and not something that determined anything else about me. So, I don't know why I'm apprehensive about it now—with Isaiah, of all people.

Maybe it's the years we lost. Maybe it's the injury making me doubt my body's abilities. Maybe it's just my stupid brain, who won't leave me alone.

And I hate how weak sharing vulnerabilities makes me feel. Like it's dumb to admit that I'm human.

"My body is—it's different now. What if you don't like it? What if you aren't attracted to me anymore?" It all comes rushing out, and I turn, facing the shower head instead of him. The water hits my face, dampens my hair, and still, I can only focus on the quick beating of my heart.

Isaiah's hands slide over my waist. "Rora, that's not fucking possible."

He moves his hands up, over my small breasts which are fully at attention, and back down my rib cage. Every trace of his hands makes me feel like I'm floating. The slow, sensual touches light up the surface of my skin, like being touched by the sun's rays. It feels like the word twinkling. That's the only thing I can think of. His fingertips, his hands, his touch—it makes me feel like I'm fucking twinkling.

"Your body is different. So is mine. We're older. But that doesn't mean I don't like it." He chuckles against my throat, kissing me there. "I've never had a single negative thing to say about your body, not even a thought. If you need me to prove it, I'm happy to do so every single day. Minute even. I'll get down on my knees and worship you if you want."

There goes my cheeks. "Not necessary."

"To be determined." Isaiah's hands roam over the swell of my hips, his lips not far from my skin. "There isn't a single thing about you I don't like, Aurora. Inside or out. You're beautiful and smart and strong, and I promise you, I'm still attracted to you. I always will be." He presses against me to prove it. "Anytime you feel like this, you tell me. But stop worrying. Stop thinking something is going to scare me away. And if you can't make it stop, you tell me."

My breath is gone, and there isn't any oxygen left in the room because Isaiah stole it. He continues his self-appointed job of soaping up my body, bending down and soaping my legs, gentle on my knee. Gentle on the curve of my butt, where he places a kiss on the swell. God, I haven't felt like this in so long. That euphoric feeling of being touched by someone who you want to touch you. Of feeling like you're the only two people on the planet.

Isaiah kisses his way up my spine and lands on my neck in the spot he quickly discovered drives me insane. Teeth nip at the sensitive skin, and a shiver runs through me despite the heat and the steam. I take the soap from him and turn around, facing him now that my unnecessary insecurities have taken a backseat.

"There's that beautiful face." Isaiah presses me forward until my back's against the shower wall, the hot water running over both of us.

He leans forward and kisses me slowly but passionately. I feel the kiss all the way to my toes. His hand is curled around my neck, pressing into the sides just so, and I'd like to say I'm not putty in his hands, but I am. Away from Isaiah, I am strong enough to get through the day, I can take care of myself and my friends and my loved ones. And I can put on a tough face. But with him, it all fades away. I don't have to be anything or anyone else but me.

I sigh into the kiss, hands draped over his shoulders, and let it all wash away. The rest of the world falls away because right now, Isaiah is the world. And I'd rather not miss a second of it.

"There she is."

I nip his lip. "Shut up."

"As you wish."

"Is this really the time to quote *The Princess Bride*?"

His thigh brushes against mine, grazing against the most sensitive part of myself. Heat fans out over my skin, and my breath hitches. "There is never a bad time."

I laugh, and so does he, our lips quickly fitting back into the rhythm. Then and there, I know without a doubt I never would've found this with someone else. The intricacies of intimacy. Being comfortable enough to tell a stupid joke in a desire-filled haze and jump right back into it. No date I ever went on even once gave me hope that it could become this. Maybe I always knew it wouldn't have mattered if it did—-because in the end, they never would've been him.

My lips press harder, hoping to convey all those lovesick thoughts onto him. He groans, and the sound is music to my ears. After too long of ignoring my lungs crying for oxygen, I pull back, short of breath, but Isaiah doesn't let up. Kisses are plastered everywhere on every inch of my face. My fingers press into his skin, holding myself tightly to him so he can never consider letting me go. The water cascades over us, and his grip on me never lets up. Teasingly, his hands move over the curves of my body, planting themselves on my waist.

"Can I touch you?"

Our eyes meet, and like always, there's so much to see. So much that is only for us to know.

Being looked at like that does something to a person. Changes you from the inside out. It peels back the layers of all the parts of yourself you've deemed rough and unpleasant, and it presents them to a person who will still find the beauty in something you've decided is ugly. It makes you feel like everything, every part of you, is beautiful and won't be looked at as anything else. Isaiah sees all of me, and I see all of him. Like a telescope into each other's personal galaxies. Every star that's burnt out, every icy planet, every uninhabitable surface is simply another layer to the person you love. Another part of them you get to discover and hold as gently as the rest of them.

His brown eyes are unwavering. Warm and open. And they're all for me. Isaiah is all for me. And I am all for him. No one else.

"Yes," I breathe out.

And he does—featherlight at first, tracing over the details of my body with a loving focus. Isaiah doesn't look away as his hand explores. I take in the details—how his eyes lighten when my breath hitches or how my fingers tighten on his skin. There isn't an ounce of space between us, the firmness of his body pressed against mine. Neither of us can get enough; we never will.

Isaiah finds my shoulder and kisses every ounce of skin he can until I feel his lips at my ear. "Ro, I hope you know I will never get enough of you."

He works me up, and it's like coming alive again. Seeing the sun for the first time. Seeing falling stars and feeling the ocean touching your skin on a hot day. All the while, his mouth finds the column of my neck and my cheeks and attacks them playfully.

I giggle in the midst of it all. "Isaiah," I say, the word turning into more of a plea.

His touch turns more frantic but never less attentive. Inside my chest, my heart attempts to escape, blood rushing through my veins, turning my skin hot and my brain to mush. Sensations burst and bloom, my eyes fluttering closed of their own accord as Isaiah takes me up and up. I know with him, it's safe to fall—in more ways than one.

A moan makes its way out of my mouth, and he catches it, kissing the side of my mouth with a smile I can feel. "That's it, Ro. It's you and me. Always."

Thoughts are useless, and he plays my body like a perfect chord.

Part of me could cry at being treated like this. The way he feels about me is shown in every breath, every caress. I couldn't ask for more, but I want to. I want to ask for everything. Everything he's willing and able to give me. Overdrive is the only word that comes to mind on how I feel. My skin, my nerves, my brain. Trying to catch up with it all.

"Let me have it, Aurora."

My nails dig into his skin at his words, at his encouragement. And my body is wound so tightly, I can sense the impending snap as it attempts to get closer to him, even though it's impossible. Isaiah tugs my head back, his fingers firmly in my hair, and kisses me again—deeply, thoroughly—and I fall apart by way of his hand and his lips. Stars blink behind my eyelids, and the tightness in my lower stomach unfurls in the most intoxicating way, fanning out in pulses, making it difficult to breathe. Making it difficult to do anything but lean on Isaiah and hold onto him like he's my lifeline.

"That's it, baby. Good." He presses a soft kiss to my lips. The shockwaves continue, sporadically firing out. "I've got you. Good job, baby."

He takes every sweet, desperate sound that leaves my lips and every tug and press of my fingers until it all slowly fades away. A shooting star falling into the horizon. When I blink my eyes open, I'm met with a gentle smile and hooded eyes. I place my hands on his cheeks and pull him to me, unable to keep myself from kissing him again. And again and again.

"I like greedy Aurora," he murmurs against my lips. I can feel his heart beating in his chest against mine.

"Shut up."

"You know, you say that a lot, but I have evidence that suggests you'd rather me not." I give him another kiss, my hand sliding lower over his damp skin, but he stops me. "Later," he says, kissing the center of my palm. "We're gonna be late, after all."

I roll my eyes, my lips forming a pout. "But it's your birthday." And besides, I want to touch him. Want to make him feel like I did. I want him to see stars when he thinks of me like I do him.

Isaiah shakes his head. "I got my gift."

With a fluttering heart, I know the world gave me the best gift of all when they created Isaiah and sent him to me. There'll never be another like him. I could've spent every day of my life looking to find something that didn't exist. Isaiah is irreplaceable. No one could touch me the way he does or look at me the way he does or know the ins and outs of who I am like he does. He's got this way of making life feel fuller. He makes the world bigger.

For the rest of my days, I know I'm lucky to be here with him.

And nothing on this earth could ever compare.

# My Little Secret

"I'm almost done," I say, running the product through my curls one last time when Isaiah appears behind me in the mirror.

He leans against the wall, ready to go aside from the fact that his shirt remains unbuttoned and the black ink is visible on his brown skin. It's proven to be quite the distraction.

Isaiah steps closer. "No rush. I'm enjoying the show."

I pull out the diffuser I've now started keeping here—along with a few hangers in his closet and a drawer and a bag in his bathroom. The sound overpowers the music playing, and Isaiah watches as I roam it around, fluffing my hair as I go with the gentle heat. When it's enough, I shut it off.

Before I can do it myself, his hands are in my hair. "I love your hair like this." And to my surprise, he fluffs it exactly as I would, tugging a few curls as he sees fit, but I'm too entranced by his hands in my hair and how good it feels. He plops a kiss on my cheek and taps my butt.

"You look gorgeous. Get dressed, and let's go."

"Bossy." I raise a brow in the mirror, touching up the gloss on my lips. He watches the movement.

"If we don't leave now, we never will, and I'll personally drag you into bed," he says, beginning to button his shirt, which makes me pout. "No. No pouting at me. Or we will really never leave." Isaiah presses this thumb to my lips, and my tongue gently taps it. His brown eyes turn molten, and I can't help but smile.

I run a hand over his chest as I exit, dragging my fingers over the skin before it disappears, and wiggle my eyebrows playfully. Quickly, I slip my dress over my trusty, athletic spandex that are required under any dress, and the brown fabric contrasts my skin and sticks to my curves.

"Jesus Christ," Isaiah muses from the doorway, his eyes taking a slow path over my body. "We have to leave. Now."

I smile, enjoying the power he gives me, whether he's aware of it or not. "I'm coming, I promise." I search for my shoes in the midst of my stuff and slip them on. Every second that passes, the heat from his gaze singes my skin. Moments later, we're heading out the door, my jacket draped over my arms, and on the way to the restaurant for Mr. Birthday Boy.

"Oh, no."

"What?" He looks over at me, hand squeezing my thigh.

"Everyone is going to learn that you're younger than me. What if they call me a cougar?"

Isaiah snorts. "It's three months, Aurora."

"Have you met Maazina?"

"Fair enough."

Smiling, I turn up the music and sit back, tracing my finger over his knuckles and the ink on the back of his hand. Little does he know, being late was absolutely on purpose. I had excuses lined up if needed, but it worked out in our favor. We're having *dinner* at a bar similar to our air hockey bar. Only this one has much more than just air hockey… It has ski-ball, pool, darts, pinball, and so many others. And I rented the entire thing out.

We park quickly and approach the restaurant, which appears as if it's open as usual. When we walk inside, a big cacophony of voices shouts, "Happy birthday!", and surprise flickers over Isaiah's face. He gives my hand a squeeze, and I smile up at him.

"Happy birthday."

I was nervous about this because I know he hasn't made many friendships of his own here yet, so once he invited the idiot brigade, I took over planning. It's my family and friends, but I wanted him to know they're his, too. There's a cake on the bar top that I had made and a personalized menu for his birthday for drinks and food. And the restaurant has a photobooth, which I prepaid for.

"You didn't have to do all this, Ro," Isaiah murmurs, a hint of insecurity in his eyes. Like he doesn't deserve it.

"I wanted to. First birthday together again. I wanted to make it special." I squeeze his hand, my thumb running over our birthday tattoo.

We approach, and not only does Maazina have on a plastic party hat but also a kazoo that she blows way too loudly, hand in hand with Joey and Zaza, who have also been given said kazoos. "Ready," she says to the kids, and they grin. "Happy birthday, Isaiah!"

He grins and immediately opens his arms for the girls. With full arms, he still finds a way to somehow hug Maazina. "Thank you."

She winks at me. "Of course." It thrills me how much she has welcomed him in. It's a small group, but they all come forward and wish him happy birthday. Maazina threads her arm with mine, resting her head on my shoulder. "I can't believe how pretty he is, and *you*, of all people, got him."

"I resent you," I say, though it's a moot point when I laugh anyway.

"Seriously, what kind of deals did you and Soph make with the devil?" Maazina's eyes flicker between Isaiah and Kian. "They're fucking beautiful. It's not fair."

"Your crush on Kian is deeply unsettling."

"Oh, get over it." Maazina sighs, and I watch Sophia and Kian, hand in hand, talking to Isaiah. "I just want my own unfairly beautiful man. Is that too much to ask for?"

"Not at all." There's no one more deserving of love than Maazina after all she's been through. After the obvious, Maazina is the person I'd lay my life down for. I want her to be happy like I want the sun to keep rising.

She turns her eyes up at me. "Are you going to become all optimistic and sappy now?"

I snort. "No."

"Good. You optimistic would be…weird."

Sylvia and Viv are talking to him now, along with my mom. It's funny; he looks shy now with all the attention. A nice reminder that I get the full, unfiltered version of him.

"Can I be sappy for a minute?" Maazina asks, leading us to the open bar to grab drinks.

"By all means."

"It's funny watching you two interact with each other versus other people."

"How so?" I take a sip of my requested apple juice.

"Obviously, I've only seen tidbits, but you guys both come alive with each other. Not that you aren't with us, but you're lighter with him. More open. You laugh more. Like you suddenly feel like you don't have to be on guard with the rest of the world. And he's the same. I've never seen him look shy with you—not like he does right now. But when it's you two, you both come alive."

Pretty sure my heart grows three sizes. At that exact moment, he looks over his shoulder at me with a soft smile.

"Good God, you two make me sick." Maazina downs her drink. "I love it."

I clear my throat. "Thank you for that."

Maazina rests on my shoulder. "You deserve to be happy. You know that, right?" I hum, not willing to answer. "And I'm happy he's back. I know it was hard, but God, you love him. I'm happy the person you love gives you the safety to be soft."

In response to her words, my throat tightens. I haven't told Isaiah I love him yet. He hasn't said anything since the carnival. Obviously, I love him, but I've been fearful to admit that I *love* him. You know? That I was in love with him. That I'm not sure I ever stopped being in love with him.

Isaiah stands in the center of the room. Looking at him here and now, it sinks in. How deep it goes. Each of our roots intertwined with each other at such a young age. Underneath the layers of who we are individually is a layer made up of who we are together. There is no undoing them, no untangling the roots beneath the soil. Not without ripping out pieces of who we are in the process.

I thought—hoped—that the love would fade away. That if I couldn't have him, I wouldn't be reminded of that every single day. I succeeded in acting like it was. In pushing it down and burying it. But I know it never left. The love I had for him was a part of who I was, and I would've recognized the void if that root had died.

Instead, I simply acted as if a part of me didn't exist.

But no matter how hard I tried, the moment he came back and every moment since, that part of me has rebloomed and demanded to be seen.

It sounds fucking ridiculous, I know, but nothing else makes sense.

A part of me came back to life when he came back into mine.

I don't think either of us is the other's moon and stars. We aren't these grand things that came and changed the course of our lives. We are just two halves of a whole. Two kids that grew up together and whose lives became so intertwined, there was no use in trying to separate them.

When he was gone, it was like missing a puzzle piece. A piece that found its spot immediately upon return. Flowers that had been living in a drought were watered again.

We are whatever the other person needs. A grounding force in a crowded room. A safety net when fear becomes overwhelming. A life vest on a rough sea. A light in the dark. For me, Isaiah is everything in one. Home, safety, friendship. Love.

I could've spent years searching for it—searching for a house to call home—but it would've been like haunting the hallways instead.

Maybe it's naïve to think I never would've gotten over Isaiah, but it's honest. It's a truth I feel down to my bones. Days and months and years could've passed, and it might have gotten easier to ignore the sharp pains when I thought of him, but they never would've stopped. I would've only been able to share minute pieces of myself, a shallow version that offered nothing of substance or sense of permanence.

It wouldn't have been fair to others, and it wouldn't have been fair to myself.

Isaiah meets my eyes, and something settles within. As if my heart was holding its breath and got to exhale. Heat spreads out from my veins to the tips of my fingers—a warm embrace on a cold night.

Even from a distance, I see it reflected in those gorgeous, brown eyes. In the softness that comes over his features when he looks at me. It's a strange feeling, looking at someone and knowing they love you back. There is always fear there. That maybe the love isn't as full or it's a different shape, but with Isaiah…the reward is worth the risk. I know Isaiah loves me as I love him.

"There is more sap in your eyes than in a goddamn maple tree," Maazina muses.

If anyone can break me out of a reverie, it's her. "I hope you plan on donating your brain to science one day."

She grabs another drink. "I do."

We gravitate toward the center, and Isaiah is next to me in the next breath, his hand immediately finding my hip, our bodies pressed together. Maazina raises a brow at us but says nothing. Everyone is chatting with one other. Kian is playing one of the games with the girls, and Isaiah and I have a moment of just us.

"Can I have a sip?"

I hold out my drink. "It's apple juice."

"I expected nothing less."

Though other people are around, it doesn't feel like it. When he's finished, Isaiah moves closer, giving me a sweet kiss. He tastes like apple juice and Isaiah. Safe and warm.

Against my lips, he murmurs, "I thought you weren't going to kiss me in public anymore."

I did say that. What a shame. I've been blinded and eaten alive by how in love with him I am. Disgusting. "Well, we all say things we don't mean sometimes." I peck him with three soft kisses before pulling back.

Isaiah turns to me, and I see so much reflected in the encompassing brown of his eyes. A twinkle, as silly as that sounds. He looks at me like I'm his whole world. The sureness in his gaze is overwhelming, stealing my air the longer I'm entranced. Six years without him was hard. So much was happening in my career that I was proud of, excelling in, yet the entire time, the ground underneath me felt unsteady. Being here with him again has carefully filled every crack in the ground, given me a solid path to walk on, and to be able to do that without fear that it's going to fall away again.

"Hm. Give me another one." His hand presses into the small of my back, leaning in and nudging my cheek with my nose. I'm overwhelmed at the affection that emanates from him flawlessly. Of course, I give in— there are no conditions required, no hoops to jump through for him.

Against his lips, I murmur, "Happy birthday, Isaiah. I'm happy you're here."

Here with me. Here by my side.

Isaiah exhales. "Me, too." He pulls back enough to look me in the eyes. They're full of life and warmth. They, much like the rest of him, feel like home. "You're the best gift I could've gotten."

Just like that, my heart locks itself away in his hands and throws out the key. And that's exactly where it belongs.

The city skyline shines in the distance, cool air wrapping around us as it whips through the grass. Isaiah's party was a success. He smiled the entire time—even when we all sang "Happy Birthday" with his mom on facetime. I love seeing him happy, surrounded by people that have known him, and people that are getting to know him and beginning to love him.

Underneath us, the blanket crinkles as I adjust on my stomach, resting my face in my palm.

Between us is dessert from the party—also containing the famous chocolate cake. Music hums from the tiny speaker Isaiah pulled out of his car. Above us, stars twinkle in the sky, visible out here away from the bright, city lights.

"Favorite part of the day?" I ask. "Besides me, of course."

Isaiah chuckles. "Kian getting a cupcake shoved in his face by his daughters."

Chocolate melts on my tongue. "Those girls are going to give him hell."

"Yeah, I wonder where they learned that from."

"If you are implying that Sophia and I are anything other than perfect angels, I'll shove a cupcake in your face."

"Would never." Isaiah fixes me with a gentle look. "Besides, you said it yourself. You were the best part of my day. Start to finish."

Leaning over, I brush a crumb of chocolate from above his lip, and he catches my thumb with his teeth. A steady pulse thrums through my blood. "Flattery isn't needed here, Isaiah."

"I like to see you flustered."

Isaiah pushes the desserts out the way and crawls over to me. "What are you doing?"

"You're too far away," he says, settling on top of me. My hips bracket him in, his forearms resting near my head—just enough of him on me that I feel his weight.

I hope we can always be this close.

Reaching up, I run a finger over his jaw, down his neck, and find the ink on his skin. Isaiah leans into the touch, a soft sigh escaping his lips. "Earlier, when I said you were the best gift I could've gotten, I meant it." Our chests brush on my inhale. "You are that and much more, Aurora. To me, you're everything."

"Isaiah—"

"Let me finish." A quick kiss has me agreeing, not that I wouldn't have anyway. "You are at the center of my life. Everything I do, everything I dream of in the future, has you front and center. From the moment I came back, I was not going to settle for a life without you in it. Because a life without you isn't a life I'm interested in."

Every word is punctuated by the steady beat of his heart against mine. The movement of his chest against mine, his body against mine. Thankfully, the weight keeps me in the moment and not floating off into oblivion.

"Aurora Jade," he murmurs against my lips. Around us, the air is statically charged. A tiny flame from a match could set it on fire.

"I've been fighting against telling you this already so soon, but I don't know why. You are the light of my life. The sunrise in the morning and the sunset in the evening. You are every moment in between—from the minute to the grand, you are in every detail of my life. "

Our foreheads touch, and the depth of my heart expands, carefully latching onto every word he says and tucking it away in the crevices. Isaiah never stops looking at me. Not for a second.

"I've wanted to tell you the moment I saw you. even though you were hurt and furious, I wanted to say it. To make up for the time I put between us."

I'm caged in by him, his arms resting near my head, fingers trailing over the curls near my ears. By his body pressed against mine and wrapped up in the gentleness and heartbreaking tenderness of what he's saying. What I think he's about to say.

"I love you, Aurora. And it's about time you know it."

Like the deep-down sap I am, I can't help the few tears that fall. Tears that Isaiah kisses away.

It's not the first time he's said it. At the carnival, he told me he'd never loved anyone like he did me, but this…it's different.

This is everything he didn't say.

"I've loved you since we were little kids and you punched that boy for breaking my glasses," he says, his lips turning up. "I have loved you every day for as long as I can remember. Walking to school together, watching you play. Growing up with you. You cemented yourself in my life a long time ago, and you never left."

My voice is wet when I say, "Isaiah, you're killing me." I brush my thumb over his lips.

He nips it with his teeth. "Shut up and let me then."

I chuckle as more tears fall, heat unfurling over my skin like petals in the sun.

"I'll never forget the day I realized I was in love with you for the first time. You just finished a rain game, and you came off the field with this smile on your face. Your cheeks were flushed, and I just remember you being so alive. It was such a simple moment but something so integral to who you are, and I fell in love before I even knew what love really was. I have fallen in love with you over and over again since that moment. With the way you are so strong and steady for the people in your life, your unfailing determination, your kindness. Your vulnerability that not many people get to see. Your stubbornness, your playfulness. The way you love people."

Boy, oh boy, do I want to fucking die. But like floating up on a cloud die. That doesn't make sense, but I stopped thinking straight moments ago.

"I have fallen in love with every aspect of you multiple times. And every time, I get to discover something new. It never gets old. Falling in love with you is like discovering new constellations. But one that only I can see. Every freckle, every scar, the varying degrees of your laughter, the inflection in your voice when you're teasing me, the blush on your cheeks at all times. Each part of you is a star in my constellation. It makes me obsessive."

"You're so dramatic," I say, though it comes out like a sob.

Isaiah smiles softly, his brown eyes a direct line to his heart, and there is so much love there. I feel like I'm drowning in it, yet in the next second, he's the oxygen that saves me.

"And you are the love of my life."

His hands push my curls away from my face, and he dots kisses over the entirety of my face. Even the tears that will not stop falling. When my brain starts working again, my arms wrap around him, and with a firm hold, I pull him fully on top of me. I don't need real air. I need him.

Isaiah's answering chuckle vibrates against my body as our lips touch. The salt from my tears mixes in, but it doesn't stop him. Doesn't stop his tongue from swiping over my lips or his hands from holding me tight.

My heart wants to burst out of my chest. I do love him. So much. Yet there is still a part of me that is scared to say it out loud. Scared that if I admit how in love with him—how pathetically, irreversibly in love with him I am—the world will take it away from me. So, I show him as best I can. With hands that are begging him to never let me go and kisses that I hope tell him how desperate I am for him.

Another sob breaks through, and I pull back to inhale.

"I know, baby." Isaiah brushes another tear. He rolls us over, cradling my knee as he does so, and pulls me into his chest. For moments, I stay there, cradled in his arms, letting him know me better than I know myself.

I blow a raspberry when I'm able to breathe again. From this angle, I look down at him, my lips finally turning up into a smile.

A strong hand squeezes the back of my thigh. "There's my Aurora." From the back of my thigh, his hand starts a slow crawl upward over my spine until it lands at the base of my neck. "I love that you let me see this. Given how much you like to act impenetrable, I'm grateful that I get to see this. Your feelings out in the open."

"Don't tell anyone." Our lips brush when I speak, and heat flares in his eyes.

"Wouldn't dream of it. It's my little secret."

"So much of me is." A kiss seals my words between us. Nobody gets me like he does. There's an intimacy between us that doesn't exist with anyone else.

Parts of me that belong only to him.

With my hands cupping his cheeks, my thumbs brush under his eyes, and I whisper against his lips, "I'm all yours, Isaiah."

## Tomorrow, I'll Love You

Isaiah was sculpted by some greater life force.

That's the conclusion I come to as I stare at his sleeping form. Without a shirt, I admire every inch—the curve of the muscles and the leanness of his body covered in ink. His face is serene and gentle, his lips slightly parted and his eyelashes fanning over his cheeks.

Raven is curled up on his abdomen as she has been since I fed her an hour ago. I rest my mug on my nightstand and sit back against the headboard with my poetry book in my hands. The one he annotated for me. The one with pages decorated with tabs and highlights and folded corners.

To no surprise, the pages are dotted with teardrops.

I run my thumb over my current page, over the pen scribblings in the margins that he left. Even so, I fan back to the dedication page, where he wrote, *To Aurora, the dawn of every one of my days.* There's something to be said for hearing—or in my case, reading—just how important you are to someone. To know that even apart, he felt this way about me. It's a gut-wrenching feeling. One that makes me both happy and sad. Happy that he loved me that much, even then. And sad that we were apart.

I bring my good knee up and rest the book against it, thumbing through the pages. His scrawl is on every page, some sections underlined, sections of entire poems rewritten, and personal notes to me. I love the way certain letters curl underneath and become this hybrid print-cursive mix. I love that it feels like something he needed to do. And I love that it's mine.

On "Still You", he notes he once called it "Still Yours" and wrote about all the ways I still had his heart, that part of him would always call me home.

On one titled "A.J.M", after my initials, he wrote it was once a prose poem. The final version is a long form, where the first word of each line spells out my name. The first time I read it, I could barely get through it. Once again, tears fall when I read his notes.

And it goes on and on. From "Surefire" to "Five Letter Word" to "Still Feel It All", I collect all of it and lock it away close to my heart.

"Rora?" Isaiah's sleepy voice breaks through the silence like a sunray through the dark.

I glance over at him, intoxicated by how beautiful and peaceful he looks. "Morning, sleepy head."

His eyelids flutter, remaining closed, but his lips turn up to a smile. Raven stretches out on his stomach and plops over to the end of the bed. Isaiah rolls toward me, stretching his long, tattooed arms above his head before his hand lands on my left leg.

"How's the knee?" he asks, like he does every morning, while his fingers gently press around it and run gently over the scar. It's such a gentle, thoughtful touch and one that he does without thinking. It makes my throat tight every time.

"A bit sore but okay. I have another MRI next week."

Isaiah kisses my arm in response but finally blinks those beautiful, brown eyes open. They widen when he sees the book in my hand, then the tear tracks on my cheeks.

"I feel like I've made you cry a disproportionate amount."

I snort. "No shit."

He sits up and pulls me to him, a gentle finger under my chin turning my lips to his.

"I have coffee breath."

Without a word, Isaiah practically crawls over me to grab my mug. He takes a long sip before he sets it down and returns to hover over my lips. "Happy now?"

Heat floods my cheeks. "I suppose."

"Good. I'll take that kiss any minute now, Miss Matthews." Isaiah's voice is raspy, and it sends a chill down my spine. My smile grows without thinking. I do as he says. Sinking into the ease of this—of this kiss. The kiss feels like the morning sun. Warm and gentle, growing stronger with every second.

After a moment, he pulls back, giving me three quick pecks before pulling me into his chest. His right arm snakes around until his hand finds my curls. "Did you read the last one yet?"

"No. I haven't read that one ever." Looking up at him, he raises a brow. "Emotional damage and all. Had a feeling."

Isaiah's lips quirk. His fingers roam over the sensitive skin of my neck. "Can I read it to you?" he asks, words soft in the early morning light.

With my heart puttering and pattering in my chest and my tear ducts on high alert, I nod and settle into his body. He takes the book and flips to the final poem, "Today, Tomorrow". Under the tangle of my curls, his palm settles on my neck, fingers firm and tangled in my hair. The touch is grounding and comforting, I think, to both of us.

Isaiah clears his throat and begins, "Today, I miss you."

The first line tells me I was right to be emotionally nervous. Isaiah's voice becomes tender with a smooth cadence as he reads. The first verse or two feels like that moment before something big: a break up, a jump scare. Something your heart races at without yet knowing why.

He continues, "Confusion looms like clouds in the sky, wondering where you have gone? And where have I? Hope is the guise of which I stand under. It blooms in the rays of sun you left behind, breaking wondrously through the dark sky of heavy silence. Left to my own devices, I ruminate, what day was it, when I left you?"

With one hand he holds the book, and with the other, he holds me. Every word has drawn me closer until I'm as pressed against him as I can be. Every time we discuss the time apart, in any capacity, pain is strung on the words like Christmas lights. My throat tightens as I try to hold the tears back.

"Today, I miss you because that is all that I can do. But if you let me, tomorrow, I'll love you."

His fingers tug at my curls as he sets the book down. My chest rattles as I inhale, and his arms wrap around tight, pulling me into him. I feel his breath on my neck, under the stray curls and the kiss he places on the hot skin. Turning, I pull his lips to mine.

A few stray tears slide down my cheeks, finding their way to our lips. It's more of an embrace than anything, holding ourselves to each other for all the years we didn't.

Isaiah pulls back, our lips still touching. His eyes glisten, but no tears fall. The unshed water illuminates his brown eyes that know me better than I know myself.

"Sometimes, when it felt especially unbearable regarding us," he whispers against my lips so quietly, I strain to hear him, "I told myself all I had to do was make it to tomorrow. That if I made it through the day, there was a chance I'd get to love you again."

My hand cups his cheek, running back and forth over a tiny scar on his cheekbone. My heart is beating heavily in my chest, and I know his is doing the same.

"It was silly. But the slim possibility of loving you again kept me going day after day, Aurora. You were everywhere. You are everywhere."

If this was a cartoon and I was a character, I would've exploded into heart-shaped confetti.

I exhale, kissing him again. Trying to show him all the things I'm unable to say yet. To kiss him until he understands that all my days were spent thinking of him, too. Even on the days I wanted to forget, he was there. Haunting me. And today, I'm more grateful than ever for him. For this.

Isaiah squeezes tighter, playfully nipping my lip, and the air in the room changes. Like he's bringing us back into the present, where we're tangled up in each other. A giggle—a goddamn *giggle*—leaves my lips. Despite the tear streaks and the emotions dancing on my nerves, the touch of his lips and teasing touch makes me smile.

His brown eyes find mine. "And now, I have you here." Playfully, he nips every inch of my neck, up to my chin, tickling my sides as he goes. "Right where I want you."

And that's right where I want to be.

I know I could do anything anywhere as long as Isaiah is by my side.

Requesting a trade has been on my mind more than I'd like to admit.

An ache spreads through my veins as I watch the team from the sidelines. Could I leave this team? Could I leave them? In front of me, soccer balls pass in and out of my view as they complete their drills.

There's an ache that I've had since I went down on the field, since my knee gave out on me. It's endless and constant. I want to be out there with my hair flying around my face, sweat on my nose, and my body burning with the exertion of something I excel at. But I'm here. On the sidelines. Wondering what my future holds.

Across the field, with a second group of girls, stands my dad. There's an ache there too, one fueled by anger. I'm not willing to stay here if it's going to destroy any hope of us having a relationship in the future. Or if it's going to make me more resentful.

But then, there's Isaiah. I won't do anything without asking him first. Not that I'm even sure if this is feasible, but I won't do it if he can't find another job or if he wants to settle here. Because I want to settle here. I don't want to leave.

Philly is home. This team, this field, my family—this is home.

But if part of my home is going to act like I don't exist, I can't stay.

Turning away, I finish my exercises on the sidelines as the team finishes up their drills. I approach the stands, where Isaiah sits with a notebook. He got here about thirty minutes ago after his class, with a notebook in hand and glasses over his eyes.

Brown eyes meet mine just as I stop, resting my hands. "You okay?" I look over my shoulder again at my dad, at the team, at my coach. "Rora," he muses knowingly.

"Yes and no." My teeth pick at my lip, but Isaiah leans forward, plucking my lip with his thumb.

"Just tell me."

I roll my eyes, though my stomach does its own gymnastics routine. "Would you hate me if we had to move out of Philly?" I sniff. "I mean, assuming you would come with me if you had to, or if that's not even something I should be think—"

"Breathe, Ro." Isaiah smirks. "Number one, I go where you go. Number two, why do you think we need to leave Philly?"

"I was thinking of requesting a trade." Shock filters down over his features, but he waits for me to go on. "I can't…I can't work with him anymore. It's always been hard, but it was manageable. Normal. But now, it's unbearable. I think about coming back and I'm overwhelmed by the fear of what he's going to think if it takes me a game or two or five to get back into the swing of it. Terrified of what happens if I'm not the same player. And that's not what I want."

I swallow, looking at my girls with big smiles on their faces, despite the hard practice. "I want to be excited to play again, to play with them. But I can't do that under his thumb."

"Have you talked to your coach?" Isaiah leans forward, pushing his glasses up the bridge of his nose.

"No. I wanted to talk to you first."

His eyes soften. "I'm not going to tell you not to do something if you think that it'll make you happier. If leaving is what you need to do, fine. But talk to your coach first. Let's take some time, okay?"

"Okay." I twist my lips. "Thank you."

"'Course."

"What are those?" I point to the photos peeking out of his notebook.

"Elijah. He must've gotten my letter." Isaiah pulls them out, fanning them between his fingers.

It wasn't much of a letter—not that he had to respond at all. Mostly just expressed that he appreciated it and that he was glad he was doing well. I watched him write and erase, *I love you, and I miss you*, almost ten times. I was sure Elijah could probably read the words through the eraser markings. But I understood why he didn't, given how scary it is to be vulnerable with someone who's hurt you in the past.

"It's short. He said that these were all photos he took that he wanted to share with me. Postcards with notes on the back."

Handing them to me, I flip through photos of Elijah getting into med school, moving to Boston for his residency, photos of books he loved, movie tickets, meeting his other residents, getting a cat who looks scarily like Raven. It's memories upon memories of times where he writes he thoughts about Isaiah.

"You okay?" It's my turn to ask.

"It's fucking weird. Seeing all these things I could've been a part of." He runs his hand over his curls, and when it drops, I wrap my fingers around his wrist, resting on our tattoo. Under my finger, I feel his pulse increase and then slow, steadying. "I wish I could be mad. I *want* to be mad. But I can see how happy he becomes as the time passes. How he settles into himself and his life."

"It's okay if you are. It doesn't mean you love him any less. You can be mad at the people that you love, Isaiah," I say. He twists his hand, intertwining our fingers over the barrier. When he doesn't speak, I continue, "And it wouldn't surprise anyone if you wanted to talk to him. Doesn't make you weak if you want a relationship with your brother again, okay?"

Instead of answering, he squeezes my hand three times, and I squeeze his in response. The two of us read each other like pages in our favorite book. We could probably do it blindfolded on memory alone. It's a strange sensation being able to see and know someone with that kind of confidence. To know what they're thinking before they do.

In the haze, a whistle blows in finality.

"Go on. I'll be right here waiting." Isaiah kisses my cheek.

I walk backward towards the team, his kiss lingering on my cheek, as all his kisses have. He sits back, arm stretching out over the seat next to him. Even from a distance, the heat of his gaze singes my skin, setting every nerve ending ablaze.

Six years was a long time without him.

But I know that we have the rest of our lives because he'll wait for me. He'll follow me. And I him.

We will be there every step of the way for each other, for every tomorrow to come.

# FLASHBACK

## *Isaiah, Spring 2015*

It was downpouring. The rain hadn't let up for hours, plastering all of us, including the girls on the field. My eyes fall back to Aurora at the center of the defense, the curls loose from her ponytail plastered to her cheeks, only held back by a thin band of pre-wrap. But she loves the rain, loves playing in the rain.

I swear she just likes the mud.

On the scoreboard, it remains zero-zero with less than twenty minutes left to the whistle. Until overtime. Aurora and her defense have been unstoppable but so have their opponents. The offense continuously stopped on each side of the field. Behind me, the stands are filled to the brim under the pouring rain. I was too nervous to sit, so I've been watching from the fence.

This would be Aurora's only championship at this school. Her first two years were a rebuild. They made the playoffs but never got all the way. Last year, they lost in a nailbiter—scored in the last five minutes of the game, something Aurora blamed herself for. So, I know how much she wants this. I can see the fire in her eyes on a game day, the adrenaline rushing through her veins.

She's already got a scholarship for college in the fall. The championship isn't a need for anything other than herself. Aurora needs it.

All of a sudden, the other team makes a break. A forward heading straight down, straight toward Aurora. Even from a distance, I see the smile that wants to break free. This is her domain, her joy, her life. Her feet are lightning quick as she moves into position. The rain batters the players, but they barely look phased. Aurora backpedals with the forward for a moment, containing her and forcing her one way. I see the moment as she does. With a sure, quick foot, Aurora steals the ball right from under her and quickly finds her open midfielders.

As she goes to pass it, the forward tackles her—a low blow considering she's coming from behind, but it's useless. Aurora already got the ball off her foot. When she stands, she's covered in mud and has a huge smile on her face.

See? I knew she just liked the mud.

Unfortunately, her pass doesn't end in a goal, but the team keeps fighting. Though I should be focusing on the game, I can't help but let my eyes remain on Aurora with more focus. Somehow, there's a streak of mud still on her cheek. Her uniform clings to her skin in the rain. With every stride, the muscles in her legs are prominent. Even now, a senior in high school, she is phenomenal. And she's only going to get better.

Exhaling, I turn to watch them lead another attack, but all I can think about is kissing her after this.

The crowd behind me starts cheering in harmony as the girls push up into their opponents' half. And I just feel it. This is it. There's less than five minutes left, but they move the ball around the field smoothly, confidently. A beaten defender. Another. A beautiful crossing pass and our top forward is right there to put a foot on it.

And it goes easily into the corner of the net.

The crowd explodes, and the girls find each other in the center of the field for a quick celebration. Now, they just have to hold it. Aurora claps, backpedaling to fall into position as they reset. The clock ticks down, and my heart is at a constant state of anxiety.

Finally, the clock stops—a steady two-minute warning on the display. And the opponents make one last effort. Already in Aurora's half, they push, connecting three solid passes. Aurora surges back, taking the space of one of her defenders. Her eyes are narrowed and focused as the girl approaches her.

She has to tackle her. It's a dangerous play, given the opposition's position. But it's that or risk a shot.

Aurora goes for it. For a second, as they fall, it's chaos. No idea if she went and got the ball, or if she'll be called for a dirty tackle. But the play goes on. Aurora clears the ball up field, and no whistle sounds.

And that's it. Everyone knows it.

A slow smile spreads over her beautiful, rain-soaked face.

The whistle blows three times, and the crowd goes wild.

I watch her with a grin as she celebrates with her team. I love seeing her like this. Jumping up and down with adrenaline, a big smile on her face after a game, especially one where she played incredibly well. She's a force to be reckoned with. From the chaos of her team huddle, she finds me in the distance, wearing her jersey. And I didn't think it was possible, but her smile spreads wider. My pulse steadies. The world clears, as it always does when I look at her.

Watching her, seeing her come alive as they lift the trophy, I realize how head over heels in love with her I am. I've loved her as long as I've known her. As fully as we can in our adolescence, but this is different.

It feels different.

Though I'm pretty sure I've been in love with her for a while now, it's just decided to sink in.

Like an epiphany.

It felt like there was this vague picture in the back of my mind, but it wouldn't come into focus. Similar to when I'm writing. Sometimes, I know what I want to write, but I can't see it. And I can't force it. It has to come to me. And this feels like that. When the blur clears and suddenly the pen is flying across the paper.

It's crystal clear.

Eventually, after pictures and celebrations, she makes her way to me. She greeted her parents, Sophia, Kian, and Azalea first, and they were trailing after her, but they've fallen back. Probably Sophia's doing. She knows things, even when Aurora doesn't tell her.

Aurora's smile is bright in the dim rain. "Hi."

Without hesitating, I pull her in for a hug. "You played fucking great out there."

"Isaiah," she whines, "I'm sweaty and drenched."

"I don't care," I say, into her wet, tangled mess of curls. And I don't. Not in the slightest. All I care about is the way my nervous system calms down. Pulling back, my hands cup her cheeks. "You won."

She's beaming. "We won." Aurora is the one that pulls me back in for a hug, wrapping her arms tightly around my abdomen. We sway side to side in the pouring rain.

Over her shoulder, I find Sophia and Kian watching, amused as Zaza swings between their arms. After a shared look, Sophia dips her head and pulls her parents a bit further away. I smile. We're together, and we're not hiding it. But neither of us have wanted to hear the opinions of our parents, so they don't know yet. At least, not explicitly.

As soon as they're distracted, I pull back just enough to press our lips together. Under my palms, she softens. It's soft, unhurried, and gentle. She tastes like rain water and Aurora. As simple as that. Aurora very gently pulls my lip back as she moves away, then leans back in for a quick kiss.

"I got voted MVP for the game," she says breathlessly, wiping water from under her eyes.

"Of course, you did."

Reaching up behind me, I unclasp the chain around my neck. It's got a simple gold pendant on it with my initials engraved. I snake my arms around Aurora's neck and re-clasp it. She reaches her fingers up and tugs it.

"What's this for?"

I don't know, really. But I look at the pendant against her brown skin, and it looks like it was always supposed to be there. Maybe it's the idea of college a few months away. We're not going to the same school, though they'll be close. Maybe it's a way to be with her the whole time. Maybe I just needed to see something of mine close to her skin. There is no logical answer. It just…is.

"I don't know. I just want you to have it."

Aurora smiles. "I love this necklace. Did you know I asked my parents for one similar? They never got it. I wasn't mad, but I've always loved this."

It's funny how often we're on the same wavelength without even realizing it. Sometimes, I swear we have the same thoughts, share the same brain. The only person I know better than Aurora is Elijah, but even that, it's different. He's my brother.

She is…Aurora.

The girl I'm in love with. The girl who's been my best friend since that day on the playground. I didn't know that emotions could run this deep at seventeen, but apparently, they do. I feel them below the surface of my skin, a low hum of energy that is constant. They belong to her, like much of me does. I mean, God, how the fuck does anyone get anything done? It feels like everything revolves around her.

I brush her cheek, finding her hand and twining our fingers. "It's yours."

Her hazel eyes meet mine, looking into the deepest parts of me. And in her own, I can see all the emotions she has. Not about me but about the game. About all she's worked for. About the sport she's played her whole life. This was it. Her last game with this high school team.

"Uh-oh."

"Don't uh-oh me," she says, her lips trembling.

My lips twitch. "If you cry, no one would know. It's raining."

Aurora swallows, and I know it's all going to overflow here in a quick second. Wrapping my arm around her shoulder, I pull her into my chest just as a quiet sob breaks free. "I've got you," I whisper into her ear, my fingers wrapped around the end of her curly ponytail.

"This is so dumb." Her words are muffled by her tears and my chest. I hold her as it passes. I know later, she'll cry again when no one's around. But for now, a quick moment is all she needs. We stay like that until her shoulders stop shaking.

When she pulls back, you can't even tell unless you were to look closely. Only I notice the slight puffiness under her eyes. No one else will. I squeeze her hand and nod to her family. "We should go."

"Yeah." Aurora turns those puppy dog eyes up to me, playing with the pendant now around her neck. I raise a brow. "Will you carry me?"

I laugh. "Of course." I bend down so she doesn't have to jump so high and hold her confidently on my back, my hands cupped around her legs.

Her arms fall over my shoulders, loosely held together. Aurora rests her head on my shoulder, her lips inches away from my neck.

Those three words pound in my head over and over again, begging to get out. Today is for her though. I can tell her I love her tomorrow. Or the next day. It doesn't matter.

I'm going to love her every day and every tomorrow there is. And beyond that, too.

Aurora is forever.

# 29

## You Always Have Been

The simple things in life are often overlooked.

For example, no one told me that some of the things I would miss most about a person were the simple things. The everyday fundamental moments.

As Isaiah moves around the kitchen, singing wildly, it hits me.

Sure, I missed *him*. But I missed all these tiny moments, too. All the minute things that people wouldn't notice in passing about him showcase themselves in moments like this.

How no matter how quiet and reserved he may present himself, in the car or at home with his favorite songs, he is anything but. How beautiful he looks when he does because the left side of his mouth turns up in a crooked smile. How he purposely sings off key sometimes to make me laugh.

Or like earlier, at the drive-in theater, how I hate when other people talk during movies but when Isaiah quotes a line he loves, I think it's the most endearing thing in the world. Or that when he greets someone, if I'm there, his eyes often glance my way for just a second before he says hello. And now, as I lean over the arm of my couch, watching him dance through the kitchen pulling out all the ingredients for hot chocolate. There's such beauty in seeing this side of someone. The side usually reserved for the safety of an empty house.

I missed him with an ache like no other when he didn't show up to that first game. Missed him when I was sad and when I was happy. When I had something to share or needed him to lean on.

But I didn't realize how much I missed everything else.

Isaiah makes the mundane extraordinary. Makes everyday life exhilarating. I don't have to live for a single moment when I'm living life with him.

He turns, fixing me with a heated look. "Rora?"

"Yes?"

"Why are you staring at me?" he asks, placing his palms flat on the counter.

I shrug, heat thrumming over my skin. "I was thinking about how much I love this."

"Me making a fool of myself?" Isaiah puts the kettle—that he bought me—on the stove. I kick my legs down and pad over to the kitchen, pulling myself to sit on the counter.

"Well, yes, of course." I pull down the sleeves of his hoodie that he pulled over my head earlier at the drive in. "But I don't know, this—doing nothing, I guess." I reach out a hand, flexing my fingers until he steps toward me with a smile. My fingers wrap around his tattooed skin and pull him closer.

His hands land on my hips, fingers gently tapping the curve of my thighs, and my heartbeat accelerates like always whenever he touches me.

With other people, the quiet can feel overwhelming to me. A living thing trying to suffocate me. Not with him. The nerves I had, the overthinking that was drowning me—they've dissipated with Isaiah's gentle care. I know he sees all of me and wouldn't run away from it.

More so, I don't feel I have to run away from myself.

With a steady hand, I cup his face, my thumb running over his jawline, and I pull him forward the rest of the way to press our lips together.

"I could do nothing with you forever," I murmur against his lips.

In the warm glow of my kitchen, Isaiah pulls back to fix those deep, winding, brown eyes on mine, a promise shining in them. That if that's what I want, that's what I'll get.

As I take him in, the strong, quiet, beautiful boy that is more of my world than I'd admit to anyone who asked. I'm overwhelmed with it. The possibility of the future. A future I thought no longer belonged to me.

Isaiah pushes my hair away from my face, tangling his fingers in my curls. "What's going on in that brain of yours?"

"How do you always know?"

"Because I know you."

I slip my hand in his back pocket. "It's really nothing. I'm just grateful that you're here. Back—with me again."

A moment of silence passes between us.

"I'm sorry it took me so long."

"You've apologized enough, Isaiah. Stop it."

He kisses me again, sweet and slow. But underneath it burns with passion, kindling for a fire we've yet to set.

I pull him in with the hand happily in his back pocket, my other hand tracking up his arm until I feel the slight stubble on his chin. Behind us, the kettle whistles, and Isaiah loudly groans.

A laugh bubbles past my lips, and I pat his butt. "You've got plenty of time."

His forehead rests against mine, hands sliding to my waist. "There is not enough time in the world to kiss you as much as I'd like."

Heat floods my cheeks, which he proceeds to place frantic, sweet kisses all over my face until he pushes himself back. I grab the whipped cream can beside me and shake it, shooting it onto my finger. Isaiah makes up the mugs, taking them over to the coffee table. When he returns, there's a curve to his lips.

"You missed," he says, eyes locked on my lips. As he stalks toward me, heat starts to bloom in the pit of my stomach, traveling over and in between my thighs. My nerve endings come alive like sparklers in the night time.

I tip my head back. "Better clean it up then."

He chuckles just as his lips touch my skin. Isaiah finds the stray whipped cream on the side of my mouth, and my breath catches in my throat. To my surprise, he doesn't stop there. A moment later, he moves to the other side, his tongue barely grazing my skin as he makes a soft hum. Every beat of my heart, I feel in my fingertips and the hot rush of my blood under my skin. Isaiah makes a slow, tortuous path over my jawline, over the sensitive skin of my throat, and presses a kiss to the hollow of my neck.

"I don't think there's any whipped cream there."

"No, there isn't." He flutters kisses around my neck until he's hovering above my lips. "Couldn't help myself."

With a firm hand on the back of my neck, Isaiah closes the distance. The flames burn hotter, heat growing with every breath, every movement of our lips. My mind turns into a hazy mess, where the only clear thought that remains is Isaiah. The pull and press of his lips against mine, the sheer *need* that exists between us. We are bodies full of want and need and desire, and we are only each other's. We were only ever meant to be *this* to each other. Isaiah pulls back instead of pressing further, and I can't help but whine.

He laughs, the sound settling in my heart. "Plenty of time for that."

I'm still a bit hazy, all love drunk and what not, and pull him back for a few more short kisses. When I sit back, I find those beautiful eyes looking at me. I could get lost in them forever—a labyrinth with every shade of the deepest browns. Isaiah slides his hands down my arms until they find purchase on my hips.

The smell of chocolate wafts in the air, and Isaiah taps underneath my chin. "Wanna ride?"

My brows furrow. "To the couch?"

He shrugs. I smile and lift my arms, whipped cream in hand. Isaiah chuckles and cradles me in his arms for the literal ten-foot walk. Who am I kidding? If he wanted to carry me a foot, I'd let him. Anything to feel the familiar touch that I went so long without. Intimacy I never would've found anywhere else.

"Down you go," Isaiah says, purposely sliding me down his body until my feet touch the floor. He begins to unwind his arms, but the song changes, and I tighten mine, keeping him against me. A pure warmth spreads over his features, and my lips curve into a gentle smile.

"Dance with me?" I ask, keeping my hands twined behind his neck.

"Always." Isaiah slips his hands under my sweatshirt to land on my skin and tug me close. Heat emits from his palms, creating pockets of warmth that spread out in waves around my skin.

The apartment is quiet aside from the music, twinkle lights illuminating the space and the city lights through the windows. From here, we can see the moon shining bright in the distant sky. I rest my head on his chest so I can hear his steady heartbeat in my ear.

"I couldn't listen to this song for a long time," I murmur. The last time I heard it was when we were at the bar together. Before then, it was on no playlist, and I never reached for it.

Memories flash in my mind of how often this was the soundtrack of our lives. A song both of our parents played on slow Sunday mornings became ours. In the quiet of our room, when we first learned to drive, road trips to the beach, and every moment in between. It is quintessentially us.

"Me either." Isaiah rests his head on top of mine. "I'm surprised it came on."

I tip my head up so I can look at him. "I added it. I've been making a playlist since you've been back."

"You have?"

To no surprise, I blush. He rubs his thumb over my cheek. "Yeah. I—I wanted to. Every time I would come home or we would do something, there'd be a song I couldn't stop listening to, so I just started adding them." I shrug. "I want to remember exactly how I felt with you."

"When did you add this one?"

"After the carnival."

He smiles. "The kiss, you mean."

"That took place at a carnival."

Isaiah raises a brow, playfully squeezing my waist, causing me to squeal. He kills the space between us, our lips so close, they brush against each other. "The only thing I need to know about that day is that it was the day you kissed me again." The pad of his thumb presses against my bottom lip. "I've kissed you more times than I can count since, yet that kiss, that moment, is embedded in my thoughts."

"It was just a kiss, Isaiah." I say the words, but I know it's not true.

Isaiah gives an almost imperceptible shake of his head. "No, it wasn't."

There's a knowing look in his eyes as we sway. In my chest, my heart beats a bit faster at his penetrating gaze. For a while now—most of my life if we're being honest—I've had a deep-seated fear of admitting that things might mean something more. If I give people those pieces, an inside look to how deeply I may feel about something, it's like I'm setting myself up for pain or embarrassment.

"You don't have to do that, you know. You never used to be scared with me. I don't want you to be now."

"I'm not scared."

Isaiah raises a brow, and I sigh. Being called out is unsettling. As much as I want him to know me (as he does) and every part of me, that doesn't take away from the sheer vastness that creates in my gut. It feels like standing on the edge of a cliff with nothing but gray sky around me.

And it's not that Isaiah is the problem. I want to be fearless with him. But I've guarded myself so closely the past few years, I have to unlearn that.

"I'm not…scared. But I have to—" I exhale. "I have to remember to let my guard down. To remember to breathe when I get too close to the edge."

"Aurora." Isaiah's hands cup my face again, making sure our eyes meet. "Then, let me help. Let me help remind you that you aren't alone. I'm not going to laugh at you for telling me something means something to you. I'm not going to shrug it off or shake my head. I care about you and the things that you care about. All of it. All of you. Not just the parts that you think are acceptable to share. All of it.

"And I want to share it with you. If it's a kiss, a line from a book, a song, a movie, a moment you lived and want to live again. It's not something to be scared of. It's what makes you, you. It's the layers to who you are. And I will never look at anything you share with me with an unkind eye. It's not possible. Because everything about you and everything that you love is beautiful to me, Ro."

Well, shit. What does one do with all of that? Where do I put that? All the love he's just handed me. All the love he hands over on a daily basis. The cup is overflowing, and it's overwhelming. Yet, at the same time, it's like I'm floating. It feels like pure, unadulterated joy—like chasing fireflies on a late summer night or holding a trophy over my head.

Except it's free. Isaiah's love is free.

I haven't had to prove myself a million times to earn it. He loves me.

Isaiah just loves me.

No conditions. No rules. No hoops.

I swallow down the thick emotions choking me, gripping my heart like a vice. There's so much I want to say and so much he's worthy of hearing. "I can't—"

"I don't need you to say anything, Ro."

"You deserve to hear it—"

Isaiah presses a finger over my lips. "You say it whenever you can. You tell me what you need to tell me when you're ready. Telling me now or in a few months doesn't change anything. I love you. I love how nervous you get, even though it's me," he says, smiling with my dimple. "I'll still be here, loving you every second."

My head dramatically drops to his chest, my arms tightening around him. That's all I needed, just for a second, to hold him. To remind myself that he is real.

"How much do you want that hot chocolate?"

"Um—"

"Bedroom, Isaiah."

Light blooms in his eyes, all hesitation gone. "Yes, ma'am."

I squeal as he lifts me up, his arms directly under my butt. His strides eat up the short hallway and enter my dimly lit bedroom. I watch him take in the room, never letting me down. His eyes focus on a few things: the keepsake box on my dresser, his old hoodie hanging from my closet, pictures I've printed out and empty frames, and lastly, the octopi on my bed.

Isaiah gently drops me on the bed, picking up one of the stuffed animals—the one he won me. "I remember this little guy."

"I've slept with it since you showed up at the first game."

A cheeky grin comes over his face as he sets it back down on the pillow, eyes focusing on me again. Slowly, he crawls over me, hands planted on either side of my head. My breath hitches at the fire in his eyes, all directed at me. In my chest, the beat of my heart is so loud, he has to be able to hear it. I trail my hands up and grip the bottom of his shirt, giving it a little tug.

"Not wasting time, I see?"

I shake my head, meeting his eyes. "Not with you. Not anymore."

Isaiah softens and gives me a searingly gentle kiss before rising and reaching back to pull his shirt off. Maybe one day, I'll be used to the ink on his skin, but right now is not that day. With a tender hand, I trail over them as I always do, interrupted only by Isaiah drawing my attention. With only him to focus on, I take in every detail. The slight laugh lines, the dimple fighting to make an appearance, the silver stud in his nose, the tight, tiny curls on his head, every line on his face, and the person beneath it all.

"You're so pretty," I say, the words falling out of their own volition.

He laughs, the sound soft like falling snow, and leans down, pressing a kiss to the tip of my nose and then to my lips. Swiftly, he flips us, cradling my knee as he does until I'm straddling him.

"Your turn." Isaiah pulls the hoodie over my head, my curls falling out haphazardly, leaving me in a simple tank top. My senses are on overdrive. I move back, stepping down off the bed, the edge of his sweats in my hands. Meeting my eyes, he gives me a nod, and I tug them off, leaving him in black briefs. Yeah, my breath hitches at the sight, and my heart melts into a warm, heated puddle.

I climb back up, trailing my nails over the outside of his leg, over the ink on his thigh, enjoying the goosebumps that follow in my wake. My eyes narrow in on yet another tattoo I hadn't noticed—a fish bowl with two tiny fish inside.

"You didn't."

Isaiah reaches down, intertwining our fingers. "The fish?" I nod, and I'm given a tiny smile in return. He tugs me upward until my hair cascades around us. "Remember after you first learned how to drive? You had a phase where you wouldn't stop playing that damn Pink Floyd song. I think your mom had made you a CD and that was always one of you guys' favorites. And then after, you would randomly sing or shout the two lost souls lyrics for like a year straight." Isaiah laughs as he tells it, his free hand crawling up my leg to land on my butt. "Every time I heard it, I thought of you. Had to get it."

I grin. "Two lost souls."

Isaiah flips us again, playfully biting at my skin, over my neck and my jaw, his hands tickling my waist. I squeal, trying to get away, only to fail and succumb to his hands. "Okay, please! Isaiah!" He laughs against my stomach, grinning up at me.

Something shifts. The mood deepens from a colorful moment to a hazy red in the blink of an eye. "May I?" he asks, fingers toying with the band of my gym shorts. I nod and watch with bated breath as he tugs them down, making sure to drag his fingertips over the exposed skin as he does.

Isaiah places tender kisses as he rises—over the sensitive skin of my thigh, my hips, and my rib cage. With steady hands, he pulls the tank top up and over my head, leaving me almost fully exposed. My body is a live wire, a chord strung tight that only responds to him. As he crawls up, settling between my hips, I feel him against me, and sparks explode over my skin in a shower of fireworks.

"Gorgeous, gorgeous girl," he whispers against my neck, nipping his way up until he's at my lips. "Are you sure?"

My nails dig into his back, pulling him down onto me, my hips moving of their own accord. "I've been sure, Isaiah. I'm sure of you." I nip his bottom lip, pulling it back as I do. His chest rumbles, his grip on me tightening.

"Now," I whisper against his lips. "Get naked please."

Isaiah laughs and pushes up, pulling his briefs down. A heavy wave of heat settles in between my thighs, traveling up my spine and setting my entire body on fire.

With a confident prowess, he bends, gripping the lace of my underwear. "Your turn." His eyes are dark and gorgeous, a heady focus within as he pulls them down. Unexpectedly, he picks me up roughly, yet so fucking hot, moving me up the bed until my heads on the pillow.

"Someone's impatient."

"Someone has dreamt of this a million times," he whispers on the inside of my thigh before centering himself, tongue sneaking out quickly, yet enough for my breath to catch. "Someone has imagined every single way this could go, and so far, none of them are living up to the real thing."

I squirm, but he firmly takes control, one hand pressing on my hips, the other gripping my thigh. He grins up at me devilishly before dipping his head again. Heat pulses in sporadic waves as he settles in, my eyes fluttering closed as my body is left to his mercy. I reach down to the top of his head, trying to find purchase on anything, even his small, gorgeous curls.

Isaiah has other ideas, his hand moving to catch mine, pressing them into my hips to keep me locked in place. I exhale, a small sound escaping my lips, now fully at his control. His tongue and his lips work in tandem in the most delicious way. Pressure builds, traveling over my hips, over the nerve endings under my skin, and I feel my entire body flush with constant heat. It's undeniable and pleasurable and unbearable all at once. I want to breathe again, but I never want it to stop. And Isaiah doesn't.

Isaiah presses in with his fingers now, all of it too much and still not enough. Up and up and up, he takes me, and I'm not sure I'll ever come down. "Give it up, Ro. I know you want to."

The feeling of his skin on mine, his hands wrapped around my own, is too much. My chest tightens and releases as Isaiah works me through it, elongating the moment and making me feel every blissful second. Stars burst behind my eyelids, and the pressure explodes like fireworks under my skin. Waves of pleasure undulate all over my body.

After what feels like years, Isaiah pulls back, pressing a kiss to my inner thigh again, sending a tiny, residual shockwave down my spine. "Good mamas. Good job."

He kisses a slow tortuous path up to me, the coolness of the thin chain on his neck a contrast to the heat of my skin. After an impatient moment, I tug the chain, pulling him up to my lips. Neither of us says anything. We just let our lips and bodies do the talking. My hands trace the person I've memorized all over again, familiar paths I've relearned and new ones I've discovered. He presses his weight onto me, a hot, constant pressure that I love, that I'm addicted to. His hands roam over my skin in featherlight touches, making my nerves stand at attention, giving me no reprieve from the pulsing heat he just brought to the surface.

I wind my legs around him, encasing him in my hips while my hands hold him to me.

"Let me see you," he whispers against my lips before pulling back just enough to take me in with his eyes.

"Why?" I exhale, brushing my hand down the column of his throat and over this tattooed chest.

"'Cause I didn't get to for so long. Making up for lost time." He presses quick, playful kisses to my lips. "In more ways than one."

"Shut up," I murmur, pulling him back down, exhaling against his lips.

He tangles his hand in my hair, moving his fingers against my scalp as his tongue leads us together. I trail my hand down until I wrap around him, confirmed by the small grunt that escapes from his lips and the circle of his hips. And we kiss until my brain goes hazy and I have to pull back to breathe. I keep a steady rhythm with my hand, Isaiah letting his head fall forward into the crook of my neck.

Moments later, he unwinds my hand, intertwining our fingers and resting them near my head. "Do you want me to grab a condom?" he asks, his other hand winding my body back up.

I blink, finding my words and shake my head. "I don't if you don't. I'm on birth control. Saw my doctor a few months ago." I smile.

"I'm good. If you're sure."

I press up to kiss him, sucking on his top lip. "I'm sure. Such a sexy conversation."

Isaiah chuckles against my body, a mini shockwave going through it. "It is. Means we can do whatever we want."

My breathing deepens. "I suppose that's true." I tug his thin chain again, pulling him as close as I can get him. "Better get to it then."

Isaiah's eyes twinkle, and he does. Lining us up, Isaiah sinks in, and I exhale, trying to come back down to Earth. But he's got me so high already, I'm not sure Earth is a possibility. I wanted to land on that elusive cloud nine, and I did. Isaiah took me there. Reality is drifting somewhere in the back of my mind, but all I know and all I care about is him. Our hands grip tighter as he pushes one leg upward, effectively connecting us in the deepest way possible. My stomach tightens at the continuous pressure. Slow and steady but firm, building the pressure brick by brick.

Isaiah whispers a million things against my lips, and I can do nothing but follow his rhythm. "Rora," he murmurs against my skin, hand gripping the back of my knee tightly, and my name sounds like a prayer on his lips. I memorize it, lock the sound in a sacred place that belongs to just us. With the firm movement of his hips, I tip my head back, overwhelmed by the sheer intensity of it. Of us. Isaiah adjusts, placing a quick kiss on my knee before sinking back down, intensifying the heat. Fireworks on New Years have nothing on this.

Being with him again, having him again, in my arms, in my body, in my heart, is better than anything else this life has to offer. My heart grows with a love I've never felt before. Not like this. I loved him when we were kids, I loved him when he wasn't here—both don't compare to this. To the connection we have, that he's fostered like a garden since returning. This is deeper, all-encompassing, and life altering. This is what they meant.

The poets I mean.

This has to be what they meant. I'd do anything and everything for him. Would sacrifice myself without a second thought or a wayward glance.

Sparks fly over the surface of my skin, crawling up my spine in tiny explosions as the pressure reaches another peak. He releases my fingers, only to wrap around my throat, his thumb adding just enough pressure there. My brain short circuits.

"Isaiah," I moan against his lips, "more, please. *Fuck.*" It's the only coherent thought I have.

He smiles against my lips, his teeth nipping and tugging playfully.

"Greedy."

I laugh, which quickly turns into a soft moan as he increases his pressure—the movements—until I'm withering underneath him. Succumbing to the pressure he's built. My nails dig into his back, and his hand gives a gentle squeeze.

"Look at me, Ro," he demands. I blink my eyes open. Isaiah looks like a dream. "I don't want to miss a single second." His hand digs into my curls, tugging enough to sting, and shivers dance down my spine. "I love the way your breath hitches, how your hands tighten. I love the flush on your cheeks," he murmurs, brushing his lips against my cheeks and my nose. "I love the way you feel."

I swallow. A wave of pleasure threatens to drown me.

We share another kiss, sure and solid. He whispers, "You're all mine. You always have been." My heart expands.

I feel the flush of my cheeks, the heat of his skin pressed against mine. The pressure builds and tumbles over the cliff, taking me with it. And he watches me fall apart, works me through it. Fans the flames licking my skin, sending sparks into the air. Every second feels like years as the shockwaves ebb and flow over my skin, washing over me, drowning me in the undeniable feeling of bliss. A tiny grunt escapes his lips, and I know he's right there. Never taking his eyes off me, our hips move together, tiny fireworks still going off, sheer pleasure bubbles still bursting over me, but I watch him, too. I watch him fall apart onto me, his beautiful brown eyes fluttering just so as he lets go, letting me feel all his weight.

Our chests move rapidly against one another, our frantic heartbeats in sync—like they always have been. A sense of bliss, of contentment, wraps around each of us as we come down. Funny because the fall doesn't really feel like one because he's here next to me. Not a figment of my imagination or a nostalgic memory but a real tangible part of my life again. The fall is more of a float—what I imagine laying on a fluffy cloud might feel like.

I practically roll over on top of him and crush our lips together, twining our bodies back into one. Because I can't get enough. A million kisses aren't enough, but I give them to him anyway.

"What was that for?" he asks when I pull back, his hand resting on the nape of my neck.

"For being here. For being you."

Isaiah smiles, pushing my hair out of my face, tracing a finger over my nose and my cheeks. Heat starts to unfurl like petals in the spring the way he looks at me. With so much love in his eyes—a level of love I'm not sure I really ever knew was possible. The euphoria never fades with him, with being seen the way he sees me. The way he takes every version of me: put together, falling apart, or all the others in between. I didn't know until he showed me how much that being seen was a part of being loved. It's all I've ever wanted, to be seen the way he sees me and has *always* seen me.

"Thank you for seeing me the way you do." I fold my arms over his chest, running my forefinger and thumb over the texture of his necklace.

Isaiah's hand tracks up and down my spine. "You are the sun in my sky, Aurora. I've had the pleasure of knowing you my whole life. Of studying you. I know every part of you, every ray. I couldn't imagine a life where I don't know you."

My heart swells, molding to his words as it always does. I kiss him gently, hoping he feels all the things I'm still scared to say.

"There is no parallel life out there worth living if you're not in it."

I look at him, and I see the rest of my life. In brief flashes, images of us together through the years in technicolor. If life has taught me anything, it's that nothing is perfect; the world won't always be in bright beautiful colors. There are moments where it's going to knock you down and make you wonder if it's worth it to stand up.

And I will never be anything short of grateful for those who've been there for me. Without them, I don't think I ever would've found my footing. But the realization that Isaiah is now a part of that again—back in my life—is like watching a sunrise over the ocean after weeks of rain. Knowing that he's going to be here to catch my fall the next time the world goes gray, that we'll have each other's hand to hold the next time the world turns volatile, is like having a safety net for life.

We might fall. We might cry. We might yell at each other when nothing else seems to be enough. But we'll bounce back up. I'm not scared of him leaving again. There are other fears, self-inflicted ones, but not about him. Because he loves me.

And has proven time and time again that he will love me no matter what. Sometimes, the love and the grace I have for myself is fleeting, but what Isaiah feels for me is not.

If there is one thing to trust, it's that Isaiah Bryant is not going anywhere.

He's going to love me every day for the rest of our lives.

## About Time

Whenever I hear the word 'fearless', I never relate it to love.

To me, being fearless is reserved for cliff jumping, changing careers, moving states—things with tangible measures and logical risks.

Love does not have that.

I can't empty it all out on a scale and measure how well I'm doing. There is no meta-data for the areas that need improvement.

Love is a vague leap of faith. A fearless endeavor that you don't even realize you're in until you're in it. I knew I loved Isaiah.

I mean…duh.

I've loved him as long as I've known him. But I didn't expect falling in love with him now—again—to feel like this. Like my heart could leap out of my chest at any moment, like my cheeks might fall off from smiling too hard. I want to tell everyone and simultaneously want to keep it close to my chest.

Falling in love with him now isn't an anxious freefall. It's easy. It feels like walking down a street I've walked a million times, except the sun shines a bit brighter. As comforting as my old favorite songs. Colors are fuller, wind feels like a warm caress on my cheek, and the world spins a little slower. Like it wants me to experience every second.

I love him as fearlessly as I know how.

What I didn't realize, however, was that loving someone so effortlessly would uncover all these other fears and put you face to face with them. Forcing you into flight or fight. It's easy to let myself be when Isaiah is around. I'm unafraid when he's standing in front of me, helping me chase any lingering fears away.

But when he's not…

A million what-ifs keep the small hum of fear alive. It thrums in the background of my mind and sits idle under my skin, waiting until I'm alone or vulnerable to strike.

If I voice it, what if the world tries to take it away?

If I admit how much I love him, what if something happens?

What if I get my heart broken again?

What if all love is, is a distraction?

What if it's all fucking pointless?

It doesn't stop me from loving him. I'm not sure anything could. Just makes my own head a bit of a fucking mess.

I exhale, staring up at the sky before pushing myself back up and repeating the exercise. My knee aches. And it shouldn't. But I keep going. Stretching and working the muscle like it hasn't been in so long. Around me, the field is empty post-practice, aside from Kian. The rest of the team is long gone, and the coaches are in the office.

From his spot on the bench, I know he's watching me. Can probably sense my inner turmoil and is waiting to drop some intelligent, brotherly wisdom. I cross the field twice more in repetitive motions that give my brain a rest. Kian hands me a bottle of water as I approach, the electrolytes inside leaving a salty taste.

"My young grasshopper, what's wrong?"

I snort, collapsing on the grass. "Nothing." The sun shines above, making me squint as I meet Kian's eyes.

"That is not a nothing, *nothing*. That is a something nothing." Kian studies me, warm, perceptive eyes not giving me any reprieve. "So, you're in love. What's the issue?"

"Kian!" I groan, digging my fingers into my hair.

"Are you insinuating you are not in love?"

I groan again, throwing my back flat against the ground.

"You know, I'm well-versed in the Matthews girls' non-verbal communication." A hand on my cheek causes my eyes to spring open, and he pats it twice more. "Come on, sit up. Sophia will be here soon. Better talk to me while you can." He's got a cheeky grin on his face, looking at me expectantly.

"You're so fucking annoying." I sigh, taking a long sip of water. "Why didn't you tell me it felt like this?"

A love sick look appears in his eyes. "Ah, yes. It feels like your heart is falling apart, right? And you can't focus on anything. Ever. And your hands feel clammy for no reason."

I give him a deadpan look.

"I couldn't tell you. It would ruin the experience," he says, leaning back. "It's such a weird thing, how insane you feel, even though you're in love with someone. Like I'm in love now. Shouldn't I feel on top of the world? And you do, but you also feel like the world's going to fall out from under your feet at any given moment." Kian glances at me, a gentle smile on his face. "But you also feel like laughing at the stupidest fucking things because you can't wait to share it with them. There's so much happening, you're sure that your heart will burst if they aren't around, but it feels like it's going to burst when they are. I'm sure it's different for everybody, but I think the insanity remains.

"I couldn't tell you because you wouldn't have believed me. And it would've ruined all of this," he says, motioning to my obviously distraught body. "And for you two—two peas in a damn pod—I'm sure it's even stranger. You grew up together. You fell in love before the meaning of that sunk in, and now, you're experiencing it as an adult. I'm sure it feels like finding a lost key that was right in front of you the whole time. Which is great but also makes you a teeny bit crazy."

A laugh trickles out, but I settle because he's right. Having Kian put it out there, knowing he felt that way, makes me feel less alone. I begrudgingly say, "Thank you."

"Ah, anytime. Have you told him yet?"

My brows furrow. "What?"

"You Matthews girls have a knack of being a tad bit fearful of accepting good things." Kian crouches down. "It took your sister like two months to tell me that she loved me back. Granted, we were teenagers, but, you know, it's not surprising to me that you haven't. It was one of the best days of my life though, learning that she loved me as much as I loved her," Kian says. "And I'm sure he understands. He loves you, after all. And I know all about being a sucker for a Matthews girl."

I begrudgingly smile up at him. Sophia and I are different in so many ways and similar in others. This being one of them. "I will soon."

"Good." Kian holds out a hand, pulling me up. "I'm serious, Aurora. Anytime, okay?"

"I got it, you big sap."

Kian turns his gentle hold into a playful chokehold as we walk. "You're such a fucking smartass. I oughta kick your ass."

"In your dreams, idiot," I say, kicking my good leg up to kick him as best I can. My heart skips a beat when I see Sophia's car, all for the simple fact that she's dropping me off and that means I'm one minute closer to seeing Isaiah again. Ridiculous.

As if Kian can sense it, he squeezes me. "You're such a love sick fool."

I reach around and give him a push in his abdomen, just enough to get him off me.

"Oof. Asshole," he calls after me as I speed walk ahead of him. Sophia pops the trunk, and I toss my bag in the back before sliding in the rear.

"What is taking my husband so long?" Sophia peeks out the window.

I shrug. "I did punch him in the gut." When she shoots me a look in the rearview, I shrug. "It was gentle." Sophia laughs, and eventually, Kian slides in the front seat, glancing my way.

"What's with the look?" Sophia asks.

"Kian, don't—"

"Your sister's in love," Kian says quickly, and I kick the back of his seat. I cross my arms like a scorned child.

"Asshole."

Soph gives us a bemused look. "You two are so fucking weird." She pulls her sunglasses down, but I feel her gaze in the rearview no matter what. "And yeah, Kian, I know she's in love. She's my sister. And it's about time."

I purse my lips, trying to hide my smile, but what's the use? She's right. It's about goddamn time.

"Okay, give me your hands," Isaiah says, stepping up behind me. I hold my hands out and watch as he pours olive oil over them and over the bread loafs that have been rising for four hours now. Against my back, he presses his body firm against mine.

"Alright, ready?"

I nod, tipping my head back to look at him. "I think I can handle this on my own, you know."

He smiles, pressing a kiss to my neck. "Not sure. Your cooking skills scare me."

"But this is baking." A shiver dances down my spine at the lingering heat of his lips.

"Ro, shut up." He centers us in front of the focaccia loaves he made and instructs me that all we're gonna do is make dimples in the dough. Behind us, sauce is simmering on the stove, the smell of tomato, onion, and garlic permeating the space. In the living room, Isaiah turned the space into a fortress. The electric fireplace is going, emitting heat in pulsing waves. An air mattress has been blown up in front of the couch, decorated with a million pillows, and the small glow of a few candles offers a little bit of light.

Isaiah threads our fingers together and begins pressing them into the dough. It's sticky but easy, like he said. Standing here, dimpling bread with him, I know I could do this for the rest of my life. Heat traverses over the surface of my skin at the affectionate intimacy in this moment. The press of his body against mine, the warmth of him surrounding me, the little puffs of air from his breath on my neck.

When it's been properly dimpled, Isaiah pulls our hands back. "Good job."

"You just wanted to touch me."

He laughs against my skin, blowing a raspberry against my neck. "I always want to touch you."

My stomach does a little dip and dance as we wash our hands and then sprinkle salt and rosemary over the two loaves. I hop up on the counter and watch as he takes over the kitchen again.

Even though he's cooking, we're celebrating his continued book deals. His second will come out in the late spring of next year, and he's signed for two more.

Earlier, I surprised him with his favorite chocolate cake and cheesy party hats. It was dumb and silly, but when his eyes lit up at the hat placed over my curls, I knew he loved it. I even printed out the deal from Publishers Marketplace and laminated it for him. I hated that he celebrated by himself for his first book. As far as I'm concerned, he's never going to celebrate alone again.

I take a sip of my apple juice, my eyes tracking every movement he makes. There's a smoothness to them, a naturalness as he moves around. Moments later, he approaches me with a spoon. "Here," he says, and I taste the sauce, licking my lips. Isaiah leans in, his tongue swiping right over my lip. My breath hitches as heat blooms in my chest and spreads out in waves over my quickly flushing skin.

"Delicious," he murmurs against my lips, pecking them once more before pulling back.

I don't let him get far, wrapping my fingers around his wrist to pull him back. With his hands on the counter next to my hips and my legs trapping him in, we're equally caged in by one another. Reaching up, I run my thumb along his jawline.

"I'm really proud of you." I rock forward, bringing our lips together again. Isaiah's hand presses against my back, toying with the band of my sweats.

"It's nothing."

I frown. "Ah. That's not true. It's something. It's big and exciting." Isaiah rolls his eyes, trying to brush it off. "Stop it, Isaiah. You can do that with anyone else but not me."

His eyes deepen as he exhales. "You never did let me hide."

"Never will." I kiss him again.

"Thank you." Isaiah's dimple fights to appear. But he turns the focus to me. "How are you feeling about tomorrow? About the MRI?"

"Nervous. But it is what it is. Hopefully, we're on the right track," I say, shrugging. "And if they're not, I'll deal with it." A thread of fear burns hot for a moment. At hearing something that I don't want to—wondering if I could handle it if I do.

"We." Isaiah brings my eyes back to him. "We'll deal with it together." Gentle hands cup my cheeks, holding his gaze to mine until I nod. He presses our lips together in a kiss that is comforting and steady, both of us telling each other we're here—always.

He leans back against me, and I wrap my arms around him, finding the crook of his neck and tucking in. His hand is wrapped around my leg, holding himself to me as I hold him. I exhale, feeling lighter than a cloud.

This is what love is. This is what I always wanted love to be. Simple, filled with tiny moments of affection and intimacy, like teaching someone how to make bread or celebrating someone's accomplishments, even when they try to diminish them. In all the relationships that I cherish, the thing that makes them so full is the ability to share these quiet moments. I think we are taught that love is these grand moments of declarations and moments of pure bliss. That love should be loud and happy.

But sometimes, most times, it's quiet. It's personal and compassionate. Tenderhearted and faithful. Real love is there, even when you aren't perfect. It's there with no expectations and no conditions. And it's there even when you feel you don't deserve it. It's loving someone, even when you're annoyed with them or when the world feels like it's going to crumble out from underneath you. The love still remains.

Love may be different for everyone. For some, it may be as bright and as blinding as the sun. For others, as gentle as a stream. For me, it is the constant of the stars in the sky. Even after the moon disappears and the sky turns blue, I know they're there. They are constant. At times, more beautiful than others, more distinct. But they are always there. Sometimes they are drowned out by bright lights and cityscapes, and other times, they're the entire night sky. As expansive as the world allows.

And Isaiah loves me like that. Constantly, quietly.

And at times, more extensively than I ever thought possible.

Isaiah is my night sky and every star within.

# 31

## The Other Shoe

The room is silent.

Coach Teller stands with her arms crossed in the back, and I sit anxiously on the PT table, waiting to see the results of the MRI scan. My teeth worry at my lip.

"Matthews?"

"Yes, Coach?"

She raises a brow. "Breathe."

My chest deflates. In and out. In and out. The weight of the pressure I've placed on my shoulders is heavy. So, I decide to make the already tense room worse. I blurt out, "Would a trade be possible, Coach?"

Coach Teller's eyes have never focused quicker and sharper than that moment. "Say that again, Matthews?"

Exhaling, I rub my palms against my legs. Strange that I can feel the slight difference in the muscle tone in each leg. "I'm not sure playing under the coaching of my father is a good idea anymore." Her stare burns. "We haven't spoken. He doesn't look at me. He doesn't coach me. And it's going to affect the way I play. If I ever step foot on that damn field again," I joke, but it falls flat.

"When," Teller corrects. When she raises an eyebrow, I know she's waiting for me to continue.

"I don't really know what else to say…just that I won't let it affect the team, and I won't let him ruin this for me. It's my sport." I swallow. "I'm not saying I'm definitely going to do it, but I thought I'd bring it up."

"Noted."

I groan. "Coach, come on."

Teller shrugs, adjusting her ball cap. There is anger simmering under the surface. Whether that's directed at me, my dad, or the whole situation, I'm not sure. "Got nothing else to say right now, Aurora. It's noted. If that's the decision you make, we'll deal with it. But I don't plan on losing you."

There's an uncomfortable feeling in my chest. Rubbing it with the heel of my hand does nothing to alleviate it. It's nice to be wanted, to know that she wants me to stay. But is that at the cost of my dad's job? I may not want to work with him anymore, but that doesn't mean I want him out of a job.

Two knocks on the door send my heart plummeting, and the doctor enters. It's a different doctor from my previous, and my eyes narrow on his name tag—Dr. Walsh. I watch as he grabs the stool and takes a seat, wheeling over, the folder resting on his legs.

"May I?" He motions to the knee.

"Sure."

The cool touch of his hands takes me by surprise as he feels around. Pressing the ligaments, rotating the knee. Up and down. In circles. Yadda, yadda.

"How's it feeling? How's PT?"

A small pit of dread sinks further in my stomach. I know he's asking to get a full picture, but my gut is telling me something is wrong. "For the most part, good. PT has been going well. If anything, I've had to slow myself down on doing the work. But sometimes, it aches." I try to wave it away, spinning the ring on my finger. "It's only with certain exercises, certain movements. Not a sharp pain, by any means. I just become more aware of it. But I figured that comes with the injury."

Dr. Walsh hums and removes his hand. "You need to have a second surgery."

I swallow thickly, pressing my lips together. In my lap, my hands are wrung so tight, the skin is turning white, and I can't bring myself to look at anyone else in the room. "There's no other option?" I ask, my voice shaky.

"It's a simple procedure. There's a secondary tear that was missed. Minute. Miniscule. Only exacerbated by the work you've been doing."

Huffing, I throw my head back, willing the tears to stay in my eyes. "So, because of the PT I was doing, I worsened something else?"

It's so stupid, but I feel foreign in my own body. Previous injuries, the more I did, the better I got. Each recovery requires something different. I know that. Some require you to push through, some force you to rest. But I've always excelled at that because I wanted to get better. And now, I've made myself worse?

"Aurora." Coach Teller's voice is stern, and I clear my throat.

"That's not exactly it. The tear was most likely caused at the same time as the MCL."

"How long will the recovery take?" I meet his eyes.

"It will add about four weeks of recovery."

Blowing out a breath, I bow my head. Four more weeks. The first showcase usually takes place in February. Sometimes the very beginning of March. Right now, based on the recovery I've already done, I should've been ready to get back on the field at the start of February and to go all out to prepare. But now…I'll be lucky if I'm even ready to go by the time the first camp comes around. The time to find my groove again has basically been eliminated.

"Okay." My voice is small. The world feels like it's closing in and pressing on my chest.

The wheels of the stool echo in the quiet space. "We'll get you in for surgery next Thursday, the seventh."

I can't believe it's already November. October was here one second and gone the next. It was such a blissful blur. Falling in love, being in love. Watching the leaves change while Isaiah and I melded more into each other's lives. But why does it feel like this sport is trying to leave me behind?

Dramatic, I know. To feel like a failure because of an injury, to feel like a fraud because of something that happened and the way my body responded. I can't out train an injury, no matter how hard I try.

"We'll have you back in PT the following week. You'll be alright. Get you back on the field in no time. Okay?" Dr. Walsh clasps his hands together. He places the folder with the surgery details next to me.

"Okay."

With a deep sigh, Dr. Walsh leaves the room with one last pitiful glance. I gather up the materials and hop down. Though maybe I shouldn't have. Maybe my fucking knee will decide to tear again.

"Come on." Coach Teller rubs my back, but the touch feels like a painful scratch. I push my shoulders back, evading it as we head down the hallway.

Every footstep feels like a mile.

I climb into the passenger seat, and every word that Coach says is a buzz in my ear. I can't…I can't focus. I can't comprehend. It doesn't make sense. The drive back to the facility is a blur. I step out of the car into the cool air. It wraps around my throat and makes it hard to breathe. Exhaling, I try to remember what it feels like, but I just feel lost. Like I'm floating on a cloud above it all.

Like my biggest dream isn't slowly slipping out of my fingertips because of a fucking injury.

"Aurora?"

I blink. "Sorry, Coach."

She sighs. "Come sit down for a minute. You're not driving yourself home right now." I let Coach Teller lead me to the sidewalk and sit down on the curb. Teller bends down, crouching in front of me. "You're gonna be okay, kid."

Kid.

Funny how the smallest things are the last straw. Kid. As many times as Coach has called me kid herself, all I can think about are all the times my dad has.

That's the real shit stick of it all. Right now, all I want is my dad.

"I have something for you in the office. Do you want to come in, or will you wait?"

"I'll wait."

Coach gives me a steely look but dips her head. She knows I want to be alone, but I know she cares. My ears ring. Thoughts pounding in my mind, the wind chilling my exposed skin. And maybe I'm crazy, but I swear I can feel the tear in my knee—where the tendon has weakened and torn.

Tears fall down my cheeks in slow pathetic drops, staining the folder in my hands.

I don't—I don't understand. Why? Why now?

It seems so fucking stupid, but it's my whole life. This sport is my life;

it's everything I ever wanted and the one thing I have always counted on. The one thing where the work and the effort was worth it, even when I was downtrodden. But now? It feels like being kicked in the gut. A dream handed over, only to be taken right back.

A painful sob creaks out of my chest, barely a sound at all but enough to make my eyes sting.

The sound of footsteps draws my head up, and I see my dad stepping off the curb a few feet away.

Time moves in slow motion as I take him in. He walks right past me.

"Are you fucking serious?" I ask, sounding slightly deranged.

Dad stops, hands tucked in his pockets, and squares his shoulders. When he turns to face me, his face is unreadable. Like it always fucking is.

Like he's above it all.

But the thing is—everyone else accepts that about him. Or ignores it.

It's me that it agitates. Me that it affects. Me that suffers from it.

Because I've seen the few times he lets it slip. Shedding tears at a movie that catches him off guard. The notes he writes in all of our birthday cards. How playful he becomes with Joey and Zaza. I've seen the best, like I've seen the worst. More than anyone.

I stand on shaky legs, pushing my sleeves up. "How do you do it?" Confusion flashes over his features. "How do you hear your daughter sob—because I know you did—and see her cry and continue to walk away? For the second time, no less!"

The memory of him being nowhere to be found at the initial tear flashes like a neon sign.

I step forward. "Seriously, how the hell do you do it?"

We stare off. I wonder what he sees. The stubborn daughter he raised? Or an insolent girl who became this way on her own?

"It didn't seem like you wanted to be bothered." He stands rock still.

It's infuriating.

"But it didn't cross your mind to check on me?" My voice cracks.

"Didn't seem like the time."

I laugh dryly. "What do I have to do for you to love me?"

Finally, there's a fissure in his stoic face. Barely. But I see the crack. "I do."

"Not enough. Not the way I need you to. Not the way I've been begging you to." It all comes tumbling out. One by one.

I didn't understand. Why me? Sophia was a momma's girl. She escaped the pain of being his favorite daughter. Never had to live with the pressure of living up to that on her shoulders. But I—I was always a daddy's girl. Always reaching and searching for him as a kid. He was steady when I was standing on a crumbling cliff. Until it changed. Or until I saw through it.

But he was always just out of reach.

"I've always loved you, Aurora. I always will. More than anything," he says, but I shake my head.

"We used to talk about other things, you know. Used to do more stuff together. Until life became soccer 24/7. And then, you just kept hammering. When I was down, when I needed a sliver of encouragement, you never stopped. You'd offer ways to get through it, ways to improve, but never an ounce of understanding of how I may have felt. Sometimes, I just wanted you to be my dad, not my coach. Instead, you just kept raising the bar for both, making it impossible for me to reach it."

The wind breezes between us, cooling my cheeks where the tear tracks lay.

Dad sighs. "I just wanted you to be great. I only ever wanted you to be great."

Jesus Christ. I'd rather him take a knife and drag it across my skin.

"Yeah, well, all I wanted was to be loved. Unconditionally. So, I guess neither of us can get what we want."

Logically, I know he loves me, but it's not enough.

Love that has conditions and requires me to jump through hoops isn't enough anymore.

I wipe my eyes and find my keys in my jacket. Coach Teller might be mad, but I have to leave. Stalking past him, I locate my car in the parking lot and head that way.

"Aurora," Dad calls, and I stop, but I don't turn to look at him. "You know I'm not good at all this shit." Emotions, he means. "I don't know how to…show it any other way."

I close my eyes, grip tightening on the folder in my hands. "Well, no one can teach you. We've tried. You've gotta figure it out yourself."

And I walk away.

## Runaway

The sensation of being suffocated diminishes the further I get away from the city.

Behind me, Philadelphia fades away. Cool air creeps through the window, caressing my hot skin, and the loud music blares out all my thoughts. Aside from the one telling me to go.

Above, the highway signs point to the Delaware Beaches, a drive I could do in my sleep. We grew up going here in the summers and for special occasions in the off-season. When my parents were still together, they bought a second house nearby, and it became a reprieve for all of us. Now, I don't go nearly as much as I should. Back then, I used it as an escape. Just like I am now.

The three-hour drive passes quickly. While the suffocated feeling has faded, the pain in my chest hasn't. At the doctor's news. At my father.

I naïvely thought Isaiah leaving was the worst pain I had felt so far. Would be the worst to feel for a while.

But this…is equally as bad. In a different way, but the cracking of my heart aches the same; the pressure behind my eyes is one and the same. Sometimes, I think if I had quit before or after college, my and Dad's relationship wouldn't be quite as fragmented. That I could've found new dreams, something else to pursue. When I was twenty-two, I was so confident that I was getting selected that year. I had an incredible four years in school, three championships, and multiple awards. A breakout season in the professional league. I had done everything to the best of my ability.

It just wasn't enough.

Afterward, I understood there were other factors. The team at the time had a solid defense, a core group, and legendary players in the wing. Eventually, I got it, but for a few months, I thought about quitting more than I'd like to admit. Because if my best wasn't enough, what was?

I dig my free hand in my curls, my elbow on the window, ignoring the tears that won't stop slowly rolling down my face.

Because this—getting the invitation, getting selected, doing the thing I always dreamed of, and then getting injured—feels a million times worse. And it won't stop. The well keeps digging deeper in my chest, hollowing out every second, with every breath.

Logic is not winning the battle right now.

Because logically, I know that this isn't the end of the world. That there's still a chance I'd be back in time. Or get invited to a camp before the Olympics. But that's all so far away. That all feels so unattainable.

Because right now, I'm injured with a shit knee and no hope.

Soon, the cool air turns salty. The smell of the ocean gets closer by the second. I head down the main stretch until I turn left toward the boardwalk and the ocean. In the summers, the boardwalk is full of families, young and old. Weaving in and out of the shops along the avenue and heading to Funland, where all the carnival games and rides are. Usually, the salty air is mixed with the salty smell of boardwalk fries and long lines up to the famous ice cream shops. But right now, it's quiet. Small groups walk up and down the sidewalks, and some staple shops are open, while others are closed.

After parking, I walk until I reach the shore, slipping my shoes off until I can dig my toes into the cool sand. Pulling my sweatshirt closer, I walk past the tipped over lifeguard stands and find a spot just far enough back, the cold water won't touch me. The sun starts to lower in the sky, but it's still high enough to warm my cheeks against the breeze.

I let out a deep sigh.

*All I ever wanted was for you to be great.*

I am. I believed that. Believed that I was great at my sport, great at my position, great at what I did. But it doesn't seem to be enough for him. Because my father's perceived level of greatness is different.

For him, greatness means solidifying yourself in the sport. For him, greatness means being the best. Being the one to beat, the one that's talked about on ESPN long after retirement. As if women's soccer is talked about on ESPN at all if it's not a major tournament, but that's not the point. The point is, no one knows the kind of legacy they're going to leave while they're living it.

No athlete can predict what their efforts or accomplishments will mean for people to come.

So what if I don't meet my father's idea of greatness? What happens then? And that's what he doesn't get. If I'm not the '*best*', then what am I to him? A failure? Untapped potential? A player instead of a person? Instead of a daughter?

I get he wants the best for me, to be great, to do great, but what is the peak? What peak does he expect me to climb? Where does it fucking end? It's not measurable. It's not like he's given me a roadmap of accomplishments he wants me to do—so, *what* does he want from me?

What more can I do?

What *more* can I do?

I don't understand what he sees when he looks at me. Why isn't what he sees enough for him? He wants me to sacrifice everything in order to become something else? Well, why isn't what I am and who I am enough for him? Why is the person I have become and worked hard to become not great? What is it about me that my dad sees, as less than?

Maybe if he told me…I could fix it. Maybe I could mold myself into being the perfect version for him, and he could get what he wants. But wouldn't I lose everything else in the process? Everything that makes me who I am and worthy of the love and the friendship and the life I do have…wouldn't I lose that?

So, who wins? Do I bend to the point of breaking just to get my dad to look at me with pride for once? To tell me? Or do I stay here, stay who I'm supposed to be, and…hope he loves me anyway. And if he doesn't…

Because the way he loves me right now isn't enough. It isn't enough.

There was no comfort after my injury, after having the dream given to me and taken away. No calls to see how I was. No texts. No nothing. Nothing because he couldn't put his pride aside for me when I needed him. When I just needed my dad.

Once again, I wipe away tears with the back of my hand. Standing, I walk down to where the ocean meets the shore. The waves are quiet, gentle swells, but they splash gently against my skin as I move closer, salt on the breeze. Against my legs, the cold water makes me inhale sharply.

I'm his daughter. His kid. He's supposed to love me when he hates me. He's supposed to do so much more than I accept. He's supposed to believe in me when he's disappointed, when I've made mistakes, when I'm less than perfect. But instead, when I fall short, I don't feel like anything but gum on the bottom of his shoe. It doesn't make sense to me.

And the reality is, all I asked was if he was proud of who I was…not who I could be, and he said nothing. He let me leave. And then proceeded to dig the knife in deeper. As if I wasn't struggling under the weight of my own expectations, as if I wasn't falling apart at the seams.

This relationship is circling the drain, and I've tried. I've been the one to fix it in the past, to apologize, to beg for him to forgive me, to let it go. I can't this time. I won't.

But wondering if I'm good enough for my dad is going to break me if I let it. And I can't. I can't live my life trying to meet some conditions that I shouldn't have to. No one else has them for me. No one else expects me to be something I'm not when choosing to love me.

If Dad doesn't want to like me, to love me—fine.

I guess I'll just have to learn to live with that.

# THE GIRL THAT I LOVE

## Isaiah

It's been two days since Aurora's MRI.

Since she's been home. Obviously, I know something happened. Bad news, I assume, but I can't quite figure out what. Aurora…she likes to hide—she always has—but it's not usually *just* one thing.

As long as I've known her, she carries the weight of things that bother her until she can't. Tends to treat it like a heavy backpack until it's forced her to the ground.

And I'm trying to give her space. Once she confirmed by answering my text with a simple 'yes,' I left her alone. But it certainly feels a lot like floating on a raft without an anchor. I sigh, removing my glasses and rubbing my eyes as I ball up another piece of paper.

Writing isn't coming easy right now. Not the letter to Elijah, not any new words for my book. Nothing. Worry clouds any coherent thought I have. Raven meows from next to me on the couch, where she's taken a liking to sitting on Aurora's lap. Two days and the both of us are lost souls searching for the girl that fills the space.

Reaching over, I scratch between her ears, and she pushes her head into my hand. "She'll be back soon."

And she will. There is no running away from this anymore. Not for me. Not for her.

I ran away for far too long. And if she wants to run away from this city, fine, but she's not running away from me. Maybe I don't deserve that, but without her, my path in life gets blurry, fractures into a million directions. It took a long time to get back here, on her path, and I'm not giving it up again.

Reaching over to my phone, I scroll past the text messages from Sophia and Kian, asking if I've heard anything, and find Maazina's name. I had figured it was the first person I should have on my side regarding Aurora, aside from her family. We don't talk often aside from the group message between the two of them and myself, but occasionally, she'll send me a strange meme or a stray message about her crush on Kian.

A strange girl, that one, but someone I'm eternally grateful is by Aurora's side.

The phone rings twice before she answers. "Y'ello?"

"Maazina?"

"Hey, Isaiah. Sorry, trying out greetings like old white men these days."

I snort, running a hand down my face. "Understandable. Do you know where I can find the head coach?"

"Teller?" Maazina hums. "She's probably at her office by now. We have practice in two hours, so she should be there. This about Aurora?"

"Yup."

"I can send Coach a text and let her know you're coming by. I'm sure she won't mind but just in case."

"Thank you. That'd be great."

There's a pause. "Can I ask you a question?"

"Of course," I say, shutting off the music and the lights. After closing my empty notebooks, I pocket my keys.

"Do you think she's okay?"

Images of Aurora flash instantly in my mind. The gentle shape of her lips, the slope of her nose, and the star shaped freckle. Hazel eyes that seem to see right through me. I know what they look like when she smiles and when she's sad. She's been gone for two days, and life already seems off-balance.

"I do. I imagine things just got too loud."

Maazina exhales through the phone. "Yeah, you're probably right. And Isaiah? I know we just met and all, but I'm glad you're back in her life. Though she may never admit to our faces, we could tell she needed you. Thanks for, uh, taking care of her the way that you do."

I clear my throat over the emotion that builds in my throat at that. Those girls had her back when I didn't. Made her laugh when I wasn't around. They solidified themselves in her life as family. I'm grateful she had them then. And I'm grateful she has them now. "Thanks Maazina."

"Of course," she says. "Let me know if you need anything. Since I'm sure you know where she is, let me know when you see her, okay? And that I'm giving her a friendly love tap whenever I see her again."

I chuckle. "Got it."

After hanging up, I make sure Raven has enough food and water for the rest of the night and next morning in case I don't return before I head out the door. Aurora likes her routine, her comfort. If I know her like I believe I do, I know exactly where she is. Everyone has asked me—the girls, Sophia, Kian, her mom, though I think she knows, too—but I don't tell them. Aurora wants to be alone, and she's gotten that.

My fear is if she's left alone too long, she'll lose sight of the way out of it.

First, I've got a few stops to make. The drive to the field is short and quick, and I follow the signs to Coach Teller's office.

I knock, and her voice follows shortly after. "Come in." She's leaning back in her chair when I enter, unsurprised to see me. "Isaiah, I presume? Nice to officially meet you." Coach reaches a hand across the desk, and I return the handshake firmly.

"You too, Coach Teller. I've heard a lot about you." I motion to the chair opposite her, and she dips her head. Taking a seat, I rest my elbows on my knees. "Can you tell me what happened?"

Coach Teller purses her lips, eyes focusing on a photo on the wall. One of the team after a championship—I think in 2022—with Aurora and the defense holding up the trophy with everyone else. "She's one of the best players I've ever seen. One of the best I've ever gotten to coach. Aurora has worked so hard for this, for that National Team invite." With a sigh, she turns her gaze back to me. "She has to have a second surgery next Thursday. There was another, smaller tear. Adds four weeks onto her recovery."

My heart breaks for her. When she was a little girl, she'd scribble out her dreams about the National Team. When she was a teenager, we'd talk about it on our bedroom floors, staring up at the neon stars she had on her ceiling or the starkness of mine. To know it may be out of reach again or delayed pains me.

"That makes sense." Leaning back, I meet her coach's eyes. "Is that all?"

Coach Teller's lips twitch. "You know, not sure I've ever had a conversation like this with a player's partner."

I huff a laugh. "Somehow, that is unsurprising."

Her dark skin wrinkles with a smile, but it's there and gone. "You've known her for years, correct?"

"Since we were kids on a playground. She punched a kid because he broke my glasses. She was five."

She laughs. "That sounds about right." Coach tilts her head, gives me a long look. "So, I assume you know her father?" I frown but nod. "I wasn't there, so I can't say for sure, but I told Aurora to wait on the curb while I grabbed something, but when I came back, she was gone. Her father, one of our coaches, as you know, was standing there."

I suck my teeth, my hands tightening around themselves. "Has she talked to you? About a trade?"

"She mentioned it when we were waiting for the results."

"She means it," I say, trying to keep my voice level since none of my anger is directed at her. "She will leave this team. He wasn't her official coach before, but he was always there. Extra drills, extra hours on the field. It was fine. But he's hard on her. I know I haven't been back for long, but it doesn't seem that that's changed. Never congratulated her for the invitation because they had a fight recently. He never once called her after the injury. I won't tell you all the details because they aren't mine to tell, but it's too much for her."

There's anger in Coach Teller's eyes now, too. A tenseness to her shoulders.

"I'm not sure how serious she was when she mentioned it to you, but she asked if I would leave the city. She loves it here. Her family is here; her life is here. She loves those girls, the team. She loves you. And she will leave it all behind if he doesn't fix it."

"I have a meeting scheduled with him."

I nod. "Is he here?"

Coach Teller raises a brow. "He is." Understanding flows between us.

She could tell me not to say anything, but I'm not a player. And I wouldn't listen. "No violence on the property."

I snort. "Not my forte."

"You're good for her. I'm glad she has you." Coach Teller stands and reaches out a hand for me to shake again. "Thank you for talking to me."

"Thank you." With a final shake, I head out.

The hallways between the offices are short, and it only takes me a second to find her father's. Steeling my features, I knock. Aurora has no idea that I've talked to him and obviously has no idea that I'm about to again. I'll tell her when I see her, but I'm so fucking sick of no one having the guts to say anything to him. They make snide comments or a line here and there, but they never really go for it. I can't find it in myself to care anymore. Whether he hates me for the rest of our lives or not, I don't care.

My obligation is to Aurora. The girl that I love.

And that means looking out for her. No matter what.

I enter after his voice travels through the door. Upon my entry, he sighs, exhaustion taking over his features. "Isaiah."

"Mr. Matthews."

"Is this going to be a friendly visit?"

"Not particularly." I stay standing. I have no plans to be here longer than needed. "She's going to leave this team."

Shock filters over his features and clouds his eyes. "She's going to quit?"

"I didn't say quit. She's not a quitter." I give him a pointed look. "She's going to request a trade if you don't fix things."

So quickly, his defenses come down. "That doesn't make sense. Why would she do that?"

"With all due respect, you know exactly why," I say, pulling in a deep breath. "She isn't willing to jeopardize the team, their coaching, and their abilities because of what's happening with you. You haven't spoken to her in—what, almost two months? And you think that she's okay with that? You're not just her father. You're her coach."

Remorse flashes in his eyes so quick, if I had blinked, I would've missed it. "She doesn't need me." He clears his throat, but I'm angry. He wants to throw himself a pity party? Fine. He can do it in private and act like he cares about his daughter.

"That's bullshit, and you know it. If she didn't need you, this wouldn't matter. She wouldn't be considering leaving her team that she's helped build. If she didn't need you, she wouldn't do anything and everything to gain your approval."

We stare off for a minute or two or five. I'm not sure. His approval means nothing to me. Not anymore. "I don't know what you said or didn't say to her that made her disappear. I don't really care because I know that it hurt her. You hurt her. Again. She'll be okay; I'll make sure of that, but you? Can you go the rest of your life without speaking to your daughter? Because you're too prideful to apologize?"

Mr. Matthews sucks his teeth and averts his eyes.

"To be clear, I'm only here because of her. Because I love her. And she deserves better from you," I say, working to keep the bite out of my words. "I'll follow her anywhere, to any team. But we both know she shouldn't have to leave. If anyone should leave, it should be you. And if you want a relationship with her going forward, I expect you to take a good look in the mirror while you still can. While there is still a relationship to be fixed."

Once again, he's silent, eyes unreadable, but there's a low hum of tension in the room. He knows he's walking a line, and there is no coming back from this one if he crosses it.

I turn to leave, my hand on the door. "Have a nice day, Mr. Matthews." The door snaps closed behind me, a feeling of finality floating through the air.

## My Aurora

Going 'off the grid' isn't easy when you have people that care about you. A champagne problem, I know. But with a cell phone that won't stop buzzing and people who are worried, there is no getting away from all the noise.

Though today, it's quieter. I imagine they've all gone to Isaiah.

Isaiah.

Sighing, I let my face fall into my hands. I thought being here, being alone, would eliminate the weight, pick it up off my shoulders, and set it down somewhere else, but it hasn't. And I haven't cried since the drive down here, which is…wrong. I keep waiting for the dam to break, the pressure behind my eyes to burst. But it all just sits there. Fucking heavy.

I've been selfish. Running away like this, leaving Isaiah there with nothing more than a simple *yes* when he asked me.

Selfish. Distracted.

Maybe Dad's always been right. I'm always focused on the wrong thing. Always focused on the problem and never the solution. But he never showed me how to get through things; he just expected me to do it. To show up on the other side with no scrapes or bruises, no scars.

Mom tried. But I was so obsessed with his praise and his approval, it just didn't matter.

And it all feels like a crock of shit.

The air brushes my skin as it rustles through the leaves still hanging on the branches of the tree. Many of them crunch under my feet as I walk through the neighborhood.

Right now is one of those times I wish I was a little kid. So I could kick and scream and cry in public where everyone would politely look away and brush it off due to adolescence. Without a glance to the house, I collapse on the front lawn in the slightly overgrown grass and let it cool my skin.

Unfortunately, I'm not a child, and I can't throw a tantrum. And for that, adulthood is grossly overrated.

Something steals the sun from me, a shadow casted over me. "You alright down there?"

I blink an eye open. "Isaiah?"

He crouches, running a thumb over my cheek. "That's me."

"You're here?"

"I'm here."

Oh, man. My God, does the dam break.

I spring up, throwing my arms around his neck, and hold on for dear life.

"Oof." Isaiah comes tumbling down on me, and I welcome the weight. This weight feels normal—right. Takes the place of the tears and the pain and chases them away. Cradling me, he holds me on top of him, and I find the safe space in the crook of his neck.

"I've got you, sweetheart. I've got you," he murmurs against my neck.

His arms hold me tight, one cupping the back of my neck and the other roaming up and down my spine. I feel bad always crying on him. But he's the best at catching the tears. With him, it doesn't seem like a weakness. My emotions don't feel like a burden. And they don't make him think any less of me.

We lay there for a while without speaking. My apologies and my thank you's caught in my throat, overtaken by quiet sobs instead. Eventually, he carries us inside and settles us on the couch together. I'm latched onto him like a koala, unable to let go because I'm scared the world will crumble as soon as he's not touching me.

"Can you look at me?" Isaiah whispers against my neck.

Taking a few deep breaths, I lean back, and he brushes my hair away from my face. His thumbs roam over my cheek bones, over the tear streaks. Isaiah studies me with gentle, brown eyes.

"What?" I ask, my voice scratchy and raw.

"I just needed to see that you were okay."

Fuck. The damn breaks all over again, tears streaming from my eyes without my permission. "I'm not." Air is not easy to come by. It feels like all I'm doing is gasping for it. "He doesn't see me. He doesn't get it. He just wants me to be some…" I can't—I can't find the words because there aren't any. I don't know what he wants me to be. And even if I did, I can only be who I am.

"Why can't he see me?" I sob, wishing it would stop. I want all the pain to go away. But it won't. "Why can't he like me as I am?"

Isaiah pulls me as close as possible from my seat on his lap. "I don't know, sweetheart. I wish I did. All I know is that you are a brilliant woman. On the field and off. You are caring and strong, and you love more deeply than anyone I have ever met. You care more than anyone else I know. You are enough. In every facet. In every way. You are the best person I know. You are my favorite person in the world." His hands are warm and steady, keeping my eyes locked on him. Those brown eyes are strong and determined, like he's ready to piece me back together on his own. "You do not need to be anything or anyone else but the person you are."

I wipe my eyes to no avail. Those tears aren't stopping any time soon. "But—"

"But nothing." Isaiah's hands are firm. "You are perfect as you are, Aurora."

I let my head fall to his chest and revel in the feel of his arms wrapped tight around me. His hand moves in calming motions up and down my spine, the other buried in my hair. Isaiah is such a steady presence. Especially for me. Sometimes, I feel like I should be stronger in front of him, more put together…able to deal with the punches life throws. But I just…don't want to. Not with him. Not when I know he's going to love me when I'm on top of the world and when I feel like I'm being crushed by it. Isaiah loves me weak or strong. Happy or sad.

"How do you always know what I need?" I murmur, lifting my head when the sobs have stopped.

Isaiah gives me a gentle smile, brushing his thumbs over my lips. "Easy. I was made for you, Ro. And you for me."

Pulling me in, he presses his lips against mine, salty from my tears. Isaiah kisses up my cheek, where the tear stains remain, and over the bridge of my nose. Each little flutter starts to repair the cracks in my heart one by one. I don't know how to explain what it feels like, being loved by him, being the person that receives his love. All I know is that it feels right.

"You're my saving grace. You're my sunshine. You're my Aurora." He kisses me, whispering the words against my lips.

For a second, nothing else exists. Nothing else matters. He's here. And he's here for me and every version that exists. The pain will exist tomorrow and days after that, I'm sure. But...so will we. So will Isaiah.

Isaiah lets me fall apart.

And still I know, he loves me as I am.

# Say It

Steam fills the bathroom; the smell of almond and honey permeates the room from the bubble bath. Outside, the sun has set, darkness settling in its place with stars above. My eyes are still swollen from all the tears, but they've stopped now. For a minute there, it felt like a well that wouldn't empty.

Isaiah eventually dragged us off the couch when the sky had started to darken. He set me on the counter, gently picking twigs out of my hair as he started dinner. Apparently, he came prepared—both for my emotional despair with a box of tissues and copious amounts of candy, and for practical matters, like ice packs and ingredients for dinner. I watched as he cooked, and he cut up apples and cheese for me to snack on. He even had a warm washcloth for my eyes. They insisted on leaking out a few tears every few minutes until they seemed to dry up. Isaiah said nothing to indicate he was annoyed by them, just wiped them away whenever he saw them on my skin.

And then, he ran me a bath.

Bubbles float up around me, hot water splashing over my skin.

"Would you please get in the tub?"

"I don't want to crowd you," Isaiah says, reaching out to tug a curl that's fallen from my bun.

"You're not. I…please?" I soften my eyes and blink my eyelashes rapidly. His lips quirk, tugged by an invisible string, but I see his resolve fall away. Though I'm not sure why he was fighting in the first place.

Isaiah sets the bag of candy down, to which I grab a rainbow-colored candy and lean on the edge of the tub. I didn't realize love was finding joy in the moments where that feels impossible. Smiling when it feels like nothing else is going right. Butterflies in your stomach when there was previously only dread.

"You checking me out, Aurora?"

"Yes," I state. "I expect a good show."

A throaty chuckle escapes him, traveling over my skin. Instead of saying anything else, he drags his t-shirt up slowly, unveiling the taut planes of his stomach and the ink on his skin inch by inch. I lick a stray sugar grain from my lips, watching as my heart beats deep and slow in my chest. Isaiah continues, stepping out of his sweats, and I trail my eyes over the fully-inked leg. It's not fair really how hot men look with a little ink and short shorts on. Of course, those short shorts are boxer briefs, but that's beside the point. He strips them off too, my breath hitching at the sight, to which Isaiah smirks because, apparently, he's attuned to every little sound that comes out of my mouth.

Isaiah's eyes soften when they land on my face. "I hope I make you blush for the rest of our lives."

At that, the heat already in my cheeks spreads further. The water and the bubbles slosh as he slides into the tub. It's not huge but big enough for us both to be comfortable. I crowd him instantly, his legs cradling me as I move as close as I can get.

Cupping his cheeks, suds run over my hands. Unabashedly, I stare at him. Eyes roaming over the face I wake up to and fall asleep with. The eyes that have seen me break down in tears or shout in anger, that have seen me disheveled in the mornings and sweaty on the field. Lips that I get to kiss every day, that kiss me every day, lips that whisper jokes in my ear while we watch movies or TV, or instructions when he tries to teach me how to cook.

"What are you looking for?" Isaiah asks, his voice deep.

"A flaw."

"I'm serious."

I raise a brow. "Me, too." I run my thumb over the bridge of his nose and the curve of his lips. "You are perfect."

A strong, firm hand lands on my hip. "That's not true, Ro."

"Maybe not. But you are to me. For me." I press a kiss to his lips. It's tender and simple, and I feel it all the way to my toes.

He looks cheeky when I pull back. Between us, he cups bubbles in his hands and blows, making them land over my cheeks and skin. Giggling, I splash his chest. "Come here," he says and tugs me around, pulling my back into his chest.

Against the warm water, Isaiah is the warmth that I need. That brings me the comfort that I crave. I lean my head back on his shoulder. His lips are as light as butterfly wings against my skin.

They brush right below my ear. "I talked to your coach."

I sigh. "So, you know?"

"About the surgery? Yes. I mean, I figured it was something with the knee when you didn't come home the first night. But…"

"But you knew something else had happened to make me stay away."

Instead of responding, he kisses my neck. His arms wrap around me, caging me in. "What did she tell you?"

"That she saw your dad standing there and you were gone. Do you want to talk about it?"

Tipping my head back, I find his eyes. "Not really. Not tonight."

"I should tell you, I've spoken to your dad. Twice."

A bemused smile forms on my lips. "You have? About what?"

"You." Isaiah tugs me closer, not an inch of space between us. Before he continues, I grab a few candies, holding two up for him. Isaiah grabs them, nipping my fingers in the process, sending a chill down my spine. "I couldn't take it anymore. The first time was after the fight at Sophia's. I told him to grow up."

My eyes widen in surprise as I suck the sugar off the candy.

"And this time, I told him if anyone should leave the team, it should be him. And that he would regret doing this to you for the rest of his life. You know, the basics." He smiles against my skin. "You deserve to have someone stand up for you, to be on your side. Of course, your mom and Sophia are. Kian, too. But it's different. I don't really give a shit, Ro, whether he likes me or approves of me from here on out. I didn't come back for anything else but you. I'm on your side, no matter what. And you shouldn't have to do it on your own."

In my chest, my heart feels safe enough to slow, to release the tension it's been holding. The low hum of anxiety that's been thrumming over my skin settles dissipates.

Isaiah tips my chin up with a gentle finger. His lips are close, almost brushing mine. "You don't have to do it alone. Anything alone. You don't have to carry the weight and the pressure alone. You don't have to figure it out alone. You aren't alone. I'm here. I'm *right* here."

All the love crowds in, pushing everything else out of the way.

"I shouldn't have run away."

Isaiah gives a slow shake. "You can run if you want, Aurora. I'll be right behind you."

Smiling, I give a slow shake of my head, disbelief at being this lucky. I'm not sure I'll ever get used to it—him being here. But I guess we have the rest of our lives for me to come to terms with that.

Leaning up, I press our lips together again. He lets out a tiny sigh of contentment, his hand burying itself in my curls. As it always does. Like I hope he does for the rest of our lives. I brush my nose against his, brush my lips over his cheek and his jawbone. And I kiss him again, soft and sweet and slow.

I pull back so I can see him. Isaiah is beautiful and kind and my best friend and the person I'm going to love every day for forever.

Against his lips, I whisper, "I love you, Isaiah."

I swear he goes as still as a statue. A small laugh bubbles out of my lips before I kiss him again. And still, he doesn't move. Reaching up, I tap his forehead. "Hello? Professor Bryant? You in there?"

"Say that again."

My heart flutters. "Professor Bryant?" His eyes clear and narrow on mine. "I love you."

Under my palms, his body relaxes. On instinct, the fingers of my left hand trace the ink on his skin, taking bubbles with it. It took me too long, I know that. Too long to tell him, but the words were not going to come if I forced them. But now, they've broken the door off the hinges.

"There was a time I was sure I'd never really be all the way happy. You know I had the career, the girls, Soph, Kian, but the reality was, I didn't have you. And I'm not saying this to make you feel bad," I ramble, his eyes never leaving mine. "But I want you to understand how deep this goes. Because I think that if you hadn't come back, there was always going to be a break in the cracks."

Isaiah's features soften as they look at me. He brushes his thumb across my jawline. "I understand. Do you still feel like that?"

Holding him tight, I shake my head. "No, Isaiah. And maybe unhappy was the wrong word; it was more so that I felt lost. Homesick. And I was resigned to the idea that a part of me was always going to feel lost. Because I longed for a place I couldn't go anymore, a place I forgot how to find. That isn't true anymore because you're here. With me." I meet his eyes. "And I could find you if I was blindfolded in the dark."

There's so much love in his eyes that I don't know what to do with it all. Part of it makes me feel unworthy. That I won't be as good at this as he is. But I get to learn. And I get to learn with him.

"You are my home. You are the missing puzzle piece of myself. If we never met, I wouldn't have known I was missing something, but there was always going to be a part of me that existed only to love you. You are part of who I am, Isaiah. You are the steady ground when it feels like the world is falling apart underneath me. Getting to be in your life, getting to love you, is my favorite thing I'll ever do in this life. And I love you so much that I don't know what to do with it all. I don't know where to put it all, and I didn't know that was possible."

Isaiah nuzzles into my neck, kissing the soft skin until he finds my lips. "You give it to me, Aurora. That's what you do with it."

My breath catches. I smile against his lips. "You sure?"

"I'm sure. You are just as much a part of me as I am of you."

Spinning in the water isn't easy, but I do it. My fingers curl around the back of his neck. "I'm so in love with you, Isaiah."

He hums against my lips and stands effortlessly with me in his arms. I squeal as the water sloshes off of us and leaves droplets on the floor. As he walks, Isaiah grabs two towels on the way to the bedroom.

"I wasn't done." I pout, fighting a smile as he tenderly dries me off. He stops every few seconds to give me a searing kiss.

"Done what?" he asks. Demanding, his hands roaming up my leg, pinching the skin of my inner thigh. Heat unfurls over my skin, sparks lighting up like fireflies.

"Telling you how much I love you."

Isaiah's lips quirk. "You can tell me." He presses a kiss on my lips and to the tip of my nose. "While I touch you and while I make you forget the rest of the world, you can tell me." His hand gently squeezes under my butt before moving me onto the bed "You can tell me over and over and over again, Aurora." Isaiah climbs over me, his tattooed thigh pushing my legs apart, his body weight settling over mine.

If euphoria was something tangible, it would be this. The intoxicating, tender touch of his hands on my skin as warm as a livewire, or the heavy weight of his body on my own, or his eyes looking at me like I am the only thing in the world that matters.

Against my chest, I feel his heartbeat racing along with my own. His hand travels over my ribcage, stealing my breath with every inch. "I look at you and I don't know how I got so lucky." Isaiah's voice trembles just so—no one else in the world would ever notice it. But I do.

He traces a pathway with his lips, nipping the skin when I inhale, flicking his tongue out when the tiniest of moans escape my lips. Everywhere he goes, he tracks and memorizes me. My hands roam over the hot skin of his back, still slightly damp, and hold him tight to me. Moments later, his hand finds my thighs, finds the center of all the heat roaring through my body, and drags his lips away from me.

I groan. "Isaiah," I breathe out, squirming. Pressure builds in my stomach. My brain is unfocused and hazy. The only thing that matters to it is him.

His eyes are pouring into mine, brown eyes alight with stars. "Say it."

"I love you."

A cheeky smile takes over his face. His lips kiss a path over my collarbone, and his hand moves with a sureness that takes my breath away. Moving with tenderness that can't be faked. He loves me. In so many ways, he loves me. And loves all of me. The good, the bad, the ugly. Every freckle, every dimple. When I'm angry, he loves me. When I'm smiling and laughing, he loves me. Right now, he's choosing love through delicious and yet torturous methods. Featherlight touches over my skin that make me hungry for more. I kiss him hard, and he tastes like sour candy and the love of my life.

"It's not enough, Bryant. More." I nip his ear, and he spins us, pulling my legs to straddle him.

"Does that hurt?"

I lean over him, my curls brushing his naked skin, and rub our noses together. "No. And right now, I wouldn't tell you if it did." Rolling my hips, I pull a groan out of him, his fingers tightening into my skin.

He pinches my butt, tingles traveling up my spine torturously. Adjusting us, he presses in and finds the magic spot that makes my head spin and stars dance behind my eyes. I press down, but he stops me, a smirk on his face. "Say it."

I smile, kissing him, and I whisper over and over again that I love him. Every thrust of his hips, every burst of pleasure that follows. It spurs him on, makes him ravenous, and I relish in it, burying my face in his neck and breathing in only him. Heat licks at my skin in small flickers and in large, enveloping flames. Pressure builds and builds slowly, then all at once. It's like flowers blooming and stars shooting over the sky, leaving tiny sparklers behind.

"Aurora Jade, I love you beyond measure," he whispers against my lips.

With a firm hand wrapped around my neck, he holds me to him, swallowing my small, breathless moans, and drags me up the peak. Up and up and up. I fly past cloud nine and land in the stars. And this time, Isaiah whispers it over and over and over again in my ear until I fall, tumbling down the other side of it. My heart beats erratically in my chest with no sign of stopping—that very same heart belongs to him.

"That's it, sweetheart. I'm right here." Isaiah's own heart increases under my palm, the only connection to reality I have.

His other hand digs into my skin as his movements become frantic, chasing the very same euphoria he's given me. For a second, he never stops, instantly building me back up with steady, beautiful, addicting movements. The nip of his teeth, the press of his hands. It's all too fucking much, but no feeling in the world could ever compare.

"Aurora," Isaiah groans, my name escaping his lips like a tortured prayer, and I roll my hips until he's teetering on the same cliff that he's dragged me back up. Both of us, together, disgustingly in love, tumble over it for what feels like forever.

Stars burst, and in the darkness of the room, new constellations form. My skin burns with the aftermath against him. Both his arms are wrapped tightly around my body as if I'm going anywhere. As if I would ever dream of going anywhere without him. When my lungs don't feel like they're fighting for life, I kiss underneath his chin and over his jaw until he blinks his eyes open.

They're warm and as beautiful as a labyrinth that only I know the way through. "My heart belongs to you, Isaiah." I tug his bottom lip. "To you and only you."

We share another long, searing kiss—a swipe of his tongue, a slow dance of our lips that makes me feel like I'm in a dream. Of all the things I've dreamed of, of all the things that I've accomplished, Isaiah is my favorite dream of all.

# THE BIG GUNS

**M**ist lands on our skin from the ocean waves.

Isaiah's arm is a steady weight over my shoulder, his fingers threaded through mine. The sun is hidden behind a sky of gray. The heat from his body seeps into mine.

"You ready to go back?" His voice is soft, barely loud enough to be heard over the waves.

Exhaling, I turn my eyes to him. "No." My lips quirk in a sad smile. "But I'd rather get it over with. If I have to leave, I want to know now."

"I'm sure you've thought of it, but you know you don't have to, right? If you wanted to stick it out, I'd be there."

"Yeah, but I don't want to have to stick it out. It's my life. I want to enjoy it." I shake my head. "I don't want to come home miserable and upset because he can't be bothered to be an adult. I want to love it. I love them, the team. But…soccer—I love soccer more. I need to be able to play without the pressure of Dad. Without him leeching the joy out of me from the sidelines."

Isaiah squeezes my hand, pressing a kiss to the side of my head. "Understood."

"I wish I had a why. Why couldn't he get over himself and come check on me? Why is it never enough? Why is asking him to love me so hard?" I take a deep breath, tipping my head back. The salty mist lands on my skin. "Because I can't…I can't fix things if I don't know why they're broken."

"Aurora," Isaiah starts, but I hold a finger over his lips.

"Let me finish," I say, and he nods. "I know that's not my job. I'm not perfect, but nothing I've done is deserving of feeling like a throw away. A disappointment. Not from anyone but especially not my father. All I've ever wanted is to make him proud. But I'm done jumping through hoops to still fail. I'm done. I deserve better than that."

After a momentary silence, Isaiah attacks me with kisses. "I'm proud of you, Ro."

"I'm sure I'm going to fall a few more times. Be angry about PT and my knee. If we have to move, that might be—"

He places a palm over my mouth. "Whatever it is, we'll do it together." Pushing my hair away from my face, he makes sure my eyes are focused on him. "And if you fall, I'll be there to catch you. You've always gotten back up, dusted the dirt and wiped the tears. The only difference is, I'll be there to hold your hand. I'm always going to catch you, Aurora."

Who could blame me for practically tackling him in the sand?

No one.

Underneath me, he smiles. I run the thin chain through my fingers, kiss his nose, and breathlessly say, "Let's go home."

My grip on Isaiah's hand is tight as we walk up to the facility.

"If you hold on any tighter, you're going to kill my circulation. How am I supposed to touch you if you do that?"

I hip bump him, my brow furrowing playfully. "Shush."

He tugs me to a stop, tipping my chin up. "You are okay. No matter what happens in there, you're going to be okay."

I blow a raspberry. The pressure lessens, if only a bit. The fear still sits there. Yeah, it was my idea to leave if things didn't get better, but I don't want to leave. I will. But it will suck.

Isaiah taps my butt twice. "Let's go." He pulls the door open and follows behind me, but upon entry, I find Maazina, Sylvia, and Viv all standing there. Spinning, my eyes land on Isaiah, who's pocketed his hands, eyes twinkling with mischief.

Maazina skips over, threading her arm through mine. "He figured you'd be all scared, so he called in the big guns."

"I did *not* say that," Isaiah groans. I hide my smile. Their relationship reminds me of me and Kian.

Viv gives my hand a squeeze, her long, dark braids flowing behind her. "He most certainly did not say that."

"Jeez Louise, you guys are no fun."

Maazina leads the charge as she does, and I exhale—really truly exhale—with them by my side. Turning back, Isaiah trails, and I mouth, "thank you," to him. And in return, I get an, "I love you."

"I never thought I'd see the day," Viv comments quietly, and my cheeks flush.

"I did. And I love it. She's so cute when she blushes," Sylvia says, causing the rest of us to laugh.

Our footsteps echo down the empty halls. Maazina's grip never lightens, and my chest expands with gratitude at this friendship. We stop outside Coach Teller's door. The girls untwine themselves from me and take up purchase on the wall. I could go in alone, could act like I'm not scared shitless, but I am. So, I reach back, and Isaiah's palm finds my own in a millisecond. After knocking, we enter.

Coach Teller looks us over, her lips barely upturned but enough for me to relax my shoulders. "Matthews, nice to see you're alive."

"I'm sorry I left like that. I should've waited."

"I may be your coach on the field, but that doesn't mean you have to obey my every word off it." She gives me a playful glance. "Though you should. Please, both of you, sit."

Coach and I take a seat, but Isaiah remains standing next to me. "I can leave you both to it, if you'd like."

Before I can speak, Teller beats me to it. "Nope. I imagine what concerns her, concerns you. You're welcome to stay."

I wring my fingers together in my lap. "So—"

"You want a trade?" Coach Teller asks. I swear, she sees every weak spot, every fear. Even the tear in my knee under the goddamn table. It's really no surprise she's an incredible, and sometimes scary, coach.

Tentatively, I nod.

"No."

My shoulders slump. "Coach, please."

"You wanted a trade because of your father, correct?"

Again, I nod.

"Well, he resigned yesterday. So, a trade isn't necessary."

Next to me, Isaiah sucks in sharply. Meanwhile, my heart short circuits. "Wh–what?"

Coach Teller's brown eyes twinkle. They *twinkle*. And her lips fight a smile. "Now, I probably shouldn't look so excited over the idea of one of my coaches quitting, but you, Matthews, are not going anywhere.

Certainly not to another fucking team."

Nothing is making sense. "My dad quit?"

"Resigned," Coach says, but I hear the teasing tone.

I huff. "Is there a difference?"

"Well, actually—" Isaiah starts.

"Isaiah, I love you. Shut up." I point at him, ignoring his tiny laugh. I swear, it's like they've decided to conspire over my shock. Turning back to Teller, I lean forward. "I don't understand. He left?"

"He did. I suspect something made him realize he was risking a lot more than he realized," she starts, eyes flicking to Isaiah. "He stated he would see the girls through the rest of the regular season before leaving. But that was it. I'm helping him get some interviews with other teams, not that he needs my help, but I have some good connections with the coaches on the east coast." Teller looks at me with a sense of finality. "You are not leaving this team. Clear?"

Tension releases. "Clear."

"One more thing." She pulls together two manila folders. "One of these has the National Team's schedule of training camps, pulled together based on the last few World Cups and Olympic years. The first, as you know, is expected to be at the end of February. This folder," she says, holding up the thicker folder, "is a detailed schedule for you that Thomas helped make. Your surgery, doctor appointments, PT, extra exercises, massage therapists, and markers for you to track your recovery."

"Coach, I—"

"We are going to do everything we can to get you on that field and at the first camp. And if not, we will damn well get you to the second camp. Understood?"

My eyes burn, but I hold back the tears. "Understood."

"Good." Teller slides the folders over and sits back, her gaze on Isaiah.

"And you—I expect you to keep her on said schedule. No trainings that aren't in there. No extra runs. No pick-up games. No practices. If it's not in that folder, she doesn't do it. Understood?"

Isaiah smirks. "Yes, ma'am."

"Is the idiot brigade outside the door?"

I snort but nod.

Coach Teller raises her voice, "Did you hear that girls? Nothing."

Maazina answers, resigned, "Yes Coach."

"Alright, now get out of here. Keep me updated on surgery. I'll see you on the sidelines soon enough."

With the folders gripped tightly in my hands, we all stand. Before heading out, I can't stop myself from suffocating my coach with a hug. It takes her by surprise, if the way she tenses automatically is any indication, but she settles. "Thank you."

She pats my curls. "You're welcome, Aurora."

Isaiah is smiling so wide when his hand finds mine again, and I almost skip out the door. Instantly, I'm bombarded with the girls over my not having to leave. Maazina, forgetting herself, jumps up on my back.

Teller's voice booms from the office. "Get off of her now."

I laugh when she slides down but keeps her arms locked tight. Sylvia and Viv lock their arms around me as well in the thickest group hug I've ever had.

"Can I kiss my girl?"

"Ooo, is she your girlfriend?" Maazina and Sylvia coo.

I sigh.

"By all means, don't let us stop you," Viv says, raising a brow but not unwrapping her arms.

Pushing up on my tiptoes above the heads of three girls that love me more than I deserve, I find Isaiah towering over us. And in the midst of all the chaos, he presses his lips to mine.

Underfoot, the ground stops shaking. My heart feels full.

I am loved. And better, I get to love all these people.

Tomorrow is always a new day when things are rough. A way to look forward, to hope that the storm breaks. But right now—today is pretty fucking great.

## I See You

When I come to, all my drug-induced brain wants is Isaiah.

In the blur, I see Maazina and Kian sitting next to each other. My mom, Soph, and the girls must've stolen Isaiah away. Even under the fog, the lack of my father's presence once again hits a sore spot.

"Kian, stay away from her. She's in love with you."

Maazina scoffs, but her warm brown cheeks turn red instantly. "That is so not true."

Kian barely blinks, simply throws his arm around her. "It's okay, Z. I know it's harmless."

She groans, her face in her hands. "I hate you, Aurora."

A scratchy laugh is my only answer as I push myself upward. Kian hands me a cup of water and some pretzels. The sight of food right now is not ideal, but I take them anyway. The water soothes my throat.

"Where is—"

"Lover boy?" Maazina snides, and Kian laughs.

"You're one to talk, Miss, I-have-an-unhealthy-crush-on-my-teammate's-sister's-husband." I raise a brow, and she flushes again, sitting back down. At that moment, the rest of them return. Sophia takes one look at Maazina, her husband, and myself.

"Stop teasing her about Kian," Soph says, trying to fight a smile.

"Oh, my God." Maazina groans and tries to make herself as small as possible.

But I stopped paying attention because Isaiah's in the room. I reach my hands up and motion for him to come here, which he does. Isaiah chuckles and comes to my side, making me smile.

"Ah, there she is. She'll be nice now," Maazina says at my dopey smile. Sophia and Kian join her, making some quiet remarks about how they've never seen me like this, to which, internally, I resent, even if it is true.

Isaiah sits in the chair next to my bed, looking at ease. The girls run up on my other side, handing me bags of candy each for my recovery with big smiles, looking exactly like their parents. Having to have the surgery sucked. But having them all here makes it suck less. Pain surges over my knee but fades moments later.

"Here." Isaiah places a few pretzels in my palm. "You need to eat."

I roll my eyes but swallow a few down, hoping the nausea dissipates soon. The haze starts to disappear, and the doctors come in. Everyone listens intently. Isaiah even takes notes, probably so Coach Teller doesn't berate him, as they talk. Surgery went well; my knee looks good. I need to use a brace and crutches again at times, but PT starts immediately. After PT and recovery, I should be good to go. Hope blooms underneath it all, and I'm sure there will be days when I can't find it, but I hope it always shows back up.

After the doctors disappear, everyone in the room shares a quiet look, leaving me on the outside of the loop. Isaiah squeezes my hand, bringing it to his lips and brushing them over my knuckles.

"What was that look for?"

"What look?" Maazina answers quickly. Too quickly.

The only person who doesn't look apprehensive is Isaiah. And I'm pretty sure that's only because if anything, he looks a little angry, which can only mean one thing.

"Again?" I ask, my voice shaky. "You're going to bombard me with him again?"

"We didn't invite him, Ro. He found out about the surgery. He's been in the waiting room all day." Sophia adjusts Joey in her arms, resting her head on her husband's shoulder.

I scoff, focusing on Isaiah. I'm already in pain. Why did he think now was the time?

"I'll send him away if you want," Mom says.

Closing my eyes, I take four deep breaths. Then two more. "You can bring him up, but that doesn't mean I have anything to say."

After a brief hesitation, Mom nods. The lot of them exit to go collect my father. Maazina strides over and cups my cheeks, taking me by surprise. "Can't wait to have you back on the field, sugar mama," she says and plops a dramatic kiss on my forehead. Despite myself, my lips quirk. "I'll be in the hall."

The room falls silent. I lean into the pillows, exhaling.

"You don't have to let him in, Aurora." Isaiah's voice is gentle, a caress on my skin.

The warmth in his eyes dances over my skin, taking away the aches and pains, leaving nothing but love behind. He brushes his lips against the gentle skin of my hand again, each knuckle brushed with care.

"I know. But I don't want to be like him. Not this way," I say, my voice cracking.

"You're not."

I snort. "I am. I'm stubborn, and I run away, and I shut down, and I shut people out. And you know those things—it's whatever. But I don't want people to walk on eggshells around me or think that they have to prove themselves to me or—" I exhale. "Not that people do, but I don't ever want them to. And I know I have every right to kick him out the moment he walks in if I want. And I probably won't say anything at all. But I'm not going to do what he did."

Isaiah nods and leans back in his chair. "Fair enough. I'm proud of you."

Rotating my head to take him all in, my cheeks warm. "You say that a lot."

"I don't ever want you to forget it."

My heart does a little jump in my chest before settling. I'm pretty sure there's a whole section of my brain dedicated to the number of times he's told me that. And another section dedicated to him in general. Soon, my heart and my head are going to be solely dedicated to him, and I'll just be a vessel.

"Can I have a kiss?"

He smiles and obliges. Sweet and tender. One of my favorite types of kisses. Even so, the heat twirls over my skin. I peck his lips twice after he pulls away and once on his nose because I like that whenever I do that, his dimple fights to come out.

The clearing of a throat draws us out of our bubble, and my dad stands at the door. While his face is stoic, emotion flashes in his eyes. "Can we have a second?"

"He stays." I squeeze Isaiah's hand. Dad looks between us but enters the room. With a steady gaze, I watch him take a seat on my other side, and I swear Maazina peeks in through the window on the door, but I ignore it.

"I heard the surgery went well, and you'll be on your way to a full recovery." Dad rests his elbows on his knees and wrings his hands together—his own nervous tell. I'm not sure what he expects—I'm not going to roll out the red carpet because he took the time to show up this round.

It probably doesn't help that Isaiah is practically glaring at him.

Dad sucks in a big breath. "I am proud of you, Aurora. I have been proud of you every day for your entire life. You've dedicated your life to something you love and continuously push yourself to be better, even when the circumstances stack up against you. I am proud of you for things other than your athletic accomplishments."

I swallow thickly, unable to drag my eyes away.

"I'm disappointed that I made you feel otherwise. That I let you think otherwise. I know that repairing this will take time. But losing you was not an option. That team is yours—always has been. I imagine it's where you'll be until you retire," he says, adjusting his hat. The fluorescent lights highlight every wrinkle on his dark skin, and he looks tired. Exhausted. "I do want you to be great. I've always wanted you to be great at anything that's important to you. But that should've never been what you felt from me. That greatness was all that mattered. You're what matters. And my failing to make you understand that is my own doing. You have been nothing but wonderful and strong, and who you are is what matters. Not what you do. I love you, kid. Okay?"

All I can do is nod.

Part of me wants to fight back and to push the buttons I know will make him angry. As if that will further justify the pain. The other part, the logical part, which under the pain meds is a miracle for winning out, accepts this for what it is.

This is him showing up. For now, this is the best he can do.

Dad stands and exhales a big breath. I can see how heavy it's weighing on him. But he has to handle that. It's not my responsibility. "I hope that we can—" Dad sighs, centering himself. "I hope that we can find the next steps. I don't want a life without you in it. I don't want to make you feel as I have ever again. And I want to be the dad you deserve. One you want to keep in your life."

I try to ignore the wealth of emotions building up.

My hope for an apology fades, though disappointment doesn't fill the empty space.

I expected it. Sorry isn't a word that frequents my dad's vocabulary. It sucks, and it's wrong, but for now, I accept it.

He approaches me, and Isaiah tenses. "There is no use in trying to cover everything today. Glad to see you're doing okay." For a moment, Dad simply studies me before tentatively pressing a kiss to my forehead. We watch him exit, and when the door shuts behind him, I let out a big breath.

"That could've been worse, right?" I ask.

Isaiah's eyes sparkle, taking me in. "It was a good start."

"Yeah, it was."

Shortly after, everyone else returns and settles in until I'm ready to be discharged. It's a weird feeling—getting worse in a way before you can get better. The same with Dad leaving the team. It sucks in its own way. Losing him as a coach as he has been my whole life. With the surgery behind me, I can move forward. Without the pressure of him watching every move, our relationship has a chance. Who knows what Isaiah and I would be if he hadn't left. It sucks having to go down a path you'd rather not to get where you want to be.

But it happens, and we persist.

Life goes on. Sometimes, it's harder than it should be.

I look at my friend, my family. Isaiah.

Sometimes, it's better than you could ever imagine.

Raven's meow is my greeting when Isaiah pushes the door open. My stuff is strung over his shoulder, his hand on my lower back as he leads me inside. "Go sit down."

"I'm fine," I groan.

"Go."

I make my way to the couch, putting the crutches aside and collapsing on it immediately. Isaiah moves about the house—sets water down next to me, then a plate of all my favorite snacks, then a tiny cup of candy, and elevates my leg according to the doctor's instructions. Finally, he plants himself beside me. Isaiah kills the tiny space between us quickly, planting his head in my lap.

"Does this hurt?"

I flick his nose. "Stop, I'm fine. I'd tell you if I wasn't." Raven pops up and plants herself between Isaiah and the cushion, a tiny paw brushing against me. My hand lands in his curls, my fingers dragging through them repeatedly. "Thank you."

He looks up at me. "For what?"

"Everything." I brush my thumb over his smooth skin, tracing over each dark spot on his flawless, brown skin. "For everything. For being here. For holding my hand through this whole thing and sticking up for me. And for being patient and for catching my tears at every turn." My lips upturn. "I'm not sure I would've gotten through this the way I have without you."

"You're a strong girl, Aurora. You would've."

"Maybe, but you let me be…soft." I take a deep breath. "I didn't have to put on a brave face with you. I didn't have to act like I was okay when I wasn't. So, yeah, thank you."

"You're welcome," he murmurs, his eyes shining with sincerity.

We sit there together in the silence, and the love that we have for each other fills every space. It's quiet but full. And the realization that this type of love, a soft flickering flame that never burns out, is as important as those louder moments. The *I love you's* never get old, but this, simply existing in it, is such an undervalued part of a relationship. It's a steady constant, the heartbeat of being in love.

Resting my head back, I let my eyes fall close. Let myself soak it all in.

Eventually, minutes or hours later, Isaiah breaks the silence. "Question."

"Answer," I say, grabbing a candy and sucking the sugar off.

"Which apartment do you like better? Or would you prefer a house? Or a new apartment?"

My mind starts spinning. Isaiah's face turns sheepish as he gazes up at me. "Are you asking me to move in with you?"

"I'm suggesting that we should move in together because we don't sleep without each other anymore, and we may as well save money."

"Romantic."

"Ah, you want the romantic version?"

Running my fingers through his tiny, beautiful curls, I can't help but grin. "Yes."

"You know, I love that no one else will ever see this version of you," he says, and my brows furrow. "How much of a complete, hopeless romantic you are. Everyone teases you when you kiss me in public or your cheeks flush. But they don't see this. Your constant need to touch me, like I'm going to disappear if you aren't, or the big doe eyes you give me when you want something. They don't know how much you read the poems or are curled up watching a show you've seen a million times just for one scene." His lips quirk, and I melt. "I see you. Every part. And that makes me the luckiest man alive."

Reaching up, he runs his fingertips over my skin, tucking my curls behind my ear. His thumb presses on the sensitive spot under my jaw. "I want to move in with you because it's pointless not to. I don't sleep when you aren't here. And everything is too quiet. There are no random giggles from you on the couch, no sleepy kisses in the middle of the night, no hands tracing the tattoos. It's empty without you. I want to move in with you because I want to live with my best friend. And the girl who makes my world spin. So I can see your soft hazel eyes in the morning and kiss you anytime I want."

I hum, warmth spilling out of my chest. "Kiss please."

He chuckles, the sound echoing through his apartment, bouncing off the walls and falling over my skin. The press of his palms on my warm cheeks is the touch I craved for so long. Every time I walked around feeling that well in the pit of my stomach, this was what I wanted.

Isaiah's touch. Isaiah's words. Isaiah in general.

Pulling my lips to his, I exhale, and he catches it. His tongue delicately teases my lips, and I don't hesitate, kissing him back.

I wonder when his kisses will feel like just a kiss. And I think the answer is never. Because whenever our lips touch, a jolt of lightning hits my veins and runs through them until the next kiss. And so on and so on. It never ends. A cycle of beautiful addiction. I am addicted to kissing Isaiah Bryant, and I wouldn't want it any other way.

I'm breathless when I pull back. "How do you feel about renting a house? I want a dog. And a yard. You can have an office and a library—"

His kiss stops me. I love those interruptions. "We can do whatever you want."

"You give in so easily," I murmur, running my thumb over his lips.

"Only to you. Only for you."

Only me. Only him. Only us.

The prospect of our life together is such a beautiful dream. It doesn't take away from our other dreams or other parts of our life, our careers. Instead, it's a supplement to a full life. It's simply more. More smiles, more fun, more love. More everything.

And it's ours.

I rub my hand over Isaiah's back. "You okay?"

Isaiah inhales and exhales. "Yeah."

We've been staring at the postal box for five minutes now. My crutches lean on the hood next to me, and the sun peeks through the clouds overhead as we sit there. Dragging my hand back up and down his arm, I find his hand and take it in my own.

"You don't have to do it, Isaiah."

He turns to me, the tension falling away when he looks at me. "I know. But I miss my brother."

The statement is simple, yet it feels like a punch to the gut. I say nothing. Instead, I choose to rest my head on his shoulder until he's ready. It's been two weeks since my surgery. PT has been painful and taxing both mentally and physically. And Isaiah has been writing and rewriting this letter since.

He hasn't texted or called his brother, but I know that a part of him wants to. Or wants to be able to without feeling guilty or vulnerable. Without wondering if Elijah will answer. Without the fear of him disappearing again. Whether that takes weeks or months or years, I'll be here every step of the way. This letter is different than the previous—that was short. A confirmation that he received Elijah's. This one is far more personal.

Isaiah squeezes my hand and takes a big breath before letting go and stepping up to the mailbox. I watch him slide the thick envelope inside and out of his control. For a second, he stands there, hands in his pockets, staring at the box that now has the letter. I contemplate going over there, but I think he needs this. Officially opening this line of communication to his brother, opening himself up after being hurt the way he was—that's hard. So, I give him the space and know he'll come back to me shortly.

Isaiah tips his head to the sky before turning around. And when he does, there is nothing but devoted attention to me. The corner of my lips turn up as I take him in. Starting with the ink on his legs, covering one almost completely and dotted around the other, my heart beat picks up as I take it in. It never gets old, looking at tattoos on his thighs and how they disappear into his shorts. His sweatshirt covers the rest aside from his hands, but I know exactly what lines each arm.

He approaches, hands landing on my waist, heat spreading in response. I reach up, fixing the edge of the beanie that covers curls before threading my fingers behind his neck.

"Ready for the fun stuff now?"

"I am if you are."

Isaiah pats my butt. The low simmering heat turns into a steady pulse that only worsens when his lips brush the shell of my ear. "Let's go, superstar."

I hum in displeasure when he lets go of me, dragging him back for a searing kiss. "Greedy," he murmurs against my lips. His hand splays dangerously along the band of my leggings.

"You made me this way."

He chuckles before handing me my crutches and opening my door for me. "I like you this way."

"Obsessed with you?"

"Exactly."

Shaking my head, I climb into the car. Isaiah bends down, hands on the frame of the door. Everything about the move is unfairly hot; I don't know how to describe it. It's ridiculous that he exists, and that's enough for me to melt.

"The feeling is mutual, Matthews."

Just like that, my heart flutters into oblivion. And kissing him feels like landing among the stars.

The loud buzzing sound greets us as soon as Isaiah opens the door. Artwork is plastered on every surface of the bright, airy space, and colorful couches and chairs line the waiting room.

Almost immediately, the tattoo artist, Theo, greets us. He's only slightly less tattooed than Isaiah is—at least from what I can see—but still, dark ink covers most of his brown skin. Even standing next to Isaiah, I admit this is a very pretty man—not as pretty as Isaiah, but a very pretty man.

He reaches out his hand to shake Isaiah's. "What's up, man? How are you doing?"

"Good, good. Thanks for getting us in today."

"'Course. Nice to meet you. Aurora, right?" Theo asks, stretching his hand out. I balance on the crutches and shake his hand.

"That's me. Nice to meet you."

He grins at me and motions for us to follow. Isaiah walks slightly behind me, as he often does since getting the crutches. Theo runs us through the process—or me, since Isaiah's seen him once since moving here. We sign all the necessary forms, and the process goes quickly.

Isaiah scoots his chair closer, hands on both my thighs. "You excited?"

"To memorialize your existence on my body forever?

He snorts, caught off guard. "Yes."

"Yes," I say, grinning. And I am. I have a few small ones, mostly in places no one sees, like behind my ear and on my ribs, but these are going on my arm. Really, I'm just copying him. Getting each of our birthdays on my forearm and the number seventeen on my wrist. The other ones I'm getting are the name of his poetry book below the bend of my elbow and two puzzle pieces on the back of my arm.

Eventually, I'll get his initials, but I have a plan for those.

Maybe it's dumb. Some people will undoubtedly think it is, but I know that that's not a concern for us. For me. No part of me thinks we don't make it through the rest of our days without each other.

"You're still not going to tell me?" I pout when he shrugs.

"You'll see soon enough."

"What if it's something awful? Like my face?"

"I love your face," he says, laughing, both hands reaching up to cup my cheeks. "But I would never do that."

I hum but drop it. Theo returns and leads us back to his station.

"Who's going first?"

Isaiah volunteers and moves toward Theo to go over sizing and the stencils. Sitting back, I take in the view. Two beautiful tattooed men, one of whom is coming home with me. Sneakily, or not so sneakily at all, I send a picture to the group chat.

**Maazina:** Who is *that?*

**Sylvia:** Her boyfriend, duh.

**Vivian:** Sylvia…

**Maazina:** Not him. The other one.

**Me:** Your new crush?

**Maazina:** Kian's got some heavy competition. Any chance you'll send me your exact location?

**Me:** No.

I laugh to myself when she sends a sad emoji back and turn my eyes to the man in front of me. Theo is finishing up the stencils and stands back to check their placement.

"Let me see."

Isaiah closes the short distance between us, and I spot the stencils immediately. The first is on an empty space on his right arm. And it's a cute looking octopus, like an animated style, filling the empty space. My chest aches at the sight of it. When I look up, he's fighting a smile, and I wait for him to show me the second one. Isaiah holds out both of his hands, which previously, both knuckles were bare. Now, they are not.

My name is spelled out over his fingers, *Rora Jade*, along with line work stenciled on each of his thumbs. In my chest, my heart stops.

"You can't."

Isaiah crouches down so he has to look up at me. "I am."

"Isaiah."

"Aurora," he mocks, amusement clear in his eyes.

"What if—"

"What if nothing. This was always in the plan. I just figured I would do it with you here." Simple. Nonchalant. This…part of it is insane, and part of me absolutely fucking loves it. "You aren't going anywhere without me. Where you go, I follow. We are in this life together. It's as simple as that. And the whole world may as well know it." His voice is loud enough for only me to hear, and every word is a shot to the heart.

Every time I think I've hit the floor on how far in love I can fall, he drags me even further in.

Pressure builds behind my eyes and around my heart, squeezing so tight it might burst. Somehow, I hold it together and settle for kissing him on the cheek. He holds me close and whispers in my ear, "I expect an onslaught of kisses later."

"You expect?"

He squeezes my wrist. "I want to be covered in them."

My heart flutters, and I nod, heat flooding my cheeks. Isaiah kisses my forehead as he stands, heading over to Theo.

"You doing alright over there?" Theo asks, a smirk on this face. He and Isaiah partake in a simple handshake.

I narrow my eyes. "You were in on this?"

He shrugs. "I read his book. He told me the story." Theo pulls on tattoo gloves, an amused smile remaining on his face. "I got invested."

Isaiah shakes his head with a laugh as he gets comfortable. There's a glint in his eyes—cocky or confident or both, who cares. I like it.

I lean back in the chair, eyes never leaving Isaiah. "Can't say I blame you. It's quite a story."

At that, Isaiah grins big and wide, bright and full and warm. That man, my man, loves me more than I ever thought someone could. It's funny watching the tattoo gun get pressed against his skin. I remember viscerally how I felt seeing him for the first time with ink covering his skin and being jealous of it. Feeling empty and lost at him showing up physically different than he was when he left. I thought the years lost would never be found. That nothing could've been done to reconcile them. But my God, haven't we? We changed, sure, but not to the extent I'd believed. Not in ways where we couldn't relearn those changes, adjust to them, and in the ways that matter, we are the same. At least to each other.

My soul recognizes his. As his does mine. Two halves of one whole.

From thinking I would have to spend the rest of my life without him just months ago, to knowing that I'm going to spend the rest of my life with him is something out of a fairytale.

Maybe it's magic. Maybe it's just how the tables turn, but either way, I like our story.

And I wouldn't change a thing.

# EVENTUALLY

Isaiah is seated in his armchair, typing away on his laptop with Raven curled under his arm.

Even though I'm doing what I should be—my stretches and exercises—I pout. I *want* to be curled up under his arm. He pushes the glasses up the bridge of his nose, and his foot taps to the rhythm of the song spinning on the record player. Sometimes, I like when he doesn't notice me staring. This way, I get to stare as long as I want without any questions.

I smile to myself like a love drunk fool and turn away, continuing my stretches on the floor. The amount of time I spend daydreaming about him, about the love of my life, could be pathetic. But I'm too in love to care. The moment he brought me back here after surgery almost a month ago, I gave up my apartment. I'm here all the time like he said, and I don't want to miss anything. Not the big stuff and not the small stuff. And this way, I get to kiss him anytime I want.

Soft hands land on my shoulders. "Isaiah!" I squeal, my heart jumping out of my chest. "I hate when you do that."

He chuckles, his lips pressing to my neck. "I couldn't help it. You were so focused. What were you thinking about?"

"Nothing." I try to keep my cool, not looking at him, but he presses his fingers into my sides, tickling me until I laugh. "Okay, okay. Stop!" Isaiah kisses and bites his way up my neck until he's kissing my lips. "I was thinking about you."

"I figured when I saw you pout."

"Well, I was pouting because I was jealous. Of the cat."

Isaiah laughs, hands pulling my curls away from my face so he can see me. "You never need to be jealous."

I roll my eyes, even as my skin warms. "I know that, logically." Isaiah taps my nose before taking a seat on the floor beside me, stretching out.

I sigh, content. This is…enough. If this was the rest of my life, sitting here with him, on the floor, I'd be happy with that. There are still things I want to do—play on the National Team, play in a World Cup and the Olympics, but this…this is good. And pure. And *happy*.

A buzzing phone breaks my happy, dopey daydreams. Isaiah picks up my phone, and I watch his eyes widen. "Who is it?" I ask, and he turns the screen, only for me to see a photo of me and my dad taking up the screen. "Oh."

"Do you want to answer?" He sits up, handing me the phone. My eyes flash between the two, and without responding, I slide the answer button.

There's a beat of silence.

"Aurora?"

"Yeah, hi, Dad." I lean against the couch beside me. Isaiah joins me, his hand landing on my bad knee, and he begins massaging it with his fingers. My heart races. This is the first time he's called me since the fight when Isaiah first arrived. The first time since surgery.

"I, uh, wanted to check in. See how you were coming along. With recovery and all."

The phone's on speaker, and Isaiah gives me an encouraging look. "Yeah, I'm—I'm alright. Pain is mostly gone, just discomfort now. PT throughout the week, still using the crutches."

"Good, good," he says, and I can practically see his awkwardness. I can envision his nervous ticks. "Doing your massages, too? And calf stretches? Make sure not to forget about your ankle and your hip."

I almost laugh. It's so like him to focus on the things he can fix. "Yeah, I know. Thanks. You been alright?"

"Yeah, yeah. Start with my new team in two weeks." The tension is still palpable. I mean, how could it not be? But it's something. It's a call. That he made. "Well, I don't want to keep you. I just wanted to check in and make sure you were doing okay. I'm sure Isaiah is taking good care of you."

I look up from the phone at him. And he's already looking at me. His brown eyes are light and warm. He taps my knee twice. "He is. Thanks for calling."

"'Course. I'll let you go now. We can talk again soon. Love you, kid."

I swallow, and a beat passes. Another. "Love you, too."

When the call ends, I exhale. I feel a bit crazy, an array of emotions flying around, trying to find a place to land inside my head. Isaiah scoots forward, one hand cupping my cheek and the other on the back of my neck. His thumb brushes back and forth against my skin. It brings me back to Earth, back to my happy, very real, very dopey life.

"He called," I say, trying to fight a smile. It's so small, it's fucking minute, but he called. And he called first. It's one large step for Dad. Isaiah grins, and so do I, but it turns wobbly. No rhyme or reason for it; assume it's just an overload, contrasting feelings trying to find their place.

"What's wrong, sweetie?"

I shake my head. "Nothing." I exhale and try to smile again. "Can you just give me a hug?"

"Always, Aurora. Always." Isaiah does as he says, pulling me tight into his arms.

I close my eyes and lean into him. My very real, very safe, very constant person. My *person*. Through it all. Always.

Sophia and I watch our two favorite boys from our spot near the fire pit. The blanket draped over her shoulders brushes my skin as she sits behind me, tugging on my curls one by one. Joey and Zaza are running around the backyard, playing tag with them. And I can't look away.

"You are so painfully in love," Sophia says with a laugh. "It's pathetic."

I scoff. "You fell in love with him, that man, at what? Fifteen?"

"Touché." My sister inhales, and I know she's watching her husband make scary, googly eyes at her youngest with a stupid grin. "He's so…"

"Dumb?"

She laughs. "Yes. But also perfect."

"Who's pathetic now?"

"Both of us."

I turn, not shocked to see a dopey smile on her face at all, and climb up into the oversized lawn chair next to her, pulling the blanket over my shoulders, too. We sit there, stupidly in love together. The air is cool around us as December approaches quickly, and the fire flickers in the late afternoon sun.

"I want another."

My heart swells. Of course, she does. Of course, *they* do. They're great parents. "Works for me. Another one for me to corrupt."

Sophia laughs, resting her head on my shoulder. Even in the winter air, she smells like spring time. "Enough about me—"

"No, Soph, really." My cheeks heat, which is so fucking annoying.

My sister waves me off. "Shut up, Aurora." I do because she uses her mom voice. "You're so…happy. And that doesn't mean you weren't before. I know you were. But I was there a few months ago when you were worried you'd never stop missing him. Seeing you in pain wasn't easy for me. Especially over something I couldn't help you through."

"Soph," I start when her voice starts to tremble.

"Shut up, and let me finish. I'm emotional, and I have baby fever," she scolds, exhaling. "You light up around him. You always have; it's nothing new, but even after all these years, you two are brightest when you're together. I remember watching you guys as kids, teenagers. I remember when it changed into something more, and I was sure you were both too young to feel that much. Not that I had any room to talk given my dumbass husband, but I was scared that it was too much and too strong."

She looks at me, and to no surprise, she has tears in her eyes. "He used to look at you like you put the sun and moon in the sky. Like you placed the stars individually. And you looked at him the same. Like he was your own personal sun. One that only shone on you. And I was scared when he came back that those things wouldn't. That the friendship wouldn't be there as it once had. That it was going to be different, tainted by the distance. And that the loss of those things would've hurt more than never being with him again."

Sophia's grip on my hand tightens. I guess I never thought what it was like for her, raising kids and watching me deal with a pitiful, broken heart. She's my sister. We hurt when the other does.

Sophia continues, "I was scared that I was going to watch you get hurt again, and there would've been nothing I could do."

And now, I'm going to fucking cry all because she had to be sappy and emotional.

"But," she says, snorting out a laugh with wet eyes, "you're so stupid happy. And it makes me so happy, Aurora. To know that it's all still there."

"Shut up, or I'm going to snot all over your shirt."

She laughs, and so do I. We were always told our laughs were similar, and when both the boys look over here, I believe it. Isaiah gives me a slightly concerned look, but I give him a half-ass thumbs up. The boys bend down, whispering something in the girls' ears, and shortly after, they're sprinting full force toward us with Kian and Isaiah trailing after them.

Joey approaches me. "Auntie Ro, can you play tag with us?"

"Of course—"

"She cannot." Isaiah glares at me. I pout.

"Why not?"

He approaches me, attacking Joey with kisses until she squeals and makes a beeline for her dad. Isaiah's hands land on the arm of the chair closest to me. "Because I said so. And because you know you can't yet."

I meet his eyes, my heart fluttering away in my chest. "Yes, Professor Bryant."

Sophia makes a faux vomiting sound and unravels herself from me to stand. "Enough." Isaiah snorts and traps her in a headlock. "Isaiah, get off of me."

I watch with amusement. "How the tables have turned. How's it feel?"

Sophia flips me off but stops fighting the hold. "You're lucky I like you, Isaiah."

Isaiah grins, his dimple poking out, and places a kiss on her cheek before letting her go. Azalea watches the whole thing.

"Auntie Ro?"

"Yes, baby?"

"Are you going to marry Uncle Ziah?"

I choke. On what, I'm not sure. The air? My spit?

Behind their daughter, Kian and Sophia try not to laugh. Kian especially looks like a puckered fish. Idiot. My skin turns hot, and I know my cheeks are red as hot flames. Zaza just blinks at me expectantly. Isaiah is crouched behind her with a glimmer in his eyes—amusement and love.

Finding my words, I clear my throat. "Eventually, yeah. If he wants that."

Kian rolls his eyes. And all Azalea does is shrug. "Cool." I'm left in some strange stupor as she strides towards the house. "Mom, can I have a snack?"

Sophia rolls her lips, trying not to laugh as well. "Dinner's almost ready, sweetie. Come help me finish up." She starts walking with Joey in her arms, and her husband just stands there. "Kian, let's go."

He looks between us and his wife, understanding coming over his face. Kian taps his head twice. "Got it."

Behind us, the fire crackles. Isaiah's hands land on my knees—one in a brace, one without. He taps his fingers over my leggings, crawling up my legs. The clouds are darkening above us, the sky as well as the sun dips lowers. There are streaks of orange and red appearing like a haphazard paint brush.

"She's just like you."

I roll my eyes. "Come here," I say, patting the spot next to me. He obliges, pulling my legs over his lap. Adjusting so I can see him better, I lean my head back. Unable to help myself, I trace my finger over his face, his nose, over his cheek bones, his jawline. His lips. He gives my calf a squeeze from where he rests his hand.

"Eventually, huh?" Isaiah grins smugly, lovingly. "I do want that."

Nerves I didn't even know were on edge settle down. "Me, too."

"Obviously."

"Hey." I pout, and he chuckles, grabbing my hand with his. He kisses each of my fingertips, little sparks sent down each one.

"She asked me first," he says, lips brushing my palm before pressing a kiss there.

A smile starts to grow. "She did?" Isaiah nods.

"Glad you were put on the spot first."

"You're such an idiot," he says, pulling me closer—as close as I can get in this chair. My fingers find the thin chain around his neck, running it through my fingers before tugging him to me with it.

"As Maazina says, I'm your idiot."

Our noses brush, and it feels like a bubble comes down around us. With a hand on my cheek, he pulls me in for a kiss. Our lips touch, and the whole world falls away. Isaiah's my anchor when I'm lost in clouds. His teeth nip the gentle skin, and his tongue teases my lips, and I sigh, turning into putty like always. It happens every time we kiss, and I'm not sure it will ever stop. I hope it doesn't.

Isaiah smiles against my lips, and my heart soars. His touch, his kiss—they sink past my heated skin and into my bones. Where they belong.

Whatever else the future holds, it doesn't matter because it'll be me and Isaiah against the world.

## ALWAYS

*I* always loved the end of November and the beginning of December. The last of the leaves are still clinging on to the trees. There's still a spot of color before the winter gray settles, and most days, the sun still shines.

And everything feels…happy and exciting with the holidays. It's a bit different these years—in two ways. One, Dad and I are still distant—and I'm still learning what that looks like. But on the other, I have Isaiah. And that's enough to be thankful for in one. Despite the injury. Despite my father.

Isaiah is here.

"Alright, ready?" he asks, his voice almost lost in the downpour of the rain outside. I smile and nod. Isaiah goes first, pushing open his door and comes around to my side of the car, picking me up out of my seat. I squeal, holding my crutches in one hand as Isaiah runs us to the door of the diner. Rain splatters on each of us, but both of us remain smiling.

The diner is packed, hence the mad dash to the door. Isaiah sets me down when we're safely under the awning. "Thank you, Zay."

Isaiah kisses my cheek and reaches around me to get the door. The warmth of him sinks into me. We enter and are thankfully seated quickly in the back at a small booth. There's a jukebox in the corner, and the seats are cracked. Giant menus sit on the table with an array of milkshake options. We've been going to diners every weekend in the city and in the surrounding area, trying to find our new favorite spot.

"Are we getting a Christmas tree?"

"Of course, if you want," Isaiah says, studying the menu, even though I know what he'll order. "Real or fake?"

"I'd prefer real, but what about Raven?"

"She'll be fine." He eyes me. "Don't forget, we have those ornaments we made from when we were kids."

I rest my head in my palm, taking all of him in. We went through his keepsake box the other day. It was painted in shades of green and dotted with poetry along the top and the sides. Inside, it was filled with an array of things that meant something to him, or to Elijah, or to me. There were pins from some of my soccer tournaments, statues I had bought him if I went anywhere exciting, some of his early poetry, pictures of us or him and his brother. There were pairs of old glasses in there, old comics, and other notes. There was also a little glass octopus that painted a rainbow on the walls in the sun. And the Christmas ornaments we made.

They were wooden Christmas trees and snowflakes that we got to paint and decorate with our initials on the back of each.

"This is the first time they'll hang on the same tree," I say, tapping my fingers on the table. Underneath, Isaiah has our legs intertwined. "The first time we'll celebrate together. It's a lot of firsts for us. I'm happy we're finally getting them."

He stares at me with a heated, loving look. "I want to kiss you."

"Nothing is stopping you, Bryant."

"The room full of people are. I can't kiss you the way I want right now."

I smile, my cheeks heating. I grab the menu and hide my face, to which he laughs at. Isaiah pushes it down with his hand and cups my chin. He leans over and gives me a tiny kiss, one that only makes me wish we were already home. So he *can* kiss me the way he wants.

Eventually, the waitress comes, taking our milkshake orders. Isaiah gets his favorite—coffee ice cream with a caramel drizzle and extra whipped cream. And I get my own—chocolate peanut butter with chocolate cookies and rainbow sprinkles. They arrive in large, silver containers that are frosted from the chill.

I spoon a big bite, knowing immediately that there's ice cream on my face. "You're such a mess," he muses.

"I'm your mess."

Isaiah reaches over, his thumb swiping the ice cream off my cheek. He pops it into his mouth, eyes never leaving mine. My cheeks heat, my body warmed by his words and the way he looks at me. "My very pretty, very beautiful mess."

I take him in. Even though we did miss some years, sitting here, it feels like we missed no time at all. It feels like we're teenagers all over again. Teenagers who knew they meant something to each other, who knew they were best friends but had no clue the type of love that would grow in the space between them.

Now, we're twenty-somethings who do know they're in love. Who are in love. Who are each other's person, each other's home. And we are happy.

There's such simplicity in that word: happy. But it's all anyone ever wants. To be happy. To feel happiness. And I feel that when I look at him. And I know that when he looks at me, he sees everything. Every flaw and mistake, every failure and every success, and I know that he *loves* me.

"Isaiah, where are you taking me?"

"Shut up and walk, Rora," he says, lips brushing the shell of my ear. Isaiah's fingers are threaded with mine as he leads us from behind. It's been a few days since the diner, but today, he woke me up by telling me he had a surprise for me. I've been living in anticipation ever since.

In my ear he tells me when to step as he has since we got out of the car. It's only been a few steps, but being blindfolded makes the world feel endless.

I hear a click, and I'm instructed to step up. Excitement starts to build, buzzing under my skin, waiting for their release. "Okay. I'm taking this off but eyes closed still, okay?" His voice is soft, but it echoes. Wherever we are is empty.

"Alright." The slight pressure disappears from over my eyes, but I keep them squeezed tight. My legs tremor with adrenaline.

"Okay, go ahead."

I blink my eyes open and am greeted with wood floors, crown molding, and archways. "Isaiah…what is this?"

Stepping forward, he grabs my hand and slowly leads me through. "Possible house. It's still a rental, but there is opportunity in the future for more. We're right outside the city."

It's gorgeous. There's a staircase leading upstairs with a detailed railing. Isaiah continues telling me about the house. Two bedrooms and two and a half baths. A full living room with a fireplace, big windows, built-in shelves, and it just goes on and on and on. He walks us around and around, hand intertwined with mine.

Oh, man.

Everywhere I look, I can see us here. Isaiah at his desk in the living room against the windows. Raven curled up on the windowsill in the sunlight or in front of the fireplace. The kitchen is gorgeous with shiny, new countertops and a breakfast nook. A big door that leads to a small porch and a backyard. Every step, I see us. Isaiah in the kitchen and me on the counter. Sitting on the porch in the sunlight, even though it's currently under a thin layer of early December snow.

We are everywhere in this house.

I didn't know it was possible to fall in love in some way every single day, but Isaiah absolutely shatters that belief. Because every day, it's something. Most days, it's small. Things that are simply a part of our routine that solidifies his position in my life. That solidifies his love for me. That exists in remembering the type of socks I like to wear to practice or what creamer I like.

But sometimes, it's things like this. Thoughts, dreams, snapshots of the future that tell me he thinks about it just as often as I do.

"Isaiah," I say, turning around to find his waiting beautiful eyes. "It's perfect. How did you—is this possible?"

"It's possible. Kian helped me find it. Friend of a friend." He rocks up on his tiptoes. "So, you like it?"

I step closer, motioning around us. "I love it."

Though I think maybe part of that is how easily it's already become ours in my head. Standing there with him, it feels like we're on the precipice of another step of our lives. But the leaps of hope aren't scary with him. They feel natural, as easy as breathing. As easy as counting to three.

Life with him, the idea of a future with him, is that simple.

Isaiah runs his knuckles over my jawbone, the knuckles that have my name on them, and a shiver dances down my spine. "I love you."

My body reacts to his touch immediately. I rest against his chest, wrapping my arms around him so I can fit my hands in his back pockets. "Kiss please," I murmur.

He smiles like he always does when I ask him to kiss me, and he does. I squeeze a hand against his firm butt, drawing a laugh out of him, our breaths mingling as we kiss in an empty house that might be ours. At least for a little while.

"I want it," I say against his lips. "I want the house. If we can do it, if we can have it, I want it."

"If it's what you want, that's what we'll get," he murmurs, his hand cupping my face. Sparks emit from his palm, burying themselves in my skin.

"I'm serious." I blink my eyes open to find him already watching me.

He's always watching me. When I expect him not to be, when I try to catch him first, I can't. Because he's always looking at me. Always seeing me.

Isaiah's thumb presses under my chin. "I want it, too. A home with you. I want that. I want it here."

A just like that, a big, bright smile takes over my lips. How could I not? Standing here with him in this house. "I love you. So much." I string an arm over his shoulder, my hand cupping his neck. "You are the only person in the entire world I have loved like this. That I will ever be in love with like this. Just you. It's you and me."

His dimple shines through, and his eyes hold the entire universe. "Always has been. Always will be." Isaiah tugs me into him as close as he possibly can. Lifting me slightly, my toes are on his, and he walks down the hall through the house. "Now say it again."

I furrow my brows. He squeezes my butt in response.

"Say it again."

"Hm," I murmur, our lips touching. "I love you." With his hand buried in my curls and his arms around me as tight as they can get, I whisper it again and again. "I love you. I love you, Isaiah."

He hums, content. "I love you."

I shake my head, wiping away a tear that escapes from his eye. "Thank you for making it so easy." I kiss the tip of his nose. "And it's not something I do. It's just something I am. Loving you is a part of who I am."

Love is so simple with Isaiah.

It comes as easy as breathing. It's not just something I do; it is integral to who I am. It's in my blood and in my bones. Loving Isaiah is a part of my DNA. Without it…I'm not sure who I would be. But we don't have to worry about that. We are one. IsaiahAurora. We are forever.

The two of us are as simple as flowers blooming, as solid as the ground beneath our feet, and as full and free as two people could be. It may be cheesy and dramatic and extremely fucking sappy…but we were made to love each other. I believe that with my whole heart. We are two halves of a whole. Two puzzle pieces destined to be together.

Isaiah is my forever. My future. My love.

I smile against his lips and repeat his earlier words,

"Always has been. Always will be."

# EpiLogue

## *Eight Months Later*

Being on this field in New Zealand does not feel real.

Underfoot, the grass is manicured and soft. The afternoon sun shines down on us and the crowd—the *crowd*—is absolutely unreal. Looking around, I cannot believe my eyes.

I cannot believe I am here.

It's the last round of knock-outs, and we're up two with ten minutes left. If we win this, we make it to the quarter finals.

Another win with the National Team does not feel like real life. Being on this field as a starter does not feel real. Not after the injury. Not after the painful months of recovering from two surgeries and fighting tooth and nail at every team camp. But I did it. *I* did it. No one can take that away.

The crowd is filled with red, white, and blue. Everywhere I look, there are young girls with their faces painted and their parents holding their hands. And at the fence, I find my family.

Kian. Sophia. The girls. My mom.

Isaiah. In my jersey, like he always is.

We move up the field, maintaining possession in the opposing half. I look around at these girls. They aren't the Royals, but they're pretty fucking amazing. And together, we dominate. We've won every game so far by at least two and given up a total of one goal. Above, the stadium lights are bright and welcoming.

I belong here.

I love it here.

Every pass we get off is smooth, landing on the targets foot with a smooth touch. There are smiles on our faces—small but there. We earned this. Holding onto possession, we move the ball up and down the field, side to side, tiring out the opponents as best we can.

We do not let up until the ref blows the whistle in three long successions. And it sinks in. We're through the first round of knockouts. The cheers are deafening, and the excitement emitting off the girls as we meet in a big huddle is an absolute drug.

"We did it!" Lucy, the right-side defender, says, cupping my face in her hands with a big smile.

"We fucking did it!" I pull her in for a hug, latching onto her like a koala. The other two defenders find us and join the mini-huddle. It's different than Maazina and Viv and Sylvia, but it's another home I get to call mine.

I can't stop fucking smiling.

Not through the post-game talk, not while getting my stuff. My smile never wanes. I'm itching to go find Isaiah. And as soon as we're set free, I set off, as do many of the others, in search of their families and loved ones.

Quickly, I find him waiting for me. My smile is so wide, my cheeks hurt. Seeing him, I get all my energy back.

"Hi," I say breathlessly as I approach, dropping my bag.

He leans over the short barrier, cupping my cheeks and pulling me into a searing kiss. My entire body flushes as I go boneless with his lips against mine. When I regain use of my brain, I wind my arms around his neck, feeling the soft, short curls on the back of his neck.

"Hi," he murmurs, out of breath. My hand finds the chain around his neck, and I tug him back to me. Our lips smile against each other, and it settles warmly in my heart. I love those moments where everything is good and right for no particular reason at all, except that we're together.

Pulling back, Isaiah drops a kiss on the tip of my nose. With ease, he tightens his arms and lifts me up and over the barrier. I don't let go. Instead, my legs are wound tightly around his waist, and I bury my face in his neck.

"You were fucking amazing, Ro." Isaiah whispers the words against my neck, placing kisses over my skin until he pulls my head back. His left-hand cups my face gently. Lovingly.

It's so annoying how much I miss his touch when I don't have it. I sink into it without even thinking, a dopey smile on my face.

"Thanks for being here."

Isaiah gives me a look. "There is nowhere on Earth I'd rather be."

"Just let me say thank you, you asshole."

Isaiah laughs, squeezing my butt. "Yes, ma'am."

Eventually, my feet touch the ground again, and we find the rest of my family.

Including my dad. We've been slowly working toward a relationship again—a functioning one this time. Him not being my coach made a drastic difference, which, honestly, I hadn't expected it to. But without it…without him watching my every move and without worrying if he was judging or criticizing, the moment I touched that field again, I came alive. The game felt like mine again. And slowly, with casual visits at Sophia's or Mom's, Dad just felt like Dad again. Not a coach. And he apologized. Sincerely.

And while everything isn't perfect, there are still times when my insecurities kick in and times when I wonder if we'll ever have that relationship of my younger years again, but it's there. For that, I'm thankful.

Every member of my family is draped in a version of my jersey. Kian is the only one in the Philadelphia Royals' colors, and I appreciate that more than he'll know. They're *my* team. I'm grateful to be here, more than I ever thought possible, but that place is home. Everyone else is decked out in red, white, and blue with my name and my number on them.

Zaza is the first to jump me with a hug, and we rock back and forth. Her curls are wild from the wind, her hazel eyes bright but tired. "Good game, Ro!"

I grin, pressing kisses against her cheek, even though she claims she hates that now. "Thank you, baby."

Her hand holds onto mine as I approach my mom, Sophia, and Kian, who is holding a sleeping Joey in his arms. His other arm is wrapped around his wife, palm splayed protectively over her growing belly.

"Thanks for being here." My cheeks hurt from smiling so hard.

"We literally wouldn't miss it," Kian says, pulling me in with his free arm in a suffocating hold. He nuzzles me as any annoying older brother would. "Good job out there, kid."

I pat his stomach. "Thank you." Sophia practically jumps on me, her curls going wild and her brown skin sun kissed.

"I'm so proud of you."

"Don't use your mom voice on me. You know it makes me emotional,"

I say, flicking her nose when there's space between us. Sophia, also dressed in my jersey like the rest of them, puts her hands on her hips.

"I'm the pregnant one."

"Okay?" I raise my brows. "I'm the one playing in the World Cup?"

Sophia narrows her eyes playfully. "Fine. You win this round. But only because it's your first time."

"Ha! I always do."

Kian and Isaiah share a look before my Isaiah steps forward to wrap his arm around my waist. "Alright there, hot shot."

I turn, pressing a kiss to his cheek. Looking past them, the fans have all but left the stadium. The only people remaining are other players and families and those in charge of managing the field. Above, the stadium lights are on, even though the sky is barely turning pink with the beginning of sunset.

"We're gonna head back and get ready for dinner," Sophia muses, taking a still-sleeping Joey from her husband. "You coming, or you going to meet us there?"

I glance at Isaiah and at the field. "We'll meet you there. I need a minute."

Sophia smiles knowingly. Leaning forward, she presses a kiss to my cheek. "This is everything you wanted. Everything you worked for. You did it."

Looking around at the field I just stepped off of, I let it sink in. At the fact that we're making it to quarterfinals. The fact that this jersey is on my back. "Yeah." Wrapping my arms around her as best I can, I hold onto my sister for a few seconds. "Yeah, I did." She pats my head with a grin before exiting with the rest of them.

I sit down on the bleachers, Isaiah joining me shortly. "You okay?"

Before resting my head on his shoulder, I nod. "Yeah. It just doesn't feel real." I laugh lightly. This is unbelievable. Even now, after multiple games, I can't get it through my head.

"You belong out there." Isaiah reaches over and grabs my left hand, his thumb running over the tattoo on my ring finger that holds his initials. Bringing it up to his mouth, he runs a light kiss over my palm. "You look so happy every time you touch that field. It never gets old."

Turning my eyes up at him, I squeeze his hand. Sophia was right. This is everything I wanted.

The field. More so, Isaiah.

And having both? Well, it's unbelievable.

"Come with me?"

He furrows his brows. "Where?"

Standing, I pull him up, and his hands land on my hips. "To the field." With that, I take his hand and lead him down. We won't stay long, but I watch one of the older forwards chase her little girl around. She's got on pink pre-wrap and a ponytail just like her mom. Isaiah follows me, never letting go of my hand until we're on the grass.

I thread my fingers through his other hand, capturing them both. My heart swells when I see my name on his knuckles, like it does every time I see them. "This wouldn't be the same without you," I say quietly, but he hears me. Isaiah always hears me.

"Ro," he starts, but I shake my head. His brown eyes are as gentle as the morning sun, as they so often are when they look at me.

"You have been as integral to my life as this sport has been. I've known you for pretty much just as long. I grew up on the field and with you, off of it. This sport is everything to me. You know that; everyone knows that. I spent my life dreaming of being here."

Isaiah smiles. "I remember. I remember seeing you scribble it all over your notebook, all the times we would talk about it late at night, like it was a dream you didn't want the light to touch."

I let my head fall forward onto his chest for a moment. Remembering all those times. All the late-night dreams we both shared. Isaiah's hand wraps around my back, pulling me to him, and I look up. "Yeah." I smile. "But I also dreamed of a life with you just as much. But I knew better than to scribble it in notebooks where you could see."

A warmth settles in his eyes. A yearning. I know it's love. That's how I look at him all the time. There is no questioning what is between us. I don't have any fears regarding the two of us. I know that deep down, this is for life. Isaiah and me are for life. The ups, the downs, and everything in between.

The two of us are forever.

"Every time I dreamed of this jersey, of being on a field like this, you were in the stands. When I thought of your future, I was there cheering you on. All of my biggest dreams involve you, Isaiah. And all my small ones. Celebrating this, enjoying this, would not be the same without you. You are my best friend in the entire world, Isaiah, and I sincerely do not know what I would do without you."

"You tryna make me cry, Aurora?"

I snort, my hand wrapping around the back of his neck, my thumb roaming up and down. "No. Though I should be. I still haven't gotten you back for all the tears."

Isaiah pinches my butt, making me squeal. He bends down, nuzzling into my neck, and I hold him there.

I continue, "No, I'm trying to make you understand that as thrilling as this dream is, it really does not compare to having you here with me. You were in every dream I ever had. You *are* in every dream I have now. You're my strong man in a storm. You are who I count on when I can't count on myself. You are who I look for in every room, in every stadium, everywhere I go."

Taking a deep breath, I force him to look at me. His eyes are watering, but no tears fall. Not yet, at least. I rub my thumb over his cheekbone, pressing a quick kiss to his lips. "I'm not sure I'm even making any sense anymore, but I'm saying, standing here, I recognize I'm a lucky girl. That I'm standing in a place where so many girls dream of, and I worked hard for it. But getting to stand here with you, being in love with you right now, in this moment, on this field, is my favorite part of it all. As much as I wanted this dream, I wanted you all the same. There is no feeling in the world that could compare to being in love with you, Isaiah. Not a single one."

Isaiah's hands cup my cheeks firmly, and he kisses me like I created the sun and the moon and all the stars in the sky. His lips are gentle and confident, and they caress my own in a way that is both searing and tender. I slip my hand in his back pocket and hold us together as tight as can be. One of his arms snakes around me, his hand spreading out over the small of my back. Euphoria dances down my spine and settles into my being.

Isaiah pulls back, our noses brushing. There's a tiny tear streak on his cheek. Between our lips, his thumb presses my bottom lip. "I love you. Thank you for letting me love you. Thank you for loving me in return."

My lips quirk, a slight tremble in them. Every day with him feels like falling in love for the first time. "I think it's what I'm best at," I joke, trying to hide the shake in my voice.

"Loving me?" I nod. Isaiah lets out a tiny laugh, the air floating over my lips. "You're pretty good at it."

"Pretty good? That's all I get?" And this—*this*—also feels like love. Joking and teasing. Being able to do so. I love it. But who am I kidding? I love everything about loving Isaiah.

"Fine." He pecks my lips. "You're the best."

"Number one?" I smile against his lips.

"Number one."

I kiss him this time, leaning up on my tiptoes and slipping my tongue past his lips in a dance we created and only we know. Isaiah lifts me off the ground, my toes barely grazing the grass, and just holds me in his arms. It feels like a montage in a movie. It feels like seeing a shooting star for the first time or listening to a song you know is going to be your favorite. Sometimes, I think this isn't real life, and then, he reminds me it is.

Isaiah pulls back, hands still buried in my curls, my feet still dangling. "Alright," he says, putting me down. "Hop on."

Turning, he crouches, and I hop on his back like I have so many times before. Isaiah stands, hands cupping the back of my knees as gently as ever. Isaiah lifts me up, and above us, the bright stadium lights shine overhead. Up here, in his arms, I feel weightless. My arms are wound around his chest, and I sneak a kiss to the underside of his jaw. And because I can't help it, my arms find their way to the sides, feeling the warm air on my skin under the lights. Isaiah's laugh reverberates through my bones. I've never smiled so hard in my life. My arms fall, holding onto Isaiah again, smiling against his skin and staring at him the whole goddamn time he carries me.

He notices, casting me a sly, sexy look, and I ache at the strength of the gaze. He's going to love me forever. He *has* loved me forever. And he stops, adjusting me in his hold just so, *just* so he can kiss me. I'm love sick—like always. My heart might burst, and I feel like the luckiest girl in the world, like I have my own personal sun to chase me around.

I'm on a field I always dreamed of. With the man I always dreamed of loving.

This is the moment, the dream come true. I don't know how it gets better than this.

I don't think it does.

This is my life. This is our life.

This is love.

# ACKNOWLEDGEMENTS

Wow. This book was a labor of love. A love—for writing, for publishing—that I wasn't sure I had left. I am so intensely proud of this book and these characters. And I am proud of myself for overcoming self-doubt and imposter syndrome and my own perceived ideas of failure or success. This story is one of resilience and strength. Of knowing the hard days and the lows are going to be just that: hard and low. And sometimes impossible. In spite of that, it's hoping and dreaming that the highs will be worth it. To that, I don't know. For me, the high was finishing this book and subsequently choosing to self-publish it. As my good friend said, *Tomorrow, I'll Love You* may be my softest book yet. I wanted to show all the little ways love remains between two people. All the unbreakable threads that tie two people together. This love story…is one that I can't really describe in a concise manner. All I know is that I love it.

To my friends, who supported me in all my downward spirals and on the days the dark clouds seemed permanent, I cannot thank you enough. You held my hand and told me you'd be by my side whether I wrote another book again or not. You never made me feel less than or unworthy. Thank you for never leaving my side.

To my sad girl libra squad always, I love you. (And happy birthday, Jordan!)

To my beta readers—this book would not have become what it was without all of you. The comments and the tips and suggestions and the screaming and crying are some of my favorite parts of this process. It is fulfilling and thrilling. Thank you for being a part of the journey.

To Kayla—thank you for editing my third book. Your comments and notes were brilliant. I cannot wait to keep working with you. To Tiffany, for proofreading—you are amazing! To Sarah, for once again blowing me away with the formatting, and to Silver, at BitterSage Designs—thank you for the cover beyond my dreams.

And to you, the reader, thank you. From the bottom of my heart, thank you for all that you have done for me thus far. I cannot wait to see what the future holds.

# Connect with K. Jamila

Website
Newsletter
Instagram
Discord
Spotify
Goodreads
Twitter
Pinterest

www.ingramcontent.com/pod-product-compliance
Lightning Source LLC
Chambersburg PA
CBHW021411010826
48972CB00014B/1092